S K Y

I C E

Copyright © 2023 by E. G. Sparks

Cover Design: *Infixgraph Designs*

Copy Editing: *Jen Boles*

Proofreading: *Lisa Fox*

Interior Formatting: *Fox Formatting*

ISBN (paperback): 979-8-9880450-1-4

For my angels—Emma, Anabel, Alicja.
Don't let anyone clip your wings.

PROLOGUE

Floating fabric of foreign colors carried me forward as if smooth sailing. I recognized the purples, pinks, and azure mixed with other mesmerizing hues. They blended with fluidity, one evolving from where the other washed out. My body and mind were at eternal peace; nothing mattered in this place. When a thought floated up to the surface, the pattern fluctuated and marked it irrelevant and soon forgotten. I could exist in this state forever.

But as my life would have it, nothing so beautiful comes at no cost.

A sensation of suction tingled my feet. I gazed down. A cobalt blue hole materialized, and a force dumped me out of the colorful bliss onto a solid floor. It was a miracle I landed on both feet. Maybe I was getting better at my balance. My feet connected with ivory marble floors. I scanned the area to assess the threat. My eyes nearly bulged out, seeing scores of angelic warriors lounging on beige leather sofas in a cavernous room reminiscent of ancient Greek architecture. Thick crystalline pillars supported this gargantuan structure with arch-shaped windows framed in white stone. The windows held no glass panes or curtains and the views of idyllic green hills stretched beyond them unobstructed. The men and women in this room possessed other-

worldly beauty. They wore full-length golden armor that clung to their bodies, emphasizing sinewy muscles. They were oblivious to my presence. I knew it wouldn't be long before they discovered me.

Why was I here? An internal tug drew me toward a long vitreous display cabinet in the adjacent room as if on cue. My eyes narrowed in search of the thing I yearned for. Before I could locate it, shouting broke out nearby. In no time, a small group of armored warriors surrounded me but kept their distance as if they didn't know how to act. Emboldened by their restraint, I continued perusing the cabinet's offerings. I halted, my gaze settling on the object of my desires. My pulse quickened, and sweat broke out on my palms, itching to reconnect. Under the enclosure lay the most beautiful crystal I'd ever seen in my life. The sapphire stone radiated with a brilliant blue aura and called to my innermost being. Divine. Its beauty lay deeper than its physical appearance but in what it meant to me and what I meant to it. High frequencies rolled off it in waves, basking me in contentment, fullness and all addictive pleasant feels. And I craved them all. It was an inexplicable feeling—all the sensations tugging at my soul at once. They existed beyond humanity's perception, and only in this realm—or dimension—was I granted a small glimpse of this higher knowledge.

Swoosh! Air blasted my face. A warrior swooped down from a Shakespearean balcony I hadn't noticed until now. To be honest, I'd noticed little else since I laid my eyes on the gem. The new warrior took my breath away. He was godlike perfection. His angelic wings were silver entwined with golden strands, as was his shoulder-length straight hair. Probably a full two feet taller than me, he loomed over me, invading my personal space. Fury vibrated off him, and I tensed. Even in this dreamscape, I didn't want to cause conflict. I knew I'd come here for this crystal alone; that was all I wanted. I needed it. And I feared he'd stop me from getting to it.

I cleared my throat to explain myself, but the words came out muted as they left my mouth. The warrior's eyes reduced to slits. I pointed to the stone and then to myself, hoping that'd do the trick. He tensed, his head swinging in definite denial.

"No," he mouthed.

"But..." I began.

Out of the corner of my eye, I caught a glint of long metal hurtling at my midsection. A sword glided through my waist as if I weren't there. Astonished, I touched my abdomen, feeling...nothing. I was still complete and unharmed. A giggle escaped me. The leader's brows pinched together over a murderous scowl destined for my attacker. I grabbed for his arm, but as expected, my hands went through it. They prickled but could not grasp any matter—as if I was a poltergeist. I reached into the display case through the glass. My fingers met the crystal, triggering a palpable wave of energy to surge up my arm. It did something unexplainable to the matrices of my energetic blueprint. I closed my eyes, listening to harmonic whispers boomeranging around me as if I was in an echo chamber. Sky Ice... Sky Ice... Sky Ice... Over and over again.

The crystal's life force rushed through me, and I let it until I was fully restored. The echoing loop subsided. "Future proves past," it whispered at last into my mind, prompting a memory within my reach but too distant at the same time. I released the crystal. My gut told me it needed to remain in this unknown place. It was safe here.

Feeling accomplished and rejuvenated, I smiled at the silver-haired warrior. His gaze filled with warmth, and he called to me. One word. A name I didn't recognize. I shook my head. "Arien," I whispered. He swayed his head slowly, an all-knowing smirk gracing his lips. The moment froze in time as I explored the depths of the warrior's glacial blue eyes. There was something familiar about them.

My scalp began heating, and I looked up. A deep blue tunnel resembling a wormhole was forming above me. I swallowed, apprehension settling in my gut again. Where would the tube of multicolored light dump me next? The warrior noticed it, too. He reached for my arm, but his fingers only grazed the air. It was as if we existed on different dimensional planes, together but apart. His gaze communicated the intensity of unidentifiable emotion. He pointed at himself and said what resembled "Sylvan."

I repeated it, and satisfaction overrode his darker emotions. Without warning, the tunnel descended upon me, obstructing my vision. The contours of Sylvan's symmetric face diminished as the vibrant pattern of contentment sucked me in. Sylvan's last words traveled to me this time, and a strange ache settled in my heart. He vowed he'd find me again.

ONE

I was on the verge of peeing in my pants. The embarrassment wouldn't bother me as much as ruining my only pair of jeans. Squeezing my thighs together, I whispered, "C'mon, c'mon, c'mon." I curved my neck around the burly man in front of me to glance at the shelter's front entrance. I sagged back against the wall with disappointment. They hadn't opened yet. And they wouldn't open for another twenty minutes. All homeless shelters opened at eight o'clock now thanks to New Seattle's green ordinance. The ordinance also prohibited feeding the homeless, including "no outside food" policies. The newly elected city mayor prided himself on putting a stop to homelessness by cutting the city's charity budget in half. That was some stupid politics if you asked me, but nobody asked and no one would. I was one of the homeless people now who were an insignificant minority, and I'd been standing there, in thirty-degree wintry weather, for over two hours. Splurging on a large Coke from a nearby fast-food restaurant had not helped my current dilemma. But I was so thirsty... I slammed back against the red brick wall and crossed my legs as tight as I could. I didn't realize I had squeezed my eyes shut until the man to my right addressed me.

"Having to go, yeh?"

I peeked from one eye. He was a mountain of a man with long, grayish-brown hair and a toothless smile.

I nodded. I couldn't open my mouth because squeaks and moans were all communication I was capable of at the moment.

"Go on. I will keep ye spot." He grinned.

"You'd do that for me?" I whispered. Kindness and self-lessness were not common traits among the homeless of New Seattle. I'd outgrown the foster care system a few months ago. Unable to find employment right away and afford rent, I'd frequented homeless shelters whenever the weather wasn't suitable for sleeping in the open. I didn't mind having to sleep on park benches, in the alleys, and in cardboard boxes. I didn't mind it because it meant I was free. I gained freedom from the system that transplanted me from foster home to foster home every few months. From people who didn't care about me or my well-being, whose primary objective was the support money government so generously distributed to those who took "problems" out of the system's hands. I'd gone without meals at the so-called homes I had. My all-time low was stealing my foster parents' daughter's underwear because clothes shopping for me was not in their books. Life had sucked then. Now, it sucked less.

"As long as you return before they open the door, this spot is yers." He inclined his head.

"I'll be quick," I said. I peeled off the wall and sprinted for the fast food chain on the opposite block's corner. I ran nonstop to the restrooms. There, I faced a new problem. A line of about seven women of all ages stood outside the facili-ties. I considered skipping the line and forcing my way in, but the intimidating looks I received told me that maybe this wouldn't be the wisest move. I didn't need to cause any commotion. Besides, assuming the women each took two minutes, I should make it to the shelter in time. And I could always use the men's restroom—possibly. I got in line and the women relaxed.

C'mon. C'mon, I cheered for us all. It surprised me to see the men's restroom door open and a woman leaving it. The next one in line went into the men's restroom, too. After a couple of minutes of waiting, the scenario repeated. And again.

"What's with the women's restroom?" I whispered to an older lady in front of me.

She looked back at me with mild exasperation in her eyes. "She's nursing a baby," she croaked.

I had nothing against babies getting the best nourishment nature provided for them, but here? Now? At a restaurant with a single restroom for each sex? I checked my watch. Fifteen minutes left until the shelter opened. *You can do this.* There was just enough time to go in, take care of business, and return to my place in line. After all, I couldn't turn around now. My bladder was refusing any movement on my part. So much so that if I attempted returning to the shelter now, I feared a leakage of some sort was inevitable.

When my turn came, the relief was indescribable. Leaving, I dashed for the side exit door. I hit a man's chest and bounced off of it, falling to my ass. At least, I expected to land on my bottom. Two powerful hands caught my forearms and brought me upright from mid-fall. I'd never seen anyone act so fast. He had great reflexes, and he stared at me with raw intensity. A sudden feeling of warmth and what I could only call familiarity spilled from my core, but I was certain I'd never met him in my life. My rescuer had gorgeous chocolate eyes, a handsome bone structure, dark brown stubble, and... What was I doing? I shivered. The weight of my situation came crashing down on me, and I removed my hands from his, breaking into a sprint.

"Sorry!" I yelled over my shoulder. Running, I cataloged the strange encounter as irrelevant, requiring no further thought. After all, déjà vu moments were no stranger of mine. It was eight o'clock now, and I prayed the Mountain Man had not yet entered the shelter. If I missed him, I'd have to go to the back of the line... And there was a high chance they'd run out of beds tonight. It was too cold for me to sleep outside. I enjoyed having my toes on my feet. Out of breath and hunching over, I sprinted down the line, searching for the Mountain Man. I got to the front where the homeless were being let in one at a time; he was gone. *Shit. Shit. Shit.* I kicked an imaginary object and raced to the end of the line, hoping there'd be at least one bed left when I got to the entrance.

The shelter staff let me in, and even two more homeless, a mid-aged hippie woman with the longest single braid I'd ever seen and her companion, before the shelter maxed its capacity. I stalked into the large room with beds, scouring for an available mattress. I found one in the back. I sat down, burrowed my face in my hands, and sagged in relief. I was exhausted, physically and mentally. Inclement weather limited my movements around town and what extra shifts I could pick up.

"Hey, you!"

I dropped my hands into my lap, confused. The couple who came in last set their eyes on me and prowled in my direction.

"Can I help you?"

"This is our bed," the man said, dropping a large duffel bag on top of said bed.

I opened my mouth; no words came out. How could this be their bed when I was here first? I eyed people nearest us who conveniently turned their backs my way.

"Er... Isn't there another bed you can have?" I asked.

"This. Is. Our. Bed," the man enunciated with a raised eyebrow. My imagination had either played a trick on me or his hands tightened into fists.

"Um, okay. This is your bed." I stood up.

"Oh, bless your heart. There is one more bed. Over there in the corner," the woman said. She beamed as if her boyfriend didn't just threaten to manhandle me.

"Oh." Relief washed over me. I strode in the direction she pointed me.

There was a single bed in the corner, away from others. I almost flanked myself on it—ready to surrender to blissful sleep —when the most repugnant odor hit me. Nausea came over me and I gagged. I changed the course for the bathroom instead. I dry-heaved over a rust-covered sink. No wonder the couple didn't want this bed. It reeked of stale urine, a lot of it. If that was the last bed they had available tonight, I was screwed.

"I'm afraid you have to leave, Miss Blair," the shelter's director said, unaffected. The director was an older woman with grayish hair piled up high, held up by a colorful brooch-like hairpin. She regarded me from above her purple-framed glasses. She recited the new shelter rules and promptly returned to her Sudoku puzzles, shaking a chewed-up pencil above the paper. Ironically, the pencil was adorned with red hearts and the black ink spelled *I Love You*.

"Don't you have any spare beds put away somewhere? It's not my fault the mattress reeks," I said with a pinch of irritation in my voice.

She exhaled and glanced up again, but this time with an emotion. It was annoyance.

"That's all the beds we have. You cannot sleep on the floor; you must occupy a bed. That's the protocol," she said. The director had no intention of addressing the situation. Why wasn't I surprised? But I wasn't planning on leaving either. I crossed my arms and gave her my best impression of a fiery glare.

"Is there a problem?" The security guard sauntered over. He was a middle-aged man with a barrel-like frame. By the twisted set of his mouth, one could presume he didn't tolerate bullshit. He scrutinized me, and a small spark twinkled in his plain grayish eyes.

The woman sighed. "We are over our quota tonight. I've been explaining to Miss Blair our regulations do not permit her to stay."

"That's true." The man tucked his thumbs behind the belt and rocked on his heels.

"But I had a bed, a perfectly good bed. The last people coming in forced me to give it up. They should go, not me."

"Tsk, tsk. What stories they will tell to save their asses. Everyone's for themselves here," the guard said to the director. He made sure I heard him, too.

"I'm not lying." Tears pulled into my eyes, blurring my vision. I shook them off. Crying never helped. I had long discovered the shelter staff had no compassion for those whom they served. I didn't know whether that was their inherent disposition or whether the years on this job calcified their hearts.

"That's enough! Follow me," the guard said.

Dabbing my eyes dry with the ends of my sleeves, I

followed the man. When we entered a narrow corridor, he halted and faced me. He took a long, assessing perusal of me. I wished I knew what he was thinking. Instead, I waited. A flicker of hope ignited in me.

"I have a spare cot in the storage room," he said in a low voice. I raised hopeful eyes to his, momentary euphoria warming my core. He skimmed the back of his hand on my cheek and shivers ran down my spine. Shock and revulsion shot down any hope I'd felt. I stepped back.

"I can't." I shook my head. I'd pay a lot for a place in a shelter right now, but not that. I'd rather freeze my toes off in the cold.

"Suit yourself." He unlocked the heavy metal door. Ice-cold air blasted my face and I took an involuntary step back. The guard chuckled before he shoved me outside without a single word, closed the door in one swift motion, and slammed the crossbar in place.

TWO

I lingered outside the shelter, dumbfounded. I stuffed my hands into my pockets. Gloves would have been a great accessory right about now. I had a warm black turtleneck and a brown leather jacket that'd seen better days but was reliable. My boots were warm enough, but the jeans were not much so. From where my jacket ended at the waistline to where my boots reached mid-calf, it felt as if I was sitting in cold water. Snow flurries drifted in with a howling wind, forcing my eyes shut. I wanted to pull my hair out for missing out on a shelter bed tonight—for being so inadequate.

The headmistress at the halfway house used to recount my flaws since I could remember: unlovable, waste of good air, worthless rat, and my all-time favorite—the reason my mother died. "She took one look at you and died," she'd say and cackle away. I rubbed my wrist where my bracelet usually wrapped around. The action soothed my mind and heart. I had no recollection of my mother. I'd only known life in the system, under the state's custody and now relying on the city-run shelters. But not for much longer.

I trudged to the nearest bus stop. Paulie lived outside the

city limit, but he had a warm place to stay in and right now that was worth more than gold. Paulie was an elderly home-less man, a kindred spirit. I'd asked him once how old he was and he said he couldn't remember—that he'd forgotten when he was born. Paulie could be peculiar at times, but he was a survivalist. I'd first met him shortly after I turned seventeen. He'd often sat in front of a small chain grocery store near my sixth or seventh high school with his hat on the ground. One afternoon, I'd caught some juveniles stealing money from Paulie's hat. They pretended to drop money in it but instead skillfully removed most contents of the hat. It was good, perhaps even a masters-of-illusion worthy act Paulie couldn't have detected from his point of view. But from my angle, I'd seen enough. I'd confronted the culprits right there and then, and with a small crowd backing me, the boys returned the money and apologized. I'd introduced myself to Paulie and spent some time with him that afternoon.

In my then financial state and living conditions, I couldn't help him materially. He appreciated speaking with someone just as much, though. Since the incident, I'd seen Paulie a few other times. I'd told him about aging out of the foster care system, and he graciously offered to share his living quarters with me whenever I should need them.

My eighteenth birthday was in April. I was a senior in high school and abruptly homeless. The family who'd provided a roof over my head for the past three months gave me a pat on my shoulder and showed me out the door as my birthday gift. At first, I'd stayed at shelters and attended school religiously. I kept all my belongings in the school locker. Washcloth baths and the laundromat had become my new reality. But after a while, it became clear I needed food. More than what a school cafeteria provided. My clothes became loose, and my head was no longer in the right place during classes. I'd always been a straight-A student, but when the reality of life punched me in the gut, I reevaluated my priorities. I could've stayed in school and graduated. I'd suffer and lose another ten pounds, but I'd have a diploma, and then...what? Or I could go out there, find a job, and start making life for myself. No one cared what I did with my life. I had no friends. I was new and a foster kid at that. Boys noticed me. But I never returned their attention, and that petered out as well. My teachers never asked about my personal life. No one cared enough. So, I didn't even bother to give notice to the secretary. I simply stopped attending.

Two days later, I found a decent job. A local bakery needed a dishwasher a few days a week. It paid minimum wage, but the morning schedule and the solitude of my work provided the perfect work environment. With little expenses of my own, I'd been putting away money every week, biding my time until better things came my way. The owner never complained when I left my oversized backpack in the storage room for a night or a couple of days. These days, I always left my backpack there when I stayed at shelters. I learned it the hard way too.

I'd visited Paulie twice since I ventured out on my own and abandoned the idea of educational achievement. He lived in a long-forgotten junkyard with metal scrap, a few miles outside the northern city limits. He'd built a shelter of sorts from leftover building materials and had comfortable living quarters there with a bed and a few random pieces of furniture. During my last visit, I spotted a recent addition of a coal stove.

The city bus commute to that part of town was close to two hours long, and I preferred to remain in the south. Occasionally, local bars needed help, and I got in the habit of checking with them daily. But with the temperatures dropping to teens tonight and a windchill of zero, visiting Paulie was my best bet for staying warm tonight. The bakery didn't need me tomorrow, after all.

As expected, in this part of town, the bus was brimming with young people heading for the clubs and bars a couple of stops ahead. A group of rambunctious teenagers occupied the back. Older folks preferred the front seats. I perched on the bench in the mid-section of the bus next to a lady engrossed in a book. She and others from the bench opposite mine soon left. That's when I heard it.

"Hey, that girl went to our school," one boy said.

After a pregnant second, another male voice chimed in, "Nah, are you sure?"

"Yeah, man, she went to our school for like two months. She was an orphan or something."

"That's her," the third voice said with something more than an interest. "She didn't let me cheat off of her algebra exam, bitch." An impending silence followed.

Oh, boy. I didn't dare to glance up or give them any atten-tion. Attention was the worst enticement for their kind. I dug my hands even deeper into my pockets and lowered my head, letting long pale blond hair fall around my face. I wished I was invisible at this moment. When I didn't hear any other comments directed at me, I relaxed a little. Until someone's leg rubbed against mine. A person dropped in the seat to my right, and another figure followed suit to my left.

"Hi, gorgeous. Remember me?" I glanced sideways at the boy to my right. I remembered him. He was one of the popular rich kids at Montech High. He'd asked me on a date once, which I'd refused. He'd made my life a living hell after that. I swallowed a clump of nerves. Satisfaction and malice crossed his dazzling rich-boy features.

"Long time, no see. We still have a date to go on." His hand glided up my thigh, stopping haphazardly close to my crotch and squeezing. I froze. I knew I shouldn't have allowed it, but I freaking froze in place.

His companion wrapped his arm around my shoulders and whispered, "How about a double date?"

Fear and repulsion rippled across my body. With one assailant pinning my leg down and the other holding my torso, I couldn't move. My heart rate turned into a pitter-patter.

"I-I-I haven't bathed in a week!" I panicked and said the first thing crossing my mind, which was true, by the way. Although, I wasn't dirty, and I didn't think I stank, thanks to washcloth baths. But they didn't need to know that. I'd make myself sound as repulsive as possible if it helped my cause. I always drew male attention—a boy once told me I resembled a lifelike Barbie doll, but better—and most girls hated me for it even though I rejected all the vain advances. The boy to my left yanked his arm away, and someone chuckled. I thought it was the asshole to my right, but a quick check assured me it wasn't him. His eyes narrowed upward. Something in me prickled with apprehension when I traced his gaze.

The handsome man I ran into earlier today stood in front of us, scowling. Two equally good-looking men flanked him. The shorter and wider one to his right clammed his mouth tight, his eyes sparkling with amusement. My attention snapped back to the leader, though. He was menacing, beautifully menacing. His deep brown eyes bore into mine, and warmth ignited in my core. This time, I didn't like the sensation. A part of me wanted to rip away and run to him. What was wrong with me?

"I think this is your stop," he said to the boy on my right. I expected my chief assailant to argue or draw a fight because he wasn't the type who followed orders. But to my awe, the boy stood up and headed for the bus door. As if someone programmed him to do so, he never looked back. The bus was slowing down. His colleague trailed behind, mumbling under his breath.

"Wait for us!" one girl squealed. She and the rest of their company sprang up from their seats and rushed after their friends, giving the towering men as wide of a berth as possible. They exited. Bewildered, I returned my gaze to the three stunning men in front of me. How I'd missed them getting on this bus, I did not know. I was grateful for their help but growing suspicious at the same time. What were the chances of me running into them for the second time in one night? Maybe I truly needed to stop bathing.

Feeling their scrutiny still on me, I realized I hadn't thanked them.

"Thank you," I whispered.

The shortest of the three men winked at me, patted the chocolate-eyed man on the arm, and pointed at the seats in the back. The leader stalled before striding away. I sighed with relief. They didn't small talk to me, which was a good sign. Perhaps honorable men who rescued damsels in distress because of their chivalry and not a prospect of the said damsel's good graces still existed in this world. I wondered who the men were and where they were going. I fought the urge to steal a glance. Eye contact was my adversary, however. Once I made eye contact with a male, they always read that as an invitation. Brie used to joke I possessed a superpower. I wished I had a superpower, but that wasn't it. It was a curse.

The men didn't matter. I stared at the floor for the rest of my trip. I refused to peek through my hair when three pairs of boots stamped past me, one pausing momentarily. He didn't utter a single word. Two stops later, the bus line ended. The driver flicked all the interior lights on and I squinted with the sudden change in lighting. I scanned the seats—all empty but mine.

THREE

I so wished I had a beanie, or at least my hooded sweatshirt, with me tonight. The chilly wind picked up at intervals, blasting my face with icy moisture. The gated neighborhoods were quiet, and road traffic was nonexistent. Everyone stayed indoors. They knew better. I trudged through slush covering the fine sidewalks of the north's suburbs. The street narrowed and the red brick fence ended. The sidewalk became a dirt path. A couple of hundred feet of wilderness preceded sparse middle-class houses with fences and clusters of mobile homes. I was almost there. The abandoned industrial district was now visible. Its landmark was an old warehouse with parts of its metal roof blown away a long time ago. I turned left at the warehouse and continued on a gravel road. Behind the buildings, a wire fence surrounded the junkyard with a makeshift gate erected behind a trunk of a burnt tree. Thinking of the warm interior of Paulie's shack made me giddy inside. The tips of my ears numbed, and that added expediency to my gait.

I lifted the aforementioned gate and shifted it to one side a couple of feet, enough for me to pass. Why did Paulie even bother with this contraption? The fence was full of man-made holes. Not wanting to ruin the effect, I shifted the piece of scrap metal back into its place. The night hid the path from me, and I tried to remember which way led to Paulie's place. I recognized a derelict wheel-less rusty pickup truck with scarlet red paint visible where rust hadn't yet taken over. I headed to where it was sitting on the remains of some other car that had met its end there.

From that point, I had to walk another hundred or so feet to the right. That was better. A gust of air blew a piece of metal scrap across the alley. It clanked its way around the path, heading for my feet. I jumped over it —this place would be a death trap if a tornado touched down in the center of it. Another small clearing opened with a two-way fork split, but I was certain now I should keep going right.

I headed toward the selected path but stalled when a cat bolted from the left alley as if its life depended on it. The little fellow scared me to my core. A second cat rushed out of the same alley. This one didn't even slow down on the corner. It slammed into a refrigerator and relentlessly dug its paws in place for a few seconds to regain its momentum. That was... weird. One cat, I could explain, but two... I'd never seen a wild animal around here. There was no food here, after all. Unless Paulie's cooking had attracted a bear from the nearby woods. A sudden fear for Paulie rose in my chest.

I froze in place, listening for wild creatures. Ominous silence filled the air as if someone sucked all life out. I pulled an iron rod from a pile of whatnots nearby and grasped it with both hands. Loud hissing echoed, followed by a rattle. I shuffled backward, cowering behind a heap of metal. A snake came to mind, but that would have to have been a beast. This had to be something else, but what? A pitch-colored shape emerged. It glided along, mere inches above the ground. Amorphous in shape and, at least, two feet in diameter, it halted and stretched upward two stories high. It was... A dark cloud? Smoke? I couldn't wrap my mind around what I was seeing, except that this creature was semi-transparent. It sniffed the air around it. It was searching for something, but what? The cats? If so, I was glad I wasn't it right now. The billow of dark fumes turned what I presumed was its head in my direction. The head rotated a complete three-sixty, followed by the creature's soft cawing.

Oh, shit. It spotted me. I withdrew behind the pile. But I had to maintain a visual of this abnormal life form. This wasn't an out of sight, out of mind type of situation. I got on all fours and peeked around the corner. I stayed low. The creature was still there, in the same location. Its entire body revolved, creating a whirlwind. It dropped down with a whoosh, revealing a shadowed figure behind it. The man wore a black cloak with a triangular hood over a concealed head. Where his face ought to have been was an empty chasm, an illusion he was using without a doubt. I sensed him staring right at me as if an invisible charge passed between us. My heart leaped to my throat. *What did I do now?*

Two men stepped into the clearing. They took stances between me and the scary man and his even scarier pet. The men carried swords sheathed on their backs, attached to bandoliers holding a menagerie of sharp objects. Black sleeves on one man's forearms revealed silver flatware of some sort concealed on the inside. Reaching overhead one-handed, the men drew their swords with deadly stealth.

There was a moment when everything stood still, and then a round disk the size of a baseball rolled in towards the dark cloud animal. It exploded, and the animal transformed into a corporeal form. It was a snake-like creature, ebony and tough-skinned. The snake rose on its tail and squealed in a terrified high pitch. It wanted to retract, but before it could do so, a silver knife plunged into its underbelly. The creature collapsed into a puddle of inky liquid.

In the meantime, the hooded figure reached his hand out to the side. A ball of dark mass appeared, spinning faster than my sight could discern. A third, familiar-looking man, perched on top of a metal mound behind the phantom. He held a large onyx blade in both of his hands and launched himself downward with it. Before he connected with his target, however, the hooded figure tugged the ball of darkness toward himself. The orb absorbed him, leaving no trace of him ever standing in that space. The broad-shouldered man I ran into earlier today hit the ground. The blade slid halfway into the dirt underneath.

"Fuck, I had him!" The man twirled around, scrutinizing the spot the figure occupied a moment ago.

I crouched. I was heaving, and my body trembled. If he was the man from the bus, that meant the other men were... *Oh shit, what did I get myself into?*

"Where is the girl? Are we too late?" one of the men asked.

"No. She's here." The sultriness of the owner's voice glided over me. I don't know how, but I knew when his chocolate eyes zeroed in on my hiding spot. Loose gravel crunched underneath his heavy boots.

"You can come out now. It's safe," he said in a soothing tone as if he hadn't just slain a sci-fi creature whose owner disappeared into a pocket-sized black hole!

Safe, my ass. After witnessing the killing and the disappearing acts, I was safer far, far away from these guys. When his footsteps reached the corner, I surged and swung the rod at him. He caught it with ease and tugged on the bar, pulling me to him. I narrowed my eyes. My fighting skills were nothing to brag about. Even so, no one should be able to catch that rod the way he did.

"How did you do that?"

He shrugged. "Years of practice, I suppose."

The closeness to him unnerved me.

"Let go," I demanded. He did, and I stepped back, clutching the rod in both hands and ready to swing it again.

A corner of his mouth lifted. "What are you doing?"

What was I doing?

"Who are you?" I was irate, which was surprising given the circumstances. I held onto the feeling though. Afraid I'd lose it all if I allowed myself to think about what I'd just witnessed.

"All clear," the taller of the two henchmen said, appearing behind his leader. Thick leather bands wrapped his forearms, the inside slits holding a dozen silver blades. They had to be throwing knives, but they were nothing I'd seen before. All silver, even the hilt. The hilt was the smallest part, maybe two inches long. I surmised it required precision, skill, and practice to wield such a weapon. One blade was slimed with a dark substance. A memory of where this wicked object was embedded only a few minutes ago made me sick to my stomach.

"She doesn't look so good," the broad-shouldered one said.

Gee, thanks.

"You need to come with us. It's safe now, but they will find you again." The leader offered me his hand.

Did he honestly think I'd go with them? We were crammed into a tight space. Fighting them off was not an option. I could run. Judging by their bulging thighs, that wouldn't work well for me, either. Think...

"Why? Why should I go with you?" I stood a little taller.

The leader's eyes slit. "You're in danger, and it's my...*our* duty to protect you," he said through gritted teeth.

Apparently, he took his self-assigned task very seriously.

The audacity of these men was beyond comprehensible. No one barged into my life, proclaiming their unsolicited services. Who did they think they were?

The one I called broad-shouldered stepped in front of the leader, placing a hand on his arm.

"Chill, sir. We don't want to scare the orphan away," he said. The man glared at him, but to his credit, he didn't flinch.

"Make her do as I say, or I will use my methods," the leader said. He clenched and unclenched his fists, zeroing his danger-filled eyes in on me.

Fear rippled down my spine with something else, some foreign feeling. They exchanged some words. I backed up a few paces. I hooked my foot underneath a truck bumper sticking out of haphazardly stacked car parts five times higher than us and yanked it out. The tower squeaked like an unoiled hinge. I tensed, waiting.

A car door fell first. It struck the taller man's head with a thump. Then, it was a chain reaction. The entire wall rushed toward us. The leader's gaze blazed with disbelief and fury. He maneuvered toward me but was socked with a large, unidentifiable, metal object and thrown out of his path. I scrambled to the other side of the fallout and climbed the remaining stack where a new alley opened. I led them away from Paulie. Who knew what these guys would do to him if they found him? I tumbled down and fled. I didn't dare to look back. At every corner, I yanked at rubbish to hinder their pursuit.

Something close to an explosion sounded off and metal pieces dropped from the sky like volcano rocks. I huddled behind a stack of car doors, avoiding flying objects. I didn't know what to make of the explosion, or why I hadn't heard a single footstep following me. My heart clenched at the thought that something dreadful might have happened to the

three men. I didn't wish them dead. After all, they saved me
from the extraterrestrial creatures.

As I listened to silence and bird wings flapping in the air,
I leaned into a large car door. I rested my forehead on a
tinted window, welcoming the cool touch. When I thought
my life couldn't get more complicated... The door swiveled
under my weight, and I fell onto all fours. It opened into a
dome surrounding an iron trapdoor. I scooted in, gliding the
car door behind me to a close. I propped the heavy hatch
halfway up and peeked in. A ladder stretched downward into
the darkness. I lowered the cover, grunting, and crawled
toward a window to survey my surroundings. I scratched the
back of my tension-filled head. *What if what I saw was a
figment of my imagination? Was I hallucinating? Or worse?*

The crescent moon illuminated the sky and cast shadows
of flying birds. They circled like vultures. Hunting. Some of
them were unusually large, and as one of them neared the
surface...I gasped. It couldn't be! When they swooped down,
the silhouettes resembled a human. A winged human. My
heart drummed as if it wanted to catapult out of my chest. I
was swaying on my heels, and my ass landed on the trapdoor.
I darted for the handle with renewed determination. I was
getting the hell out of here.

FOUR

I descended a metal ladder shrouded in darkness, stopping at intervals to listen for anyone following me or any movement below me. Only the echoes of my boots hitting rungs resounded off the walls. I reached the ground surface and pulled out my prepaid flip phone. I had little use for a phone, but it was essential. It did everything I needed it to do, and the best thing of all was that a prepaid minute card lasted months with my spare usage. This time, however, all I needed it for was the soft glow of the screen. Yes, a flashlight app would be ideal, but my phone was not "smart" enough for it. The phone's screen illuminated a narrow tunnel going in both directions. I started to the right because...why not? And if I was correct, this direction was northeast. I needed someone trusted to talk to, who could ground me in reality again. And I knew someone who fit this description. Although, we hadn't spoken in over a year.

Brie and I met at New Seattle's halfway house, a place housing minors in between family placements. I was nine. Brie was a year older, yet I consoled and guided her through the system. Contrary to my story, Brie had been recently orphaned, a sole survivor of a devastating car crash. With grandparents long passed on either side and an aunt who'd claimed she couldn't afford to keep her, the state assumed custody until her eighteenth birthday. Three weeks passed, and the state sent us into different family placements, but as luck had it, we'd often attended the same schools or ran into each other on the streets or at events our foster families attended.

Brie aged out of the foster care system a few months ahead of me in the summer. She'd visited often at first. She'd given me her new address and urged me to join her and the others who lived there once I turned eighteen. At our last meeting, Brie had been acting strange, though. She no longer advocated for me to move to the Fringe. And the boyfriend she'd brought with her hadn't uttered a single word. I'd tried to speak with her in private, but she'd only smiled, dismissing any concerns I might have had.

Altogether, she'd acted as if it was the last time we'd see each other, and that was precisely what happened. Ever since the strange encounter, I'd received no word from Brie. It had bothered me then, and it still bothered me now. I had made up my mind to locate her in the past many times. Each time I'd found a reason to scrap the plan, such as the guilt I harbored since I'd landed Brie in isolation for a straight month.

I begged my foster mom for movie tickets for me and Brie to celebrate her sweet sixteen. When she refused, I stole from her and hid the money in Brie's backpack, certain no one would suspect her. I miscalculated. When I confessed to the crime, no one believed me. Everyone assumed Brie stole the money, and she lied, saying she'd done it, too. She'd known I was on the mistress's special list of repeat offenders. I'd never forget Brie's lifeless eyes when I visited her for the first time after her isolation. She laughed it all off, but for months, I glimpsed a hidden trauma. I'd never forgiven myself for hurting my best friend.

Having survived a brush with death and a kidnapping attempt, I ran out of excuses to keep away. Tomorrow wasn't guaranteed. There was one problem with my plan—the new mayor had declared the Fringe was now an outlawed territory, and I was headed for it. That was after I navigated my way through this long-abandoned tunnel.

The tunnel seemed to stretch on forever. To preserve my phone's battery, I powered the phone's screen on and off every few steps to confirm no turns or exit shafts sprang up as I continued in silence. I found it rather unusual there were no exits in sight for the amount of distance I'd traversed. In the city, emergency access caps on the overflow drain lines stamped the roads and sidewalks at frequent intervals. This tunnel must have had a different utility. I slowed down to pay closer attention to the ceiling and the walls. When I scanned the floor ahead of me, it reflected the light. I tapped one foot into the liquid, and it responded with a gentle splash and ripple. Water. But where was it coming from? I meandered another ten minutes through the shallow water puddles before the sounds of flowing water reached my ears. The idea of seeing something other than this same never-ending tunnel got my adrenaline pumping. Dimmed yellowish light appeared at the end of the tunnel. I jogged toward it.

Below the edge was a large dome-like space with water rushing inside a cement corridor, sloshing and splashing in response to uncontrolled currents. The attached ladder passed my amateur safety inspection, and I descended about three stories. I crossed the metal bridge above the water to inspect the four tunnels on the other side.

Someone had etched the tunnels' destinations into the concrete wall. There was the Central Station in the City Center, St. James's Abbey on the west side of town, and the Queen's District located more southeast. A letter "F" marked the last tunnel. An "F" and nothing else. Could that mean the Fringe? I didn't intend to meander in an underground tunnel and find myself in Franklin, Missouri. On the other hand, all other locations were hours away and nowhere near the Fringe.

I entered the unknown-destination tunnel. I had to be close to the Fringe by now, and if this tunnel led there, I would be quite lucky. I should make it there within half an hour. If I didn't get anywhere in that time, I'd turn around and head into the city. Sleep evaded me, and I had to keep moving to stay warm.

Goose bumps broke out on my arms, and I hugged myself. The tunnel, crafted with stone and wooden support beams, resembled an old mining shaft. The sound of water rushing through the corridors faded away. A few minutes later, my ears picked up on the rustling noise. I halted in the darkness, listening in. The noises were not of a person but rather of vegetation scraping the rocks on the outside, accompanied by howling winds. Was this the end of the tunnel? I shuffled towards the noise. The sound grew louder, and soon streams of moonlight danced on the tunnel's floor. Bushes swayed from side to side outside a wrought iron gate. Layers upon layers of thick metal chains wrapped across the gate with several locks securing them in place. Unless someone came in with a bulldozer, I wasn't getting out of this tunnel.

"Fuuu—Fox!" I tugged at a few locks with all I had. This stupid gate was all that stood between me and my freedom— and my sanity. I sniffled and rubbed my eyes with the pads of my palms. I wanted to sink to the ground and cry my eyes out, but I sure as hell wasn't going to. I lit up my phone screen. I inspected each divot and shadow. There, a few feet back, one wall cratered out, unusual from what I'd seen so far. I jogged up to it. The opening was a foot or so deep, and unfamiliar carved symbols decorated it. The intricate patterns connected in the middle with a central caved-in circular point. Guided by instinct, I placed my index finger on the hollowed button. I held my breath and...nothing happened. I closed my eyes and laughed at my stupidity.

The ground shook, and I backed away to the wall behind me, except my palms found nothing there. I spun and dug the toes of my boots into the soft earth at the edge of a cliff that had erupted, chopping my arms backward and landing on my ass.

Panting, I stared wide-eyed into the deep gorge. I wouldn't have survived the fall. Thanking all that was *holy* for my continued existence on this planet, I scooted backward. Towering trees and thorny shrubs guarded the chained gate of the tunnel I was in a moment ago.

I stood stock-still in one place, running through all the logical explanations in my mind. Yet, in my heart, I knew what I'd experienced was not logical. Neither was the hooded creature, the gargantuan snake, nor the armor-clad men— who, I suspected, could fly. *Don't faint, don't faint.* I inhaled deeply and exhaled with control.

A small trail led to the right, down an easy slope. I blew a breath of relief, realizing I didn't have to jump off of the cliff to get the hell out of there. I'd probably attempt it too. With what I'd witnessed today, the line between the rational and the implausible was blurring. I'd stepped into a parallel dimension where sci-fi creatures, sorcery, and magic were common. A dull headache threatened to overpower my senses. I traversed down the narrow path twined with lush vegetation that hindered my descent. After turning at a ninety-degree angle and pushing through a thick branch facade, I emerged to a familiar view I recognized from the newspapers. The Fringe.

I crouched. A corrugated metal fence at least ten feet high surrounded the area. From my vantage point above the main camp, I could see beyond the exterior walls. Houses and apartment buildings, streets and walkways, and foot traffic resembled a scene out of New Seattle's well-to-do neighborhoods, and it surprised me to find it here. At the center, stalls, tables, and shipping containers formed a market illuminated by street lamps with solar panels. Some street lamps shone in housing areas, but not all of them. Darkness set over most of the camp. A vehicle's headlights rounded up a hill and came to a stop at what appeared to be a front entrance. Someone walked up. A soldier-like figure, or security. They chatted before the security man inclined his head to somebody by the gate, and it opened outward. The vehicle disappeared inside. The faint glow of headlights traveled above the various buildings until it stopped deeper in the camp in front of a sizable house resembling a Spanish villa.

This camp was more than I had ever imagined the Fringe living quarters to be. It was a thriving city just outside New Seattle's borders, and yet no one spoke about it. Was it possible that no one knew? I doubted it. The New Seattle authorities knew, and yet they turned a blind eye. My suspicions about the new mayor's shadiness only grew. Star citizens didn't live in the Fringe. Outcasts ruled this area, tax-evading crooks and the criminal element. The thought that I ought to have checked on Brie sooner boomeranged again to the forefront of my mind. What if she was being exploited here? A slave, or worse a sex slave? Bile rose in my throat, and I choked on my spit, water filling my eyes.

A movement in the wall drew my attention. A section of the metal wall, roughly two feet wide and five feet tall, fell outward. A lithe teenage boy stepped out through the makeshift opening and set the metal sheet aside. Two girls and a pair of boys around the same age emerged. They wore regular clothes, and nothing about them screamed criminal, more like teenagers sneaking about past their curfew. The boys scouted the perimeter wall while one of them put the piece of the wall back in place. When he secured it, they were off, running toward the Avalon River. I waited for them to disappear before proceeding toward their secret hole. No one patrolled these walls. The occupants either had an acute sense of security, or they were ignorant of dangers lurking nearby like black-orb commanding hooded creatures. I shivered, but not from the cold.

I located the two-by-five sheet of metal and inspected it. Two large loose screws held it in place on the top. The bottom rested on the wall partition beneath it. I undid the screws and placed them on the grass by the wall. Hooking my thumbs into the holes, I pulled on the piece. The sucker was heavy, way heavier than I'd expected, and I widened my stance to stop myself from tipping over. With a last-ditch effort, I pushed it to a side. How the hell did that boy make it look so effortless? I didn't think I could get this patch back in its place. I peeked inside; vegetation camouflaged this particular spot. At least no one would find this opening soon.

I sneaked into the compound and peeked out through the bushes. A singular swing squeaked in an empty playground. Behind it, rows of townhouses lined up perpendicular to the wall. I didn't have a plan beyond this point. Not yet. I sat down on the bench, allowing darkness to shelter me. I tried to recall what Brie had told me about this place, but it wasn't much.

Girly giggles reached me from the direction I'd come from.

"Can't believe you forget the keys again?"

"I know..."

"We're lucky Mark left the wall open."

Two girls stepped out of the bushes, and I rose. I wasn't sure why, a stupid reflex. It was enough to draw their attention to me.

"Ah..." One girl elbowed the other one. They appeared to be in their early teens, maybe thirteen.

"We were just...taking a walk," the taller girl said. She swallowed hard and bumped her friend with her own elbow. That was almost cute and gave me an idea.

"Outside the walls?" I raised an eyebrow.

"Ah..."

"Please don't tell our parents. They will be so angry." The taller girl spilled her guts out on a single exhale.

I pretended to consider.

"Fine. I understand young people need some freedom from time to time. Be sure not to abuse it," I said.

"Oh, yes, we don't get out much at all. I swear." The taller girl grabbed the other one's hand and, with lowered heads, they marched past me.

"I wonder"—both girls peered up—"can you tell me where Brie Thomas lives? She gave me her address, but I'm afraid I've forgotten it already." I hoped I played this right.

"Oh, yes." They both nodded enthusiastically.

The taller girl pointed to the second row of the townhouses.

"Right there, the fourth door down. I think it's number four-o-five." They waited until I nodded my head and scurried away. I turned in the direction of Brie's apartment and drew a long inhale. *Thank you, girls. You've been most helpful.*

FIVE

Showing up at my all-ties-cut friend's doorstep was not a situation I'd ever thought I'd find myself in. How should I act? Admittedly, it hadn't been me who cut the ties between us. But I hadn't exactly tried to remain close. After seeing Brie at school with her mystery man, we hadn't spoken to or seen each other since. She'd been in my thoughts, of course, and maybe she'd been in there for a reason. Perhaps I was about to walk in on an unpleasant situation. My only consolation at this point was that the teenage girls knew her and that she lived in a nice house. As I ambled down the street to the door marked four-o-five, I noticed everything was orderly. Pavers lined a narrow but clean street. Ceramic planters held miniature trees at regular intervals. No one was outside at this hour. One street lamp stood erect halfway down the block. It cast a faint yellowish light—the rotten shade of my guilty conscience.

I skipped the steps leading to the main door two at a time. There was an intercom with resident listings on one side. Sure enough, it listed Brie Thomas next to apartment C. I pressed her button before I could chicken out and waited.

Nothing happened. Not even a buzzing sound. I rattled the handle, and the door opened right away. So, the intercom didn't work. They might have a limited power output around here. I stepped into a dark corridor with a staircase and tiptoed up the steps. When I located the door with *C* engraved on it, I put my ear to it and listened. Silence. I knocked twice. After a moment of eerie stillness, feet shuffled in the apartment. Someone undid the lock, and the door cracked open. Brie stuck her face in the opening, candlelight in front. Her eyes rounded in a mixture of surprise and fear. She scanned the corridor, grabbed my hand, and pulled me into her apartment. I was too shocked to object to her nails digging into my skin. I found her. After a year without my best friend and the hell of a day I'd had today, my eyes welled up, and I hiccuped.

"Oh, come now. It's going to be okay," she said. Her words, which I had yearned to hear all this time, soothed me. I enveloped her in my arms and squeezed back. I didn't expect our reunion to be this...emotional. Until this moment, I didn't realize how much I'd bottled up. Months of pent-up feelings of loss, betrayal, and loneliness in this world broke me into thousand pieces. Brie said something, but I couldn't make it out. I released her, took a step back, and swiped my eyes dry with the ends of my sleeves. Her face paled with worry.

"I'm sorry. I'm just relieved. I've been worrying about you," I said.

"Oh, sweetie." She gave me another hug and guided me to a couch. "You're freezing." She shivered from holding me close and tightened the robe around her, scowling at my inadequate outfit. Before I could answer her, she ran off toward what I presumed was the kitchen and whisper-shouted on her way, "I will brew us a hot drink."

I sat in the darkness. The moonlight shone in a striped

pattern of wooden blinds, revealing a modestly furnished living room. A couch and a recliner lined the back wall, facing a bookshelf and an average-sized TV. A small coffee table completed the decor. Brie returned with two large mugs in her hands and placed them on the coffee table. This time she didn't carry a candle with her but relied on moonlight. After setting our cups down, she'd gotten a blanket for me, too.

I had *so* many questions for my best friend, and yet now that the initial emotions subsided—and I could see for myself that she was all right—I didn't know where to begin. I felt out of place and embarrassed for barging into her life like this. Still, this was the only way to get into this secured compound that was nowhere to be found on the maps. Well, at least not the maps available to most New Seattle residents. We were told it was out there, north of the city, but the media never ventured out to investigate. And amateurs who did had their posts removed. Something was off about this place, and a renewed fear for my friend solidified. I picked one mug up and wrapped my cold-as-ice palms around it. The heat radiating from the cup warmed my hands instantly and reminded my body of how cold it had been outside and how I'd probably frozen my toes off, after all. Brie turned quiet. I studied her profile. The long auburn hair now hung low, caressing her slim waistline. Her face appeared rounder than what I remembered, but as lovely with defined eyebrows and long eyelashes I'd envied when we were kids.

"So...what is this place?"

Brie let out an overdue breath. "I can't—" Concern reflected in her gaze. She swallowed. "Tell me again, why are you here? Did you come in through the gate?"

"No, Brie." I took a sip of the hot drink Brie had made for us. The luscious sweetness of hot cocoa breathed some energy back into my body. "I sneaked in through a hole in the wall. I came here looking for you, but I didn't expect this." I motioned with one hand around me. Brie nodded her head with understanding.

"I didn't like how things ended between us. I always had this feeling that you might be in trouble. That... I don't know... The guy you showed up with, for example. I thought he was your pimp or held some kind of power over you. I wanted to believe that I was making things up because I was grieving the loss of someone close to me. But lately, I've discovered that there is more to lurking shadows in the corners, and I had this need to find you and witness on my own that you were fine." I shrugged a shoulder and sucked in a lip. I didn't want to sound lame, but that's all I heard while listening to my explanation. I couldn't reveal to Brie what took place earlier today. At least, not until I had a full grasp of reality. Worry lines already underlined the smiles and looks she was giving me. I didn't need to have her question my sanity.

Brie seized one of my hands in both of hers and in a strangled voice said, "You can't even imagine how sorry I am for what I said that day. Please know that I'm okay. Actually, better than okay. I'm happy, and the man you saw me with that day is my boyfriend. I'm here completely out of my free will."

"But—" I was about to protest. Why had she said we could no longer be friends? She didn't let me voice my thoughts out loud, though.

"I know it's confusing. Trust me. I didn't understand much at first myself. But life here is different. People here are very private." Brie searched my face for something, but all I could convey was utter confusion. What was with this place?

"I still don't understand why we had to stop seeing and talking to each other?"

Brie sighed. "I can't tell you any more beyond that. Trust

me." She clutched my hand harder. "I'm fine. I'm safe here, and I'm happier than I'd been in a long while." She smiled.

I wanted to scream. I should've been thrilled I'd found my friend alive and doing well, but here... Why the Fringe? I inhaled deeply.

"Tell me this one thing. Are you or your boyfriend involved in anything illegal?"

"No." She waved her hand and chuckled mildly. "Ashton works security here, and I teach kindergarten."

My jaw fell slack open. Another baby chuckle came from Brie.

"Don't look so shocked. This is a pleasant place. A little alienated from the rest of the world, maybe, but you can make a decent life here. Better than what we were accustomed to, anyway."

Somber silence fell between us. Yes, this was undeniably better than a broken foster care system and vile foster parents. If Brie was content in this strange place, who was I to judge?

Brie deflected all further attempts at talking about the Fringe. We reminisced most of the night about our past together. We laughed, and we cried. I told Brie about my eighteenth birthday, and how I ended up doing odd jobs here and there. She listened intently through those parts. I told her about the men saving me on the bus and that earned me some questioning eyebrow twitches and "hmms." The old Brie resurfaced once again. I said nothing about the junkyard, only that I rode the bus to the last stop on the northwest route and that I hiked from there to the Fringe. Brie rolled her eyes when I mentioned the teenagers sneaking out through the wall. After talking for hours, we drifted to sleep on the opposite ends of the couch, but closer than we'd been in a long time.

SIX

S omeone gave my shoulder a shake. I sprang upright. Events from last night flashed in front of my eyes, and shivers ran up and down my body. My friend's face came into focus, and I smiled at her. *It wasn't a dream after all. She was real.* Brie's grim expression put a damper on my mood.

"What's wrong?"

She grasped my hand in both of hers and squeezed, looking paler than she had just moments ago.

"I am so sorry, Arien. You must leave," she said.

My mouth opened and closed while she pleaded with her eyes for understanding. She didn't want me to go, but she needed me to leave.

"What's going on, Brie? Are you in danger?"

"No." She shook her head, and a stray tear leaked out of the corner of her eye. She stood up. "The Fringe doesn't look kindly at intruders. You cannot stay here, and you most definitely can never return again. I was selfish keeping you for as long as I did." Right, I'd kind of trespassed last night. And I didn't want to run into Fringe's security or whatever they had in this militaristic city. This place made my skin crawl.

I scanned the room for my backpack, realizing I had nothing with me last night, only a jacket. I hugged my friend fiercely, and she returned the sentiment. We let go of each other. I swept my eyes over her apartment again now that the dawn had dissipated the darkness. My initial assessment of the place was accurate. Brie had accentuated the simple décor with splashes of warm colors and accents like the fuzzy throw she'd laid across a recliner.

"Come with me." I don't know who was more surprised by my sudden words, me or my best friend. "I saved up . We can rent a two-bedroom apartment like we always wanted to. There are plenty of jobs available if you don't mind hard work..." Brie's eyes twinkled, but the light in them flitted. She pursed her lips. There was something she wasn't telling me. Finally, she lifted her eyes to mine.

"I'm happy here." She shrugged in lieu of an explanation. "This is my home, and the boyfriend I told you about... Well, he's my fiancé."

A sheepish smile spread across her radiant face. If I didn't believe it before, I sensed it now with my entire being. Brie was happy here. It hurt, on some level, to see my best friend move on without me, but I couldn't begrudge her that. She was and always would be my best friend. My initial shock soon turned into pure joy and I beamed at her.

"Congratulations," I said, choking a little on the emotion.

"You need to let people in, let go of the past. Sometimes that leads to beautiful things."

"I've got Paulie." I balked at the insanity of her suggestion. Hadn't we grown up in the same system? Just because she had a fiancé that didn't make her a relationship guru.

"Your imaginary friend?" She raised one eyebrow.

"No, you've met him." I racked my memory. Maybe she hadn't.

"Anyway, an old man seeking the company of a schoolgirl? That doesn't sound creepy at all." Brie nodded in faux agreement. I grinned.

"I missed you," I said.

"I bet you did. Now, get out."

I stuck my bottom lip out. I wanted to ask if she'd visit me in the city, but I feared the answer would be another "*no*." There was nothing else to say. Except maybe that I loved her; she was my only family after all. But I'd never said the words out loud, not to Brie, not to anyone. It was an unspoken agreement between us to never use these words to define us. Because what was love? An abstract. A formless idea long removed from our reality.

"So, how do I get out of this place undetected?"

Brie winced. "Dumpster."

Bags of trash jostled around me and pummeled my crouched body inside a freaking trash bin. Today was Brie's turn to take the block's trash bin to the dumpster chute embedded into the northern wall. "It's a short distance," she'd assured me when my expression soured at the visage of me inside the filthy container. But it was the only idea we'd come up with, so here I was. I squatted in the center of the smelly trap helping Brie to balance and to avoid raising suspicion. I jostled upward, and the bags skipped along with me. We must have gone over a road bump. Thankfully, the bags around withstood the impact, and no contents spilled out. When we came to a stop a few minutes later, the lid lifted part of the way. Before I could gulp fresh air, Brie slammed it down. A stranger's voice traveled to my outstretched ears.

"Jason, you startled me!" Brie said louder than necessary.

"What are you doing pushing this around?" Jason *tsked,* cajoling. The trash bin rocked and hit a hard object, my head whipping to the side. *Ouch.*

"Oh, it's no biggie. I can manage."

Brie attempted to regain control of the receptacle. The plan was for me to come out of the trash bin and slide down the chute on my own so that I could control my descent. The trash bin began lifting on some sort of machinery, and my heart stilled. Unless Brie succeeded, I was about to be shot out of the container like the trash surrounding me. That was not part of our plan. The lift's engine muffled the conversation outside.

"I'm gonna have to talk with Ash," Jason said in a friendly manner. "I wouldn't let my fiancé, especially one in your cond —" The bin upturned violently, and I went airborne into a dark tunnel. I hurtled downward with bags of waste bumping about slimy and rot-filled walls. The drop was at a sharp angle, and I struggled to find a purchase to slow my descent. Light filtered through ahead, announcing an opening. No wonder they said, "to go to the light at the end of a tunnel." The light was true salvation. I screamed as the chute spit me out and I went flying. My legs sank into a pile of garbage, not all of it bagged. I gagged before drawing my turtleneck over my mouth. This wasn't how I imagined a rebirth.

I shielded my head from the last few bags following me down to a football-field-long dump field. I landed on the very top of a mountain of trash. But as comedic as it was, the position wasn't completely inutile. Above the surrounding foliage, I could make out the furthermost river bank of Avalon River that ran through the city. I wrangled out of the hip-deep trash, slid down, crawled to the edge, and climbed up by way of protruding tree roots. I brushed off pieces of unidentifiable substances from my jacket and pants and sighed mentally. I had a river to follow back into the city. This was going to be one long, cold trek.

SEVEN

A s the sun began to set, I finally reached the entrance to the bakery. The warm aroma of baked goods twisted my empty stomach in knots. I was lucky the owner hadn't closed yet for the day. I apologized for the inconvenience and grabbed my backpack when the owner's wife dragged me into an employee bathroom equipped with a small shower and ordered me to clean up. The owners were generous and loving people. I suspected they were aware of my living situation, but they never treated me any differently.

I protested at first, but in the end, I couldn't resist a hot shower after my journey. My entire body ached, and some parts of me suffered from frostbite. Brie had forced a pair of gloves and a knit hat on me, which prevented the worst of the damage. I showered and changed my clothes, stashing the dirty ones in a plastic bag. I thanked the owner and his wife with a warm smile and promised to scrub the bathroom squeaky clean tomorrow after my shift. It needed it.

I rummaged through a secret packet in the back of my backpack and pulled out a golden bracelet. This was the only jewelry I owned, and I missed it like I'd miss a limb whenever

I had to take it off. I snapped the closure around my wrist and my spirit uplifted—as if I was whole again.

I ruminated over yesterday's events for several long hours while I trekked from the Fringe to the south of the city. Half of the time, I convinced myself I hallucinated the hooded monster, the giant snake, and the three warriors. The other half of the time, I felt certain what happened yesterday was very real. And it was that gut feeling that compelled me to reach out to Paulie. What if he'd been harmed? I would've never forgiven myself if Paulie had fallen victim to the monsters last night while I ran away.

I repressed the rising fear of the possibility I'd be walking into the monster's hands. Or the warriors, since they wouldn't take a no for an answer when they demanded I go with them. I desperately clung to the idea that daylight would keep monsters at bay. Because monsters didn't come out before dark, right? At least, that's what they say. Stepping outside and heading for the bus stop, an ominous feeling of déjà vu hit me. Did all my paths lead only one way? When had my life become so, so...repetitive? Monotonous? I huddled deeper into my hoodie and leather jacket as icy winds picked up, obstructing my progress. A bus stopped on the opposite side of the street. About a dozen occupants stepped out of the bus and dispersed in various directions, except for one. As the bus departed, an elderly man stood transfixed, facing the narrow alley in between tall buildings. I ran up to the busy street and stared in disbelief. The man wore a green fedora, Paulie's favorite hat. I waited for the man to turn around. Loud honking alerted me that I'd nearly stumbled into the traffic. I sprinted to the crosswalk and jammed in the call button. When I glanced at the bus stop, the person I spotted earlier was gone. Gone! The traffic light couldn't have turned red soon enough. I raced across the crosswalk and searched the area in a frenzy. He couldn't have just disappeared. A wide straight sidewalk stretched for blocks ahead, and I would have seen him. Wouldn't I? Unless he entered a store or a building. I passed a narrow alley between an apartment building and small business units and retraced my steps. I peered into the shadowy alley again. Trash cans blocked most of the view, but at the end of the alley a figure was visible. And it wore a hat.

Some scrambling ensued. There was somebody there with him, hidden behind a large container. Paulie, or a Paulie look-alike, kept speaking in a quiet yet harsh tone. I skulked alongside the opposite wall, coming closer. Too close. Contorted eyes of a rugged-looking man in his thirties with shaggy wavy hair connected with mine. Paulie's look-alike held him by the arm with one hand and the man's face twisted in pain. He was younger and bigger than his assailant, yet he seemed to be immobilized and scared shitless. Stricken by the scene playing out in front of me, I stumbled on an empty can. The thing clanked and skipped across the alley, rattling my nerves.

"Arien!" Paulie wrapped his arms around me, pulling me upward from my near slip down the wall. Though his movements were a blur, I'd recognize Paulie anywhere. That was his voice, his woodsy scent on the wind he somehow carried with him everywhere he went. A plume of green smoke erupted behind him, drawing my attention back to the strange man. Except he was no longer standing there. There was no one around but Paulie and me. My friend let go of me but didn't even glance back.

"What was that?" I whisper-shouted, bewildered. Didn't he notice the smoke that had since self-contained itself and evaporated? Where was the man Paulie held up against the wall just a moment ago?

Paulie grabbed my arm and attempted to haul me away. I balked, staring at the spot where Paulie held the terrified man. The place was empty. Someone swiveled my head gently, and Paulie's face came into focus.

"Arien, look at me," he implored. "Good. Now listen, we need to get you out of here. I promise to explain everything, but right now, we need to go."

His eyes begged my acquiescence. I nodded and followed him out of the alley. We walked at a brisk pace up Main Street, blending in and out of the late afternoon populace. When the first shock eased off, I pulled Paulie aside. We stopped in front of one of Main Street's banks. The security guard behind the front glass windows cast us a dubious glance.

"Who was that, Paulie? And what are you doing here?" I asked.

"I was searching for you." His eyes darted around the street and sidewalks. The temptation to follow his shrewd eyes was there, but I feared Paulie might poof into thin air like someone I just witnessed had. My eyes remained glued to his face.

"What is it? Is someone following you? Are you in trouble?" I creased my brows.

He sighed and put his large, withered hand on my shoulder. Gazing into my eyes with raw intensity, he asked, "Were you at the junkyard yesterday?"

I gulped. The terror of yesterday displayed on my face. Not thinking about it and most definitely not talking about it had helped squash those fears. They were multiple, and none the least of them was the fear of having gone insane.

"I was," I whispered. Paulie's beseeching stare urged me to continue, but I couldn't. I could say I'd gone to the junkyard looking for a car part. That was plausible, right? The problem was, I had no car to speak of.

"You didn't make it to my hut," he said. "Something happened to you." He paused, and I dipped my chin.

"There was a...complication on the way. But I'm fine, and you are too. Phew." I wiped off imaginary sweat from my brow. "I'm *so* happy to see you're okay, in one piece," I said with sincerity. The crow's feet around Paulie's sparkling blue eyes softened.

"Don't you worry about me, child. I'm not helpless." I had to agree, judging by the iron hold he'd kept the alley man in. I saw Paulie in a different light now. He was not the elderly gentleman I'd befriended all those months ago. The discovery disturbed me, and I took a small step back.

"You know what happened last night, don't you?" I narrowed my eyes.

Paulie's face fell, and he hunched over.

"I promise you. I'm not a threat to you. What you witnessed yesterday is from my world, my old world..." He smiled wryly. I blinked several times, replaying Paulie's words over and over in my head. As I was opening my mouth to ask some important questions, a loud knock sounded from the bank's window. The bank's security guard gestured rudely for us to scatter.

"Come on," Paulie said, and we resumed walking. Possibilities overwhelmed me. And as much as it frightened me that Paulie knew something about the creatures from my newest nightmare, I still trusted him.

"Where are we going?" I asked.

"To my place." I didn't protest. "Ever since I learned about what transpired last night, I've been searching for you. If the Archon got to you before me, I'd never forgive myself." His face contoured into an angry grimace.

"Well, it didn't...get to me. Three men showed up and fought him off."

"Powers," he grunted. "How did you get away?"

I explained how I'd loosened a stack of metal scrap and hid in a car door structure with access to an underground tunnel. It turned out Paulie knew about it and revealed a second tunnel entrance was hidden south of the city.

"I've never heard of anyone escaping three trained Powers," he mused.

"Who are they, Paulie? And how do you know all this?" A million-dollar question.

Before he could answer, we turned a corner into New Seattle's own Chinatown. I'd never been there. Once, I'd passed by its large ornate entrance, and the place gave me willies. The entrance was a typical Chinese gate with red metal pillars and a Paifang archway decorated with Chinese tile and motifs of mythical beasts.

We crossed below the monstrous structure, and my skin started to crawl. All my senses on high alert, I cinched myself to Paulie's side and walked in silence. Several vendors yelled out their specials from their street stands. The place was loud and busy. Only foot traffic and bicycles were allowed here. Although, you could hear motorbikes coming through occasionally, too. As we neared a group of bicycle rickshaw operators, they perked up, hoping for a customer. We strolled by, and they renewed their conversations except for a couple of drivers who seemed rather pissed off. With their arms folded, they kept glaring at me and Paulie, and something told me they were not upset about us refusing a cab. I broke eye contact. A few other vendors and shoppers cast hostile glances at us as well. No wonder my skin prickled as soon as we passed through the gate—denizens of Chinatown hated outsiders.

Although we weren't the only ones here. Most of the customers lived outside Chinatown. My brows drew together in contemplation. Paulie steered us away from the street onto a sidewalk. It took me a minute to get by a traveling rickshaw, several shoppers, and a vendor. A young man bumped into me, and I spun around. *What the hell?* Why were these people so antagonistic? I swiveled my head in search of Paulie, but he was already on the sidewalk. That man could blend in and out like a chameleon. He held the door of a dry cleaning establishment open and waited for me to enter.

Inside the building, Paulie pulled me to the back. A young girl sitting by the registrar glanced lazily at us from above her magazine but otherwise didn't object as Paulie lifted open the counter slab to let us through. The girl wore black-on-black attire, and her eyes popped with heavy black eyeliner. She blew a bubble of black bubblegum. A muted *pop* traveled to my ears as we reached the first of several rows of hung clothes. I'd never dry-cleaned clothes myself, and I marveled at the sheer amount of various outfits occupying row after row. We entered a narrow hallway that divided a spacious workroom to the left and office spaces to our right. Paulie guided us into the first office. Granted the doors were ajar, but it baffled me that Paulie hadn't even knocked. How did Paulie know all these people?

"Malcolm, I require your services," Paulie said as a way of greeting.

A middle-aged, bald man peered up from the documents he'd been studying and gave Paulie, then me, a perfunctory glance.

"I see." He rose from a large leather chair. He was tall and robust, with a potbelly protruding under his dark green dress shirt. Ill-fitting beige dress pants and black loafers completed his look. He redefined the casual dress code, inflating it with an air of sloppiness.

"This way." Malcolm pointed to the door behind his desk. We followed him through to the adjacent room that didn't seem to belong there. The room resembled an old apothecary. Simple rustic shelves lined the largest of the walls. Malcolm kept a plethora of jars, tinted glass bottles, and baskets with what appeared to be dried herbs. He rolled up an exquisite handmade Persian carpet covering the center square of the wooden floor.

"Malcolm will transport us to my place," Paulie said. My mouth hung open in disbelief. *Transport us?* What did that mean?

"Um...how?" I asked.

"I know this must be overwhelming for you. Trust me"—he rubbed my shoulders in a way fathers did to calm their children—"I will explain *everything* once you're safe."

"I trust you," I whispered. Sweat broke out above my lip as I observed Malcolm placing crystals in a circle about three feet in diameter. The man had spoken little to either of us since we arrived at his shop. He acted as if this was an everyday occurrence. When Malcolm completed the circle, Paulie tugged me to the center.

"Thank you, my friend. I will bring payment next time. The usual?" Paulie asked.

Malcolm's mouth thinned. "That will do," he said.

Without warning, he raised his arms to the sides and closed his eyes. His large nostrils narrowed as he inhaled and relaxed with a deep exhalation. For a moment, I thought I'd gone crazy. *I had to be out of my mind.* I stood within a crystal circle, waiting to be teleported to Paulie's place.

As my resolution to step out of the circle formed, the crystals vibrated. I startled when an opalescent light shot up. In the next moment, I felt weightless, as if someone had turned the gravity switch off. My adrenaline levels spiked, and my breathing quickened. I clutched Paulie's arm and held on for dear life. Something was happening to us, and the idea of space folding I had read about in *Dune* for a school paper was suddenly a stark possibility. As soon as the thought flitted through my mind, the light dimmed out along with the crystals, and we stood on the barren ground of the junkyard, facing Paulie's makeshift abode.

EIGHT

My legs trembled. I couldn't move. Not immediately, anyway. Paulie marched inside his home as if nothing had happened. He left his front door ajar. *How nice of him.*

"Paulie!" I hugged myself.

When he failed to return, I forced myself to take a tentative step out of the circle burned into the ground. I quickened my pace and stepped inside. The old man was collecting various items and depositing them on a wide table—dried plants, pestle and mortar, and jars with unidentifiable living things suspended in liquids. His hands became a blur of practiced motions. When I approached to examine the table's contents, Paulie shooed me away. I bristled at his treatment at first. But I was of no use to him. And no matter how long I observed his work, I couldn't make sense of it. I strolled over to a single narrow bookshelf in Paulie's abode, but paid no attention to the book spines in front of me, either. My head was spinning from the "travel."

"Angel blood runs through you, my child." I faced him.

Paulie's brows pinched while he dripped droplets of tangerine liquid into the concoction.

"I know you're oblivious to this world—the true world you and all of humanity live in," he said, concentrating on his task. "I am weaker now than I was in my prime days, but I sensed your essence during our first chance meeting. I thought you recognized me too, and I was pleasantly surprised you didn't treat me with contempt. But as we kept meeting, I surmised you didn't have the slightest idea who you truly are."

"Angel blood? Are you an angel?"

"Not even close." A sad smile emerged on his aged face. "I'm a druid." Paulie bowed.

"Why didn't you tell me...back then?" I asked in a small voice. I had many questions for Paulie, but I needed to know the answer to this one now.

He shook his head, grimacing. "Your life..." he began while grating a root over a large wooden bowl. "Your life was...*is* already so complicated. I knew I had to tell you, to prepare you, but I wanted you to get on your own two feet first. And the chance of them finding out was nonexistent."

"Them?"

Paulie paused. For the first time since we arrived at the junkyard, he made eye contact with me. Genuine concern and raw sadness marred his mature features.

"You weren't supposed to be here last night. We agreed to meet in two days." Accusation stained his tone. I had no words. It was true; he'd made me promise to stave off my visits to the junkyard until Thursday. I hadn't questioned it, knowing Paulie's eccentric nature, and I had no intention of breaking my promise to him either.

"I'm so sorry, Paulie. The shelter was full, and it was too cold to sleep outdoors..." I left it at that. Paulie squeezed his eyes shut, his mouth flattening. It pained him whenever I mentioned my housing arrangements. Like me, Paulie had no regard for the new city mayor and his new ordinance. He resumed crushing dried herbs in the mortar with added vigor.

"What are these for?" I inched up to the table again.

"The creature you encountered yesterday, the nefora, is a tracker. Neforas place markers on everyone they encounter with their unique vibratory trachea. It's a frequency overlay that lets it locate you instantaneously when it enters this dimension. The nefora is not of concern here since the Powers sent it back to its dimension. The Archon intercepted the frequency."

"The hooded man?"

"Don't be fooled. He's no man. He's pure evil. And he will return. I have no doubts about it. This balm"—Paulie gestured at the table—"once rubbed on the inside of your left arm will camouflage the marker."

"Oh..." I recalled the moment the gigantic worm rotated his head in my direction and cawed at me. The auditory sensation had preoccupied my senses, but there was another sensation present in that moment of an invisible vibrational wave that prickled against my skin. Was that what Paulie was referring to?

"Paulie?"

"Yes, child."

"Why is this Archon after me?"

In succession, three somethings landed with a thud on the ground outside Paulie's door, and my heart began pounding.

"Pau—" The door dented inward and folded in half, flying off the hinges and landing several feet away. Three intimidating men leaped inside. They appeared human except for red-hued angelic wings flexing at their backs with agitation. They wore black skin-tight shirts and utilitarian dark pants with hefty belts. Those belts held wicked weapons. Were they Powers? I didn't recognize any of them, but then Paulie didn't get far explaining the angel-like warriors to me. Judging by the entrance, they didn't come in peace.

Paulie rose up, shoving me behind him.

"Xavier," he boomed with surprising force, "you and your Seraphs are intruding on my property. May I ask what warranted this uncalled-for behavior?"

The warrior with shoulder-length blond wavy hair and chiseled commanding facial features tsked in response.

"Kwanezerus, my friend, our command center received the most disturbing report this morning. An Archon sighting in your area, and a human girl who witnessed it. I must say the description matches well with your friend over there."

Paulie blocked most of my view, which was both a relief and a curse. I was relieved the terror incapacitating each cell in my body wasn't on full display. But I hated cowering. I should've been facing the enemy alongside Paulie. Instead, I stared into the back of Paulie's head and prayed this was just a bad dream—or more like a continuation of one.

"As you see, I'm working on a memory-altering potion so that she can return to society." I blinked. Had Paulie deceived me?

Xavier tsked again.

"There is but one problem with your plan. She is not human, is she?" The following pause charged the air.

"She's an innocent. She knows nothing—"

"Quiet!"

Paulie complied.

"Hand her over nicely, and we'll play nicely, too." Except his tone promising violence and retribution of sorts was nowhere near "nice."

Paulie spun to face me.

"I'm sorry, child. I only have enough power to relocate myself."

Defeat and resignation sounded off in his voice. Green

smoke billowed around him and he vanished. The angel on
Xavier's left side bounded into the fading fog, chanting as his
wings flapped ominously.

"Let him go, Anhelm," Xavier said. At the command,
Anhelm cut off the chant. His wings snapped tight behind his
back. I didn't know Anhelm's intentions, but I was immensely
glad that Paulie left when he could. Was I upset he left me to
deal with these three overgrown angelic beings by myself?
Well, it stung a hell of a lot. But I trusted Paulie wouldn't
have left if he believed my life was in danger. If what Paulie
said was true, they wouldn't hurt me. I hoped. What did they
want from me then? And why were Xavier's intense lapis
lazuli eyes trained on me like I was prey he'd like to catch and
run off with?

"We got what we came for," Xavier said with a hint of
reverence. His eyes never left my face.

"He was hiding a fledgling. He broke at least four edicts, if
not more," Anhelm spat out. My gaze shifted to him. Was
that what I was? A fledgling. As if I'd spoken, all men fell
silent. Their eyes locked on me. My heart pounded in my
ears, and my breaths, although deep and long, were nothing
but calm. I stared at Anhelm, pondering his words, when his
lips curved into a subtle, inviting smile. He took a step
forward but backed away when an unusual sort of growl
rumbled from Xavier's chest. My eyes flicked back to him. I
didn't know what to make of it...of them.

Escape was impossible as the ogres in front of me blocked
even the slightest rays of sunshine streaming into Paulie's
abode. A table edge dug into my rear, or maybe it was me
pressing against it instead, and I sneaked a hand behind my
back to explore it. Otherwise, I stood there as stony as the
men before me, glancing from one to another and trying to
decipher their next move. I rejoiced on the inside when my
fingers grazed what seemed to be a small knife handle. I

seized it. I hoped the piece of cutlery in my right palm was, in fact, not a butter knife but more of a scalpel caliber that would do actual damage when I needed it to.

Finding my voice again, I spoke to them for the first time.

"What do you want?" The question came out steady, harsh even.

"I assume Kwanezerus explained what you are?" Xavier asked.

"He wasn't sure what I was initially—" Anhelm hmmed. I ignored him. "He'd just begun telling me about...this"—I swept my hand in the air in lieu of the words I had difficulty speaking. Only two days ago, demons and angels existed in the bible, lore, and legends, and now? "And what I am when you arrived. Why did he call you Seraphs?" Stalling was my most effective defensive tactic.

Xavier's face morphed into exasperation.

"So, you know nothing."

His disparaging comment irked me.

"I wouldn't say that. I don't know who you are and why you think Paulie broke any of your laws. But I think it's time you tell me what you want with me." I raised my chin a notch. My second-best defensive tactic was playing tough. Because I didn't look like it, if I played the tough bitch act right, I'd confuse the hell out of my opponent and gain time.

This didn't have the desired effect on Xavier, however. He narrowed his eyes as if a new idea had struck him.

"What do you know of the Underground?" he asked.

"The what? Do you mean the Underground Den? The nightclub on Fourth Street?" Xavier's expression soured. He side-eyed the Seraph to his right.

"She's telling the truth. She must not be with them. She's a true orphan," Anhelm said with awe.

What did that even mean? And why did these creatures care if I was an orphan? I was eighteen now, an adult. I wanted to tell them that, but they were not DFACs. I doubted they came here to place me in a new foster home.

"You're one of us. Human with angelic genes."

"I'm a Seraph?"

"Not necessarily. There are other kinds. There is a lot you have yet to learn and acquaint yourself with. You'll come with us to Invicta," Xavier said matter-of-factly. *Come where?* Did they think I'd just follow some strangers to who knows where?

"Er...it's nice of you to offer, but I think I'll pass." Xavier's eyes darkened. "But we can certainly revisit this conversation some other time..."

Anhelm's mouth twitched. The second Seraph hid his smirk behind a fist.

"This is not an offer you can refuse. Now, let's go," Xavier said with finality. Blood boiled in my veins.

"*Excuse me?* I don't know you, nor do I trust you. I've never heard of this place you call Invicta something or other, and I'm nothing like you. For one, I don't have wings. If there truly are some angelic genes in me, they are definitely recessive because, believe me, there is nothing angelic about me."

"Are you finished?" Xavier quirked an elegant eyebrow. That's when I decided I'd slice Xavier into the tiniest pieces and feed him to the fish in the Avalon River. At least, I'd try. Gritting my teeth, I opened my mouth to retort.

"Mezzo," Xavier said, and the man to his right advanced at me. Before I could react, he passed his hand in front of my face. It sparkled with thousands of tiny diamonds, promising dreams of paradise. Sluggishness overtook me, and I began slipping to the floor. *Wait!* I willed my mind to resist this undeniable urge to succumb to a blissful sleep. I caught myself on the table behind me. My arms were all that held me up now. Outstretched arms appeared in front of me.

"Don't touch me!" I yelled at the intruder. My head lulled

side to side on my limp neck. Three sets of black combat boots halted too close for my taste, and I couldn't do anything about it. Anger rose in my chest.

"What did you do to me? If this is supposed to convince me to go with you, you've failed spectacularly." Some nonverbal communication took place above my line of vision. Then, Mezzo whispered how this had never happened to him before.

Hands reached for me, again. "We must take her to our healers," Xavier said.

"Screw the healer. Screw all of you!"

Xavier closed in, his hands finding my back. My face pressed into his expansive chest. I struggled to pull back. My arms were the only body parts that functioned at the moment and I chose to cling to the table. Fear shot through my veins, and my ears drummed a battle cry, propelling me to action. My fingers grazed the hilt of the knife I must have dropped when Mezzo did his thing.

Without thinking, I grabbed it and thrust it into Xavier's side with all my remaining energy. The knife slipped in up to the hilt, grazing a thick rib I now felt under my palm. Not a butter knife. Xavier hissed but never let me go. A glittering hand passed by my face again, and this time my mind abandoned me, wandering towards silver sands and undulating lapis lazuli waters.

NINE

I bounded in and out of the water and drew angel wings in the purest sand I'd ever seen. Everything around me was perfect— sunny, balmy day with froth on the tips of waves and relaxing sounds of tides breaking in shallow waters—and I didn't question a thing. That's when I should've realized this wasn't real because life isn't perfect. Not my life. Circular black spots reminiscent of cigarette burns on old picture films popped up on the horizon and expanded, eating at the picturesque beach landscape from all sides. When the sand under my feet dropped away, I plummeted into nothingness and my consciousness made a fanfare of an entrance. About damn time.

Returning from the dead would've been more pleasant than this feeling. My body was a heavy lump that ignored my commands to move. Not a single eyelid would slide open. Not even the slightest tweak of my fingers. Voices traveled toward me. They sounded muffled as if a barrier separated us, but not too far off.

"How much longer until she wakes up?" a young female voice asked.

"Hard to say. Mezzo had to subdue her twice," a sedated male voice said.

"Yeah. I've never seen him this concerned. He checks in on her every day," another male said.

Every day? Did that mean I'd been in this...coma for days? Once I came out of this shitty state, I'd avoid Mezzo like the bubonic plague.

"Hafthor isn't pleased. He sent Xavier to report to the council in person," the female said, a note of irritation underlying her tone. Someone whistled emphatically.

"Yeah, well, let me know when she's up and ready," the female chirped. Her hurried footsteps echoed in the chamber.

Feet shuffled away and men's voices quieted with growing distance. Relief comforted me. It was one thing to have been unconscious and not have a care in the world, but another to have had awareness but no control over my body and the strangers around me. They didn't know when, if at all, my condition would improve. Add the fact that I had no idea where I was and what these creatures wanted from me. The only thing going for me right now was time—I had time to think and plan.

I recapped the events of the past few days. Certain pieces fell together, but mostly, I still had no clue where I was, who my captors were, or even who I was anymore. Paulie said I belonged with the winged half-human, half-angelic creatures. But that made no sense at all. I was one hundred percent human. There was nothing out-of-ordinary about me. *Tell that to the supernatural freaks after you.* Images of the mammoth snake began haunting me yet again. I shivered. At least the winged men spared me from being its meal. Time passed, and sleep tried to claim me again.

"No..." I whimpered. I tested my body again and my eyelids peeled open. Moisture immediately filled my eyes as bright lights assaulted them. I made out a frosted privacy curtain that partitioned off my section from the rest of the space and a lonely side table by the bed. With great care and anticipation, I curled and flexed my fingers and toes next. They resisted me at first. But, with each repetition, they bent faster and wider. I was on the mend. A mixture of trepidation and excitement rushed through me. Because the scary angels might have worse plans for me once I was awake than the coma overdose they'd put me in. The goal was, of course, not to find out what they had planned for me. I'd try to leave this building undetected. But the realist in me knew escaping these super-enhanced beings right from underneath their noses and from their base, I might add, was no easy feat. Where would I go if I succeeded? They must have known where I stayed and worked by now. *I'll have to leave the town.* Sadness filled me prematurely. First, I'd have to succeed in escaping this hellhole.

I refused to wallow in the gloom and doom of the situation, I forced myself to flex my feet. Several silent minutes later, I continued to push myself to do more. I could be discovered at any time. Occasional beeping sounds disturbed the stillness. By my estimation, I was alone. There was the risk of guards stationed inside or outside this room. I couldn't detect security cameras in my section, but it didn't mean there weren't cameras hidden in this ward. That added another layer of difficulty to my escape.

As I pushed up and swung my legs over to the side of the bed, I took two deep breaths in and out to prepare for one of the hardest tests in my life. *Would I be able to walk?* I needed my legs to hold my weight. The ability to run would come in handy, too. With shaking hands, I rubbed my face up and down.

"Here goes nothing," I whispered and hopped down. I nudged away from the bed and took the first couple of steps like a wobbling toddler. On the upside, my lower extremities worked, and if needed, I should be able to run. The eerie silence lingered. I slumped by the wall and peeked out through an inconspicuous opening, where the curtain met the wall not quite all the way. Dimmed open space greeted me outside my ward. Similar-looking hospital beds ran up and down in line, butted against the wall. The beds were empty, curtains drawn back to one side. A glass-front cabinet was stacked with prepackaged medicines. Other shelves held medical supplies and equipment. A row of monitors lined the long tables in the center of the room. All monitors displayed screensavers of an emblem I didn't recognize with a sword on angel wings. The words below read *Invicta*.

I tiptoed across the room to the computer station in search of a keyboard. Except for a pile of stacked files, the desks were bare, and all drawers were locked with a finger-print reader. I had nothing to go by, not even a map of this place. Based on the proportions of this room alone, the building had to be as large as the New Seattle Hospital, but older. The plaster on the walls had turned mustard-yellow in places and began peeling off in others. Greige stone covered the ceiling.

There was only one way out of here, that I could see, anyway. Large dark cherrywood double doors stood between me and my first step toward my freedom. I scanned the area for any footwear. But there was nothing in here. At least I had my jeans and a plain gray T-shirt on. Someone had taken my jacket off, and I missed my backpack. It might have remained at Paulie's. I crept to the double doors and laid my ear on them. Nothing.

I cautiously lowered the handle and eased the door open, concealing myself behind it. When no one entered, I peered around it. The hallway was cavernous and stretched the length of a football field, branching off into different hallways at intervals. A thin line of luminous light ran about a foot above the floor on both sides. The stone in the ward extended into the hallway. Large red stones polished by traffic formed flooring. This didn't bode well for me. This place was monstrous, and without windows, I had nothing to orient myself with. I could've been levels under the ground for all I knew.

I had to be smart about this. Follow my instincts...or something. I hobbled to the left. Another hallway opened. I paused, not knowing whether to follow this hallway to the end or turn here. I shut my eyes and inhaled. Before I could question myself, I turned. I came to a staircase at the halfway point on the opposite wall. If I was underground, I'd have to make my way up. I climbed the stairs one by one, tuning into my surroundings. I poked my head into the hall on the first floor above. Although similar in build and shape, this corridor held more doors. Fear rose in me. I flattened myself against the wall and squeezed my eyes shut. *I have to do this. There is no other way*.

I scaled the next set of stairs with heaviness settling into my chest. I glanced back—I could still return to the medical ward and hope for the best. A decidedly better option than getting killed during this escape attempt. I froze and ducked when I heard two male voices exchange a greeting. One male congratulated the other on a difficult...kill. If I had hackles, they'd be all at attention right now. The conversation ended and both men walked away. When I dared to lift my head, at first, I thought I was hallucinating.

A handsome male face hung over me, staring at me with a delightful smile. The head was attached to an outstretched torso leaning on the staircase railing, propped on crossed arms. The delight gave way to mischievous amusement. I yelped and jumped to my feet. The motion had my equilibrium at the heels of my feet, which teetered on the edge. My spine caved out, and I threw my arms forward in hopes of grasping something. They grasped something, all right.

Xavier's corded forearms. Repulsed, I released his arms, expecting to plummet down a flight of stairs. I didn't, however. Xavier clawed my elbow and dragged me up to the floor where his lower body had stayed during the entire three-second-long ordeal. We stood on the same level now, and yet we were not. *I* faced his chest.

TEN

"**F**inally decided to join the living?" Xavier smirked. "I nearly ventured in search of a prince to kiss you awake."

"D-did you j-just reference *Sleeping Beauty?*" I croaked.

I gaped at him, stunned. He made no sense. He defined formidable. The air around him crackled with power, and my hair stood on end. He was a beautiful being, though. His face was clean-shaven and sculpted by an artist. Dirty blond locks framed it. His pupils swam in aquamarine waters. If his wings were visible at this moment, I would think him a god. But they were hidden—put away or something. And the supercilious twist of his mouth reminded me he was no deity. More like an angel of doom and misery. My misery.

"I had no idea your...*kind* had an interest in folktales. Wouldn't that be too...mundane for you?" I tried to hide the tremble in my voice.

My heart pounded, and the ringing in my ears intensified. I didn't know how much adrenaline one's body produced; my reservoirs were beyond exhausted at this point. A part of me demanded I run, but the other warned me about leaving the lethal being in front of me out of my sight. I listened to the latter.

"Hmm... The sarcasm doesn't suit you, little one." His eyes twinkled. "I'd advise, though"—Xavier leaned in until only uncomfortable inches separated us—"that you do not forget your place in this new situation you're in."

He picked up a lock of my hair and wound it on his finger. I refused to react. Even when he tugged at it until my head tilted, I maintained eye contact with him. He grinned, displaying his pearly whites. Weren't there any flaws in this humanoid creature? Between his attractiveness and harshness, cruelty even, I was getting whiplash. My tongue stuck in my mouth, paralyzed and indecisive...as was my brain.

"They will need to train you right away. Such behavior can get you killed. Although, in your case, I'd suggest punishment instead." He leered. "It'd be a waste to kill you," he breathed into my face. The innuendo hung heavy between us.

I cringed, but this wasn't the first time someone had threatened me with death, physical abuse, or sexual exploitation. I stood my ground.

"You know, laying there in a coma, I almost regretted stabbing you," I gritted through my teeth. It came out in a whisper as if we were sharing a secret.

Xavier released me but remained in my space. "Almost?" He raised an eyebrow.

I folded my arms over my chest.

"And now?" he asked, with another hike of his eyebrow.

"Now, I wish I'd aimed higher," I said on impulse. It was not smart to provoke him this way. Words spilled out of my mouth whenever I felt cornered as if some defense mechanism switched on inside I wasn't in control of. I tensed, waiting for the promised punishment. But instead, he tilted his head back and guffawed. The sound was rich and oddly... pleasant. But annoying, yes, definitely annoying.

Fast footsteps resounded on the staircase, and a male figure approached. He was young, twenty-ish maybe. His face was red and his breathing was labored. When he laid his eyes on Xavier and me, he spoke into his smartwatch. "I have her. Abort code orange." The man scanned me up and down with his clinical eyes as if I was a test subject.

"Lost something?" Xavier asked.

As if on cue, something snapped in the man's demeanor and his posture straightened. His irregular breathing quieted as he forced a large swallow down his throat.

"Sir, the fledgling left the infirmary...unattended. We did not anticipate she'd wake up today or...leave." The man's face and neck broke out with more red splotches. He lowered his gaze to the floor.

Flicking my eyes to Xavier, I sensed a wave of anger rolling over him. "Weren't my instructions clear when I delivered her to your ward? You will report your incompetence to your supervisor, or do I need to file a report, secondborn?"

"Yes, sir. We alerted Malcolm."

"Good," was his stern reply. Returning his attention to me, he said, "You will go with this secondborn back to the infirmary for your assessment. Then, you will follow directions from your assigned counselor as to your quarters and training. Straying from these orders is not an option. Do. You. Understand?"

My mouth dropped open. Was he expecting me to listen to his commands and to hand-deliver myself to some kind of testing? As if I was staying here. I *did not* intend to remain here or anywhere near these creatures. I opened my mouth to voice the protest, but Xavier cut me off.

"Unless you prefer I hunt you down?" His expression morphed into elation—but in a dark sort of way. He encroached on my personal space again. I didn't falter, but I could not bring myself to look into his stormy eyes. I stared at his exposed collarbone and the sinewy muscle of the side of his neck. A wisp of warm air carried his words to my ears and my petrified heart.

"Make me hunt you, little one. I'd so enjoy hearing you scream," he whispered. I closed my eyes. He... This wasn't real if I couldn't see it, I reasoned. Xavier promised pain. Would he want to even out the score?

"He's gone," the newcomer said.

Startled, I fluttered my eyes open. How long had passed since I cowardly recoiled inside? I squinted at the man. He appeared human, which I recently discovered meant little. But he also lacked the air of disdain and self-veneration I attributed to the half-angels. Was he human or something altogether else? He cleared his throat.

"I'm a... I'm Zed." He held out his hand to me. After a moment of hesitation, I shook it for what it was worth.

"Arien."

"I know," he said, a small smile gracing his lips. He scratched his temple with an index finger. "Listen... I mean, could you...walk with me to the infirmary? Please."

I contemplated my options with Xavier fresh on my mind. I shivered and nodded. Zed released a long sigh as if he'd accomplished an arduous feat. He stepped aside and gestured toward the staircase like a true gentleman would.

"They need to establish a protocol for this," he muttered to himself as we walked down the steps. Chills ran up and down my body in protest. I shouldn't listen to Xavier. I should try to break out again. But those glinting blue eyes kept slipping into my head as if monitoring for any sign of dissent. I shook my head and preoccupied myself with studying Zed's profile instead. He was too deep in his thoughts to notice. Zed was handsome in a bookish way. Although he was tall and slim, he ambled with a slight hunch, indicative of a more sedentary lifestyle or job. His dark brown hair was cropped short; he had a straight nose and almond-shaped eyes. The olive tan of his skin highlighted the rich amber of his irises. The plain dark green long-sleeve shirt hung loosely on his upper body in contrast to the form-fitting skinny jeans. He wore tanned loafers, and that made a corner of my mouth twitch. Too stylish for partaking in demon-catching activities. I chewed on a lip. I had much to learn about these beings—and the demons, the denizens of China-town, even Paulie.

"You don't like them, do you?" A gravelly voice drew my eyes away from Zed's shoes.

"Hmm?" I asked, confused.

"The shoes." He pointed a slim finger downward.

"Oh." I studied Zed's face. His question caught me off guard. A few minutes ago, someone threatened my life, and now I was discussing fashion.

"They're...okay." I winced. Telling untruths was not my thing, and I hoped he was not a prideful type. His face fell crestfallen at my admission, causing a tiny pang of guilt to flip in my stomach. Argh, I needed to work on making friends, and allies, and not complicating matters further. Especially if said people were my captors. Zed pushed open one side of the mountainous double mahogany doors. Inside, he guided me toward the computer and medical supplies station, where another male figure sat in front of six monitors. When he swiveled to face us, I faltered. My gaze hopped from one face to the other. Zed scratched the back of his neck.

"Yeah, we get that a lot. Arien, meet my brother, *twin* brother, Dez."

The mirror name play took me by surprise as much as the mirror image grinning back at me. Dez stood up to his full six feet and extended his hand.

"Nice to meet you, comatose girl." The corners of his mouth spread farther apart.

"Um...uh...hello." I offered a limp hand more on autopilot than a true greeting.

So far, the angel beings I'd met had been rude and presumptuous. The brothers didn't exude any of these qualities. Maybe they weren't like the others and were human, like me? Yes, until I was proven otherwise or grew wings, I contended I was human. Human beings were no longer the only denizens on planet Earth. But I'd be damned before believing Paulie or my captors that I wasn't human either. No, I was falling back on the good old principle of "innocent until proven guilty," and, in my eyes, I was "human until proven angel."

"Causing havoc among the orders and running around with a druid. I *like* you." Dez winked and slumped back into his chair, sliding towards his computer station. I blinked. So that was...different. I glanced at the first brother, who seemed to share my dismay. He ran his hand down his face and made a noise in his throat.

"Anyway...come with me." Zed strolled to the cabinets holding various unidentifiable panaceas, including some regular generic medications I recognized.

I rested on a swiveling stool he'd pulled out from underneath a massive ebony desk. Setting several implements down, he first reached for a blood pressure monitor. He secured a cuff to my bicep and pressed a button on the unit. The roaring of the small engine filled the silence, pumping air into the sleeve until it compressed my arm. Numbers flickered on the monitor as the cuff deflated. They settled on one hundred ten over seventy and my pulse at sixty. Recalling some of my human anatomy studies, I knew my vitals were good. Zed gave a brief nod, too engrossed in his task. Next, he shone a light into my eyes and examined my throat and ears. Up to that point, I hadn't minded his intrusion. Not until Zed grabbed a handheld tool I wasn't familiar with. It resembled a small paddle. One side, the one Zed pressed buttons on, seemed to be a control board. The other side had a two-inch metal strip stretched across its length.

"What's that?

Zed beamed as if I asked about his favorite football team. If they even followed human sports. "This is a nuclear magnetic resonance or NMR scanner. Works similar to the MRI chambers mundane medicine employs." He thrust the NMR closer to my head, and I swayed to the left.

"I'm not injured. I don't need an MRI." I might have warmed up toward Zed a smidge, but I wasn't about to drop my guard. Especially not when the likes of Xavier breathed in this building. I gave him my best unwavering stare. At last, he sighed and laid the NMR tool on the table. He typed into his laptop.

"NMR scans are standard procedure with new candidates," Dez said. I shot him a blank stare. "You know, new cohorts accepted into the training."

"I did *not* apply," I said dryly.

Dez chuckled, and Zed joined him.

"True," Dez said. Both men sobered up upon noticing my sour expression.

"Right, just one more thing, and we can wrap this up." He rummaged through a drawer and pulled out a syringe. I gripped the edge of my stool. No way in hell was I letting them inject me with anything.

"What's this for?" I hid the quiver in my voice.

"A blood draw." He assessed me with his trained eyes, placing the syringe on the table between us as if to say, "Nothing to fear here."

"The report says you learned about your angelic heritage a couple days ago," Zed said. Dez turned away from the monitors and concentrated on our exchange. "There are different factions of the Earthbounders. Some are more pure-blooded than others, but in general, there are Seraphs"—he gestured around him to point out this fortress—"less common Powers who are top-level assassins, and lesser groups descending from the Tribunes, Archangels, Cherubs, etcetera who dwell among the people. We are the hybrid progeny of ancient beings who walked this planet a long time ago."

"Oh...are you part alien or something?" I winced because saying that sounded odd. Aliens were fictional creatures in movies and books. They didn't walk this planet, did they?

Dulcet laughter drew my attention toward a walking figure of a petite female.

"Leave it up to you two to educate new fledglings, and they'll think we're small green people parading in human costumes," the newcomer said. "Sorry, I'm late. I'm Nelia." The female offered up her hand. "I'm your assigned orientation leader." Her large emerald eyes softened around the edges as our hands parted. Nelia was stunning, with thick golden-blond curls hanging past her shoulders. She wore enough makeup to accentuate her soul-searching eyes. Her casual clothes—white sneakers, black leggings, and a long dark green sweater with a loose turtleneck—altogether painted a picture of poise and calm.

Nelia scanned me from head to toe in a non-obtrusive way. She scowled at Zed.

"I'm taking over," she announced in a brooking-no-argument manner. "She'd want to have showered and changed before being prodded with medical implements." Zed's neck flushed.

"Not his fault," I said. "I kinda tried to...escape."

Nelia smirked.

"I bet you did. And how did that work out for you?" She waved her hand in the air dismissively.

"I must collect a blood sample before she goes," Zed said.

"Why?"

"We can determine which angel faction is dominant in your genome. This will help to ascertain your placement."

I didn't understand what placement Zed was referring to, but I liked the idea of getting some answers. The test could confirm I was one hundred percent human.

"Come on. I'll take you to your quarters so you can clean up. We must get you some food, too." Nelia clasped my arm and weaved it through hers. Before I knew it, we were up to the entrance. I shot a last parting look at the brothers. They sported smug expressions as if they enjoyed watching me being handled. I screwed up my face and they rewarded me with grins.

"See you around, Arien," Zed said.

At the same time, Dez said, "Au revoir." He punctuated it with a wink.

ELEVEN

I sized Nelia up out of the corner of my eye. I considered my chances of wrestling away from her. A notion I soon dismissed when she tightened her firm hold on me. I had a few inches on Nelia, but I'd bet a hundred bucks she'd have had no trouble restraining me if needed. She led us through endless hallways and staircases to a section she said was delegated to trainees. I was a trainee now, a fact I could not wrap my head around. It went along with the fact that Paulie was a druid, people sprouted wings, dark hooded creatures roamed in desolate places with ginormous snake pets, and so on. Would I ever get used to this life? I didn't know the answer to that. I knew I didn't want to stay here—or any other place—if I couldn't come and go at will. I was now a "trainee," but in reality, I was a prisoner here. I had to be clear about that with myself. No matter how friendly people might or might not—thinking of Xavier and his weird-ass buddies—be in this place.

Nelia showed me to a single room with a small bathroom. The room itself was generic and pragmatic. It contained a twin-sized bed, a wooden desk with a matching chair, and one small wardrobe closet which held a few articles of clothing, all my size. Nelia explained she'd had this room prepared when I first arrived—*arrived* used loosely since I was comatose upon entering these premises—and guessed my size from the clothes I had on me. She pointed out my backpack stashed under the bed and promised everything in it was intact. At last, she stepped out, affording me privacy.

Under any other circumstances, I would've enjoyed the hot shower, but not today. Not in this unfamiliar place. I chose a sparring outfit with loose gray pants and a T-shirt because they seemed the most comfortable out of the entire wardrobe. I liked the cozy feel of the material on my skin, too.

When I opened my room door, Nelia was there, flipping through a thickly bound book. She looked like she'd never left.

"Nice. You almost look like you belong here," she said with a cheery note. I wrinkled my nose.

"I said *almost*," she said. "Why don't we get you some fuel?" She set off walking, and I joined in step with her. "And get you familiar with our history and teachings." She sounded apologetic when she dumped the volume into my unsuspecting hands. My eyes bugged out of their sockets. This tome was thousands of pages long.

"You expect me to learn this *tonight*?" I whisper-shouted. Anxiety gnawed at my insides.

Nelia clapped me on my shoulder, amused. "Don't be silly. It takes years to master the material and a lifetime to perfect combat techniques. And that's for those who grew up Earth-bounders. But the sooner you start..." She didn't finish. She didn't have to. There was no consolation in what she implied. I pinched my mouth, inspecting the tome. I could use a Cliff Notes version, but somehow I doubted they had one.

"Oh, don't worry. You're a secondborn, like me. We

seldom engage in combat. Most of us get assigned to more *mundane*"—she air-quoted—"tasks. There are various fields available to you. Intelligence gathering—that's mostly for computer geeks, but if you have an aptitude for it... Then, there are managerial positions like secretaries, accountants and so on, scientists and healers, weapons handlers, kitchen workers, washers, and room service to recount a few. So, the lifetime of combat training doesn't apply to us. Only a couple of years of basics."

I swept my eyes over her, wary of the physical strength she exuded.

"You work out a lot?" I asked before I could stop myself. Nelia laughed softly.

"Staying fit is part of our way of life. We are obliged to be ready to defend ourselves even if we are secondborn, and we'll engage in a battle when necessary. Think of us like a backup."

"A reserve?" I asked, trying to equate Nelia's explanation to something I understood.

She nodded.

"What is a secondborn?"

Nelia frowned. "I heard you have little knowledge of your heritage." She glanced at me, her eyes filled with pity.

"I think it's safe to say I have *zero* knowledge." I blew out a long overdue breath of irritation.

"Right. The secondborns are exactly what the name implies. They are second children to full-blooded Earthbounders. We differ from our older siblings. The fundamental difference lies in that the secondborns cannot transcend."

"Transcend?"

"The first child born into an Earthbounder family is always full-blooded. Pures are nature's trick to preserve our abilities amid our scarce population. They, the full-blooded ones, can call on the ancestral magic flowing in their veins and transform into winged beings—our true forms. They are stronger and faster. They can fly, and they become invisible to the human eye when in their true forms." I paid close attention. Nelia scanned my face. She must've seen something to her satisfaction. "There are drawbacks to being a full-blooded Earthbounder, a Pure, though. The density of this realm is not compatible with their true form. They can only transcend for a defined time. For some of the seasoned Earthbounders, that could be as long as an entire day without respite. When a Pure transcends for the first time on the day of his eighteenth birthday, he will transcend for about an hour tops and will require several days of rest afterward."

There were implications to what Nelia was telling me, that I was certain of. But I pushed those thoughts aside. My brain was on an informational overload, reorganizing neurological pathways and acclimating. In my case, that required time.

We walked down a long hallway leading to a double-wide, white windowpane door. The dining hall was a cavernous space with high white ceilings and suspended fluorescent luminaries. They kept the original brick walls here, aged and hollowed in some places. A menagerie of industrial stools and chairs accompanied dark wood tables of various sizes. To my relief, the hall was empty.

"What time is it?" Why hadn't I asked that before? What day was it?

"It's mid-morning. If we're lucky, they will still have some of those delicious pancakes in the kitchen," she said with a renewed bounce in her step.

A tiny smile formed on my lips involuntarily. But it soon melted away as a prickly sensation ran down my arms. I scanned the room for its source. There was an adjacent room to our left, hidden from the view of the main entrance. It separated its occupants from the general populace in a way reminiscent of a VIP section. The room was decorated with modern paintings and unique furniture pieces which screamed high society. A small group of men occupied one of the few tables dispersed throughout this section. I suspected they were full-blooded Earthbounders. Their athletic physiques and demeanor were clues enough. I flinched. Were the three men I encountered at Paulie's junkyard among this group? But as half of them sat with their backs to us, I couldn't tell. Nelia retraced a few steps backward, following my gaze.

"Those are some of our Pures. They normally have break-fast brought up to their rooms," she whispered. Her mouth twisted like she'd tasted something sour. "Stick to my side and don't draw attention to yourself."

We resumed walking to the self-serve food area.

"What was that?" I whispered. Nelia's expression suggested she didn't know what I was talking about, but I knew better. "Come on. Why are we supposed to scamper around like mice in their presence? Aren't we all Earth-bounders?"

"It's not like that." She screwed her face in contemplation. "Remember when I said the secondborns are like a reserve unit? Well...we also take orders from the Pures. They rank higher."

"Oh." I mulled this over. "In the field...or all the time?" I hoped the answer was only during operations...

"That's not clearly defined. Definitely in the field, as you put it, and while on duty. But there's an overall expectation of deference and respect toward the Pures, no matter what Earthbounder line they're from. If they ask you to stop and tie their shoe, you stop and tie their shoe." Nelia passed me a plate and uncovered the buffet trays. Food lost its appeal. The prickling sensation on my arms traveled to the back of my head.

A loud whistle resonated in the hall.

"We need coffee," boomed a fierce male voice. My back stiffened. Nelia picked up a carafe, but before she could take a step, the same voice called out, "Not you."

She sucked in her lip, setting coffee down.

"It's only coffee. Pour it, say nothing unless asked a direct question, and don't stare." She beamed, although it didn't reach her eyes. I gripped the carafe and lumbered over. I counted six figures but didn't dare examine them closer. Four mugs lifted in the air. The men who'd been having an animated conversation when I first approached, quieted as I worked around the table. By the time I got to the last mug, the conversation had died down.

"Is this the one you caught today, Xavier?" a casual, assessing voice asked.

My hand trembled, and soon lines of coffee ran down the sides of the carafe. A single drop splashed onto someone's lap. *Please, don't let it be Xavier.* I inspected the man's face. Not Xavier's. The warrior blinked at me, brushing his pant leg off. I dared to glance around the table. Most of the men wore guarded expressions, but at least they lacked hostility. I said most because Xavier would no doubt be the exception. He lounged at the very end, obscured in shadow. When he leaned in, his stormy eyes locked with mine. Every cell in my body vibrated with the need to submit. And I ought to have cowered, but rules be damned. I promised myself not to lose sight of the predator, and I would not start now. I stood up straighter.

"He didn't catch me. I failed to escape. Something I plan to rectify."

The men guffawed. Wholehearted bouts of laughter erupted with several men clapping others on the shoulder or the table. *What does one have to do to be taken seriously around here?* I groused internally. Xavier didn't laugh unless his version of a laugh was a crooked set of his lips.

"No wonder you felt restless this morning," the man to his right said with glee.

"Sounds as though you're a seasoned escape artist." Xavier's expression remained stoic. He gave nothing away.

"You'd be surprised how many sleazy men walk the streets these days."

"And you lived on the streets." A statement, not a question.

Mortification stained my cheeks red. I wasn't sure if the reason behind it was embarrassment or the vile feelings I'd begun developing for Xavier. Probably both.

"I did."

"Excuse me," Nelia called from the entrance. "I must escort this secondborn to her quarters immediately." She made a show of checking her smartwatch. "I can't possibly keep the Magister waiting any longer."

Everything paused. Xavier's eyelid ticked as he bore his eyes into Nelia. That act alone would have iced my blood. She waited. We all waited.

Xavier's lips stretched, revealing a straight line of white teeth.

"Of course," he said.

When I replaced the carafe, Nelia had a carry-out box ready, and we marched out without as much as a glance at the privileged Earthbounders. They resumed their discussion while I begged my legs not to buckle beneath me.

"You intrigue them," Nelia said. While her act at the cafeteria was a ploy to get me away from the Pures' inquisition, she did in fact have some important matters to attend to and requested I return to my quarters.

I swiveled my head her way. "How?"

"For one, you're an orphan who was raised in the human world. That's rare. Add the fact that you resisted and outsmarted three Powers during your first capture—that's just unheard of."

"Oh." Wouldn't anyone have done what I'd done? "Are the Powers here?" Ever since Xavier brought me to Invicta, I'd been on guard about that threesome. Nelia made a sound in the back of her throat.

"Oh, no. Powers don't belong to any of our organizations. Most of them work solo. But they are part of the network, and they're required to alert their closest Seraph station of any unusual activity in our region. That's how we found out about you."

"Ha. And you always take in orphans?"

"If there's an orphan in our region, we'll provide shelter and education. Any secondborn can apply and train at Invicta. But only descendants of Seraphs maintain their residence and perform jobs at one of our stations. Other orders don't organize, and many allow their members to live among the humans."

"Let's hope I'm not a Seraph then," I murmured.

Nelia snickered and smacked me on the back.

"We'll get along just fine." She wiped a stray tear. "Just don't say it loud. In fact, it'd be wise if you don't even think it..."

TWELVE

Master Malcolm was the Head Secondborn at Invicta. He directed all operations involving secondborns, and today he was my tutor. After resting a couple of hours in my room following the meal, Nelia guided me to a spacious library. I brought the heavy manual Nelia had so helpfully provided only hours ago. Our conversation on the origins of Earthbounders and their history was captivating. The Master carried the aura of warmth and assurance. His hair was a blend of salt and pepper, yet, like all the Earthbounders I'd come across, he had an air of timelessness around him. When the conversation dove into topics he was passionate about, he embodied a young warrior with his entire stature. His smile was intoxicating, and I caught myself smiling back in response. But there were moments in history, a distant history, which he'd recounted with sorrowful eyes only personal experience could bring on.

I embraced Malcolm's openness. His presence made this place less horrifying and possibly even palatable. At least, my first day at Invicta was survivable. The Master frequently left the library to attend to his other responsibilities. Some of them required physical exercise as his change of outfits implied. I tried my best to stick with the book, but my eyes kept wandering to the broad arched windows and the fields beyond them. Groups of trainees rotated out on various obstacles and weapon stands.

I blew out a frustrated breath. Malcolm might have made progress selling Invicta to me, but who was I kidding? I was no warrior. Earthbounders were raised in this ideology, this way of life. They possessed superior strength and speed. Especially the Pures, who could tap into a plethora of gifts such as invisibility when they unveiled their hidden angel-like wings. My Earthbounder genes were so weak I was practically a human. A human in an Earthbounder world. Why in the hell would they want me here?

I guessed my capturers didn't know the extent, or the lack, of my abilities. They also suspected I was with the rebellion. Whether they believed I'd never heard of Earthbounders before remained to be seen. I understood, though, their options were to either control me or remove me, permanently.

I pushed the handbook away. I stretched and strolled around, inspecting bookshelves more out of boredom than genuine interest. A thick volume on angel marks drew my attention. I began sliding it out when a hand twice the size of my own covered mine and thrust it back in. I stiffened. He'd been so quiet; I didn't hear him approach. His body heat radiated to my back, suffocating me.

"You're so small," Xavier whispered. Expelled air ruffled the hair on the side of my face. My heart stuttered.

He squeezed my wrist, eliciting a wave of pain up my arm, and spun me around, backing me into the bookshelf. I glared at him. My lips pressed into a firm line.

"You can breathe now." He smirked.

"What do you want?"

"Why, I'm your tutor for the rest of the day."

I gaped. The obnoxious warrior played with a strand of my hair.

"Stop that." I swatted his hand away.

An angry growl caused me to freeze again. Xavier scowled as if his reaction surprised him, and he took a step backward. Malcolm reentered the library, and his eyes locked with mine briefly.

"Xavier, can I have my student back?"

"She's all yours," Xavier said with an air of nonchalance. His words contradicted the way he studied me. He stood unmoving, delighting himself in a slow head-to-toe perusal of my body. His eyes twinkled while bile rose in my throat. My palms curled into fists, and he grinned. *Jerk.* He made me think he was taking over my training. What was worse? I bought into it. Since he wasn't moving, I unglued myself from my spot and stepped past him.

"I like to see you tremble in front of me." His words were a whisper, destined for my ears only.

I swiveled, ready to retort. With what? I had no idea. Xavier eased the library door open and walked out before I came to my wits. He was gone in an instant, never looking back.

"I don't have a whole day..." Malcolm stood by my study, squeezing the chair's solid wood rail.

I hurried over and reached for the manual when Malcolm's wooden bo staff struck the book and pinned it down. I jerked my hands away, watching Malcolm for any further unexpected moves. Was this part of today's lesson?

"Don't waste my time." His eyes turned cold but were unreadable otherwise. Was he referring to the recent incident with Xavier or something else? I matched Malcolm's unwavering stare with my own. In my mind, I scrutinized the events of today and those since I arrived at Invicta with what I knew about this race of warriors. Malcolm would feel displeasure upon seeing Xavier's and other Seraph's reactions to me, but he was a sensible man. He knew that was out of my control. But what I had control over was my devotion to the cause and my commitment to becoming the best I could be in this short amount of time—to evolving into a second-born warrior. Malcolm was questioning my commitment.

"I won't," I vowed. My stare never wavered.

The master brought the bo staff to his side with lethal grace. Relief swept over me. Until this moment, I'd never realized how badly I needed to become a warrior. A life of servitude in one of the other secondborn professions was out of the question. If this was going to be my life, I'd rather hack some demon heads off or die trying. I broke our eye connection first out of respect.

I opened the manual to the last pages I'd read in his absence.

"That's enough for the day." Malcolm twirled the bo staff in one hand. I'd seen nothing like it up close. Such skill and dexterity. The abrupt stop to the movement took me by surprise and haziness came over me. I shook my head to clear it. Malcolm's eyes shone.

"Few of us use the bo staff in a battle these days. They think it a relic. And yet it never fails to hypnotize the opponent, rendering them useless for deadly seconds."

I blushed.

"We're going to the sparring center. It's time to evaluate your speed, reflexes, combat skills, weaponry..."

Blood drained from my face. "Yeah, about that, I can tell you right away I have none of...that."

Malcolm's eyes gleamed.

"I haven't been challenged like this in... No, I've never had an untrained senior classman in my long life." The gleam grew dangerously brighter. His eyes went distant as he rubbed his hands together.

"That's me. 'Challenge' is my middle name," I muttered, waiting for Malcolm to announce my immediate fate. The Master lifted his arm. His smartwatch interface activated with light.

"Cedric, I'm putting you in charge of evening drills. I'll be in the arena with our newest recruit." He pierced me with his shrewd eyes. "That's the one."

I groaned. *Here's to my brilliant idea of becoming a warrior.*

THIRTEEN

I didn't expect to dream so soon at Invicta. I was physically exhausted, battered, and mentally overwrought. Yet I dreamed of pounding on my door. No... Someone kicked my door in. There were three or four of them. Large men in dark garb, details escaping my tired mind even in my dream. It seemed to be early morning, judging by the low rays of sunlight hitting the curtain. One man approached the bed. Sculpted cheeks and a wide jawbone contoured his face. He was handsome, especially with his dark curly hair dancing around his face. But why was his face twisted into a snarl? I didn't want this dream anymore. I squeezed my eyes shut. Silence. Ahh... That was much better.

"Get up," said a damning voice in my room. "We have questions to ask of you."

I jolted upright, clutching sheets to my chest. I hadn't dreamed these men up! My heart skipped its way to my throat.

"Who are you?"

"Your worst nightmare," the man by my bedside said. He leered, and a wave of heavy air rushed over me. This wasn't good. "You have two minutes to get dressed and step outside."

He was already on his way to the door. The other men followed, smirking to themselves and sharing knowing glances. Oh boy, what sort of pile of poop had I stepped into now? Was this about the cafeteria incident with the Pures? As the door clicked shut, I threw the sheets down and yanked out a new workout set—loose black pants and a black V-neck. My hands trembled as I pulled the clothes on. *Get your shit together, Arien.* I got on all fours to fish my shoes from underneath the bed. I had stashed them there last night—a habit from staying at homeless shelters. It was that or sleeping with shoes on.

The light from the corridor lit up the room. I knocked the second shoe out of the way and dove deeper under the bed. Steel fingers dug into my waistband and tugged. I banged my head on the bed frame. The fingers clasped my arm and dragged me up to standing.

"My shoes." I tried to free myself, stumbling and jamming my left knee into the floor. The two men who'd grabbed me only tightened their grip. I gave in and tried to match their pace. I didn't see the dark-haired one with us.

"Where are we going?" I tried again.

No answer. I scanned my captors' faces, but they ignored me. I sensed tension rolling off of them, no...anticipation. They were eager to begin something. Could that something be my interrogation? I swallowed hard. The corridor was desolate. Some secondborn trainees stepped out of their rooms only to retreat in. And those who passed us lowered their eyes. I'd have called to them for help, except I didn't even know their names. Besides, why would they help a stranger? Someone fresh off the streets who did not belong?

We arrived at a door that required a punch code. When it slid open, we were met with the metallic sheen of an elevator.

Sweat began to form on my forehead. This wasn't covered in my orientation with Nelia. The second set of doors unsealed, revealing an enclosed space made of eight-by-eight steel panels. My mind raced with worst-case scenarios.

"Arien?" a soft voice carried to me. My head snapped to the side. Nelia rounded a corner, staring wide-eyed. They tossed me into the elevator and blocked the way out.

"Stop!" Nelia's footsteps pounded on the rock floor.

"Help," I wheezed out. Excruciating seconds ticked by as the door inched shut, cutting me off from my only hope at putting an end to this madness.

"No one is going to help you, little traitor." The man to my right hauled me up by the shirt. The seam ripped under my arms. I gasped and crossed my arms in front of me. I wore a sports bra, but his ogling eyes repulsed me. He smirked knowingly.

"But maybe if you're nice to us..." He jerked me closer. My arms skimmed the front of his shirt. "Who am I kidding? This is going to hurt either way." His ominous tone sent ripples of terror down my body. He jeered down at me, pulling me by the hair into a dim corridor. I had to grab his arm to regain my balance. My scalp was on fire. When my pleading for him to stop didn't work, I began punching his arm, his side. Whatever I could reach, I'd punch.

None of my thrashings seemed to faze him or slow him down. He shoved me into a dimly lit, bare room with a single chair. I scrambled to my scraped feet and pressed myself against the wall farthest from the entrance like a damn scared mouse. The men exchanged words. Something about the Soaz being delayed. They grunted and departed without so much as a second glance. I hurried to the thick steel door and threw myself at it. It wouldn't budge, not even in the slightest. I ran along the walls, tracing my fingers over them. They were all the same solid steel. I was

trapped inside a can with no pleasant prospects ahead
of me.

Hours passed by.

I'd had a few stints in isolation before. Each time a family
returned me to the halfway house like god-damned exchange
merchandise, the headmistress would throw me into a special
padded room in the basement. I'd stay there for days at a
time in darkness. The room had a small toilet and sink. There
were times when no one even brought the food down. The
mistress said she'd been teaching us a valuable lesson in life—
to appease the people who handed us food and clothes
because without them, we were nobody. She had no patience
for repeat offenders, either. I was among the few she listed as
special cases who needed extra enforcement. This cell terrified me more than the halfway house basement. There, when
someone unlocked the door, they let me out. Here, I didn't
know what awaited me when that door swung open.

Feet shuffled outside. I rose from my huddled-up position
onto stiff legs. My throat was a sandpaper and it hurt to swallow. The door swung open, and the dark-haired man walked
in. He wore black slacks and a pair of elegant shiners. His
blue dress shirt was crumpled and stained as if he'd been
working out or something. He kicked the door shut
behind him.

"Ah, the moment I've been anticipating. I'm sorry we had
you waiting. The other prisoners required extra...incentive."
He scrutinized me with his calculating eyes before gracing me
with a slow, menacing smile. An old cut split his lower lip on
one side, and a faint scar extended from it past his chin—the
only imperfection on an otherwise flawlessly sculpted face.

He paused in the middle of the space, right underneath the
source of light. To my horror, the stains tainting his shirt now
resembled blood. I tasted bile. The Soaz followed my line of

vision and his wicked grin broadened like that of a deranged Cheshire cat. Glints of madness entered his intense eyes, and his pupils contorted, stretching into vertical slits. I blinked rapidly, convinced I'd hallucinated it. When I peered at him again, his pupils were round black holes like they should've been.

"You won't make the same mistake, will you?" My throat bobbed. My captor strode forward, caging me on one side with his arm. Not that I could move or run away. He pinned me down with his eyes, and I stared right back at him. Black, intricate-patterned tattoos hugged his neck from his ears downward.

"I rarely get rebellion traitors anymore. You've done well hiding from us over the last decade." He grabbed my jaw and squeezed it. "Pray tell me, where is your hidey-hole?"

"I don't know..." As soon as the whispered words left my mouth, my tormentor slapped my cheek with such force my good cheek hit the wall behind me. He flattened me against the wall again with my jaw trapped in his crushing hold and my body pinned under his weight. My eyes welled up with hot liquid.

"I'm sorry. Did that hurt?" He sounded rather amused. He lowered his head to my neck and took a long inhale. He sniffed me! What kind of freak was he?

"Ahh, your ripening scent is rather appealing. It triggers my other senses." I had no idea what a "ripening" scent was. The Soaz pressed harder against me, making his erection known. Oh no! *Speak, Arien*, I commanded myself.

"Your other senses?" I asked in a strangled voice.

"The non-violent ones. Violence is my preference. But, perhaps, we can mix the two?" With his mouth still dangerously close to my neck, I remained still. Panic seized me.

"I don't know anything. I swear," I spluttered.

His lips stretched against my neck.

"Wrong answer," he whispered before sinking his teeth into my neck.

I yelped from the pain. His teeth were unnaturally sharp, and they cut deep into the skin. He drew blood and spat it out on the floor. His hold on me slackened as he continued to spit and wheeze. My back began sliding down the wall as my legs buckled under the added weight. He was...choking. Unfortunately for me, he recovered within seconds. He rounded on me and thrust me into the wall. His face was mere inches from mine. My eyes wandered to his blood-stained teeth of their own volition.

"What the hell! You trying to poison me?"

"No." I shook my head. My mind struggled to understand how I was poisoning him.

The metal door groaned. The Soaz abandoned me, and I fell forward, hands on my knees. I had trouble catching my breath, and my vision went out of focus. I couldn't afford to black out, though, not here. Not with this maniac.

The sound of new voices reached me. Someone had entered the room.

"There's nothing in her file," the Soaz said. Who was he talking to? I forced my head up, and I could have cried from relief. Mezzo filled in the now ajar door.

"It's there now." He threw the folder to the ground, and papers slid out from it, scattering across the floor. "Xavier signed it himself."

The Soaz leaned against the wall with arms and legs crossed in a leisurely manner, scowling at the documents.

"She's my detainee. You can have her when we're finished." *No!* My lip quivered.

Mezzo's scrutinizing gaze swept over me. His eyes zeroed in on my bleeding neck.

"What happened to her?" Mezzo sounded repulsed.

The Soaz craned his neck like he was seeing me for the

first time. He weighed his response. "I must say I haven't noticed. I just got here myself. I'll talk to the guards." He pierced me with his thundering eyes. My lips parted in protest, but I thought better of it.

The Soaz scratched his jaw in contemplation. "I'll review the report and determine if it warrants further investigation."

"I will return the recruit to her quarters." Mezzo punctuated his point by waving me over to him. I glanced at the Soaz. He dropped his hand. His hawkish stare and the conflicted vibe coming off of him unnerved me.

"Of course. She can resume her duties as assigned." The tone of his voice was in contrast to the emotions I'd glimpsed.

"I'll escort you," Mezzo said, bringing me out of my stupor. I stepped into the doorway, and a low-pitched growl emanated from my tormentor. I ignored it and strolled out of the cell with my head held high.

Mezzo followed me into the hall.

"Mezzo?" the Soaz called out. "Make sure she does not leave Invicta."

Mezzo acquiesced before scooping me up into his arms.

FOURTEEN

My vision fuzzed around the edges from Mezzo's quick pace. I rested my head on his shoulder and squeezed my eyes shut. My errant thoughts kept drifting to the darkened cell and the cruel man—err, angel being. These creatures were not the same angels one reads about in the Bible and other sacred texts. They emoted so many angelic attributes it was unthinkable for them to be evil. Yet, they could easily be demons in disguise.

The Soaz thought I was a rebel. Absurd supposition since I had only learned about this hidden world a few days ago. He said he'd torture me, and then he bit me. Nausea crippled me as the words replayed in my mind. *He bit me. He bit me...* With shaky fingers, I touched my neck and found mangled skin covered in a slick substance.

"The fledgling needs medical attention," Mezzo said while depositing me onto a cot. I clung to his arm, not willing to be rid of my safety net. Noting familiar surroundings, I lessened my grip enough for Mezzo to slip his arm out of my hold. We were at the infirmary, and Zed was at my side. His mouth twisted from side to side.

"What happened?" he asked Mezzo as he shone a light into my eyes.

Mezzo rubbed his face once, twice. "She hurt her neck during her transport to the interrogation. Besides that, I don't know."

My consciousness drifted in and out. Wait a minute. Did he say *I* hurt my neck? Was the Soaz tearing into it with his teeth some sort of hallucination? Ohmygod, was I drugged?

"Her pulse jumped over a hundred," someone said in the distance. White noise rushed over my ears, and I pressed my palms down on them, hoping to silence it. Words like "shock" and "trauma" carried across the noisy barrier. A stinging sensation erupted on the good side of my neck and I bucked. Cold liquid spilled in all directions, mellowing my limbs. Gentle hands readjusted my head on a pillow. *I should be terrified. I should protest.* But that moment fled away in mere seconds as all layers of fear and worry flaked off. I couldn't remember why I had been so upset a little while ago. This oblivion was a much better option. This was as it should be, always...forever... I sighed with relief as I floated farther and farther away.

The balmy sun radiated a scrumptious heat across my skin, and the gentle sand beneath cradled my body. I giggled and began moving my arms, drawing angel wings. Angel wings... I paused. There was something familiar about...that. Angel... Angel... I pushed up as questions began rushing in. Where was I? Why was I here? A giant figure blocked the sun. A tall, sinewy man stood in front of me. His features hid in shadow. Sunrays danced around him, painting his body contours gilded. I admired the view.

"Who are you?" I whispered. A gust of air blasted me as something materialized from behind the man with a loud whoosh and a snap. I shielded my face with my arm. My heart skipped a beat, and I tensed, ready to flee. The mute man stood before me, unwavering. His energy pulsated with an invisible force. I stared at him. Tanta-

lizing and foreboding wings stretched out from behind his back.
Nooooo!

The sand swallowed me. In the next moment, I was standing in a
cavern with pale blue lights dancing on the walls. A woman kneeled
by a pool of water. Her long golden pale hair was partially pinned up
by a diadem, her back to me.

"Do not fear," she said. "Find the stone. It will protect you."

The second I came to, I retched my stomach's contents
beside the infirmary bed. It had been a while since I'd eaten
last, so my stomach held only yellow bile. Once my eyes
adjusted and the prickliness abated, I saw my projectile had
met an object—a polished black leather dress shoe. My gut
roiled as my gaze traveled up a dark gray suit to Xavier's
blank stare. Oh, that was just great, from one tormentor to
another. My head throbbed. Covering my face with my hands,
I laid it back on the flat pillow, stilling myself for another
onslaught of violence. I should apologize for the shoe, but I
honestly didn't care that much anymore. A massive hand like
a paw rested on my arm.

"Go away." I groaned. He pried my hands off. His face was
an unmovable mask as he scrutinized mine.

"Have you come to finish what he started?" I wanted it to
sound biting and brave, but my trembling voice didn't quite
carry the bite. *Argh.* I loathed to come across so feeble. Never
in my life had I been so scared and degraded—not until I
entered Invicta.

Xavier let go of me.

"No." His jaw muscles clenched as his fists indented the
edge of my cot. The cuffs of his suit rode up, and I glimpsed a
golden band on his left wrist.

"He shouldn't have laid his hands on you. Not on my
watch." Something like regret and resentment registered in
his voice. I recited his words mentally. His tone and manner
of speaking suggested this was an apology of sorts. A round-

about way to say, "I'm sorry," but maybe Earthbounders never apologized. Not the Pures. Perhaps this was the closest to an apology you could expect from an arrogant angel-like being.

I stayed silent, allowing myself to linger on his face. Our eyes connected, and for the first time, his blue pools lacked animosity.

He stalked off. No doubt, he had plenty of more interesting things to do, and this momentary lapse in his tough, emotionless warrior demeanor was already fading. I rolled to a side and the rancid bile by my cot assaulted my nostrils. I flopped to my back again, rubbing my forehead. Xavier didn't seem to notice the disaster by his feet. On his elegant shoes. He'd probably experienced far worse. But his shoe got a generous splatter of what had come out of my stomach. I leaned over the edge. The substance smeared the floor from where Xavier's feet had been halfway to the double doors. I winced. I'd offer to clean up my mess once I was certain my legs wouldn't buckle beneath me. For now, I'd lie here and try not to dream.

"Shh, you'll wake her up, you moron," Nelia said. Boys snickered. I rubbed my eyes, surprised I had fallen asleep again. I took stock of my body. Not bad. I had no aches, not even throbbing from my wound, and mentally... Well, I guess we'd see about that. I lifted up slowly.

"Hey!" one twin yelped.

"That's for waking her up." Feet shuffled in my direction.

"Hey, sweetie. How are you feeling?" Nelia's melodic voice was weighed down with concern.

I smiled. It was nice to know not everyone viewed me as an enemy. And maybe, just maybe, I could count people here among my limited number of friends.

"Better." I combed through my hair with my fingers, attempting to look better, as well. I was still wearing black training gear, all crumpled now, and I smelled funky. I pinched my lips. "Can I take a shower?" I scanned the spacious infirmary for a bathroom. I dreaded returning to my room. Nelia locked eyes with me.

"Of course. You can clean up at my place. In fact, why don't you sleep in my suite tonight?"

"I wouldn't want to get you in trouble."

She waved her hand. "Nonsense. After all, I'm your orientation leader. I will classify that as part of your onboarding."

Dez shot up his hand in the air with enthusiasm. "I haven't had my orientation. Can I join?"

Nelia rolled her eyes at him. "You *skipped* your orientation because it interfered with your...schedule."

"I am now eager to correct my errors." Dez winked at us, and I couldn't help but laugh.

"Before all of you disappear into Nelia's chambers, I'd like to complete Arien's evaluation." Zed stepped forward. Nelia's cheeks turned pinkish.

As Zed approached with four medical instruments in his hand, I asked playfully, "Aren't you joining us in Nelia's chambers, too?"

No answer. Zed's clinical side kicked in—it's possible that it never left him—and his gentle fingers were already peeling off the bandage. I shifted my eyes to Nelia to distract myself from the unpleasant sensations and the onslaught of flashbacks. Her cheeks seemed even darker. Ha.

"Ow," slipped through my lips when Zed probed the wound. "How long have I been here?" I asked immediately.

"Mezzo brought you in last night, around nine," Zed said. I looked around for a clock.

"It's early morning. You spent the night here," Nelia said.

I mouthed "thank you" to her and winced as sharp pain pulsed through my neck.

"It got infected. I'm draining the wound," Zed said, applying pressure to the sensitive area. Shivers riveted my body as I remembered the Soaz shredding my skin open with needle-like teeth. Something else began surfacing in my mind, a memory of Mezzo's words. He said I hurt myself?

"Is anyone going to address the elephant in the room?" Dez bit out.

"We can't..." Nelia whispered.

"The hell with it!" Dez abandoned his post by the monitors and strode over to my cot.

"How did you hurt your neck, Arien?"

"I—I'm not sure..." I averted my gaze. Because I knew what had happened, didn't I? The memory of Soaz's breath on my neck was palpable.

"But you remember something?" Dez prodded. Nelia came closer and grasped my hand.

"Yes." I cast my glance downwards. "He...the Soaz...got upset because...I couldn't tell him what he wanted." I swallowed. "I don't know who the rebels are. I've never heard of them, not before I met Xavier." With hesitation, I raised my eyes. My listeners' faces remained passive. So, I took another long inhale and described what happened next. When I was done, some mental weight chipped away.

"Oh, sweetie!" Nelia said.

At the same time Dez yelled, "Knew it! That bastard is dirty. I've been telling y'all."

"That's enough," Zed said. "Stop before you're accused of blasphemy and removed from your post." The reprimand caused Dez's mouth to clamp tight. I studied their faces, trying to decipher this situation.

On a shaky breath, I asked, "What's going on?"

"You cannot talk about it. Consuming the blood of another Earthbounder is..." He paused.

"Taboo," Nelia said. "It is highly frowned upon and punishable under our law."

I didn't understand. If this was a crime, why not report the Soaz? Or was this world as crooked as that of the mortals? Where the accused bought their freedoms with favors and money and the society blamed victims for crimes perpetuated against them? Yes, that had to be it...or even worse. There was so much I had yet to learn about the Earthbounders.

"I think I understand. If I accuse the Soaz, it's my word against his, and well, he's the Soaz..." Silence followed. I didn't want to talk about it, anyway.

"There is something I've been meaning to ask you about." I sat up straighter. "When Xavier captured me, I wore a bracelet. It's rose gold with intricate designs. It wasn't on me when I woke up here, and it wasn't in my backpack. It's a family heirloom. Have you seen it?" The bracelet was my mother's. I'd guarded it with my life, and its absence chipped at my already frayed heart. Xavier's visit reminded me of it.

"I remember it. It's a pretty thing. You're sure it's not in your bag?" Dez asked.

"Yes. I swept that bag and the room a gazillion times looking for it."

"I'll track it down." Dez mock-saluted and marched off.

"Thank you!" I called after him. He had no idea how much this meant to me.

"How about this shower?" Nelia perked up, though it felt forced. I nodded and slid out of the bed. I recalled falling sick when Xavier visited and noticed the floors were free from the evidence. For a second, I convinced myself that it didn't happen. I never woke before this, and Xavier hadn't come. But there was that energetic footprint I could only describe as remnants of his aura. Most of the time, his energy repelled and didn't linger with me. This time it was different. It festered around and consoled me somehow.

"Where did you go just now?" Nelia asked. She supported me with her arm around my waist as I hobbled alongside her. Secondborns milled around the hall but gave us wide berths as if I was a plague not to be associated with. This world treated me no differently than full-blooded humans.

"Just thinking how delightful training will be tomorrow."

"Err...actually, you are to report to combat class this afternoon." She wrinkled her nose in apology that was saying *Sorry, not sorry*.

So, maybe I was wrong about my assessment. The Earthbounder life sucked worse. And I vowed at this moment, I'd master all the training they'd give me because next time the likes of the Soaz or the roaming super worms attack me, I would not hesitate to fight them the hell off.

"Which is why I brought you this." She pulled a dark glass jar out of her pocket.

"What is it?"

"Salve for your ribs. It takes the pain and swelling away instantly."

I touched my bandage-wrapped midsection. "What's wrong with my ribs?"

"Nothing major, two clean fractures. And I bet you don't even feel a thing. I applied the salve as soon as Zed completed the scan."

I gaped at her. I had fractured ribs? I concentrated; she was right. I wouldn't have known I fractured a thing; the pain was absent.

"I will need that." I snatched the jar. "Thank you."

FIFTEEN

The combat class was grueling. Secondborn instructor, Master Pietras, had no mercy or patience for me. He stared down at me from his aquiline nose. When I entered the expansive room with its high vaulted ceiling and mats scattered on the hardwood floor, the trainees practiced hand-to-hand combat. Others handled knives and swords. Some paused and got an eyeful before dismissing me. Derisive sounds and comments reached my ears. It took everything in me not to turn around or cower in a corner. Instead, I glued myself to the wall like an ugly wallpaper. My heartbeat skyrocketed.

I knew zero to nothing about any forms of fighting. Sure, I got slapped around by a popular girl once, and I'd scratched her in return. But that was in self-defense and...sloppy. These Earthbounder trainees looked lethal from their sinewy, defined bodies that could bulldoze their way through a wall to their sheer skill and speed. I was spared the impeding heart attack when Master Pietras ordered me into a small corner, demonstrated a few moves and techniques, and after instructing me to carry on, he deserted me for the proper crowd. Each time Master Pietras cast a critical glance my way, I lost focus and floundered. I dreaded him having to correct me again. His disapproval was palpable from across the room. Compared to the other trainees, my skills were beyond inferior and inadequate. If there was a scale, I'd score outside of it on the negative side. I wished I could turn invisible, but that apparently required a pair of wings I didn't have.

I shook off my sore arms and began the next round of punches and hooks.

"Your thumb, Arien." Pietras appeared by my side out of nowhere. I fixed him with a blank stare. He grabbed my fist, adjusting my thumb on top of my curled fingers. He lifted my fist to show off his creation.

"Fold it or lose it." He marched off, leaving me feeling trepidation and embarrassed. How could I ever catch up to the level I needed to be at to complete my training? Setting inhibitions aside, I devoted all my will and focus to punching and kicking. I drowned out all distractions. With time, I got sluggish, and sweat seeped out of all my pores. It stung my neck wound. Zed had applied a gauze earlier, and now it was a wet plaster I wanted to rip away. But first, water. I thirsted for a cool liquid. As if by magic, a bottle of water popped up in front of my face. I snatched it and guzzled it down.

"Thank you," I wheezed out. Master Pietras studied me with narrowed eyes. The gym grew quiet, and only a handful of trainees remained. Master Pietras and I were the only living beings on this side of the gym. I wanted to ask him where everyone had gone but thought better of it. Something in his demeanor told me he didn't tolerate nor entertain himself with trivialities.

"You didn't quit."

"No."

"Why?"

I rubbed the back of my neck and sighed.

"I cannot afford to."

Master Pietras circled me slowly. I stayed rooted in place. There was nothing aggressive, predatory, or improper in his manner. He picked up my arm and bent it at the elbow. Tapping my elbow, he yanked me forward, aligning my arm with the side of his jaw.

"Here. If you get close enough to the enemy—" He pressed the elbow to his jaw, demonstrating how to bypass his defenses and place a blow. Next, he showcased a few hand movements and kicks. While he emphasized defensive postures, he seemed most eager to explain offensive maneuvers. I followed his direction as closely as I could.

"Good, we're done for today," he said before he stalked out of the arena. I lowered myself to the mat and attempted to stretch. The other trainees didn't stretch during their practice, but that's what I knew. I began slowly, letting my body assimilate to the new sensations coursing through it. My body hummed with a newfound energy that empowered me. If I could do this, if I could master the ways of Earthbounders, and those of a secondborn, in particular, perhaps I'd find my way in this world. Find my little niche.

———

"Looking comfortable," a melodic voice called out. Nelia sauntered in, confident as ever, and plucked a sword from the peg wall. She grinned before engaging in elegant maneuvers, slicing and dicing the air around her. She finished with a bow toward the flat side of the sword, touching it to her forehead with reverence.

"I missed this," Nelia said. She returned the sword to the wall and wiped her hands on the gray suit pants she wore today. A frothy blue blouse complemented her outfit. Nelia followed my eyes and sighed.

"Business attire is in my job description," she said.

"That was amazing," I said with awe. "Do you practice often?"

"Sadly, no. I had hoped to be allocated an instructor position, but..." She shrugged. My brows dipped down. Nelia had explained that secondborns were assigned jobs after the compendium exam, which took place in the year in which they turned eighteen. Invicta granted me a one-year extension because of a steep learning curve.

Nelia laughed. "Don't look so morose. Secondborns are a servile class. This is our destiny, and we face it with pride and exuberance." She filled her lungs as if partaking in fresh mountain air. I gawked. Was she kidding? Nelia should lead legions into battles and not shuffle paperwork.

"It's clear you're not passionate about the office work. Swordsmanship, however..." I said, commiserating with her rather than accusing her of hypocrisy.

"Shh. Don't speak of it out loud." Nelia laced her lithe arm through mine. It'd become a habit of hers. We ventured into the vast hall where several secondborns rushed to their next prospective assignments. "I know I don't always sound grateful..." Nelia said. "But my position is...unique. My family connections prevent me from joining the warriors. This will not be the case for you." She beamed at my prospect. "We have a year to figure out what you excel in and perfect those abilities. How did you do in combat today? Master Pietras will post your assessment later today." Nelia retrieved a handheld device, which doubled in size upon contact. It stretched into a thin touchscreen.

She perused the contents until her face lit up in an "aha" moment. "He posted remarks. And he sees potential in you."

"Really?" I sounded dumbfounded, even to myself. I was a total wreck in that gym. "Are you sure you didn't confuse me with someone else?" I tried to sneak a glance at the device's screen, but Nelia had already pocketed it. She insisted I describe what Master Pietras had me practice in the session today in painful detail. She hung on my every word, especially when I described fighting stances.

Nelia's quarters were in the same wing as mine, but on the top floor, where rooms were sparse and access required fingerprint identification. While we walked, I shared all the knowledge imparted to me by Master Pietras, and she clarified where I had questions. Nelia's apartment was a stark contrast to mine. There was a master suite to the left and a guest bedroom on the right side, separated by a cozy living area and an open-floor kitchen. I fell silent as we entered. I expected the same level of bleakness present in my room. I figured the Earthbounders were all about their mission to remove evil from the surface of this planet and had zero tolerance or spare time to indulge in material possessions. If a secondborn secretary lived in a suite, what privileges did the Pures enjoy? Would that grant the Magister a status and riches of a king?

"I know it's a little much—over the top if you ask me—but it's safe. Not even the Soaz can access this level without clearance." At the mention of my torturer's name, I shuddered. It hadn't yet been a whole day since they had removed me from the musty holding cell.

"Who is he? And why is everyone calling him the Soaz?"

"The SOAZ is a policing organization protecting Earthbounders from exposure and, well, hunting down those of us who defy the authority. Each Magister Office has its own SOAZ force. The head of our unit had always been known as the Soaz. He has a free rein to capture and interrogate the Earthbounders, although complaints may be filed with the Magister if the Soaz oversteps."

I had a feeling not many dared to complain. There'd be repercussions.

"Here." Nelia pointed toward a large, soft-cushioned armchair. "I'll get you something to drink. And eat." I watched her round a kitchen island and pop open the fridge door. She took out containers and transferred their contents into a casserole dish. My eyes wandered around the living area. I could see the austere blandness of this place peeking out here and there. Nelia tried to camouflage it with decorative pillows, motif throws, modern wall pieces with embedded mirrors, and a large mural. Something was missing, though...family memorabilia. No pictures were decorating this area, not even of Nelia with her friends. Perhaps she kept personal items in her room. Haziness subdued my mind, and I rested my eyes.

When I opened them, a steaming plate of roasted meat with vegetables in gravy and a couple of buttered rolls awaited on the coffee table. I salivated on the spot. Master Pietras's class drained me. Not wanting to be rude, I waited for Nelia to join me. She sat at a computer desk next to the kitchen area, engrossed in something. I cleared my throat.

"Oh." Nelia sounded apologetic. "You're awake. I've just reheated this for you. Please dig in." Blush crept up my neck. I fell asleep in someone's chair while they prepped food for me. What kind of guest was I? Nelia smiled and faced the bright screen. I tore into the meal like a starved animal. I refrained from licking the plate, though. Maybe I wasn't the most social of guests, but I had some manners, at least. As if reading my mind, Nelia showed me to the guest bathroom. She'd already had some of my clothes fetched up here.

The addictive shower soothed most of my muscle aches. I forced myself to leave the confines and solitude of the bathroom. I overheard Nelia speaking to someone in the living room and stooped closer to the door. Under different circumstances, I wouldn't eavesdrop on one of a few people I could call friendly in this place. But I'd learned the hard way that information could be the difference between life and death at Invicta.

Nelia's hushed tones made it difficult to distinguish words. She mentioned "traumatized" and "assimilating." There was a momentary pause.

"She doesn't belong here," Xavier said. His deep vibrato caressed my ears.

Nelia replied in a clipped tone—she said words like "vision" and "important."

"Don't get too attached. Better yet, stay away," Xavier warned her before leaving the apartment with a resounding crack of the door slamming into its frame. Were they talking about me? The ocean-eyed Pure didn't want me here. Why in the hell was I brought into this place, then, to begin with? I cursed my alleged bloodline and all its implications.

When Nelia knocked on my door, I didn't answer. I pretended to have fallen asleep, although, with her heightened senses, I doubted I fooled her. She lingered on the other side in indecision. A minute later, her retreating footsteps reverberated on the hardwood floor. Tomorrow, I'd sleep in my small, dingy room. Enough hiding. Enough hoping that the next time I woke up it would be in a different reality. This was my reality now—my life—and it was time I owned up to it.

SIXTEEN

In the few days that followed, Master Pietras put me through the training wringer. I spent many hours perfecting the moves he taught me. I often trained alone, in what I now considered my corner of the gym. With each day, other trainees, my classmates, paid less and less attention to the orphan.

The distance from and to my room, training sessions with Master Pietras, and the office of the Master of the second-born had become my entire world the past few days, and it had been wearing me down. I didn't have much in the human world, but I missed people from the bakery, Brie, Paulie, and even some random kind homeless kindred I'd run into over the years. I wanted my life back. I felt freer sleeping on park benches at night than I did at Invicta.

Last evening, Master Pietras instructed me to join the senior class for morning conditioning. I hadn't been allowed to leave the building until now. I surmised it'd be weeks, or perhaps even until the graduation before I was rendered this privilege. Scornful gazes passed over me when I joined the group. Ignoring everyone, I made my way to the very end and stayed there during the entire run. Even though I sensed the group's ostracizing air, I was too happy to let it affect me. I enjoyed the fresh air and exercise outside the building. Soon, the group left me behind. I didn't blame them, though, as I was truly the slowest one out here. I could easily distinguish the route on my own. Besides, I couldn't get lost when the towers of Invicta's main building stuck out above the tallest trees. And because of that, I deviated from the course heading away from Invicta. Keeping up the jog, I hoped not to raise anyone's suspicion. Just a secondborn enjoying her conditioning away from the building.

I entered the forest. I'd noticed earlier during my run the border walls weren't visible, and only trees surrounded Invicta in all directions. The wall must have been hidden behind the cover of the trees. After about ten minutes, the trees thinned out. I passed the last row of them and halted. A fluid curtain separated me from the outside world. Semi-translucent, it reflected me standing by a tall tree and revealed hilly fields beyond it—a perfect reflection of both worlds. I inched closer. The skin on my arms warmed up, drawn into the thing. I picked up a stick and tossed it at the barrier. The stick was suspended within it. The barrier flashed. *Aww.* When my eyes readjusted, the stick was gone, and my horrified expression reflected off the surface. *What the hell was that?*

I retraced my steps and headed for the cafeteria, looking forward to their hot, fresh breakfast. I hesitated outside the large doors. My rumbling stomach quickly made the decision for me. I stepped inside, and feigning confidence, I strolled to the back of the line. I didn't think anyone would notice me, not until the rock-solid body in front of me turned and a male face scrutinized me. He narrowed his eyes as if trying to place me. His features lit up, and he stared at me with renewed curiosity. I realized, at this moment, I didn't know how to interact with these beings. And maybe, just maybe, I was partially to blame for my own isolation. I didn't recall ever trying to speak to anyone there.

"So, you're the orphan," he said.

"That'll be *me*," I nearly squeaked. *Get hold of yourself.* The warrior sported a spiky hairstyle with sides clean-shaven. Brown spikes on top of his head were mussed back, and a line of sweat beaded his hairline. He had clear molten eyes and a handsomely cut face. He also carried that air of arrogance I'd come to associate with all Earthbounders, although some exuded more of it than others. I was surprised he deigned to speak with me. A large hand clapped the male's shoulder from behind, and soon another male head appeared over the other shoulder.

"Who do we have here?" the newcomer asked in a mocking tone. "She's pretty. We should have her come to the hangout tonight."

"I think we should, Mark. I think we should..." the first man said.

My skin bristled. "Thanks, but I'll pass."

The men snorted and exchanged knowing glances. The second man, Mark, had curly blond hair and a round face. If it wasn't for his bulging muscles and brawny physique I'd think him related to cherubim. The first man examined me again, amusement crossing his lips.

"Yeah, you're definitely coming tonight." Before I could utter another word, the two secondborns snatched food trays and began piling up delicious-looking eggs, bacon, and tater tots. I stood there dumbfounded for a second. I wouldn't have put it past them to break into my quarters, my only sanctuary, and drag me to the so-called hangout. I didn't even know what a *hangout* entailed. And after being exposed to the Soaz, my wariness had only grown. I searched the hall for Nelia and caught a glimpse of her stepping down from the upscale dining area devoted to the Pures. My pulse quickened, and I found myself laser-focused on the food in front of me. *Why would she be up there?* Nelia was a secondborn, but she was established here and had a high position within the organization. Both groups treated her with some regard. Perhaps she was just doing her job. It pained me that somehow, since the incident with the Soaz, we'd grown apart.

A gentle tug on my ponytail alerted me to someone standing behind me. Already on high alert, I spun around, hitting the hot-serve table behind me in the process with my rear. The Pure who'd requested coffee on my first day, stood before me. One side of his full lips lifted in a cocky smile.

"You didn't hear me?" His tone was smooth and laced with enough command that admitting he was correct felt like a crime.

"No..." My voice shook. The warrior's eyes drifted downward and stopped on my breasts. The sweaty workout shirt clung to me, and he was blatantly getting an eyeful. I'd have covered myself up but I was clenching the plate with my breakfast. And while his scrutiny annoyed me to no end, at this time, I valued the delicious meal on my plate more than my dignity. The twinkling of his eyes told me exactly what he wanted from me.

"Sit with me," he said again, a command. Didn't these men know how to court a woman? Were they immune to rejection? I wouldn't sit with him or entertain him in any way.

"Um... Can I finish getting my breakfast first? I'll come to you." I glanced at the dais leading up. He grinned.

"Just ask for Donovan if anyone gives you any trouble," he said as he stepped backward and turned around. I sighed from the exasperation I was withholding. I finished loading my plate and made my way to the nearest table occupied by a group of seniors, among them two girls who aspired to be selected for warrior posts. They occupied the opposite side of the table and cast curious glances at me when I joined them.

"Ahem... What are you doing?" one of the girls asked.

"Eating." I pointed at my mouth as I shoved forkfuls in. I intended to leave before Donovan realized I was standing him up. The second girl snickered.

"Aww, she thinks she's cute." I ignored the comment and kept shoving.

"Donovan Wright asked you to dine with him, you moron. You don't flout a Pure."

This sounded foreboding, but I played an ignorance card again.

"Why not?" I knitted my eyebrows together.

"Because..." she began, but she was interrupted by her friend with an elbow strike. The girl's smile widened with delight. When her eyes traveled past my shoulder, I started panicking for good. A chair scraped the floor to my right, and soon a hulking figure straddled it, facing me. I stole a sidelong glance. Donovan wore a bemused expression.

"You made me look like a fool," he said in a tone meant to tease but implying his displeasure and possibly a veiled threat all the same.

"One doesn't have to try hard." I winced as the words flew out of my mouth. A hush fell over the entire table. The girls' eyes bugged out and locked in place. I lowered my eyes to my plate, appetite all gone. Rich baritone laughter filled the silence. Confused, I lifted my eyes to Donovan's face. Still laughing, he picked up my plate and offered me his hand.

"Would you like to join me at my table?" His gentile manner was a nice change, yet I had no choice in the matter. If I refused him again, I'd be walking on doubly thin ice. I slid my hand into his. When we reached the upscale dining area for Pures only, I focused my attention solely on Donovan. I feared being surrounded by these lethal warriors who could crush me like a bug at any moment would cripple my survival game. I knew when I had to fake compliance and now was that time. Donovan placed my plate down in a spot immedi-ately to his left. With my appetite absent, I simply waited for Donovan's next move. Moves and counter-moves, that's all there was to it, regardless of the opponent.

"You're an orphan, I hear. How interesting." Not a ques-tion, so I remained quiet. Donovan brought a cup to his lips, his eyes never straying from my face.

"And you're a secondborn?" he continued relentlessly.

"That's what I'm told. I turned eighteen in April." I kept it curt. Nelia had explained that pure-blooded Earthbounders gained their full power and wings on the day of their eigh-teenth birthday, therefore taking that possibility for me off the proverbial table. I was a newly transformed secondborn. I had a specific transformational scent only those of pure blood and creatures that hunted the Earthbounders could sense. But, apparently, that was the only gift—if one would call it that—I'd inherited from my bloodline. And it would soon vanish, leaving me with nothing but an Earthbounder gene in my screwed-up genome. Many secondborns could wield supernatural powers, and some were as strong physically as the pure-blooded Earthbounder in front of me. They could never grow wings and turn invisible to humankind. But, over-all, some secondborn warriors placed high on the badass scale, along with the Pures. I wouldn't have made the scale unless it measured sub-zero.

"How interesting." I sensed he was feigning interest in the subject. This wasn't a social call. Donovan wanted something from me, and I grew agitated.

"I saw you training with Pietras earlier."

I nodded. No need to elaborate there. Donovan leaned a little closer, his eyes glistening with intent or some subdued emotion.

"I'm the best warrior at Invicta. I can shape you into the best fighter in your class." His hand snaked to the back of my chair. His eyes scrutinized my face and traveled lower. Normally, I'd shy away from such scrutiny, but my body was paralyzed. Donovan's eyes blazed upon returning to my face. "I see a lot of potential here."

I glanced down. My cheeks burned with rage more than anything else.

"You're blushing." His finger skimmed across my cheek and tucked a loose lock of hair behind my ear. Of course, the maniacal, supercilious being that he was, he thought I was actually vying for his attention. *What a jerk.* I was better off not flat out refusing him, though. I peered up at him through my lashes, going for the gooey-eyes act.

"Master Pietras keeps a tight training schedule."

"I will make it happen." Donovan winked, his sly smile showing off a perfect row of perfectly white teeth. On the exterior, Donovan was perfection, in a fashion model way, and I was certain his one look melted panties off of female specimens wherever he went. But his overconfidence was off-putting. He was assumptive and arrogant. Not a surprise, really, based on what I'd observed so far about the Earthbounders. They deemed themselves superior to the simple mundane folk living their everyday lives absent supernatural creatures. Yet, they clearly had a caste system in which lower-born Earthbounders served the others, an unjust and brutal judicial system, and a dictatorial or even militaristic government. One was no more free being an Earthbounder than your average Joe walking down the street.

I could only hope that Donovan wouldn't be able to "make it happen" at this point. I excused myself. As I neared the steps separating the Pures' elevated dining hall from the cafeteria, my pulse picked up a notch at the sight of Xavier, Mezzo, and Anhelm climbing the same steps. They wore combat gear that had slashes and foreign substances stuck to it. Xavier took in my crimson face and balled fists with a half-second-long glance and dismissed me. Apparently today he was in a mood to ignore me. Fine by me. Mezzo stepped to the side, allowing me to pass first, and I inclined my head to him. I wanted nothing more than to leave the cafeteria as soon as possible. The back of my head tingled from the many eyes trained on me as I walked out. I hoped Donovan's attention would not hamper the fragile progress I made with my secondborn class today. Establishing some form of rapport with my fellow classmen had suddenly become a compelling need. I wasn't naive enough to hope for friendships, but I needed to belong somewhere. And I'd have rather been a secondborn who earned her place than Donovan's mistress. At least I still had this choice.

SEVENTEEN

I stepped out of the shower when a knock sounded at my door. My heart vaulted and spasmed, remembering the last intruders who dragged me out of my room to underground dungeons. But they wouldn't have knocked. I crept towards the peephole and spotted Nelia. She was alone.

"May I come in?" she asked, wringing her hands. Of course, she'd known I was here. If it weren't for her heightened senses telling her that, it was the tracking system she had access to as my orientation leader. Even with the sudden, silent rift between us, I yearned for her company. With only a towel around me, I asked her to wait while I got dressed. I'd been going through my training garb at lightning speed, yet there were always clean sets tucked into my dresser's drawers. The room service here was beyond efficient and stealthy. I had yet to spot them in the enormity that was Invicta.

"Come in," I said, pulling the door open. I, for once, refused to get my hopes up on striking a friendship with Nelia. Xavier had ordered her to stay away, and if I'd learned anything in the past few days, I knew secondborns did not defy their Pure brethren. Nelia stood in the center of the small space, gazing up and down. I leaned against the wall, biting my lip.

"I need your help," I blurted.

"You do?" she cocked her head.

I bobbed mine. "I was invited to a hangout tonight." I air-quoted the "hangout." "What do Earthbounders do when you all hang out?"

As I spoke, Nelia's complexion gained brilliance and a genuine smile blossomed. "Ohmagod, you serious? I knew you'd eventually fit in, but so soon..." The wistful tone in her voice was reminiscent of a proud mother.

"Well, it wasn't as much as an invitation as it was a compelling request..." I wrinkled my nose. Nelia's faltering grin made me regret my comment. Aside from the unfortunate run-in with the Soaz, she acted as if this was one big sorority or fraternity house where everyone was everyone's best friend.

"My senior class was known for camaraderie and excellence. But as of late, the secondborns will act worse than Pures. Full of entitlement and arrogance," Nelia griped. She propped herself against the desk.

"I'm coming with you." She brightened again.

"Can you?" I didn't think the "hangout" was an event proper for someone in her prominent position in the Magister's office.

"In your own words, *you need me*. I will scope the details and bring reinforcements." Enthused by the idea, she spun out of the room.

"Wait, when will I see you?"

"Your room. Seven."

After poring over illustrated demon books and reading lists upon lists about each demon's strengths and weaknesses, I itched to burn off tension from the morning. Again, Master Pietras surprised me by allowing me to warm up with the class. Some secondborns darted their condescending stares at me, but the majority either didn't care or shot acknowledging glances my way. The two jocks who'd "invited" me to the hangout belonged to the latter group. I rolled my eyes at them, a gesture that earned a chuckle or two. Yes, they were pushy but not stuck-up. Halfway through the session, the Master called for sparring exercise. My cue to move to the corner of the gym for individual work. I went through a sequence of hand moves and kicks I'd memorized. Next, I directed my hits at the dummy.

I sensed rather than saw Master Pietras's approach. He picked up pads, and without missing a beat, I directed strikes to the new shifting target. The pads were for my benefit. When we'd started this exercise, he instructed me to aim at him with no protection, and while in my mind I knew I couldn't have injured him, part of me rebelled at the thought. When I did land a punch, it was soft because I couldn't, or wouldn't, hurt anyone unprovoked. So, pads had become my friend, but knowing the Master, not for long.

"Donovan approached me earlier today," he said. "He inquired about your training schedule, saying you accepted his offer to train one-on-one." I slowed my kicks as soon as his name fell out of Master Pietras's lips, furrowing my brows. *What? He's got a nerve!*

"He…" I sputtered. "He wasn't…didn't…" I struggled to get words out of my mouth with the added adrenaline spiking from this shocking revelation. I bent over and took a few deep breaths. When I straightened, I was unsure of what to say. What was the protocol for that? Would I breach any Earthbounder dogmas if I told the truth? Donovan lied.

"I see." Master Pietras nodded. "I refused his request to coach you." I blew out hot air, and gazed heavenward, mouthing a silent "thank you."

"And thank you," I said to the Master. He inclined his head in acknowledgment, nudging me with the pads. I resumed the workout.

"He won't stop. He will most likely go over me to the top leadership if he has to. But it will buy you some time." Time to do what? The Master was conveying something to me, and I needed to pay attention. One thing was clear. It was up to me to figure out a solution.

***

Nelia froze, her mouth unhinged.

"What? I have nothing else to wear, I swear." I chuckled at her stunned reaction. She wore cute, no doubt designer, denim cutout shorts and a loose-fit asymmetrical red top that flowed around her when she walked. For me, the choice was between my old worn-out jeans and T-shirt or a gray workout set. The jeans and T-shirt won. It felt as if eons had passed since the last time I'd donned them. It was thrilling to wear them again, and the notion of a hangout with self-privileged jerks from my senior class didn't sound as gloomy anymore. Truthfully, I was looking forward to it.

"Fine," Nelia said. "But tomorrow, I'm lending you some clothes." She shrugged one shoulder when I said nothing, twiddling my fingers. Moisture glazed my eyes over.

"They're old clothes, nothing fancy." Nelia's old clothes might as well be new, and they were pricey. I hadn't seen her wear a single piece more than twice.

Leaving the headquarters raised my spirit even higher. Wow! In times like these, I thought this place could grow on me. Could... Possibly... We passed the courtyard and headed out through the southern gate where open fields used for training welcomed us and with them, a chorus of cheery voices. Groups of Earthbounders sauntered toward parking lots, wearing casual clothes, and the lack of a shirt wasn't a problem either. Many of them wore beachwear, and they brought surfing boards and stashed coolers into the backs of Jeeps, Humvees, and SUVs. Nelia mentioned a lake where secondborn trainees threw over-the-top parties. "*A rite of passage*," she'd said.

A sedan with a lowered roof pulled in front of us. Slicked ash-blond hair, black sunglasses, and matching twin bright smiles became our focal points. Both men wore Hawaiian shirts, khaki-colored shorts, and leather sandals, which made it difficult to sort them out.

"Dez..." I pointed at the twin on the passenger side. His shirt had brighter colors matching his more cheerful disposition. That elicited a grin.

"Bingo." He jumped out of the car, bumping a fist with mine. My reaction was as awkward as hell. I didn't bump fists often. He chuckled and hopped back into the back seat, spreading his arms across the backrest. Lowering glasses down his nose, he said, "You just earned yourself a front seat, my friend. Nelia will have to squeeze in here with me."

Nelia leaped into the back seat, laughing. Zed glanced at the rearview mirror, his demeanor deflating. His focus shifted to me.

"So, your first hangout..."

I hugged myself. "Yeah. So far, it looks like a typical juvenile beach party."

Zed snickered. "And what did you expect?"

"I don't know." I pinched my nose. What was I envisioning? They were mostly human, after all. Well, the second-borns were. And they lived on the same planet as everyone else, with access to the same entertainment and social media.

Although I'd never heard of Invicta, Invicta's librarian showed me maps of all Earthbounder stations and training facilities on our continent—strategically placed and concealed. The librarian also answered my questions about the mysterious barrier concealing those stations from the world. It was called allura. The shimmering semi-transparent firmament trapped demonic beings trying to breach it and blocked Earthbounders from crossing it, but it was harmless to people. A human who crossed allura would emerge on the other side of the station without ever knowing it. Allura had one other useful property; it stabilized the weather within it. Today was a balmy spring day on Invicta's grounds.

"Hey, Arien. I found your bracelet." Dez popped his head in between the front seats.

"You did?" I squeaked.

"Don't get too excited. I found it, but I don't know yet how to get it back."

"Get it back?" Nelia asked. "Who has it, Dez?"

"Xavier. His team was tasked with investigating Arien's belongings and her past. They're still doing recon in this capacity. But the bracelet should've been returned by now. I can't discern without straight out asking him why he'd still have it."

"He wore it," I gasped. He'd had it on him when he visited me at the infirmary. The shiny object peeked out from under- neath his starched sleeve. Ohmygod, I was so close to it and didn't realize it.

"When? I see Xavier often, and I'm quite confident he doesn't wear any embellishments." Nelia's admission puzzled me—the part about seeing him often. They didn't seem on friendly terms, but I pushed it to the side.

"He had it on him when he stopped by the infirmary after my interrogation. I thought I saw something, but I dismissed it..." A morose silence met my confession. I scrutinized everyone's faces.

"What?" I asked.

"Arien, nobody came by..."

"But..." I faltered, questioning myself.

"Xavier never steps a foot in there, anyway. It's beneath him to associate with those of lower ranks. Besides, all of Hafthor's family have a dedicated healer," Dez supplied.

I let out a long breath and rubbed my temples. "I think I'm losing my mind."

"No, no, no." Nelia squeezed my shoulder. "You're overloaded. Angels know how any of us would adapt to your situation. You've done remarkably well, and now we're going to have some fun!" She stood up and yelled, "Yeah," fist-pumping in the air. The trainees around us responded with wild cheers of their own. Still apprehensive, I pep-talked myself. *It's going to be okay*. It would be okay. What other choice did I have?

EIGHTEEN

Tall pines and willows shrouded the lake. A grassy parking area sat above the vastness of the lake and its sandy shores. Widened paths led down from the elevation to the ground level. The lake spread out in all directions, with lush islands dispersed throughout. In the dimness of looming nightfall, there was no end to the body of water. The only sign of the shoreline was the small window lights in the distance.

The Invictus beach was expansive in either direction, stretching deep into the hill where rocky boulders held vegetation back from spilling into sandy terrain. Hundreds of secondborns milled around, enjoying upbeat music, grilled food, drinks, and company. A large group watched a volleyball match while others hung out in the water or on boardwalks lit with tiki torches. Others were showing off their acrobatic skills by diving from a mountainous oak tree that had grown under an angle as if it wanted to dip its branches in the lake's refreshing water.

The sunset colored the horizon maroon, but it wouldn't be long before all colors dissolved into the night. Breezy air carried scents of wildflowers and lavender. I took a deep breath; the scene unfolding in front of me should've been my high school years in the human world, with human people. A hand brushed mine and someone handed me a cold bottle.

"Got you a beer," Dez said, smiling down at me.

"It's a lot harder to get drunk when you're an Earthbounder," Zed said. "Perks of having angelic genomes." I didn't know if I'd call it a perk since getting a buzz was why people indulged in booze. The backward norms of Earthbounder life kept throwing me for a loop. He clinked my bottle with his and took a long swig. He sighed. "I missed this. When was the last time we took time off?"

"I don't recall, man," Dez sympathized.

We ambled in unison, the four of us. I glanced over my shoulder at the two men. They were babysitting me. All three of them. I didn't want them to waste their free time on me, but I also couldn't bring myself to tell them to leave. I didn't know anyone here, and while some had warmed up to the idea of me being an Earthbounder, most despised the idea of an orphan with no apparent lineage, importance, or skill among them. Several eyes followed me around, narrowing whenever my eyes met theirs. If it weren't for my entourage, I'd be like that volleyball being bumped and spiked around. Nelia found some friendly souls among the group, and while she chatted away, I watched the game.

Secondborns were twice as fast and strong as the best athletes alive today. Fast enough to provide thrilling entertainment but still slow enough for the human eye to capture the action. This was a co-ed match, and the female counterparts were as intent and vicious with the ball as the males were. Crowds cheered and shouted, drinks in their hands.

"Arien!" two boisterous voices yelled right from behind me. I capped my poor ear with my palm before swinging my head around. Pestilence One and Pestilence Two, the two secondborn warriors I had met in the dining hall, maneuvered through the crowd to get closer to us. Specifically, me. They crowded my space, one sitting next to me and the other one behind me. Zed had no choice but to make room for Pestilence One.

"Hi," I said and returned to watching the match.

"We're going jet ski racing later, and my man here needs a partner. It's a two-rider race. Are you game?" Pestilence One asked.

"Sorry, I don't have a swimsuit." I feigned regret.

The warrior closest to me scrubbed his jaw. Out of the corner of my eye, I caught the two warriors exchanging looks, but they said nothing. The volleyball match ended, and the crowd was thinning out in this area. The sun set low over the horizon, firing an orange haze over the sky and painting waves on the lake's surface ombre. The atmosphere grew heavier somehow. Warriors began dancing, chasing, kissing... Loud laughter and shrieks of females being thrown into the water from boardwalks filled the air. Nelia held onto my arm with fierce tenacity. The two warriors tried yet again to coax us into doing this or that. It appeared Nelia had some pull over everyone here, and they heeded her refusals. We found a snug spot around a tall log fire with Zed and Dez. Out here, away from the ebullient crowd, I finally began relaxing. A few familiar faces sat around the fire with us, and a couple was cozying up, taking advantage of the romantic atmosphere. Our conversation was light and playful. Dez amused us by recounting his worst dates ever.

"Nelia," I whispered, "is there a bathroom nearby?"

"Oh," Nelia blanched. "I'm horrible at this. I keep forgetting you have human needs." What? As if reading my mind, Nelia said, "Since we burn off more calories and more rapidly, we have less of a need to...you know."

"Well, as you said, human here." I pointed my thumbs at

my chest. "I'm just gonna, you know..." I jerked my head towards the thick vegetation down the beach and away from the party.

"Do you want me to go with you?"

"Um, no." I clasped her shoulder and squeezed. I rushed away—driven by my need and fear that Nelia would follow, or even worse, one twin would volunteer to be my escort.

I walked a short distance down the beach, away from the party. The moon would soon be full, its surface providing sufficient illumination for my tired and mostly human eyes. I slipped into wide-leafed undergrowth and deeper into shrubbery on the edge of the tree line. Turning a full circle a few times, like a puppy chasing its tail, I hid in the shadow of a broad oak tree.

Leaving my hideout behind, I strolled through waist high plants towards the beach and the bonfire. When I neared it, Nelia was no longer sitting on the log. She wasn't in the area at all; neither were Zed and Dez. Instead, two large males, the Pestilences, stood to the side, taking long swigs from glass bottles. I changed my trajectory and speed-walked around the fire. They jogged over and cut me off.

"What do we have ourselves here?"

"Pretty little thing," Pestilence One slurred. Earthbounders couldn't get drunk. They must have been guzzling.

My annoyance grew to a new level with these two. "My friends are coming."

"Actually, we may or may not have told them you got hurt and they rushed away to find you." Pestilence Two shook his head. "You're all alone."

"What do you want?"

"Nothing." Pestilence One lifted his palms in surrender.

"But it seems you disrespected our girlfriends." I looked past the two fools to a small yacht in the water. In the moonlight, I recognized two female warriors. I'd joined them at the

dining hall during the whole Donovan fiasco. My gaze drifted
back to the men in front of me.

"I don't know what you're talking about."

"They'll explain," Pestilence Two said with impatience. In
one swift move, he picked me up firefighter carry style, and
both warriors dashed for the water.

"Let me down." I screamed and thrashed on his shoulder.
When he wouldn't let go, I pummeled his back. The crowd
cheered for the two idiots kidnapping me. My head touched
the water, and my abductor swung me over, gripping my torso
like a lifeguard. Before long, he flung me over the yacht's
water access platform. I was wet from head to toe and spit-
ting water. My heart raced. I pulled myself up on shaky legs
and dashed for the water, but bulky arms seized me mid-air.

"Easy there." One man smiled. "Finally, we have you to
ourselves." He stroked strands of wet hair out of my face.

"Ugh, I'm gonna barf. Don't tell me you're into this abom-
ination." The taller, blond female warrior screwed her face.

The man shrugged. "So what if I am? Donovan doesn't
think she's trash." Judging from the female's contorted face,
he aimed the last words at her. Whatever was going on
between them seemed unhealthy. What did they call the two
female warriors on the beach—girlfriends?

"I need to return to the beach. Nelia is looking for me." I
fought against the man pushing me toward the main deck.
Pestilence One and his girlfriend lounged around a small
round table, sipping cocktails. Unlike the rest of the boats
docking near the Invictus beach, this one seemed abandoned.
No music blared from speakers, no boisterous laughter, no
bodies grinding against each other or somersaulting into the
water. Truth be told, the vibe I was getting off this boat was
ominous. And this revelation threw my heart into a frenzy.

"Sit." The man pushed me onto a stool at the minibar. I
didn't resist. My legs were the consistency of Jell-O. Taking

stock of myself, I knew I at least had my wits about me—the best weapon in my non-angelic arsenal. The boat was already speeding away from the shore. Jumping overboard was no longer an option.

"Why am I here?" I yelled over a cacophony of roaring engines and breached water to Pestilence One, who reclined against the bar. He grinned at me but said nothing. The blond female steered the boat, easing it off somewhere in the freaking middle of the lake. From here, I realized how much I misjudged its size. Invictus Lake was even vaster than my initial estimate. The bonfires around the beach were now tiny flickers like stationary fireflies. On the other side, lights illuminated a monstrous building. Faint music carried over from that direction.

A white porcelain hand slid over the man's shoulder to his pec.

"Baby, get us some drinks, hmm?" The girl nipped his earlobe. "I think our guest is too...stiff." He darted for the bar while she sauntered closer to me.

"What do you want?" I bit out. I trembled from the cold and irritation.

"Well, it appears no one has given you a proper lesson in Earthbounder etiquette. Oh, I'm Paulyna, by the way," she said, simpering.

"You've overstepped," the other female warrior chimed in. She bounced up to her friend's side, and now two minatory sets of eyes stared me down. "No one, and especially not a fucking nobody like you, talks to our men."

My brows pinched together. "Wait. I didn't... I'm not interested in any of your men. I just got here and not of my free will. Trust me, the last thing I want is to draw more attention to myself." The words rushed out of me. Did they think I was hitting on their men? I never even approached their boyfriends. They did all the chasing.

The other female snickered. Pestilence One returned with drinks and shoved a glass of bright green liquid into my hand. I accepted it but had no desire to consume anything coming from these four nutjobs. The man sat down by me, invading my personal space and caging me in. My anxiety spiked. I hated to be caged in.

"What did you tell Donovan?" Paulyna asked, her tone sharp. I fumbled my drink, shaken by the abrupt change.

"Nothing..." I said. Did she think Donovan and I had a thing? And why would it matter to her when she had a boyfriend? Said boyfriend's hand wandered to my back, drawing patterns along it that seemed sensual. His appearance altered as the tough, I-give-no-fuck attitude gave way to hedonistic lechery. Confused, my eyes swiveled to the second female warrior. Her demeanor softened while she sipped her drink. She crawled toward the other man and straddled him like a sex-deprived maniac. I scrutinized the fuzzy liquid in my glass.

"I'm talking to you," Paulyna said. Her tone dripped with condescension.

"What's in this stuff?" I inspected the glass. Tiny wisps of green smoke peaked on the surface.

Paulyna knocked the glass out of my hands, and it tumbled over the side of the boat into undulating water.

"Hey!" Mark protested.

"Oh, shut up and make her another one," she sneered. Mark charged for the bar like his life depended on it.

In a deft move, Paulyna pinned my back to the side rail. Her nails dug into my shoulders.

"You're a lying bitch and a fucking joke. No one will miss you. Bye." And with those words, she tossed me overboard. My piercing screams died out under the lake's murky water.

NINETEEN

I thrashed in the water, trying to orient myself. What had just happened? Moonlight cut through at an angle, and I pushed off to the crystalline surface.

"Hey!" I shrieked as the boat's motor roared to life. Realization set in that they were abandoning me in the middle of a miles-long lake. As much as I hated being on the yacht with green-juice-high and orgy-ready Earthbounders, I wasn't a great swimmer either. I struggled to hold my head above the water. The revving of the engine kicked me into motion. I began kicking away from the yacht before Paulyna ran me over. The boat sprang up, spewing foamy water all around me. The force thrust me farther away. I sputtered water as small waves continued to break over my face. The lake quieted with the yacht widening the distance between us.

Suspended in water, I twirled in all directions, thanking the moon for its light. Without it, I'd be sitting in pitch black. As I splashed my way toward flicking miniature bonfires, a glow radiated from within the waters beneath me and all around. I froze. Shades of fluorescent green light emanated from the lake bed upward. *It's only some light*, I assured myself. *Keep moving*.

I proceeded at a slow pace. The lights traveled with me. I paused and inspected the water again. A bubble of air floated up and popped near my left shoulder as if someone or something breathed it out from beneath me. I watched with growing horror as more and more air pockets breached the surface all around me. Breathing hard, I chopped the water with my arms and kicked harder with my legs. After a few minutes of restless motion, I collapsed. My head dipped below the surface before I regained control of my aching muscles. I scanned the surrounding waters, all dark and quiet, and sighed with relief.

I stole a glimpse of what I thought was my last location. The green shimmer emanating from the water faded. I laughed to myself. Now, I feared lake water. I needed to get a grip on myself. Pop, pop... Chartreuse shadows swam towards me, faster and faster, until they slammed in place beneath my feet. Bubbles erupted as if I hung above a boiling cauldron. My breathing quickened. This time, I didn't bother attempting to swim away. Whatever this was, it was bent on following me around.

Think, Arien. I took long, deep breaths, diluting some fear. Air bubbles hissed around me, and I closed my eyes. My leg snagged on something in the water, and I wretched it free with childlike giggles assaulting my ears. What was that? I scoured the water. Nothing but chartreuse iridescence. And bubbles. And shadows... Something stirred in the water, brushing past my calves.

"Whoever or whatever you are, I mean you no harm. All I'm trying to do is get to the shore," I pleaded with murky shadows. More giggles.

"Please...help me." All the pent-up desperation of the past few days seeped into my plea. Bubbling erupted into tiny geysers. Under different circumstances, I'd have admired their incomparable beauty. Without warning, small appendages clasped my ankles and dragged me down under the surface. I fought against the vice grip. I opened my eyes and gulped lake water upon seeing the culprits. Small, lithe women of unparalleled beauty carried my body through the water at inhuman speed. There were five or six of them, all wearing long gossamer dresses, with equally long hair and slim faces. What gave away their supernatural pedigree, apart from their unusual size and strength, were their large, round eyes. They tittered as they propelled my body, and I couldn't help myself but grin in return. My lungs no longer burned and the fear of drowning dissolved into the effervescent waters. The women's eyes shone bright with laughter and something else. They held my gaze hostage. When they pitched me out of the water, the rebound of the emotions I repressed, albeit only for a short while, hit me with a double whammy.

"Cursed lake creatures," I croaked after emptying my lungs of lake water. I lay on my back on a boardwalk expecting to hear live music and the boisterous laughter of secondborns. Unease clenched my insides when the noise sounded muffled as if it carried from an enclosed area. I lifted my spinning head.

A mansion stood before me with robust edifice. White columns bolstered the level above. A vast balcony stretched above the support and some suits wandered around there. Through expansive bay windows, I glimpsed elegant men shooting pool and sipping drinks from scotch glasses. This was a type of gentleman's club, and I recognized its patrons. The full-blooded Earthbounders. The Pures. The warriors could behave, after all, observation catching me by surprise. The party across the lake was savage in comparison. It didn't mean I wanted to run into any of the warriors, though. Quite the opposite. I planned to bypass them and wend around the lake until I reached the Invictus beach.

There was only one problem. The boardwalk ended at the foot of a wide paved terrace occupied by several warriors in the company of women. The women wore skimpy, sexy dresses with deep cleavage and cackled at pretty much everything the men said. I knew from experience the grim angels were far from funny.

I propped myself up and wrung water from my T-shirt. It clung to my skin regardless, heavy and soaked. My jeans were no better. I didn't fit in with this crowd, but I had to try blending in, at least until I could leave the terrace through a side garden. Walking around the garden was out of the question. Short thorny bushes stitched together like a rough carpet, and I'd lost my shoes in the lake. I wouldn't be surprised if those cheeky lake ladies had plucked them off. They had a terrible sense of humor.

I rolled my shoulders, readying myself to fake confidence and loftiness. The breezy air chilled me, and I fought the urge to hug myself. I strolled with measured steps and a steady pace, holding my head high and tunneling my vision on the iron garden gate. Either my plan was working or the warriors were too busy to notice a jeans-clad girl with cleavages thrust in their faces. I could see myself reaching the exit, and palpable relief warmed me up a little. The vision of my escape burst into tiny pieces when an oversized hand squeezed my bicep.

"Arien?" Donovan's eyes searched my face. While my heart pitter-pattered and my mouth refused to cooperate, Donovan perused me up and down and up again. "What... Did you go for a swim?" A sly smile replaced a hint of concern he had let slip earlier.

"W-what d-do you think?" My lips were unglued, but my teeth chattered. Man, I was colder than I thought.

"Shit. Let's go inside."

"No." Alarm bells rang in my head. Donovan expected me to join his harem, and I'd avoided him at all costs since our chat. Before I could take another step, he grabbed my other bicep and held me in place.

"I mean...I'll fetch a towel. Then you'll tell me who's responsible for this." I met Donovan's iced and calculated stare. Lost was the player persona, and the formidable warrior teetered on the edge. He'd become scarier, and I was plenty scared when we crossed paths the first time. I acquiesced. There was no way in hell I'd tell Donovan what had happened to me tonight, but I'd accept a towel for now. Besides, I couldn't bring myself to refuse when he grew so freaking intimidating. I didn't think many beings would.

Donovan draped his arm over my shoulders and pulled me closer. He walked me inside a circular foyer and into one hall-way. Doors upon doors greeted us here, and I sighed with relief when none of the warriors witnessed my appearance. I stiffened when Donovan opened the door to a bedroom with a king-size bed and modern furnishings. He gestured for me to come in, but I shook my head.

My savior smirked. "Ye of little faith. Bathroom's over there." He pointed at the door to the right of the headboard.

"I-I," How could I say "I don't trust you" to the Pure saving my cold ass? I sucked at diplomacy.

"Hold on. I'll grab a couple of towels." Donovan didn't skip a beat, surprising me again with his thoughtfulness. He reemerged within a few seconds, carrying two fluffy jumbo-sized white towels. First off, who used white towels? They would stain. My brain prided itself on feeding me such inane observations. The feel of warm fluffiness snapped me back to the here and now.

"Thank you," I said.

Donovan inclined his head. He guided me toward a bar

area with pool tables, where we settled on a comfortable couch in a corner. I didn't think anyone noticed us coming in, thankfully. While Donovan went to fetch us drinks, I worked on a breakout plan. Yet, all my ideas led to me allowing Donovan to escort me to Invicta. I did not know where I was, and I doubted he'd let me take off without him. I questioned what this concession could mean to him. Would he expect me to repay him for his help? Would this solidify his claim over me?

He handed me a Coke in an elegant glass, and I accepted with a small smile. I sipped at it, avoiding Donovan's prying eyes. But some ancient warriors did lack patience, after all. Strong fingers pinched my jaw, turning it to face his chilly eyes and compressed lips.

"Arien." A warning. I swallowed.

"It's a funny story, really..." I went for blasé. "I was at the hangout, and..." And what next? I scrambled for words.

Donovan released his grip on me and finished for me with agitation. "And you decided to go for a swim with your jeans and T-shirt on." Sarcasm, good old-fashioned sarcasm.

Well, yeah, I wanted to say. But who was I kidding? He'd smell the lie on me. Instead, I shrugged noncommittally. His mouth twisted as if he tasted something sour. I would not allow him to solve this for me. He was a stranger, and this was none of his business. I recognized he wasn't happy with my answer, and we danced on the line between polite chatter and him strangling information out of me. I wouldn't have put it past him, anyway.

"Lake beings carried me here. They looked so ethereal. What are they?" I misdirected.

Donovan's brows dipped lower. "Nymphs. They're ancient beings. We call them Sisters of the Lake. They've lived here since before Invicta claimed the terrain. No one truly knows how old they are." He adopted a forlorn look. "They seldom interfere in our affairs but can be... mercurial. They've taken Earthbounders before."

"Taken?"

"Dragged into the depths of the lake. Drowned them. No one knows because they disappeared forever."

"But why?"

Donovan found my childlike curiosity charming. The corners of his mouth quirked up. He dropped his head to my level.

"Like I said, whimsical and unpredictable. But the legend says the Sisters know your worth. If they judge you worthy of entering their waters, they will not interact. In fact, they rarely show themselves anymore. But if they rule you unworthy..." He didn't finish, wanting me to put the two together myself. His cognac colored eyes sparkled as he took in my shivering body. He chuckled—the bastard. I ignored him stroking my wet hair as I pondered his words. Something just didn't add up.

"Why did they help me? You said if they judge you worthy, they leave you be."

"I've never heard of them interacting with anyone before. I wish I had an answer to it myself." Donovan rubbed his rounded jaw, scrutinizing me anew. "If I were to guess, you bewitched them as you've bewitched me." His voice softened and the arrogant, self-righteous sexy warrior fought his way to the forefront. Well, shit. I hoped I wouldn't have to deal with that. Not today. Not after I almost drowned in the lake. But these warriors knew no mercy.

"Would they judge you worthy?" I arched an eyebrow. Donovan stilled, the light in his eyes dimming. He didn't answer right away, so I repeated the question. "Would the Sisters find you worthy?"

He nodded, letting me know he had heard me the first time. His demeanor changed from playful to withdrawn.

"I don't know." He paused. "When I was young, we'd go to the hangouts and dare each other to jump off the highest cliff into the Invictus Lake. We believed we were virtuous and morally incorruptible. We were untouchable. No creature could ever say we were unworthy of warrior's glory..." Yearning for those old days reflected in Donovan's eye. He didn't answer my question, well, not directly, but he gave me so much more. For mere seconds, Donovan allowed me to see in—to witness who he truly was underneath the tough warrior exterior. Also, his words suggested that Invicta's mission had been altered or taken a turn off the course. Or maybe the implication was personal? I offered a sympathetic smile.

"Hey, no one gets me to say shit like that." He grinned.

A middle-aged server in a black suit balancing a silver tray in one hand informed Donovan his guest had arrived. I couldn't make out how Donovan felt about his guest's arrival. His mask of indifference slipped right back onto his handsome face.

"Wait here," he said in a commanding tone. Without sparing a single glance, he departed. Stunned by his presumptuousness and sternness, I sat there like a stupid little lamb. What was I doing here? With Donovan? He was not my friend, and no matter how ordinary he presented himself, for all I knew, he was playing me. I noticed a few warriors shooting curious glances in my direction, but no one approached. It was as if they didn't dare peek my way when Donovan was here. Actors. They were all protean actors and skilled killers.

I needed a new strategy. I couldn't and wouldn't let Donovan drive me back to Invicta. I crossed over to the bar and slid underneath the bar top when the bartender served at the other end. I grabbed a spare bartender vest and fastened it in haste. Slipping under the top again, I filched an empty tray and began trotting back through the house to the garden area.

I was about to descend the staircase when I spotted Paulyna all wrapped up around Donovan's trunk-like body. Paulyna's earlier comments made sense now. She was into Donovan. She was his to-go girl, or whatever Pures called their secondborn bedmates. He wasn't oblivious to her either. His palms kneaded her ass. I wanted to gag. Since this staircase was no longer an option, I ventured forward into a vast corridor. I hoped there was another exit point if I proceeded in a straight line.

I entered a cavernous room with a triple-height alcove ceiling, which painted the illusion of airiness about the place. Mammoth sets of balcony doors opened onto a terrace, adding an extension to the room. The seating was modern milk-white leather, with a circular bar in the middle of the space and cigar smoke filling the air. I raised the tray to hide my face from the bartenders. I weaved between sitting clusters. The warriors here, which included a group of females, reeked of upper class among Pures. All elite. Expensive suits and dress shirts with gold cufflinks lounged around. Dress shoes gleamed from fresh polish. I caught sight of elegant watches, wrist bracelets, and rings. One bracelet drew my attention, in particular. As I passed the wearer, it donned on me why. I retreated four steps backward and watched in amazement as long and lithe fingers caressed the precious stones on a rose gold band. *My mother's bracelet. My bracelet.*

TWENTY

"That's my bracelet," I said out loud, surprising myself and everyone within earshot. I set the tray down on a nearby side table, dropping all pretense. They knew I was here now. *He* knew. Shoulders bunching, he turned his steely gaze on me. I didn't know what to say or do. This was Xavier. My short-time nemesis, among others, I had upset with my breathing the same air. Just as I had thought, he'd been wearing it, but why? Surely he didn't need to wear items under investigation to study their properties. No, he stole it because he put himself above anyone else, especially a low secondborn like me. My hands curled into fists.

Xavier took an elegant minute to stand up and adjust his suit jacket before facing me. His eyebrow quirked as he examined me from top to bottom. I had an idea of what I looked like—a total mess with hair plastered to my scalp and wet clothes clinging to my skin. At least, the waitressing blazer covered my chest where the wet shirt left nothing to imagination. Under the force of his gaze, I shifted my weight from one shoe-less foot to the other.

"You were saying..." Arrogance colored his masculine intonation. Tremors ran down my body, and not because of the cold.

"Um...you have my bracelet. I'd like to have it back." I cast my eyes to his chest, as Nelia had taught me since I'd arrived here. Secondborns bowed to Pures. "Never disobey a Pure" was our motto. The second motto said something about servitude, but why bother to remember when I didn't intend to adhere, right? In this scenario, however, acting meek and subservient was the way to go.

To my utter surprise, Xavier unclasped the bracelet and extended it to me. Not before he harrumphed, drawing laughs from his company. I didn't care, though. My mother's bracelet would soon be with me again, and that was all that mattered. My hand all but shot out to grab the treasure when he snatched it from my grasp.

"What?" I clipped my tongue in fear of offending and lowered my gaze again, although only to his chin this time.

"Aren't you forgetting something?" Xavier dangled the bracelet in the air. With an icy stare and lips pressed firmly, he brought his head closer and whispered into my ear, "A magic word."

He hedged away, smirking. His comrades watched our exchange. They simpered and laughed, and made offshoot comments. What game was he playing with me now? Trying to humiliate me in front of elite Pures? Bait me? So that I'd make a mistake, allowing him and other Pures to discipline this unruly secondborn. I narrowed my eyes, zeroing in on his features.

"Ab-ra-ca-dab-ra," I chanted through gnashed teeth. A wave of laughter echoed through the room. At least, now, no one could accuse me of dissension, and I didn't reduce myself to begging either. That was a win-win, right? Except, well, Xavier could punish me for anything, anytime. I wasn't daft enough to think he couldn't do whatever he wanted. I bit into my lower lip, awaiting Xavier's verdict. The skin around his eyes crinkled, and he handed the bracelet over. I exhaled with relief. I brought my treasure to my chest. My vision blurred. I opened my mouth, stopping myself in time before I thanked my torturer. My gaze drifted to his face again. He'd cataloged every one of my reactions. His brows furrowed in contemplation. Now he had a way to hurt me if he wished to. Would he hold this knowledge against me?

"Ahem, commander, where did you find this pearl?" Xavier's companion brushed past him. Five handsome warriors lounged in this square-shaped seating area. All men and, if I didn't know any better, I'd think them gentlemen. The warrior's alcohol-hazed eyes gleamed. He licked his lips slowly as if I were a long-promised dessert he'd like to savor. I cringed.

"Sublime. You must join us." Grabbing my hand, the dark-haired warrior pulled me toward a luscious cream-colored couch. He didn't wait for my response, which grated on my nerves. I dug my heels into the polished marble floor, managing to slow him down a bit.

"Actually, I was just leaving. So, if you'll excuse me..." Lowering my gaze to the floor, I tried backpedaling. But he held a vise grip on my wrist. I stilled, considering my options here and reining in overwhelming emotions.

"Let her go, Borgey. She's as green as a newborn."

Borgey released my wrist, and I was guided around the couch. Steel fingers squeezed my elbow joint when I stumbled. I peered up to find Xavier escorting me out of the cavernous lounge room. His jaw was set tight. *Shit.* I froze. I freaking froze in front of Pures. If it weren't for someone directing my body, forcing me to walk, I'd be standing there enticing those powerful men to take advantage. Shame and anger flooded my vision. Bile rose in my stomach. I yanked my elbow. A reaction that earned me slamming against the wall. Xavier's harsh azure eyes pinned me down.

"This isn't a place for you," he boomed.

Wasn't that the understatement of the century? I arched my brows, conveying a "tell me about it" sentiment. I'd been panting, so I couldn't say it out loud yet. It was for the best—I didn't want to poke the monster...again.

"I agree. Bringing me to Invicta was a huge mistake. I'm human, and I belong in that world. I mean...look at me." Whoa, where was this desperate plea coming from? And to Xavier of all beings. I shouldn't bare more of my soul to him.

"Are you looking for pity? Compassion? Consolation?" He stalked closer, encroaching upon my personal space. I raised my chin a notch, staring into his hypnotizing blue orbs. To hell with Earthbounder etiquette, or whatever Paulyna called it. When a monster tried to intimidate me, I didn't back down.

"You get none of that here. Not at Invicta, not with secondborns, and, for the glory of all that's Mighty, not in the Pures' den." His nostrils flared and hot air assaulted my cheek. "Do you have any idea what your being here implies?" No, not a clue. I thought back to the balcony—the skimpy-clad women and men were all secondborns. Realization set in, and I swallowed.

"Good, now I don't have to spell it out for you." Xavier pushed off the wall and marched towards the grand staircase.

"Wait," I called out and ran after him. I hoped he was still intent on me safely leaving their boys' club and pointing out the best route for the Invictus beach. I walked by his side, scouting potential exit points. My trust in him doing what was right hadn't grown. Although I trusted he wanted to rid himself of me. We descended the stairs, wide enough for twenty people walking side by side. The sight of Paulyna swaying by an ornate pillar twisted my guts. It made sense now, her being here. She was Donovan's fan club girl. *Gah*. Where was Donovan? Wait, I didn't care where this bastard went.

As if I called her name, Paulyna turned around. Her fancy cocktail swished to the rim of a pear-shaped glass before it righted itself again. She faltered, eyes widening, then narrowing to the tiniest pinpricks of madness. Oh, she was seething, all right. Perhaps Donovan was not her first pick? She aimed higher. I averted my eyes, rolled my shoulders, and pushed out my chest. Xavier scowled at Paulyna and slanted a single eyebrow. I shrugged, ignoring him. Xavier did not relent, though. His power or aura oppressed my energy field, threatening to cut off oxygen. I didn't know what it was and how he managed to do it. But I was certain it was him as his eyes never strayed from me.

"Fine." I coughed. "Can you stop?" We entered the garden.

"You have a lot to learn," he said.

"Such as?"

"Such as, do not ignore your superior. Do not challenge your superiors—"

"Challenge? How did I challenge you?"

He growled. "Do not interrupt." He shook his head. "Another would have you whipped. Or worse…"

I pressed my lips together, but they opened again before my brain had time to rethink.

"For one"—he pointed his sinewy, long index finger upward—"you do not stare us in the eye." A shockwave rocked through my body. *Oh shit*. I'd been struggling with this rule, even now… I focused on the path laid with river stones. Another growl rumbled from his chest.

"Unless a Pure addressed you directly. Then, you are permitted to do so." Silence. I waited.

"And since you've all but challenged me to a duel, I'll allow your forthcomings when we're in private. You will show me respect otherwise." He huffed.

What? And *what?*

"I would never want to fight you." I peered at him from underneath my eyelashes. The sentence rushed out of me; not the best answer to his teachings. A brilliant smile graced his lips. I guessed in a way that was a compliment, although I was no rival to anyone at Invicta.

"Two," he said, "you answer when spoken to immediately and with the utmost respect. You do not speak up of your own volition. Indeed, you do not eat, sleep, work, or fight without us permitting you to do so first. Do you understand what I'm saying to you?" With each sentence, he closed the distance between us. My nose scraped his collarbone as I tilted my head to survey his rough-cut face. Thoughts swirled in my head, painted in outrage over the servant-master societal caste of the Earthbounders. I could've been sarcastic with statements like "I guess Invicta is not a hotel, then?" but I'd be running a risk of enraging him even further. I watched as a vein on his temple thudded with increased pressure. Ready to explode.

I gulped. *Here goes nothing.*

"Why...why are secondborns treated this way?"

"Explain."

"Inferior. As if they're second class. But worse."

"Worse?"

I sighed. "Like slaves."

His forehead creased. He gestured to a path veering to the right, and I matched his long strides with two of my own.

"Secondborn duty is to support Earthbounders' cause. It's

the core of our values. Our mission is to defend humanity from unauthorized intrusion by evil entities from outside this realm. We pride ourselves in what we do. Each secondborn you've met would sacrifice themselves to protect this cause." He cocked his head, searching my face. I eyed him askance. If I had my way, I'd continue staring straight ahead, but his pull, his presence, demanded my compliance. Maybe, just maybe, there was a grain of substantive logic in how Earthbounders operated. Yet, I still preferred free will.

"I know what you see with your eyes," he said. "View it through the eyes of someone who's seen an absolute evil. There's no negotiating with evil. There's no good side to it. You either fight it or you get consumed by it."

I mulled over his words. "But why subjugate secondborns to obedience and servitude?"

"You say obedience, servitude. I say deferential regard and honorable conduct." As more objections formulated in my mind, Xavier's lips formed into that single curve. I should've been outraged by his attitude. But part of me understood where he was coming from. The encounter with the Archon gave me a new perspective. There was nothing under the black cloak worth saving—only an emotionless void.

We stepped onto the gravel parking lot and a silver sports car pulled up. Mezzo lowered the window.

"Mezzo will take you to Invicta. Unless you prefer another swim?" A corner of his mouth quivered. I bristled and gave him the stink eye.

"Thanks, I prefer a bed." My eyes rounded with trepidation at the double meaning. Without another word, I let myself into Mezzo's car.

We drove in silence.

"I'm Mezzo." Mezzo's gruff voice startled me.

"I know."

"Yeah, I know you know. The silence was killing me. So, now we can talk." He shrugged a shoulder.

"You want to talk?"

"It's better than not talking."

I couldn't make him out. Yes, Mezzo had intervened when the Soaz detained me, but he was under orders. I'd had only a brief interaction with him besides that. And after his sleeping spell went awry, I vowed to keep my distance. Yet, here I was, in a compact car with him.

"Uh, thank you...for giving me a ride."

"I'm only doing what I was asked." Right, Xavier arranged this. And Xavier removed the Soaz from the picture, at least for now. I should thank him. The idea left a sour taste in my mouth. I drummed my fingers on the armrest.

"Can I ask you something?"

"That's the point of a conversation, isn't it?"

I stared at him in disbelief. Was he for real? Yes, he was. Not a twitch on his face showed otherwise.

"What did you do to me when we first met at the junkyard?"

"Telesomnia."

I waited for him to elaborate, but it did not surprise me when he didn't. I knew what insomnia was and putting "tele" with "somnia" didn't take a genius to figure out.

"Is telesomnia your gift?"

"Yes. It runs in my family, on the paternal side."

"How does it work?"

"Simply put, I can will a person sleep. I only require a touch."

"How long—"

"Never longer than a few hours. Your case was unusual."

"Because I was unconscious for days?"

"Because I couldn't will you to sleep at first."

The car slowed as we entered the circular driveway at the trainee's wing.

"Why?" I asked, emboldened since he welcomed my questioning.

"Remains to be seen."

What did he mean by that? Frustrated, I reached for the handle.

"Wait," he said. I glanced back at him. He held up a crimson feather.

"What is it?"

"A gift."

"Listen," I faced him, "I appreciate you entertaining my questions and all, but I need more information. Why are you gifting me a feather?"

Mezzo's features morphed into confusion. "I forget how unfamiliar you are with our ways. Let me explain. A freely offered feather can be presented as repayment or a favor. I wronged you when I doused you with telesomnia twice that day. That could've ended deadly. My father warned me about that danger in the past. I never thought it'd come to that."

"But I'm fine."

Mezzo breathed a heavy sigh. "Take it. I insist."

If it meant so much to him, I didn't want to offend. I took the feather.

"So, a favor, huh? What type of favor are we talking about here?" I twirled the feather while my mind conjured all kinds of schemes.

"Crush it in your hand, and I will come to you. No matter where you are, it'll guide me to you."

"That's it?" My shoulders slumped.

"It will come in handy if you get yourself in trouble. Again." The implication was clear. If the Soaz crossed my path, I could alert Mezzo. The single feather was my personal emergency alert button.

"Practical." I corrected my error. "Thank you, Mezzo. This means a lot."

He nodded, his pretenseless gaze shifting to the passenger door. I rolled my eyes and stepped out of the car.

TWENTY-ONE

The morning came early. Pounding, yelling, and doors being flung open gave me unpleasant déjà vu. Before I knew it, I was up, fists ready, stance wide. I blinked hard to clear my vision. A silhouette walked into my room and threw a square of packed material at me.

"Fledgling, in the field in five." His obnoxious mock singing echoed through the hallway. My early visitor and other Pures in the hall struck their batons on the doors and hallway walls for good measure, herding my fellow classmen like sheep. As soon as my visitor left, I dressed in combat gear and sprinted out the door.

The sun had not yet broken the dawn, and the secondborns lining up the field into four neat rows looked as if sleep had evaded them. I felt wrung through myself, and I'd managed four, maybe five, hours of sleep by my calculations. I jogged into the last row, wide-eyed. A few more secondborns trickled out of the building. We stood on guard in silence, facing forward. I let my eyes wander and counted heads. I couldn't tell for sure, but it appeared someone was missing.

"Secondborns." A hardened voice drew my attention to

the front. The warrior called Mattias was in charge. I'd seen Mattias around Xavier, and I was pretty sure he was at the table when I was handpicked to serve coffee at the dining hall. He stuck out among the Pures with his hawk-style red hair and elaborate tattoos. Most Pures preferred polished looks. "Today is the day, yeah!" He fist-pumped in the air. Pures replied, mimicking his gesture and faux enthusiasm. They milled around large SUVs. They were taking us somewhere.

While Mattias explained our first assignment outside Invicta, one more SUV arrived and parked at the end of the carpool line. A female warrior stepped out of the passenger side. I'd recognize her anywhere—Paulyna. She wore a smug face as she sauntered her way to the front row. Whistles followed her. My nose scrunched up in an equal measure of disgust and disbelief. Who was I to judge, though, especially since I wasn't on my turf and wasn't playing by my own rules? One thing was for sure, though. I had a score to settle with Paulyna for her masterful recreation of the scene out of *Overboard*. One of my foster moms had been an avid fan of Kurt Russell.

My eyes connected with Donovan's. He trotted over from the car Paulyna vacated. No surprise there. More fuel dripped into my resolve to stop dallying. Since I was already here, I'd better master this secondborn stuff and fly under the radar until I could emerge my own me and, hopefully, leave this horrid place. Donovan offered a lopsided smile. Instead of analyzing his coded message, I schooled my features and devoted my full attention to Mattias.

The Pures dropped us off an hour later in the middle of nowhere. Fields of cotton, wheat, and corn greeted us with sparse outcroppings of lush greenery, all placed on serene gentle hills traversed by no one. They told us farmers didn't step foot out here until the harvest. Automated irrigation systems distributed water, plant food, and pesticides throughout the season.

"Hey you, you're with us." A secondborn whose name I didn't recall motioned me over. Step one in Mattias's instructions was to split into teams of five. I was one of the last ones selected, and I sighed in relief when I saw Paulyna and I were on different teams. Each one of us carried a large canvas bag with a pull string which the Pures had so helpfully provided during the wake-up call. The objective of our mission was to capture demon-spawned rodents called *chikakas*. They descended upon these lands each year, causing havoc by destroying the crops and drawing attention to the supernatural. The team with the most rodents captured by noon would double their overall score for the year.

"Do you know what you're looking for?" he asked me. The secondborn sounded skeptical. They had all probably known a *chikaka* since they were toddlers. I recalled something small and furry out of the books Nelia had thrown my way. I nodded in the affirmative. As if in agreement, all the teams disappeared into the cornfield—the easiest to navigate. I shadowed someone from my team, hearing the occasional squealing of captured *chikakas*. Each time I shut my eyes until the unpleasant feeling subsided. I was not a fan of this assignment. And it didn't take long for me to separate from my group.

"Typical," I muttered. Several *chikakas* darted across my path, and a few secondborns knocked me over in their pursuit of runaways. I attempted to catch a few *chikakas* here and there. I sprawled in the dirt more times than I cared to remember. It had to be approaching noon because the sun now beat down on us. I glanced at my empty bag, cringing at yet another of my failures as a secondborn.

Out of the corner of my eye, I spotted movement on the ground. One little furry thing was digging a hole in the ground. The *chikaka* was too busy to notice me hovering over it. I reached out to grab it and recoiled. *Damn it*. Fighting repulsion, I tried again and grabbed the animal by the scruff of the neck. The fella squealed bloody murder, bucked, and kicked. I kept it a full arm's distance away from me until it quieted. It turned its eyes on me, and I gasped. They were pitch-black. No irises. I'd caught a *chikaka*. Yet, something was preventing me from stuffing him in the bag. He twisted his head as if studying me. I did the same. Intriguing creature. I let out a frustrated breath. Who was I kidding? There was only one way out of this.

"Okay, here's the deal. If you leave these fields *now*, I will let you go." I observed the *chikaka* for any sign of comprehension. "You have to go." I emphasized each word.

It blinked. I blew out another breath, annoyed with myself. I was supposed to ace this assignment, and instead, I was going to release the only *chikaka* I had. I lowered it to the ground and made shooing motions with my hands. *Please, go*. The *chikaka* cooed. *Awe*, so cute. He cooed again, and I could swear he was thanking me. The ground next to him stirred up and a black nose appeared, followed by a small head. How many *chikakas* were hiding in there? The answer was one. The second *chikaka* wobbled to her friend and poked him with her nose, cooing. I squinted from one to another and it occurred to me they were together! And by the looks of it, they were about to become a family. The female slumped to the ground on her side, panting.

"What, now?" I asked the father in an accusatory tone. This was the worst time and place to birth offspring. The male stared at me with distraught black orbs. He thought I could help. His black eyes rounded and ears folded flat as he straightened on his back legs and awaited my decision.

"Okay, okay. I'll need you to get in the bag." I crouched down and held the bag open. I didn't know what to expect. I remembered little about these creatures from my studies. So far, they appeared to have some cognitive function. If I was going to be conspicuous about this, our best bet would be the bag. The male had already decided I was trustworthy, and they both scurried inside the bag. I tenderly raised it. Up to this point, I hadn't been observing directions. I pulled out a compass and proceeded north. There was a patch of greenery at the far end of the cornfields that was a straight shot down from our drop-off point. We entered a slice of open grass field before stepping into dark moss-covered trees. Absent any signs of secondborns, I lowered the bag and released the *chikakas*. The female wobbled off into thick grasses and palmettos. Her partner remained, boring those black orbs into me.

"What is it?"

"*Kwiiin*..." His little mouth moved. He stared. Ha? "Kwin, kwin," he repeated, bouncing up and down on his meaty back legs.

"Um...Arien." I pointed at myself.

"Kwin, kwin, kwin."

"All right, Quinn it is. It's not the worst of names, I suppose." At that, the strange demon departed. A sense of satisfaction filtered through my body. I'd done a good deed. I rescued a new family from certain death. I crossed my fingers. *Here's hoping they stay away from these fields from now on.* Any farmer crops, ideally. A bullhorn sounded in the distance, and my head lolled forward. My spirit deflated. The assignment ended.

I could get whiplash from the frantic sequence of ups and downs I'd been experiencing lately. I trudged out of the woods, kicking a pine cone. *Shit*. My heritage weighed me down like a curse. However, I could still dream, and I planned to survive the training, gain the trust of Earthbounders, and slowly disappear from their radar. Success in my training was a critical part of this plan. Catching a *chikaka* or two would've proved something. Unfortunately, today was a massive failure instead. Not that I regretted letting the *chikakas* go. But in the end, I needed a miracle, stat.

"Arien," the whisper traveled to my ears. I tripped over my own feet as I spun around. I narrowed my eyes at the shadow stationed between two mammoth oak trees.

"Donovan?" He inched closer to the field's edge, allowing sun rays to dance on his stately face.

"What are you doing here?" On alert, I engaged all my senses in scanning the perimeter.

"I need to speak with you."

"Now? I have to go." My unease with this man escalated to unbearable levels. I had to return to complete my assignment, and... Before I could stride into the cornfield, the jackass blocked my path.

"You're gonna make me late." A smidge of irritation leaked out with my words. The devil himself flashed a brazen smile. He stepped closer.

"You have nothing to worry about. All my pupils graduate top of the class. Even when, well, they underperform..." His gaze steered toward the empty bag I clenched in my hand. One corner of his mouth was riding up in a pretentious smirk.

"I don't underperform. It's just...an off day. That's all." A major part of me fought to say something about being Donovan's protégé, his anything, but it'd have to wait for a more suitable time.

"I believe that's yet to be determined." His brows rose. I quirked my brows in response. "Whether you can perform." I squeezed the bag. I wasn't so sure we were still talking about the training.

"Er... What did you want to talk about?"

Donovan chuckled, so confident and, yes, attractive. "I was searching for you last night—"

"Before or after you screwed Paulyna?" The words slipped out before I could check myself. In all honesty, I didn't give a shit whether Donovan and Paulyna were together. It was a relief. I didn't want anyone's special attention, and categorically, I didn't want to become anyone's *pupil*.

Donovan snickered again. "You're the most entertaining creature I've beheld in a long time."

"Because I don't bullshit around?" I wrinkled my nose. The novelty of that would soon wear off. How long could I use it to my advantage?

"So, you're looking for me..." I prompted.

"It wasn't long before I returned to our cozy corner and found it empty. I searched for you, and I saw Xavier escorting you out..." He seemed to weigh his next question. "Did he..." Donovan's jaw ticked.

"Did he what?" He waited as if he had all the time in the world. "No! As in hell no." I shook my head, sickened by what Donovan was insinuating.

"Good." Donovan relaxed. *Why? What did it matter?* Several minutes had passed since the bullhorn, and I had to return before someone noticed my absence.

"I'm so late. Can we discuss this later?" I sidestepped Donovan, committed to avoiding his further diversions when he scooped me into his arms and took off into the sky.

TWENTY-TWO

Donovan's wings sprang out of his back through the accommodating slits in his thermal as he took off into the air with me in his arms. I yelped. But words soon escaped me, and my body fell frozen solid. I clung to his neck for dear life. The travel lasted mere seconds. Nearing the land again by an old farm well, I closed my eyes to stale incoming nausea.

"Here," Donovan whispered into my ear. I bolted out of his grasp, rushing toward my group. I hoped no one noticed the shakiness in my legs. As I approached, our group leader shot me a disapproving look. He was a lean but mean fighting machine. I'd witnessed his sparring matches before. I had no recollection of his name, though.

"What's happening?" I asked all my teammates at once. Most of them evaded my eyes and ignored my question. I might as well have been invisible. They refused to play nice with me. That was fine. I guessed I had earned no favors with my troop. A singular voice broke off. The only other female in our small group.

"We dispatched our prey." She pointed to the square

makeshift stone well where the last trainees threw tied bags in. "Master Mattias will tally our scores soon. The winning team gets to accompany Pures on their next demon hunt." The way she said the last part, with a faraway look in her eye, made me realize today's prize was a coveted honor. We stood side-by-side, waiting. Mattias dragged some things around on his tablet. His head lifted, and his eyes perused the audience until they landed on me. They zeroed in on my empty bag and swiftly returned to the screen.

"No thanks to you," the same female whispered.

"What?"

She sighed. "Only that we're not the winning team, obviously." Heat crept up my neck. I let down my teammates. Maybe I proved to myself I still had a heart when I released the *chikakas*, but was it worth the consequences? Yes. No. Maybe? I ran a hand down my face. I had no freaking idea anymore.

"I expected more out of you, to be honest. I've seen you in the gym... I thought..." my team leader said. My spine stiffened. No one was a champ at receiving criticism, but at least he delivered his without malice. I turned to face him.

"This one got out of my hand. I'm sorry I let the team down." The secondborn's cobalt blue eyes swept over my face. He nodded. I faced Master Mattias again as he read the names of the winners. Paulyna was among them. I cringed, imagining how savage she must have been with the poor *chikakas*. My name being called out by Mattias drew me out of my ruminations. *Hmm, what?*

"The ten of you performed the poorest today. You will get back to Invicta on your own from here." Matthias leveled his gaze at each one of us for emphasis. I swallowed, apprehension descending upon me. Could this be my ticket out? What if this was part of my test and if I didn't return to Invicta on my own, I'd be classified as a rogue for life? My eyes snapped to where I saw Donovan last. He was no longer here.

"Better make it back in time for dinner. I'm famished," one of the Pures said, grinning from ear to ear. The Pures headed toward their parked cars on the other side of the hill. Secondborns followed. I watched in disbelief as everyone but myself and nine other secondborns drove off. I wasn't on any cozy terms with the remaining Earthbounders. A few of them huddled together and jogged away. I skirted around, observing others depart one by one. For good measure, I meandered in the same direction. Once I lost sight of the last secondborn, I cut through the ditch into green foliage. Away from the crop fields, the verdure grew thicker and formed a forest. I skipped over gnarled roots winding on the ground. A bird took off with a whistling noise and I flattened myself against the tree trunk. I scoured the treetops and fragments of the blue sky. My palms shook and turned clammy. I rubbed them up and down my thighs once and forced my feet to keep going. With every shimmer of light and rustle of leaves, my heart beat faster, and my mind conjured a thousand ways Xavier would hunt me down and send me to the gallows. Well, not precisely. Although the Soaz himself could be my undoing.

I spun in a circle again, hyperaware of the slightest movement. A deer poked its head above the brush, and my heart stuttered. Rubbing my forehead, I stumbled forward. I needed information and...some answers. If I could only locate Paulie. I wasn't happy about him abandoning me in my darkest hour—the gall! Yet, I recalled the sorrow in his eyes. His waning magic didn't allow him to teleport anyone but himself. He wouldn't have left me if there was even a slight possibility of my life being in danger.

With the sun directly above me, I struggled to get a good read on the direction. I brushed my fingers across the tree trunks instead, feeling for moisture and moss. I wasn't a Girl Scout growing up, but I knew moss settled primarily on the north side. By my estimate, New Seattle was to the west of here. I prayed I wasn't off by much...

I was still processing the fact Pures had freed me. By accident, of course. Someone overlooked an important caveat—the fact that I was a brand new addition to their crazy world and bound to be a flight risk—and knowing Xavier, they were going to pay for it. With every hour passing by, my impromptu escape seemed to be a success. I wasn't deceiving myself into believing I could have the life I'd once known, though. I'd have to leave New Seattle soon. And I'd have to stay hidden for an undetermined amount of time. The weight on my shoulders kept adding up, making the prospect of a free life less appealing.

The sun was setting down, and rust-hued skies injected sepia into the air. My tired eyes quit distinguishing the mirage of vibrant colors these forests afforded during the day. Everything was painted with yellowish-brown hues as if someone dimmed the contrast. Traffic noise alerted me to an upcoming road. Before long, I stared into a darkened tunnel below the highway. Large load-carrying trucks and cars zoomed by overhead, rattling the walls. At some point on my journey, I stepped onto a trail. A worn path extended from my feet forward. It was careless of me to miss it.

I plodded toward the moss-covered stone facade of the bridge, scanning the sky anew. I was exposed outside tree cover. A sign to the right side of the dank opening read: *Highway 24*. Yes, finally some good news. This was a perimeter road winding itself into an imperfect oval around the city. I wasn't far away now, and if I was lucky, I'd stumble upon a homeless encampment soon where I could spend a night in tolerable safety.

I examined the tunnel and beyond. Proximity to the city

meant my chances of running into someone just went up as well. My attire wasn't exactly inconspicuous. It'd pass with most of the homeless—I'd seen flashier outfits in their midst —but I couldn't risk drawing the attention of anyone else. I pinched my nose as I raced through the tunnel. The odor of stale urine reached me, and I gagged. When I emerged, I sprinted across a field of grass for cover.

I wrapped my arms around a robust tree I chose as my shelter and wheezed from exhaustion. A large canopy stretched out above like an awning. A chortle escaped me. What the hell was I thinking, running away from Invicta? From Xavier? Did I believe I could outsmart cohorts of lethal, winged, inhumanly strong supernatural warriors? Oh man, I was toast. On cue, my stomach grumbled. I'd been ignoring its demands for some time now. But there was no question who'd win this battle. I hoped some homeless fellow felt generous with their food tonight. They often traded for goods, but the only items of interest I had on me were my mother's bracelet and a utility knife. It was a standard-issue knife for Earthbounders but sharp as a demon's razor. Someone would slash their wrist with improper handling, and my conscience couldn't bear that responsibility. The bracelet wasn't an option either.

I pushed off an enormous tree trunk and strode a few yards to the side. I'd follow the trail but wouldn't stay on it as a precaution. Darkness descended, stripping russet hues out of the landscape. The crescent moon's luminescence painted strokes of white into the blackness. The air thickened. The pressure intensified, and heaviness settled into my bones. Some invisible force slowed my movements. My legs turned into two lead rods, stiff and unbendable. I peered into the darkness, my body trembling. Someone was here.

Bright lines resembling live electric currents weaved their way through the underbrush. They merged at the base of a massive gnarled tree with heavy boughs overhead. They climbed the tree's front, creating a swirl of energy on the surface. As the flow subsided, the face of a person beveled outward. The face etched itself into the rough bark but with the smooth consistency of treated lumber.

"Paulie?" I blinked my eyes. The force rooting me in place let up, and I collapsed to my knees. All the while staring into a Paulie-like face embedded into a freaking tree. The face grimaced in a Paulie-like fashion.

"I haven't done this in eiges," Paulie muttered.

"What?"

"I kno, I kno. I hav lot splaining to do." The medium through which Paulie communicated seemed to have a draw-back—articulation.

"Yes!" I sounded undignified. "But first, are you okay? Did the Seraphs do this to you?" Scenarios ran through my mind. Paulie captured and killed by the Seraphs for breaking the edicts, as Anhelm referred to them. Was his soul forever trapped in a tree? Had they seized Paulie and sentenced him to eternity as a tree spirit?

"No."

I hauled myself back to standing. The initial fear and shock dissipated to manageable levels.

"What the hell is this, Paulie?" I gestured toward his wooden likeness.

"Tis?" He shifted his eyes downward, and more of his scalp emerged as he dipped his chin. "A tree."

I narrowed my eyes, wondering whether he took me for total dumbass. A slow smile stretched Paulie's wooden lips. *Ah, very funny, old man.*

"I'ma druid, I can do tricks with nayture. I bin trying to

detec your presenz since you bin taken from my humble abode."

I mulled over his words. "But you can't do your tricks on Earthbounder grounds."

"No. That plus my magik is wik. Can only cover so much ground." His face contorted into a scowl.

"Where are you? Can I see you?" Questions spilled out. Finally, something tangible from my not-so-distant past presented itself, and the need to grab it surmounted everything else. His features pinched and closed off.

"We do't hav much time. Listen—" Wind picked up, howling around us, and I missed his next words. "But she got the wrong one."

"Wrong what?"

"The soleil, my magik. She tuk the soleil of a Great Archon this realm knew as Bezeka-ah. He waz at the junkyard that day. He waz der for me." My mouth moved, but no words came out. Paulie's explanation began sinking in. It was all an accident. I wasn't supposed to be there. The Archon, nefora, or demons were never after me. The creature was coming after Paulie. He wanted his power back. And I stopped the Archon from getting it, didn't I? Me and a trio of angelic warriors.

"Where is it?"

"No. I am not pullin' you under with me. I's my battle." His stern stare would brook no argument, and yet I had to point out the obvious.

"I'm all tangled up in it now."

"He'll stop at nothin' to regain hiz power."

"The Archon, this Bezekah, was coming for you?"

"Yez. I waz ready to fight him. I haad you swear to stay away." His inflection rose, and accusation and worry struck out at me. I brushed it off.

"What now?"

"I'm bidin' som time. I'm workin' on somethin'. I haave...connections." Some weight lifted off my shoulders. Paulie was a wise old druid. He'd fix this. "But Arien, you ca't see me or luk for me. Not until this is ove'."

"I understand." My shoulders slumped forward, and I cast my eyes downward.

"Go back to Invicta."

My head snapped up. "What? I can't..."

"You hav no choise, my child. They are the only ones who can protect you from Bezeka-ah." Paulie's fear was palpable.

"Why do I need to be protected?" I asked.

"Bezeka-ah may have discovered our connection. He will use you to get to me. Haave no doubt 'bout it."

That bit of information was scary. My enemies within Invicta paled in comparison to the hooded demon overlord.

"Swear it." Wooden eyes bulged out with Paulie's heightened scrutiny and anticipation. He worried what the Archon would do to me if he was sending me back to the place he'd vowed to keep me out of to begin with. I didn't want to add worry to his precarious situation, especially when so much was at stake. A Great Archon, Bezekah or not, could bring legions of demons into one dimension or a single planet. Our planet. With decreasing Earthbounder population, a spillover into the human realm would be catastrophic.

"I promise," I fibbed. At once, the carved protrusion retreated inward, re-scrambled into plain bark and arranged back into place. Shimmering currents traveled down the trunk into the soil and diffused with a gentle whoosh. The action was so abrupt, I couldn't judge whether it was intentional. I scanned the area for threats but detected none. I'd draw this one to Paulie's capriciousness or him running out of his magic juice. The druid often said he wasn't as powerful as he used to be. It made me wonder how powerful Paulie had been before his punishment. And what had he ever done to earn it?

TWENTY-THREE

I twisted my neck from side to side to shake off the tension. The inception of a migraine threatened to cripple my senses. A singular tentacle was burrowing itself into a central point between my shoulder blades. *Brrr*... I shook. I needed to rest, hydrate, sleep, and eat—and not necessarily in that order. But first, I forced my feet to move forward. Finding Paulie was out of the question now. Locating an overnight, inconspicuous shelter was not. A wintry chill seeped through my gear and I was in danger of hypothermia.

At last, suburban residencies rose on the horizon. I skirted through neighborhoods keeping a low profile and meandered along a major road. Small business buildings lined both sides. The farther I traveled, the more structures morphed into abandoned and dilapidated remains. I wasn't familiar with this side of New Seattle. But I understood its circular layout, with suburbs making up the outer layer and business districts congregating in the city's epicenter. In between sat a hodgepodge of apartment complexes ranging from high-end to projects, small businesses, shopping centers, and many neglected areas where the homeless often gathered. Passing underneath a highway system, I spotted cardboard boxes and a few denizens deep in slumber. To the right of the bridge, large metal cans burned into tall flames. Homeless milled around, grouped around the fire. I grabbed a long brown coat someone had laid next to their raised boxes and donned it.

"Sorry, buddy, I promise to return it in the morning," I whispered to whoever slumbered inside.

Stepping into everyone's line of vision, I burrowed my chin deeper into the coat and cast my eyes to the ground. Most homeless kept to themselves. Some were friendly, social even. Now and then, a few thugs would get territorial and toss intruders out. This bunch was quiet. I ambled over to an opening by the fire and watched flames dance around, melting tidbits of mental weariness away. A small Styrofoam box and bottled water materialized in front of me. I inclined my head as a thank you, not daring to look my savior in the eyes. The homeless of New Seattle shared a handful of unspoken rules. Staring at someone could cause an altercation, but if a stranger made eye contact, he or she wouldn't leave unscathed. Most homeless took such behavior as a personal attack. It got worse if you walked up to someone and asked a question to their face.

I dug into the offering—a melted ham and cheese sandwich. The warmth from the fire transcended into my soul and imbued it with contentment. Not long ago, visiting homeless sites was my common routine. I worked during the day and sometimes in the evening and searched for a safe place to sleep at night. Since I'd been at Invicta, my life had flipped upside down. Invicta offered a comfortable bed with my name on it at night, and the day's activities injected uncer-

tainty and danger into my existence. Some of that uncertainty
was fading away now. I eyed stacked-up boxes tucked against
the old warehouse building for communal use. I pulled out
what I needed and built a pop-up bed for the night, sheltered
by the building's sheet metal wall on one side. I settled inside
it, pillowing my head with my arms.

A noise akin to cackling haunted me in my light sleep. The
wind picked up and assaulted my temporary lodging, causing
the cardboard to tremble. Something scraped against it. My
eyes snapped open. Precious seconds passed, and no one
came for me. I sighed in relief and stretched, which made my
boots and arms push the box flaps open. The frigid air reas-
sured me this wasn't a dream. I was free. I shed the coat,
crawled out, and gulped down my water. In the dawn's light, I
surveyed the area. Derelict industrial buildings ran perpendicular to the main road. On the other side, there were used car
lots and a fast-food joint that'd seen better days.

I yawned. The heady aroma of burned coffee grinds filled
my nostrils. I pinched the bridge of my nose. I'd hide out in
the city until things cooled off. Invicta would deploy their
best teams to search for me. I counted on Invicta moving my
name down their priority list with time. I'd always remain on
their "wanted" roster, but I couldn't do anything about that.
Strolling along the warehouse, I came across a single door.
Someone had smashed the handle in and removed the lock.

These plants usually contained functional bathrooms. A
vast open space with steel-formed beams welcomed me.
Deserted cots, bottles, and food wrappers lay scattered across
the floor. But not a soul was in sight. Doors lined the far wall.
I peeked into the spaces one by one. Small offices intermin-
gled with narrow storage units. The bathroom was in the

middle. I knocked on the ajar door. Rusted hinges wailed. I paused and listened for any sounds. Nothing stirred inside. I relaxed and entered.

I indulged in the refreshing sensation of cool water running down my face. It felt like freedom. I cut off the faucet and stared at droplets falling into the rusty basin. I inhaled and ran my fingers through my tangled hair, rearranging it into a messy bun. Stepping back, I took a once-over in the mirror. It would have to do. If I was lucky, I'd get some coffee at the can fire, and I'd be on my way. And I was feeling lucky today.

The squeaking of an old faucet knob turning brought me out of a temporary stupor. I jumped up when a faucet furthest from mine began spewing water at high pressure. Nobody was there. I turned around, and still, no one made a sudden appearance. I froze when the second and third faucets started running. The knobs twisted again. An earsplitting screech bounced off the walls, surrounding me. I clasped my hands over my ears. The phantom ripped the last sink off the wall and dumped it at my feet. The water hit me straight in the face, and I backpedaled, tripped, and tumbled to the hard cement floor. The contour of a human-like being appeared in the gushing water. This being was an apparition mostly unrestricted by the physical world. As it twirled around, the water sculpted a form of a petite female figure with long, unruly hair. A kelpie.

Although I was an Earthbounder, I was an ungifted secondborn. Anything absent corporeal form was bound to evade my notice. How long had this creature been observing me? Footprints planted in inch-deep water were my only clue to its whereabouts. My status was a blessing in disguise. The ancient Law of Parallel Realms prevented foreign entities from interacting with anyone who couldn't perceive their true form. I'd committed this section of the manual to memory. Maybe a part of me knew how important it'd be in my future.

The kelpie circled me. "My master wants to see you." The creature had a dark singsong voice. Her feet splashed water as she sped up, turning in different directions. She was dancing. "Oh, he'll be so proud of me. He will reward me. My master..." The kelpie's voice drifted in and out. "He will reward me. Oh, yes, yes..."

I crept out of the circle she'd created. As I reached the entrance, the kelpie let out an earsplitting screech. Shit. I sprinted out of the bathroom. A door at the furthest wall burst open, and figures filed in. They shouted commands. My internal radar propelled me in the opposite direction. As I bolted outside onto a loading platform, heavy footsteps thudded on the metal cover above. They raced along with me. A tall barbed wire fence to my left blocked my escape route. My only option was a field of rocks ahead.

"Stop!"

Adrenaline pumped in my blood, and my pace quickened. Holy shit, I'd never run so fast before. But that didn't stop the man atop the roof from sticking with me. I abandoned the cover of the building and charged a hill of gravel ahead. Large piles of stones and clay obscured my vision. I got disoriented, tripped, and landed face-first in a pool of murky water. A hand fisted the back of my top and hoisted me up. I jerked and planted a punch to the man's throat. Well, not exactly. He grabbed my fist and pushed it to the side with ease. My eyes rounded with dreadful realization.

"Easy there," the man said. His posture slackened. He reported back through his comms device. "She's one of us... Aha... Roger that."

I fixed my outfit and wound loose hair back into a pony-tail. There was a chance I was not the reason for this group's arrival. It was time to play a badass warrior part. I eased my stance and rested one hand on my hip. No, that felt so... unnatural. The warrior observed me with the acuity of a hawk. I clasped my hands behind my back and straightened.

"You must be... new?" The questioning note hinted at his skepticism.

"Yes. I transferred," I said. I crossed my fingers that was a thing with Earthbounders and released a long breath when he nodded.

"We're investigating a report of a demonic breach in this area. The energetic signature popped up unexpectedly on our radar." He waited.

"Um... It had to be the kelpie. I was around when I saw it cross the street." I'd always heard sticking close to the truth was your best bet. Some of the doubt dissipated from his eyes, and he graced me with a fleeting smile.

"We should go back to brief the team." The warrior didn't wait for my response. I fell in step with him to not raise any suspicion. My heart hammered in my chest, but on the exterior, I was calm personified.

"You're not from Invicta?" I studied his profile, cataloging it in memory. I hadn't seen this warrior before.

"Angels, no." He laughed. "Our domain is the *superior* Praetor 6. P6 for short." The corners of his mouth wavered when he said superior. There was a sort of competition between the two factions. So far, my studies had skimmed across the political arena of Earthbounders. I wished I knew more about P6. I clammed my mouth shut. My ignorance would only lose me points with this warrior. We scaled up the clay surrounding the corridor and navigated our way around mountains of dust-laden rocks. My muscles prickled with growing apprehension.

A figure crouched on the roof's edge as we approached the building. The sun rising behind him obscured his face in shadow, highlighting his muscular build. His presence frayed my already delicate nerves, evoking instant heartburn. I averted my gaze away from the warrior demanding my attention. I creased my brows in horror as my other internal alert sounded. I halted and gazed heavenward. A birdlike figure plummeted toward us like a missile. The red hue of his magnificent broad wings gave him away. He touched down on the roof with a thud. His cerulean glare zeroed in on me.

TWENTY-FOUR

Breathing escaped me as I counted Xavier's determined steps. One, two, three... My muscles froze. My mind went into overdrive. All I knew right now was that this was bad. In a flash, a figure appeared in front of Xavier, halting his progress. It was the warrior who'd perched on the roof a minute ago. His ash-gray wings folded tight behind his back. He was a Pure but of different angelic descent. Somehow, he looked familiar. If only I could see his face. After a brief exchange, the mystery Earthbounder stepped aside, allowing Xavier passage, opening a direct path to me. Xavier's features lost some of that raw intensity. His eyes continued to hold mine hostage as he gracefully dove off the roof and got within a step of me. Steam left his nostrils with each exhale and sweat beaded his forehead. Exhaustion marred his features, suffusing the anger. I cleared my throat.

"I can explain..." I said. Xavier snorted. He requested a pickup SUV through his comms device.

"Now, I hear you ran into a kelpie." He scrutinized me up and down. "And survived."

"I couldn't see her." I shrugged a shoulder. This kelpie

couldn't have touched me physically, although that had not rendered her less frightening.

"Nothing to report, then." For the first time since his arrival, Xavier acknowledged the other warrior.

"Sir, this kelpie was hell-bound on getting to this Earth-bounder. We need to interview—"

"Request denied. Ask your questions now. I'm eager to return this Earthbounder to Invicta." Xavier's formidable eyes zeroed in on me. A spark of glee fired them up fleetingly, and a shiver raced down my spine. Xavier had promised dire consequences for my defiance ever since my first day at Invicta. Minuscule movement at the corner of his mouth made me suspect he was gloating, knowing perfectly well how he affected me. He was wired with cruelty, his default state of being.

"Yes, sir." The P6 warrior played with his wristwatch's touchscreen until a holographic blank page projected above it.

"In as much detail as possible, provide the sequence of events involving the kelpie." His expectant eyes shifted to me. I coughed, making a quick calculation of whether I needed to keep anything to myself. I came up with nothing concerning the kelpie. But Paulie was a different matter altogether. I recounted the events of the last hour. As I spoke, words—my words—were transcribed to the holographic page. That was a nifty trick.

"Are you sure you heard the kelpie correctly?" the P6 warrior asked.

"Well, she definitely preferred run-on sentences, so I may have the order wrong..."

"The part about her master wanting you, Arien." Xavier's tone scolded. Did he think I was playing daft? I had no idea the master part was a big deal. Didn't kelpies and their masters, whoever they may have been, want to crush Earth-bounders?

"Yes." As the word left my mouth, the P6 warrior pressed Xavier to detain me further. Xavier refused and refused again. I was glad he did. As much as I hated to admit it, I felt safer with him. As I listened to their heated exchange, I tried to conceptualize the kelpie incident. Paulie had warned me about Bezekah coming after me. Was this part of the Archon's plan? Was he the master the kelpie kept referring to? If so, there were a whole lot of demons rising to get me. Deep fear gripped me. For Paulie, for the big picture, and me.

I grabbed Xavier's arm. "Can we go?" The action was as much a surprise to him as it was to me. And yet, I didn't let go. Instead, I pleaded with my eyes. His own eyes turned contemplative. He dipped his chin.

"Contact the Magister's office with further inquiries in this matter."

"But, sir..." Xavier seized my upper arm and hauled me forward. When we rounded the corner out of the P6 warrior's sight, he dropped his hold on me. I knew better than to fall behind, and I speed-walked to match Xavier's long steps. Through the loading dock's now open door, I spotted other P6 warriors inspecting something inside the building. A cube-shaped glass container of some sort. I flinched when the cube rattled upon impact, and a trail of perspiration imprinted the glass wall. The P6 warriors' attention snapped to me, confirming the cube contained the kelpie. It also confirmed what I'd just figured out for myself. The kelpie was after me, after all.

Unable to divert my eyes from the cube and wet splotches left by the thrashing kelpie, I bumped into Xavier's side. I righted myself with a couple of backward steps.

"Let's go," I muttered, rubbing my nose. A wall would've been nicer to bump into. Did Earthbounders pack steel?

"As you wish."

I eyed him with suspicion. He struggled to keep a straight face. A twinkle in his eye gave him away. Smug a-hole. A black SUV pulled up to the curbside. The driver, an Invicta second-born judging by the insignia, rounded the front of the car and opened the back door.

"Key." Xavier sidestepped me and shut the door. The bewildered secondborn handed over the key fob. He glanced at me and Xavier again. Some nonverbal communication took place between the two men, and the secondborn pivoted on his feet and stalked off. Xavier ushered me into the passenger seat. We peeled off the curb before I got my seatbelt on. Xavier had foregone his. I stared at his profile, firm square jaw shifting as if he was grinding his teeth. I started to feel uneasy. I jerked away to explore the view the passenger window afforded instead. I was returning to Invicta. Not the place I wanted to be right now, but where I needed to be.

"What were you thinking?" Xavier's nostrils flared as he glared me down. I flinched inwardly. But man, if the entire situation did not grate on my nerves as it was. Add Xavier's audaciousness to the mix, and you got an ill-thought-out response like this...

"Your incompetent men practically presented me with a free card when they presumed I'd obediently follow their breadcrumb trail back to my prison."

Xavier's eyes couldn't be more glass-like, hard and full of shards.

"Did you stumble upon a witch's hut?" he asked after pregnant seconds passed on.

"Huh..." I scrunched my nose up as if I smelled something putrid. Xavier broke eye contact, directing his attention to the road. Why did that sound familiar? I snorted when it hit me. He was referring to the story about Hansel and Gretel, I think. I wouldn't give him the satisfaction of asking and, well, his cold attitude hadn't improved. The silence stretched between us.

"Will you file a report?" This was my way of asking what kind of trouble I was in with Invicta.

"Any idea who the 'master' is?"

"No."

"I can't help you when you're lying to me."

I snickered. "You...help me?" Gee, why hadn't I run to Xavier with all my problems sooner?

His head swiveled. The cerulean in his eyes spilled over the white of his eyes and disappeared within an instant. My breath caught in my chest.

"Fine. I can make your life easier, though."

Should I ask him about his weird eye condition?

"I..." My tongue stuck to the top of my mouth. I must have been seeing things. "I don't know for certain, but... well..." How much should I tell him? Xavier gestured with surprising elegance and patience, prompting me to continue.

"My only other encounter with a sentient demonic creature was the Archon attack at the junkyard, so..." I rotated my wrist palm up.

"You believe that's our culprit." Xavier completed my sentence, although it sounded as if he was only thinking out loud. "Is that all?"

Oh, yes, the Archon was Bezekah, who was after his stolen soleil.

"I can't think of anyone else. Can you?" I feigned ignorance, and I prayed I'd done a good job at it. Xavier's question wasn't specific, so I didn't lie. Not directly, anyway. His nod was meaningless. It could've meant "I believe you" or could've meant "You're full of shit" for how guarded he was.

"He could be after your young Earthbounder essence, I suppose..." He dragged the words out.

"You don't think that's it?" I couldn't help but ask. Xavier shot me a glance saying, "Isn't it obvious?" No, it wasn't obvious. I had no idea how Archons operated. If it weren't for Paulie's revelation, I'd still be in the dark. Xavier's throat vibrated with audible *hmmm*.

"I don't think that's the end goal."

Silence.

"Care to elaborate?" I wanted to know a seasoned warrior's take on this Archon's motivation. Xavier relaxed, pleased with my reaction.

"Archons are solitary beings. Highly intelligent. They never ever work together, and while they can summon lesser beings to do their bidding, that's rare by itself. Now, this Archon showed up with a nefora whose tracking abilities surpass even divine gifts of the best of us. It's obvious he's searching for something specific and of value. Blood and essence of a young Earthbounder? That was the official report. Yet I had this feeling even then that he wasn't there for you. Kwanezerus, on the other hand, that old bastard, might have had something desirable to an Archon."

"So, you suspect the Archon is after Paulie?" I couldn't shake the old habit of calling my friend by the name he'd given me all these years ago.

"I did." Xavier scanned my face, which grew paler by the minute, no doubt. "But now, I'd like to know what it is you're hiding that he'd lower himself to bribing kelpies."

A chill passed through me. Xavier was onto me! How much could I reveal? Paulie forbade me from mentioning Bezekah and the soleil. Small beads of perspiration gathered above my upper lip. Xavier chuckled, throwing me for a loop. What was funny about any of this? He ran a hand through his glossy waves.

"You're terrible at this, you know." He clapped his muscular thigh, melodic laughter echoing with his words.

Once he sobered up, his formidable persona slid back into control.

"Let's make something clear. What we're dealing with here is unprecedented." Xavier's hard eyes fixated on my face for a prolonged second. Too long. I swallowed. His attention returned to the road. "And somehow, you, the poor little orphan, are right in the center. Worst of all, I don't believe you have any idea of the role you play in this. But you know something. And I need to know this 'something.'"

I gazed down at my blueish hands. Was I that easy to read? I held my breath, anticipating Xavier exploding and demanding I confess everything. I squeezed my eyes tight in brutal anticipation.

"I can't believe I'm about to do this..." The words carried to my ears in a whisper. I cracked an eye open. Xavier continued to stare ahead. His knuckles blanched as he tightened his grip on the wheel. And I waited. At this moment, I was out of cards, out of moves, and tired of pretenses. It'd be whatever he settled his capricious mind on.

"Sleep on this tonight. We will resume our conversation tomorrow. At breakfast. My quarters." I wasn't sure which words surprised and repulsed me more. Would he wait for me to come around? To have a civil discussion over a meal? In his apartment? I decided not to protest the idea of being alone with him. All of this reeked of manipulation, but I wasn't being interrogated or thrown into an underground cell. There was still a possibility for that as he did not specify where I'd be sleeping tonight. My lips formed an *O* ready to say something.

"What?" Xavier's curtness was like a slap in the face. But maybe that was what I needed right now.

"Oh, nothing." I hid my face from him, watching the passing landscapes. The city limit sign whizzed past us. Xavier grumbled something unintelligible under his nose.

"One more thing," he said. His words warned of a grim outcome. I glanced down at his extended hand, palm up. Eyes widening, I glided them up his bulky arm to his face.

"The bracelet."

"No." I covered my treasure with my hand. I shook my head repeatedly. That was all I had from my past. From a mother I'd never met but who I'd imagined would've loved me if we only were given a chance. Xavier wiggled his fingers.

"You can give it to me freely or..."

I closed my eyes. "Why?" I asked.

"Hmm, think of it as insurance. In case you have thoughts of running off again. I'll keep it safe until your graduation."

That was a few months away. With shaky fingers, I unclasped the gold band and deposited it on his palm. He snatched it out of my view. I rubbed my wrist, already missing it. My vision blurred as I stared out the passenger window.

"If I see you wear it again, I swear I'll cut your fingers off." Xavier snickered.

"Did you secure the runner?" His comms device carried Anhelm's monotone voice.

"Heading to Invicta now."

"Superb. We've had inquiries..." Anhelm let the sentence hang.

"And?" Was it me, or was Xavier getting irritated with this conversation?

"I did as you asked. Everyone was told she's training with you, but some are more suspicious than others, outraged even..."

"Who?"

"The lover boy..."

Silence.

The only name coming to mind was Donovan. What was he telling people about us? That we were together? Ugh, this was worse than I imagined. Blood flowed to my face as much from rage as from embarrassment.

"I'll handle him," Xavier said.

Anhelm made a sound in the back of his throat. Xavier switched off his watch, and silence once again filled the space.

I crossed my arms over my chest, killing scenarios running rampant in my mind. Of course, little bitty me wouldn't be able to scratch Donovan if I tried. It was best to hide away from him. Forever, if possible.

"Are you blushing?" Disgust echoed in his question.

"Ha." I rolled my eyes. If only he knew. My face warmed all over under Xavier's scrutinizing stare. I faced him.

"Let's set the record straight. I don't want or like Donovan's attention."

"I thought—"

"That I'd worship at his feet 'cause he's a mighty warrior endowed with divine looks?" Perhaps this was a little too elaborate of a description.

Xavier's mouth twitched until a cheesy grin won over. My mouth fell agape.

"That's usually how it goes."

I blew out hot air and made use of the headrest. This conversation was pointless as if I talked to Donovan himself. Xavier's smile morphed into indifference once more. We continued in silence.

Too soon, the gates of Invicta rose before us. My body coiled into a clump of nerves. I repressed the flight instinct trying to overpower me. To my surprise, we arrived at the west wing. I'd never been to this part of the building before, but I understood the Magister and his security detail occupied it. I'd assumed Xavier's apartment was in the east wing near Nelia's.

Anhelm greeted us. Never one to bother with formalities,

the warrior only spared me an acknowledging glance. Nelia stepped out through the wing's door, and I rushed to meet her. Her hug was warm and bone-crushing, reminding me of her hidden super-strength.

"I know what you did, and I understand why. But I'm glad you're back too," Nelia whispered into my ear. At Xavier's command, Nelia abandoned me and joined the two warriors. It didn't appear Xavier wanted me to join, so I waited.

"It's settled," Xavier said while the trio approached us. I raised a questioning eyebrow at Nelia, a mistake in the presence of high-ranking Seraph warriors. Xavier harrumphed to remind me of that.

"Nelia will take you to your room. She will bring you to my quarters mid-morning. You are not to leave your room or let anyone in. Understood?"

I nodded numbly. Later, I might feel differently about it. But right now, I wanted to speak with Nelia. She was the only person at Invicta that I trusted.

"What about the, ah, *problem* we've talked about?" I asked.

"Since your disappearance, Donovan has officially proclaimed you his *Amorei*. The only way to stop him is for someone to claim you as *Ashanti*."

"Sir, I implore you to reconsider..." Anhelm beseeched.

"It's done." Xavier's eyes pierced mine with utmost intensity. Mine narrowed in return. The phrase sounded familiar. *Ashanti*. Oh, holy shit! My face turned hotter than a fire poker.

"Are you crazy?"

"Even the secondborn agrees," Anhelm deadpanned. His reasons to dissuade Xavier from pursuing this horrible idea had to do with me not being worthy of the honor, no doubt. Always protecting the prestigious warrior and leader. I admired Anhelm's devotion.

Nelia tugged on my sleeve. Xavier dismissed us with a simple raise of his chin. How did he do that? Applied body language with such clarity of purpose. And how, for all the marbles in my brain, had my life led me to be claimed as "the one" by one of my adversaries?

TWENTY-FIVE

The aroma of freshly baked bread wafted toward me, and I drooled. Abandoning the towel I was drying my hair with, I plucked a chunk off a knotted roll and popped it in my mouth. A feast awaited me when I stepped out of the bathroom, courtesy of Nelia.

"Hungry?" Nelia's buoyant voice sounded even livelier.

"Uh-hmm." I pulled a stool from beneath the desk and dug into everything on the plate at once. Let her laugh at that. Before long, I polished my plate clean.

"You're moaning."

I rolled my eyes. I reached for the takeout cup and slurped the last remaining sips. As my belly became full and satisfied, my mood improved. I stretched my arms upward and turned around on my stool. Nelia sat on the bed, legs crossed over and a book in her hands. On further inspection, the book was titled *The History of Earthbounders*. I grimaced.

"What's up with that?" I pierced the book with a slanted eye. It wasn't a terrible book; it had its uses. It was what it stood for—a reminder of my current situation—that bothered me. Nelia cleared her throat.

"And the Voice said, 'You've served well and proven your-selves worthy of this gift—a likeness of yours in heart, mind, and spirit. Her name shall be Ashanti which means The One. She shall fight alongside you. Together you will establish my Dominion on Earth. A new race of light warriors to fend off those who violate the cosmic law of the universe and the free will of my People.'" Nelia flipped hundreds of pages over to a folded corner. Without hesitation, she carried on, "'Following the original Edict's teachings, a Pure-blood Earthbounder can nominate one female Earthbounder to be his *Ashanti*, the highest honor a female Earthbounder can receive in the act of coupling between male and female Earthbounders. Once selected, *Ashanti* becomes untouchable to other prospective suitors. Her actions will forever cast a shadow or light on the character of her Devoted. The Devoted, or the selector, will bear all duties of discipline, teaching, ensuring safety, and providing life's necessities for his *Ashanti*. She will be his duty and his prize. It is a sacred distinction of each Pure-blood Earthbounder to find a female Earthbounder worthy of such a title, and it shall not be taken lightly. There can only ever be one *Ashanti*, The One. She shall be recognized and cherished by All. Anyone who challenges this sacred pact shall be met with fire and fury, a trial...'"

"All right, I get it." I put up my hands in surrender. I strolled over to the bed and curled my legs beneath me. "So, am I now Xavier's property or something?" I asked, picking at the hem of my frazzled jeans.

"No." Nelia's rebuttal packed a punch of offense with it. I raised my questioning eyes to hers. "He's granted you the most esteemed title an Earthbounder Pure could give to anyone." Nelia sucked a lip in between her teeth, giving something a prolonged thought. "It's like having a wish you treasure above anything else. That's how important choosing an Ashanti is."

My eyes rounded into perfect saucers. "Ohmagod." I shot off the bed and began pacing back and forth.

"So, you understand?" Nelia's tone conveyed a sense of hope. I stopped in front of her, hands on my hips.

"Yeah, he wasted his one wish on me. Me! What the hell have I done to him?"

Nelia froze as if I had poured a bucket of cold water over her. "Um, well, that's one way of looking at it."

"There isn't any other way." I lifted my arms heavenward in anger, in defeat—in utter confusion. "I can't go along with this. Don't I have any say in whether I want to be this *Ashanti*?" Overtaken by a new purpose, I snatched the book and sifted through it like a maniac. The answer had to be somewhere on these pages. Why hadn't I studied more?

There. I traced an index finger across the passage where Nelia had left off earlier. It continued to translate the ancient edict, in particular, the message about building dominion on Earth and the critical role of procreation... *Ughhh*. I fumbled the book and it flopped to the floor, bouncing off and then collapsing on open pages.

"Children? Nobody said anything about children." I was too young to pop babies.

"Arien, please. You're hyperventilating." Nelia pulled me down beside her. She smoothed out my hair with tender touches and wiped off unsuspecting tears. She sighed. "No matter how this situation pans out in the long run, you need to know Xavier is not all that bad."

I snorted. Nelia grabbed my shoulders and twisted me around, gaining my full attention.

"He'd never force a woman to...you know." Nelia's cheeks pinked. And yes, I suspected he could have his pick any day of the week and any time of the day. "I believe he is selfless in his decision. Being claimed as *Ashanti* by a commander will make you immune. Not only by Donovan but by the Soaz and higher." Nelia rattled my shoulders as if to emphasize her words.

I mulled them over. I didn't doubt the benefits of the claiming, but did I trust Xavier not to expect something in return? If I was being honest with myself, I didn't trust him one iota. Period. He had an ulterior motive. I just didn't know what it was, yet. Nelia didn't see it and... Wait a second, Nelia was with Xavier. I was sure of it. And yet, she acted so unaffected by this. I clasped her hands, and surprise morphed over her concerned expression.

"Oh, Nelia, I'm so sorry." I squeezed her palms.

"About?" A note of suspicion underlined Nelia's tone.

"It should've been you. If he had any sense altogether, he would have picked you! You're far superior to me. You're excellent with weapons, smart, gorgeous..."

"Wait!" Nelia withdrew her hands from my tight grasp. "You think...I'm Xavier's *Amorei*?"

I bit my lip and Nelia burst out laughing. Confused by her sudden outpouring of emotion, I waited for her to get a grip. I seriously wanted to shake her. I needed answers.

"Xavier is my half-brother. Much older too."

"Oh."

"What made you think we were in a relationship?" Nelia removed the residue from stray tears.

I shrugged. "You seemed close?" Not that I had known all of Xavier's whereabouts these past few weeks, but as far as I could tell Nelia was the only woman he spent time or conversed with.

"He looks after me." Did he look after his sister? Nelia had dreams of fighting on the front lines. Couldn't he have made that happen? I tried my hardest to withhold my judgments. I had so much to learn about Earthbounder ways of life.

"Xavier's mother died when he was seven years old. She

was Hafthor's *Ashanti Rosa, The One True Love*—the most rare
connection Earthbounders can have and limited to the
warriors of the same order. They were fated to be together
and Hafthor rarely had been seen without her by his side.
They say when you meet your fated mate it's as if the
universes collided to make that happen. The two souls pull
each other in. It's inescapable. Following his fated mate's
death, Hafthor spiraled. He became more severe. He devoted
himself to running Invicta, and Xavier threw himself into
training. Did you know he's the youngest warrior ever to hunt
down and kill a mature borelli demon?" Nelia retold the story
with pride in her voice, but my heart filled with sorrow.

"How old?" I whispered.

"Fourteen."

I gasped. Even for Earthbounder standards, fourteen was
very young to take part in demon hunts. Those who wished
to join the warrior ranks had to graduate at age eighteen first.
Who allowed a child to fight demonic creatures? It was despi-
cable. Unthinkable. But under this blanket of righteous anger,
some other sentiment lurked. The sadness for a boy whose
world had crumbled around him that faithful day. As much as
I hated to admit it, Xavier and I had something in common.
We both lost our mothers at a young age, and our lives have
never been the same since.

Hard knocking roused me from the stupor. Nelia opened
the door and spoke to a warrior I recognized. I listened to
their conversation, but it was all too hushed and brief.

"I have to go." Regret registered in Nelia's tone. I winced.
I so didn't want to be alone right now, and I still had so many
questions.

Putting on my best impression of confidence, I stood up
and said, "Duty calls." Despite my prime attempts at bravado,
a sad smile accompanied my words. Nelia nodded with as
little enthusiasm as I embodied.

"I'll be back as soon as I can." Pulling away from the embrace, she tightened her grip on my arms. "I promise."

Nelia's eyes searched mine. As swiftly as they connected, she was pivoting away from me and leaving without a second glance. I scrubbed my hands through my hair and ran them down my face. Images of water splashing as the invisible kelpie danced around me popped into my head, and I leaped out of bed. Before I knew it, I was opening my room's door, ready to do something—chase after Nelia, maybe—when I met with a uniformed warrior's broad back. Without a single glance, the warrior instructed me to go back inside.

"What do you mean I can't leave?"

"Commander's orders."

"How long?" I asked. The warrior smirked over his shoulder in response. I gritted my teeth, determined to push further. Thinking better of it, I closed my door, putting a tad more strength behind the shove. He would not tell me anything.

Xavier's orders. What a joke!

After an hour of pacing around the room and cataloging everything that had happened over the last day, I gave in to the weariness settling in my bones. The bed tempted me, and in spite of anxiety over falling asleep, I lay down and succumbed to nothingness. Tomorrow would be a new day, a new battle...

TWENTY-SIX

I woke up to banging on my door. Disoriented at first, I read the hour on the nightstand clock. It was only five o'clock in the afternoon. I cracked the door open, revealing the Magister's Office personal guard.

"Secondborn Blair, the Magister requests an audience with you."

"Oh. Now?" I was told the Magister was away for weeks to come. What made him return to Invicta so soon?

"When you're ready." The warrior raised an eyebrow. A mass of hair weighed one side of my head down. My face heated. I wasn't the mirror-looking type, but I knew what my unruly hair did when I failed to brush it out after washing. I got ready in record time, choosing a fitted tactical training shirt over more relaxed, standard-issue gear and, well, my jeans. It seemed to be the proper thing to wear to an audience with a man in charge of the entire northwest region of wicked warriors battling an unauthorized demonic presence. A tight ponytail completed what I hoped was an Earthbounder trainee-worthy look.

Something seemed off when I stepped into the hallway. I

cast a glance into my room—what I'd associated as *my* place —with nostalgia. Shivers ran down my body as the door glided to a close.

"Follow me," the Magister's guard said. The guard assigned to me by Xavier wasn't there. Was he dismissed on account of the Magister? I'd never met the man in charge. Knowing he was Xavier's father, I imagined a condescending, self-righteous, and most likely very handsome warrior. I needed to curb my impulses around him, especially those injecting hasty words into my replies.

The receiving office had modern and simplistic decor. The staged room stood in contrast to the Renaissance architecture and marble statues lining the corridor on this floor. Perhaps white walls and standard black furniture with leather-backed chairs were more suitable for audiences. A large-framed man sat in a visitor's chair. He stood to greet me as I approached. A pleasant face and welcoming smile faced me. The man had that uncommon attractiveness and air about him I associated with Earthbounders.

"Arien, it's nice to finally meet you." He stuck out his hand.

"Finally?" I asked, shaking his hand. It'd be rude to decline. The man was about to speak when the Magister drew my attention away with a loud and cautionary clearing of his throat. As if on autopilot, my body snapped, facing the authoritative and threatening figure leisurely seated behind the mammoth black rectangle of an office desk. The Magister leaned forward, his lithe forearms exposed by the folded-over cuffs of his crisp white dress shirt. The shirt and tie— although top-shelf and elegant—contrasted with roughened hands from centuries of fighting. His face was an older version of Xavier's. The eyes were as marvelous but a shade darker than Xavier's lapis lazuli orbs and a shade crueler, too. The stark difference between the two men was their hair.

Xavier must have inherited his golden locks from his mother. His father's hair was coal black and he preferred a short, clean cut.

The Magister's face screwed into pure reprobation. He grunted with dissatisfaction and pointed to the unoccupied visitor chair facing his desk. He unclasped his hands to play with a large ring on his left middle finger. There was an insignia of some sort embedded in a red square stone on the ring. The Magister gave the man in the chair next to mine a meaningful stare.

"Right." The visitor clapped his hands and leaned in. "I'm Seth, the head of Praetor 6 or P6," the salt-and-pepper-haired man said. Seth wore a tweed brown jacket with elbow patches paired with dark, boot-cut jeans and, well, boots. Something told me this was the most festive ensemble he possessed. Seth's demeanor lacked the intimidation factor. He was inviting, *likable* even.

"I'm sorry, the head of what?" I broke through the heavy haze of confusion. I glanced at the Magister, thinking he led this conversation. The Magister began sorting documents on his desk. I arched my brows in confusion. Seth's gentle smile conveyed empathy. A chunk of apprehension melted away from my heart. The P6 leader acted quite the opposite of Hafthor's dictatorship style, and since I was running rather low on supporters, I appreciated his civility.

"The P6 is an establishment for Earthbounders who are descendants of Powers. You are familiar with parts of our history?" I responded I did. Powers were the rarest group of Earthbounders. In the distant past, they'd been sole custodians of planet Earth. As their name indicated, they were powerhouses. But their primordial role had been that of builders and teachers, not fighters. They built matter, forms, and structures on Earth's spiritual plane and the physical. They were not equipped to fight evil. The *War of the Worlds*—

as named by the Earthbounder historians—had taken Powers by surprise. There'd been an unexpected shift in the far universe, causing a chain reaction. All galaxies and stars rearranged, triggering cosmic forces, opening and closing stargates at a rapid pace. The Archons and other low and dense-frequency creatures took advantage of this disturbance. Their destination: planet Earth. What happened next was the chaos and annihilation of Powers and the unsuspecting human race. According to the handbook, their battle cries were heard in Heaven, and the Light Council sent in reinforcements, the Seraphs. The rest of the Earthbounders' history wasn't as interesting—mostly politics—so I'd skipped those chapters.

"The P6 has been around for millennia. It's run by Powers"—Seth placed a hand on his chest—"and it's home to the best Power warriors. The best of the best, as they say." In the background, the Magister harrumphed, reminding me of his presence. Seth grinned. The P6 leader drew nearer and whispered, "Some of us can't handle the truth."

"As I was saying"—Seth's eyes glinted with anticipation—"P6 is officially recruiting you to join our ranks." What? No, he had said nothing like that in the prelude to this. He said "best of the best" or something like it. I was nowhere near that category. Speaking of being blindsided, he wanted to recruit me to what he just described as elites. My head swayed from side to side before I even uttered a single word. Seth's eyes dimmed.

"I understand this must be a lot to take in—" he began.

"Arien Blair, daughter of no-one-knows-whom, an orphan and a secondborn or worse"—Hafthor made being a secondborn sound like a crime—"do you think you have a say in this?" His irises darkened to thunderclouds. "Do you truly think your future is in your hands?" He laughed. Dark undertones cut through his outburst.

"Is this necessary?" Seth asked.

"We don't baby our trainees, Seth. She's a disgrace to our kind. My son thought there was some potential here, but he's biased or swayed by her looks. Donovan's field report shows her being completely inept and incorrigible. If I were at the office, I would've complied with your transfer request on day one. I'm surprised you still want her."

"You know why," Seth said under his breath. Seth's words made Hafthor consider something; he dipped his chin in silent understanding. Feelings of humiliation, anger, and betrayal bubbled up in me. Although I didn't expect any better treatment from Hafthor, he startled me with his shrewd jabs aimed at my character, aptitude, and prowess. And Donovan's report? Was he pretending his interest in me to compile some stupid report? Here I was thinking I'd made a notable improvement in training—that I'd fit in. I was a fool.

Something warm flicked to life inside of me. No, this thing was flaming. Its tongues rose higher and higher, uncontrolled, until my scalp smoldered.

"Why has your *kind* taken me in? You kidnapped me. You forced me to forget the world as I knew it. You stole my freedom from me. Do you truly think I owe you *anything*?" Each word came out louder and harsher than the one before it. I didn't know if it was my tone or that I twisted his own words and threw them back at him, but his displeasure with me grew. The blue in his eyes morphed into gleaming steel. For a moment, I feared he'd rip my throat out here and now. He remained still. He was a man in full control.

"Case in point. Good luck with that one. Seth, it was a pleasure to see you again." The Magister dismissed us. Seth shook Hafthor's hand and stepped away. To my surprise, Hafthor waited to shake my hand next. His hand dwarfed mine. He applied enough pressure to make the experience an uncomfortable one. He let me know he could've crushed my hand with one innocent squeeze. I suspected this little show of Hafthor's power was all for me. It was subtle. Goose bumps spread on my forearms. Hafthor was immensely powerful, from all angles—physically, psychically, and politically. I understood. At this moment, my fate was in his hands. My mouth turned dry, and I lowered my eyes in a sign of submission.

Seth gestured for me to precede him.

"Secondborn." I turned around to find Hafthor resting one hip on the edge of the table, his clasped hands in front of him. "For your sake, I hope you learn your place among the Earthbounders quickly. Should we meet again, I expect a show of respect to this office and your superiors and that you act with decorum. We have a special place for Earthbounders who dissent or try to ensnare their superiors into sacred vows."

Satisfaction relaxed his features. His words had the intended effect, draining blood from my face. The Magister was referring to Xavier's latest proclamation. He wasn't too keen on having an orphan secondborn and suspected traitor by the Soaz as his daughter-in-law. Did Xavier know? I spun away and hurried to leave. I had no idea what sort of hell I was in for with the P6, but right now I looked forward to it.

TWENTY-SEVEN

The P6 leader stayed silent once we departed from Invicta in a nondescript silver sedan. Seeing a mundane car brought back memories of my pre-Earthbounder life, and nostalgia planted roots in my heart yet again.

"Relax, Arien. You'll cut off circulation to your legs." I swiveled my head away from the passenger window and stared at Seth, my brows drawing close.

"Your hands." He pointed at my lap. *Oh.* Veins popped on the backs of my hands as they squeezed my thighs. I let go and flexed all ten digits. I massaged both legs just above the knees and studied the leader. His oval face had a sloped forehead and a long, straight nose. His jet-black hair was cropped short, too modern for his old-fashioned style.

"How old are you?" I asked.

A genuine smile spread across Seth's face. "Ancient."

"That's a broad term." I sighed.

He nodded. "It requires a long conversation, one I hope we will have soon. Meanwhile, we shall focus on your transition. How are you coping with the sudden change in your circumstances?" My mouth hung open. Not only was Seth offering to answer my questions, but he was also concerned for my well-being. Not one person—errr, Earthbounder—had asked how I was doing since Xavier dragged my ass to Invicta's infirmary.

"My transition sucks." I grimaced at my word choice. Seth was so proper; my foul language sounded out of place. "I mean, it's been difficult and fast-paced. I haven't had the time to process the initial shock yet," I corrected.

"I suspected as much. I think you'll find P6 quite a *refreshing* change." Hmm, this piqued my interest. I shifted in my seat to give him my full attention. If he wanted to talk, I was willing to listen. His lips curved upward.

"Are you trying to tell me the P6 warriors do not have to train at ungodly hours of the day, on and on for hours, and you serve pizza and burgers in your dining hall?" I half-joked, encouraged by his openness. Seth grinned.

"I'm saying it's a different atmosphere."

"Oh." I deflated. More disappointed about the pizza than the grueling workouts. Maybe I was assimilating after all.

"I don't house many warriors. Mercenaries come and go as they please. Some work in teams. They're all seasoned warriors who've been around and seen a lot. Reliable and self-disciplined hunters. But when we do come together, it feels like a family reunion." A sincere grin lit up his face once again. He must have truly cared about his fellow Powers.

"But you run the place, right?"

"The place, yes. The people, no." I gnawed on my lip, wondering what this revelation meant for me. Did this mean I was free to return to my former life?

"I know what you're thinking." I blinked. There it was, the freaking caveat, the *but* squashing my newfound hopes. "Arien, the world is too dangerous for a young Earthbounder to be on her own. Hence, I'm offering you a place to stay and an opportunity to train with some of P6's best warriors." He was right. I stood no chance against an Archon. Even the thought of kelpies terrified me. There was the threat of Invicta, of Donovan who now hated me, of Xavier. *Ohmagod, Xavier!* How would he react when he found out Hafthor had sent me away? Did he even care? I slapped myself mentally; nonsense. Xavier must have been relieved he didn't have to proceed with his ridiculous idea of pursuing me as his *Ashanti*.

"Why are you doing this?" What was the hook? The P6 leader inclined his head as if he'd expected this question.

"You may find this hard to believe at the moment but I was once like you. I was an orphan from a very young age and knew nothing of the Earthbounder race, not until I transformed on my eighteenth birthday. They tracked me down shortly after that. I sort of acted as a vigilante and righted some wrongs on my own. They followed my trail." He peered at me. "I know what it feels like to have your world flipped upside down around you. I think I can help. The choice is ultimately yours."

Seth took a ramp off the highway and shifted the stick shift into the highest gear. The gears in my own head kept turning. I dissected scenario after scenario, and most of them had possible dire outcomes. The P6 sounded more like Earthbounder heaven up above than reality. And I was the naïve sheep about to be rounded up. What was next?

I halted my ruminations when we arrived at P6's iron gates. Similar in design to Invicta's front gates, these giants stood taller, with a large solid circle in the middle showcasing the P6 emblem. Seth scanned his watch at a stand-alone caller box. It beeped, displaying a green light. The left wing of the gate retracted, and the *P* separated from the *6* in the carving with a zigzag line. Four side-by-side sedans could fit through the opening the left wing afforded. Trees surrounded us, among them spruce and towering Pacific red cedars. A troupe of magnificent deer crossed the road up ahead.

"How big is this place?" I asked because we'd been driving for a good fifteen minutes now. Not even Invicta's headquarters were that far off from the front gates.

"We have fifty thousand acres here, give or take a few."

"Give or take a few..." I whispered, staring out the window wide-eyed. As we rounded a corner, a massive rock blocked the road ahead. The front of the rock lifted into the cavern above it like a supersized garage door.

"We are a small group. We employ many security measures here. The gate we used to enter is an official business gate for P6 members only. Visitors are directed elsewhere."

"What about allura?" I could swear I saw the shimmery veil extend on both sides of the gate.

"Allura is an effective trap for demons. There are other bad actors out there." Seth pulled deep into the hangar. The entrance sloped down, going deeper into what I believed was a rocky hill. Motion-detection lights illuminated a tunnel ahead. Seth decelerated as we approached an underground garage with rows of heavy-duty and militaristic cars. A scary realization gripped my guts and squeezed. *Was I more of a prisoner here than I was at Invicta?* Seth said I could go as I pleased, but he also made a strong case against me leaving P6 prematurely. I wanted to trust him, and so far, he hadn't given me a reason not to. I'd keep my guard up, though.

Seth tossed a suitcase on the back seat of a golf cart. He'd explained someone was called in to pack my things while we were in the Magister's office. I recognized the green and purple paisley-patterned bag from Nelia's apartment. I wondered how she reacted when she received the order. Moisture filled my eyes, and I forced the thoughts away from Invicta. My brows lifted, studying our new mode of transportation. A golf cart was not what I expected to travel in the rest of the way. I had hoped to walk. My legs and my mind needed exercise.

After ten minutes of a smooth ride within a narrower tunnel, we arrived at yet another large garage. A motorbike drove in after us and a female figure disembarked. She wore a black fitted one-piece leather outfit and black boots with short heels. She removed her black helmet, revealing a mass of red locks. She defined sexy, badass female. A small part of me envied the way she moved, sleek and determined. She owned each step. Before I knew it, the red-haired goddess stopped before us, grinning from ear to ear.

"You're here." Her voice was smooth like honey. "I'm Zaira."

"Um, Arien?" My voice wavered.

"Of course you are." Zaira's eyes sparkled. "Exiousai, with your permission, I will bring Arien to her suite."

Seth smiled. "I was counting on it."

TWENTY-EIGHT

My hand trembled when I reached for the handle of Nelia's suitcase. Not a good sign. I took a steady breath and made brief eye contact with Zaira, communicating my readiness. She led through a mudroom into a woodsy-looking kitchen with cherry-stained log paneling and matching cabinets. The counters were slabs of some dark stone, and the breakfast bar was the crosscut of a tree trunk. Beyond it, a large living area with a high ceiling featured a wood-burning fireplace and brown leather furniture pieces. As my eyes shifted to a wicker basket in the corner filled with crocheted afghans, they widened. This place was nothing like what I'd imagined. I turned in a circle, taking it all in. If I drew a definitive former-experience-tainted opinion, it'd go something utilitarian and cold. But not this place.

Decorative carpet-lined wooden steps next to the furthest wall led one story up. At the top, an arched bay window over-looked a courtyard, sprawling gardens, lakes, and trees. Lots of trees. I brought my face closer to the glass. The building extended on both sides, creating a U-shape with a paved patio space below. Adirondack chairs surrounded a stone fire pit in the center. I almost smacked myself in the forehead for not realizing until now that the P6 headquarters was a log cabin. Thick cedar logs supported the metal roof. I spotted another building in the distance—a huge hangar-like structure. One of its entrances opened, and male warrior figures filed out. My stomach twisted in knots, already bracing itself.

Zaira stood to the side, waiting.

"Um, sorry..." I said.

The warrior invaded my personal space. "Never apologize." Her serious eyes switched from one of mine to the other. She stepped away. "Come on."

Geez. I picked up my suitcase again as I massaged a spot on my chest. My heart pounded.

My room was, in fact, a suite. Nothing fancy or large. The space encompassed a living area with a smaller fireplace, a bedroom, and a master bath separated by a set of stained-glass-filled wooden doors.

"I'm sure you had an eventful day. Take your time. Come down when you're ready. I make killer pancakes," Zaira's singsong voice pitched at the end. I wasn't sure if this was Zaira's natural disposition or an effort to make me feel welcomed. I guessed time would tell.

There was no way in hell I'd sit on my ass and wait for things to happen. After I unpacked my spare belongings, I traipsed downstairs. I listened to the voices that carried to the top of the staircase. Female. I recognized one as Zaira. The second one was softer than the other warrior's. I hovered longer, listening in. Not something I was proud of, but I no longer had qualms about it either. If I had to guess when this change in my character occurred, I'd guess Paulyna's drowning attempt was the tipping point. The Powers talked about food, specifically which pancake batter was better. A corner of my mouth hiked up. One of my foster moms used to make delicious pancakes. I'd never forget Ms. Pam. She was kind to me. Her husband... He was a different story.

Big breath, and here we go. When I descended halfway down the stairs, the voices hushed. My muscles bunched, and I ended up crossing the room over on stiff legs. Two pairs of eyes tracked my moves. Zaira stood at the counter with a mixing bowl and a whisk. Her companion, who sat at the breakfast bar, stood up and met me at the edge of the kitchen tile floor with an outstretched hand.

"Hi, I'm Rae." Her eyes shone with genuine humor as she shook my hand. "You joined us just in time. I'm trying to convince Zaira to make chocolate chip pancakes and not plain-o buttermilk."

"Hey! My buttermilk pancakes are a hit around here."

"Because those men will eat anything you put in front of their noses." Rae rolled her eyes.

"They better." Zaira simpered knowingly. I followed Rae and claimed one of the bar stools.

"What do you think, Arien?"

I froze, stunned to be addressed by my name. *Someone better explain the pecking order around here.* I assumed Zaira if not both female Powers were Pures. But I didn't know for sure. I glanced from one expectant face to the other.

"Oh, well, chocolate chips will make anything edible for me."

Rae grinned. Zaira's face fell. I inspected what I said and, crap, I might have insulted Zaira with my comment. I needed damage control, stat.

"I mean, I like chocolate chips, but I'm sure your pancakes are as lovely without them. Uhh... Would you like me to prepare them for you?" I hopped down without waiting for Zaira's response, determined to appease. As a secondborn, that was part of my purpose. A warm hand grabbed mine, and Rae's concerned eyes captured my alarmed ones.

"Heyyy, that won't be necessary. Sit." Rae inclined her head towards the stool. I obeyed her command.

Zaira raised her eyebrows, pointing a stainless steel spatula at Rae. "I told you," she said. I lowered my gaze to feign interest in the intricate tree ring patterns imbued in the bar top's surface. This introduction to P6 wasn't going as I'd imagined. Maybe because I expected to be thrown into training right away or some kind of work. Physical exertion helped my cognitive functions. The word "training" caught my attention, and my head snapped up.

"When will we start?" My eagerness took the Powers by surprise.

"Start what?" Rae's nose twitched.

"Oh, I thought you said something about training." I sat straighter but avoided eye contact. *Show no weakness and convey respect for their rank*, I reminded myself.

"We should start tomorrow." Zaira placed a plate full of steaming hot chocolate chip pancakes right underneath my nose. The aroma transported me to the bakery I used to work at. We didn't make pancakes there, but Tuesdays and Thursdays were crepe days. And they were to die for. My stomach somersaulted and growled at the same time.

A fleeting shadow swept over us from a tall window—one of many rectangular, tall windows with grids surrounding double doors on the back of the house. Opaque white curtains obstructed the view beyond them. It could've been a figure passing by, but it happened so fast I didn't know for certain.

Rae slid a glass of OJ my way, but it was Zaira's heavy presence that drew my eyes upward. A spatula stuck out sideways from her folded arms, and her brows formed a V. I averted my gaze. "Sorry."

"Forget about tomorrow. We'll begin training today. Lesson number one, we do not uphold a distinction between Pures and secondborns here," Zaira said. I hesitated. Wait, *what?* "That means you can and should look into my eyes, Arien." My eyes were already on her face, never quite capable of abiding by Invicta's rules. I exhaled. Satisfied with my response, Zaira returned to tend the pancakes despite the emotion never reaching her cutthroat eyes.

"They put you through a wringer at Invicta, didn't they?" Rae sipped her OJ. I tossed the idea in my head, wrinkling my nose at the sour realization. I'd been conditioned like a dog. Made to believe my future was not my own. Falling asleep afraid someone would be in my room in the morning, threatening me or accusing me of sedition.

"You could say that." I nodded with resignation. The idea struck a cord of sadness and embarrassment. I'd let this happen to me. And I wasn't out of the woods just yet, either. Thinking of my old life, dependent on charity and government-run programs, I questioned whether I'd ever been truly free. Was anyone ever free in this world?

The heavenly taste in my mouth lessened the punch of these unpleasant truths. Frankly, I couldn't stop the moan from escaping my mouth. That solicited a smile from Rae and a toss of hair from Zaira, which I assigned to satisfaction.

"See, chocolate chips make everything better," Rae prodded. "Zaira here hates chocolate."

The warrior gave her the stink eye. "I don't hate, hate chocolate. I think it's overrated, that's all."

Rae smirked around her drink. "Seriously, we needed more estrogen at P6. Men are...men." Rae pointed a thumb down while sticking out her lower lip in a mock "they suck" rating.

Zaira cackled out loud. "Does Vex know?"

Rae's cheeks turned ruddy as she hid behind her glass again.

I washed down the last chunk of my pancake, feeling calmer on the inside.

"How many warriors are stationed here?" I asked. It was time I learned the ins and outs of my new station.

TWENTY-NINE

My brain worked in overdrive. Following our meal, I spent most of my time quizzing Rae and Zaira about the P6 and other Earthbounder groups. Earthbounders descended from different angelic orders. While Seraphs remained the most populous group on the planet, there were fractions of Thrones, Cherubim, Virtues, and even Archangels. Members of these groups often excelled at counterintelligence and sciences, portal fissure phenomena, and diagnosing energetic signatures of objects and beings traveling through the time-space corridors. Invicta collaborated with one of the largest supernatural surveillance firms in the world. P6 relied on several trusted informants. In addition, warriors procured certain technologies, enabling them to identify immediate threats with some predictive modeling capabilities. As Zaira was describing one such gadget, I itched to see one up close.

I was relieved and disappointed when the Powers put an end to our conversations and announced a barbecue and a bonfire at a nearby beach.

"Oh, bring a swimsuit. Everyone usually goes for a dip."

Zaira walked me to my door. Her suite was the next door down. She explained female warriors stayed on the top floor. Male warriors occupied the ground floor, while couples had access to larger suites in the left wing.

I thanked Zaira, thinking I'd rather park my ass in the sand at the risk of coarse powder entering all unwelcome places than go into, and potentially under, water. A flash of a not-so-distant memory triggered goosebumps all over my body. Water nymphs were absolutely and categorically scary.

Skeptical at first, I found myself stupefied in awe at the lush flora surrounding the crystal blue water. Each step in the sand felt like sinking into pliable cushions. The clear sky above was tranquil. The sounds of undulating water filled the air. That was if you ignored a group of warriors jumping off a coral-lined cliff in the distance. In the far, far distance. My jaw slackened open.

"How?"

"Remember, this place is not truly here," Rae whispered into my ear, her hand moving across the breathtaking landscape. She was having some innocent fun at my expense, and it didn't bother me at all. Rae explained how the first P6 leader had anchored the tropical place here centuries ago. I gazed back at her with an expression of utter disbelief and incredulity. Part of me knew by now the sky was no longer the limit. I tried to be open-minded, but "anchoring" a place aka folding space between two faraway points was science fiction in my books.

I smiled to myself, removing my boots and delighting in the warmth seeping into my feet. My jacket was next. The rugged stone fire pit appeared original to the landscape. The black porous texture was reminiscent of lava rocks. For good measure, I scanned the horizon for any signs of a volcano. I sighed with relief when I didn't spot one. I kicked myself mentally. Why would a P6 leader transport a volcano to P6 headquarters to begin with?

"You know, except for you being an orphan who'd lived among humans, we know little about you," Zaira said. I caught a hint of curiosity in her tone—as if she'd been musing her thoughts out loud. I paused mid-bite. Someone brought boxes of pizza and a cooler filled with drinks before we arrived.

"Zaira," Rae hissed. Zaira rolled her eyes. "Never mind," she muttered.

I sat my plate down, losing interest in my *numero uno* food choice. I brushed my hands off.

"It's all right. It's only fair after you've shared so much with me." Zaira shot Rae a winning smile before rounding her eyes on me. They were full of anticipation.

"Yeah, so..." Where did I begin? "Didn't you read a report on me? A file?" I sounded hopeful.

"Exiousai Seth has your file. He only divulges information critical to our mission. Except for what I just told you, we know nothing about your life prior to being recovered." Exiousai, that word again.

"What's Exiousai?"

"Title. All Power leaders are Exiousai. It means 'Authority,'" Rae said, her tone soft and patient. Oh. I gaffed when I called the Exiousai by his name. Why hadn't he corrected me? Zaira cleared her throat. Right.

"What would you like to know?"

The next hour or two passed by in riveted conversation and some boring storytelling on my part. I answered all their questions about my past. Yes, all. That was until my so-called "rescue" by the Seraphs. The Powers sensed my guard was up when Invicta came up, and they abandoned the subject. The weird part about it was that I felt better, lighter even, when the questioning ended. I stretched out my limbs and grabbed another iced tea lemonade out of the cooler.

At first, there was a solitary flutter of wings brushing against my abdomen from within. Then, an unfamiliar but irresistible warmth unfurled. My heart skipped a tiny beat. *No!*

"Arien, is everything okay? You've paled..."

I shot up to my feet and whirled around, seeking him. A small group of men cleared the corner behind the dunes and stepped onto the beach. Among them were the three men I'd had a run-in with in the junkyard. Impossible! Nelia never mentioned that the Powers who had alerted Invicta stayed at P6. They were supposed to be elite assassins who worked alone. And neither Rae nor Zaira said a peep during my story time.

Overwhelmed by conflicting emotions about the situation, I somehow ended up backtracking right into the log bench on the other side of the bonfire. I tripped and squealed, hands windmilling in the air. A puff of powdery sand fluffed around me when my ass touched down.

Rae took hold of my arms and righted me in no time, asking questions. I wasn't paying any attention. My entire being focused on the Power with dark chocolate eyes and an unforgiving scowl as if I were a moon and he were a planet whose orbit I circled. His face twisted in what I could only judge as disgust. The group ambled at a leisurely pace, heading in our direction. No thanks to my squeals and ungraceful fall.

As they approached, the Power's eyes grew darker, and a chill ran down my spine. Weapon. I needed a weapon! I lurched for the nearest roasting stick propped by the fire and pointed it at the Power's chest. He halted just in front of it, scowling at the misshapen jumbo-sized marshmallow dangling from the stick's end.

"Oh, yum." The blocky, shortest warrior of the three picked the marshmallow off and popped it into his mouth. The Power's irises darkened with palpable annoyance.

"What is she doing here?" the unapologetic Power boomed at Rae, who'd remained at my side. Rae stumbled her way through a few words, trying to piece together an acceptable answer when he interjected, "Never mind. I will take this up with Exiousai."

He stormed off. I blinked. *What in hell?* Why did he hate me so much?

"Hi, babe." The marshmallow thief kissed Rae's cheek. I frowned at the roasting stick I brandished as a weapon and set it down. I hoped its owner wouldn't take offense. After all, I didn't eat the marshmallow pierced to its end. The offender nuzzled up to Rae, squeezing her waist. Rae's cheeks turned pink as she tried to pry his hands off her midsection.

"Arien, you've already met Vex." She pointed to the man glued to her hip. He winked.

"We didn't get a chance to introduce ourselves properly. We would have if you didn't pull off that stunt a few weeks back. I think Talen is still ticked about it. He's never been knocked down before, especially not by flying vehicle parts." His full-on toothy grin caused the corners of his eyes to crinkle. I grimaced at his confession concerning the third warrior. He'd called him Talen.

"I'm so sorry. Is he okay?"

"Oh, yeah. We heal fast," he said. "His biggest wound is the one on his ego." Vex picked up the roasting stick—also known as an ineffective weapon against pissed-off Powers— and began impaling marshmallows, one after another.

"You've got to tell us how you escaped. We searched for you for hours."

"Talking about me again?" I didn't notice Talen approaching. Several warriors were now headed this way. Talen retrieved a roasting stick and a bag of marshmallows. He inserted one spongy substance after another, the same way Vex did. I counted a dozen marshmallows by the time Talen finished.

"Arien, this is Talen," Rae said. Talen had the dark Power's height and build. His dirty blond hair hung in unkempt curls. Locks swayed haphazardly over his eyes, and he swept them to a side, revealing a square face with thin, determined lips and unusually large aquamarine eyes. He extended his loaded stick toward me. I put my hands up.

"Um...sorry, but I can't eat all this."

"Don't be *silly*. It's Vex's. Can you prop it on the stand behind you?" Talen's lips quivered.

"Oh, sure." I raised an eyebrow at the stick and in Vex's direction.

"He knows how to take care of me, doesn't he?" Vex asked, cajolingly. I couldn't stop the small smile from spreading on my lips, and I shook my head lightly. These men were full of surprises. They acted nothing like what I'd expected. Well, not all of them, anyway. One brooding Power fulfilled my expectations.

Vex sat on the log with Rae on his lap. They left open space between them and Talen, and feeling a bit more at ease, I joined them.

"So, how did you get away?" Talen asked.

Vex snorted. "You can't let that one go, can you?"

Talen's brows bunched. "No one has ever gotten away from us. I want answers."

"You heard the man. Spill the beans, sister. You found some hidey-hole and waited for us to leave, didn't you?" Vex asked. I momentarily pondered how much I should reveal. Should I tell them about the secret passage? My first thought was that I shouldn't. Someone had made it for a reason, and that someone could've been Paulie. He'd always protected me, even though I'd been oblivious to it, and now I needed to protect his secrets. I nodded, hoping no one would pry for details.

"I thought you were going to kill me next."

"That had to be terrifying," Rae said. I shrugged. Of course, it was. Winged creatures chasing after me, not to mention a terrifying shadow figure with a two-story-tall smoky worm. Even if they swore to do no harm, I wouldn't have gone near them. Not right then, anyway.

"Nah, the Archon was gonna drain you. We saved you," Vex said with hubris.

Talen stayed quiet throughout our exchange, and I wondered whether he was going to call me out for my omissions.

"Why didn't you talk to me at the restaurant or on the bus?" If all Earthbounders could sense my fledgling status, surely they had known what I was the first time we met.

"We suspected you were with the rebellion," a low-timbre voice answered from across the fire. I recognized it, but I leaned across Talen to get a visual confirmation, anyway. The Power's unmistakable silhouette, perched on a rock, loomed against the backdrop of the fading light. Perplexed, I shifted back in my seat. He was here, but I didn't sense his approach that time. Of course, now that I knew he was there and listening, my stomach roiled and my hands became clammy. The dark Power consumed all my senses when he was around. I couldn't deny it.

"And that's Kolerean. Goes by Kole." Rae sighed.

Kole.

———

"Wanna join us for a swim?" Zaira jumped to her feet and shimmied out of her swimsuit cover. Rae followed suit. I scanned my torn-cut jean shorts and T-shirt. I didn't bring a swimsuit. To be honest, I didn't own one to begin with. I wasn't keen on swimming either. But the alternative before me, which was being alone with three quizzical male warriors, was even less appealing. I leaped to my feet and pulled my T-shirt over my head. I wore a comfortable sports bra underneath that afforded full coverage. When surrounded by incredibly handsome people, especially men...especially *him*, a girl could get a little timid. Stepping over the log, Rae got in front of me, staring at my rib cage. Oh right, that hadn't yet healed.

"May I?" She reached out her hand to the yellow-greenish spot. I froze.

"Rae has multiple medical degrees. She's one of the top medics." Zaira stepped forward. The fracture had mended, and there was nothing more that could be done. Nelia had fixed me up with a miracle-working numbing salve I'd used religiously until now.

I inclined my head. Rea ran her delicate yet skilled fingers over my abdomen, pausing here and there, applying some pressure with her fingertips. I tried my best not to grunt when prickles of pain shot up through my body. Rae withdrew her hand, opening her eyes.

"Two clean fractures. You were lucky," she said. Her eyes searched mine. I didn't understand what they were searching for.

"Er... Yeah, too bad I don't heal as fast as you do." I fidgeted with my hands.

"I was unaware Master Pietras condoned such callous treatment of recruits. I guess he's changed along with the leadership." Displeasure laced Zaira's words.

"No," I objected. Something inside me insisted on defending Master Pietras. "He wouldn't have allowed it. I had an unfortunate run-in with the Soaz, that's all."

I strolled away, wanting nothing more but to submerge in the refreshing water. I was done talking. I dashed and plunged into it. When I emerged, some altercation had taken place between the warriors we left behind on the beach. Both Vex and Talen manhandled Kole, voices raised until they got him to settle down. Vex forced a beer into Kole's hand while Talen kept a vice grip on his shoulder, pressing him into the log. Rae and Zaira popped out of the water near me.

"What's that about?" I sounded bewildered even to my ears. Were all warriors so volatile, or was that Kole's specialty? Both female warriors turned their heads toward the beach and in unison, faced me. In the millisecond that'd passed when they spun towards me, I could swear I witnessed them share a look.

"That's nothing. Lost a bet or something." Rae shrugged. As much as I wanted to believe Rae and dismiss Kole's strange behavior, something just didn't add up. My gaze shifted to the bonfire and homed in on the warrior. Talen no longer pinned him down. Kole's hardened stare didn't waver. He tipped the bottle to his mouth and emptied it. Standing, he tossed it in the bin and stalked off. I blinked, frazzled. Water splashed into my face, and I gasped.

"You looked like you needed it." Vex popped out of nowhere in front of me.

"Gee, thanks."

"A word of advice. Don't let him get under your skin."

THIRTY

"Whoa." Vex doubled over. "You have a helluva punch there." A small smile played on my lips. I mean, Vex insisted I showcase my training using him instead of the punching bag. He'd interlaced his fingers behind his head and urged me to hit his "steel ten-pack." I refused time and time again, but Vex was a master of perseverance. I landed a shot to shut him up. Master Pietras would've been proud.

"You made your point. Let's use a punching bag next time." Vex rubbed his abdomen as we ambled over to the standing punching bags and practice dummies. I smirked to myself—I may have cheated a little bit; I'd aimed for his liver.

"Seriously, where are you storing all this power?" He shook his head. A thrill ran down my spine at his unexpected praise. I'd been training hard at Invicta. My strength was nothing compared to Pures, but enough to stupefy one long enough to break for it when the need arose.

Vex was my assigned trainer today. His first order of the day was a skills assessment. He called out different kicks, punches, and combinations until it became clear I didn't know what he wanted me to do anymore. Reality check—I was still a novice in hand-to-hand combat. And according to Vex, I needed to work on my reflexes, recognizing body language cues, perfecting restraint when provoked, and so on...

Oomph. Air whooshed out of my lungs with the umptieth body slam to the floor, courtesy of Vex. Wheezing, I peeked at him from behind arms splayed across my face. He pulled a mini notepad from his pocket and made yet another note. He'd been taking notes on me all morning. He folded pages over and stuffed them back into his pants pocket. Hands on his hips, he stared me down with amusement twinkling in his eyes.

"I'm thinking you enjoy manhandling me." My jaw jutted out. The entire left side of my body ached. I'd failed to deliver a single punch or kick that had connected since our sparring session started. It wasn't due to Vex's angelic genes, either. He'd "turned off" his special abilities to level the playing field. I didn't delude myself; even as human, Vex was stronger than me. His technique was superb, and his reflexes were impeccable. So, I ended up taking a beating. Technically, Vex didn't hurt me. He deflected my lousy attempts at besting him.

"Ha." Vex's outstretched hand hovered above me. I relaxed my legs, and my arms fell to the sides. Vex straightened, arching a brow.

"I get it. You're faster and stronger. And I have a lot of work to do." And my side throbbed.

"So...you give up?"

I wrinkled my nose. No one liked to be called a quitter, even when they were in the process of quitting.

"No," I said. "I don't see a point in us sparring any longer. The things we fight out there are not human, and they'd wipe me off the surface of this planet before I could even get close enough to think to throw a punch." I heaved myself up and brushed off my pants.

"Very good." Vex glanced at the wall clock and wrote a few more words in his notepad. "You passed today's lesson. We'll break for lunch now. I'm starving."

I stared at the man, dumbstruck. "Wait, a second... Are you telling me this was some sort of test?"

"Aha." Vex shoved the dummy into its corner. I threw my hands up in the air. I tried again.

"What were you testing?" I chased Vex around the gym as he put the room together.

"Your ability to recognize your limits and the strengths and weaknesses of your opponent. To push emotions and hubris aside and think strategically." Vex patted a spot on the wall bench beside him. "Ideally, you would've stopped attacking me after the first time I smacked your behind to the ground. When I said I'd revert to human strength, a part of you saw an opportunity to shine—to show off. You came after me repeatedly because your pride got hurt. Hubris is a state easily preyed on. I understand humans revere and admire certain characteristics like resolution and determination, overcoming obstacles at any cost. They are often guided by their hearts and their ego to varying degrees. In our world, mind"—Vex tapped his temple with an index finger—"and thinking detached from emotion is the difference between life and death."

I rested my back against the cold brick wall as I contemplated Vex's words.

"Earthbounders *do* have hearts?" I asked after a prolonged pause. I was only half-serious. Vex's sobered demeanor didn't change.

"I think... After centuries of observation, I'm convinced Earthbounders' hearts are bigger. No offense." Vex bumped his shoulder into mine. I hissed as his action aggravated an already sore spot.

"None taken." I scowled at him. "Does this mean I get to practice with weapons next?" I asked sweetly.

Vex's face contorted into a horrified expression. "It's too early for that." He jumped to his feet.

"You said I needed to strategize. I can't defeat you in combat, but I can blow your brains off with a proper weapon." Vex scratched the back of his head, looking every-where but at me. Oh my, I think I vexed Vex—pun intended—and I was enjoying it.

"Please? I promise to feel nothing when I do it, too."

Vex's head swiveled my way in a flash. "You're a hellion." He grinned.

I lifted a shoulder. Two could play this game.

"I was sure Rae packed leftovers... Oh, right, I ate that for breakfast." Vex's voice blended with the refrigerator's humming as his head dove inside. When he reappeared, he basket-carried a bread loaf, meat, cheese, lettuce, and tomatoes. I crossed my arms and parked my butt at the edge of the counter.

"You don't have to babysit me, Vex. I can manage a sand-wich, and I can meet you afterward. Where is everyone?" I hadn't seen a soul around here since I left my suite early that morning. A note under my door said Vex was waiting for me in the kitchen. I had expected to have Rae as my guide or Zaira. But I soon learned Vex was an amiable option. The Power was approachable and even-tempered.

"P6 received a call for support early today. All but Rae, Elias—one of our intelligence-gathering guys—and Exiousai are out there helping put out fires."

"But not you?" Vex smiled as he set our prospective lunch near a cutting board. It was obvious he'd much rather be out there with Talen and Kole on a mission. Instead, he was stuck here with me. I took some pity on him and rinsed the produce he selected.

"Vex!" Rae rushed into the kitchen, winded. She wore a headset with a mic and cradled a tablet to her chest. "I've been trying your comms for... Never mind. They're calling in all warriors to Sector B."

There was a millisecond when everything stood perfectly still. Vex flashed past me, his sprint a blur. Speaking to her mic and tapping on the screen, Rae raced over to the double front windows. A motorbike air-lifted from the garage entrance. Once it touched the gravel driveway, it took off at a dangerous speed, spewing dirt and rocks behind it.

"What's going on?" I asked.

Rae whirled at me, her eyes wide. "Oh, Arien." She exhaled. "Sorry, I was so focused on the task, I forgot..."

"That you have a new roommate?" I raised an eyebrow in mock humor.

"Yes. How's your training?" As soon as she posed the question, her eyes wandered to the rectangular screen of her tablet. She perched on the arm of the couch, scanning its contents. My head was full of questions, but I applied self-control and made us both sandwiches instead. As I offered a plate to Rae, she accepted it with thanks. I took a bite of my delicious sandwich and reposed my question.

"Is someone in trouble?"

"A lot of someones," she mumbled over the food in her mouth. "A summoning spell went awry. Some young mages attempted to pull a prank on unsuspecting shifters in their area. They tried summoning the ghost of a long-gone super hunter called Pavel. But when they activated the circle, demons of all types pushed through instead." Rae took another bite. "It's...as if...they were waiting...to be summoned...you know?"

I pieced together Rae's last sentence spoken in between bites. I set my unfinished sandwich down. Recalling Paulie's warning, I had an inkling this phenomenon was related. *They're after Paulie and me.* I jumped to my feet, startling Rae.

"I need to go. Where is Sector B?"

Rae frowned up at me. "We both know you're not ready to enter a battlefield just yet. Your presence will only hurt this mission." She was right. I'd be walking right into Bezekah's trap, which Paulie had me swear not to do. Hollowness gripped my insides. I wanted to—no, I needed to help. I opened my mouth, ready to confess my part in this. Yet, I stopped at a mere "eh." My confession would incriminate Paulie and, possibly, condemn him forever. I let my head fall forward.

"Come with me." Rae led me to a lounge-slash-library connected to the living area via carved wooden doors. There, in the corner, was a black pillar with an iron gate. A spiral staircase led down into a small square room with two stainless steel elevator doors.

"This leads to our operations room and a shelter, should we need one."

A ding announced our elevator car. The metallic interior looked ordinary, with white plastic level buttons that lit up. The speed, however, took me by surprise. I grabbed the sidebar when my heels detached. Bile rose in my throat. When we came to stop, my feet flattened on the floor again, and a force came down on me as if it aimed to squash me. I couldn't wait to step outside.

My eyes lit like a child's at a candy shop. What Rae described as an operations room was a futuristic-styled command center. In the center, an oval table spanning at least twelve feet had a 3D map displayed atop it. I didn't recognize the area. The mountainous terrain was positioned south of the New Seattle border. I scrutinized petite blinking lights moving around the map. They had to be warriors and other life forms. Maybe the enemy?

"Second drone was disabled. I'm releasing MDs and LIDs." A man around his thirties rolled away on a chair from his station. Surprise flickered in his eyes, and he inclined his head in greeting.

"Thank you, Elias," Rae said. I followed her to a similar station with four monitors side by side and two additional ones on top of the others. I didn't know what I was looking at. Was this what they called algorithms? Numeric sequences danced on the screen. But one screen drew my attention. It was a livestream, as seen from a bird's view. Multiple angles recorded the mayhem below. Rae clicked on something, and the visuals projected onto the wall beyond her monitors. The theater-sized screen was split into ten different views. Two squares in the bottom right corner displayed pictures of the new drones clearing the mountaintop and approaching the battlefield.

I jerked when a large object hurtled by one screen. A charcoal gray feather stuck to the corner of the lens and flapped around until a gust ripped it away. I checked the table map. Most dots blinked on the ground. About ten of them zipped in the air. My adrenaline spiked with each red and green dot diving at incredulous speeds and crashing into each other. One green dot faded away.

"Please tell me the good guys are red." My lip trembled.

"Yes. Earthbounders are coded red. Plus, we have access to our warriors' vitals." Rae typed something on the keyboard, and warrior headshots with their vitals, injury, and readiness scales flashed on two of the screens. My eyes gravitated of their own volition to a lethally handsome face. His piercing dark eyes stood out in sharp contrast as if someone

had traced an eyeliner around them. His square jaw compli-
mented a Grecian nose and full, firmly pressed lips. All set in
perfect symmetry. His dark hair was shorter in the picture.

"Bull's eye!" Elias sounded a victory cheer.

I pulled up a chair and tucked my feet under. Something
told me this battle was far from over.

THIRTY-ONE

I hugged my knees tight to my chest as I greedily watched the action unfolding on the holographic 3D map. Each blink of an eye was a nuisance, but I could only hold it off for so long. I held my breath when one of the red dots blinked off, and I hiccupped when it came online again. Ever since Rae had brought me down to the command center, the live feeds absorbed my complete attention. I studied the invading demonic creatures, hoping to identify anything that could give Earthbounders an advantage. The creatures' dark leather-like skin oozed with black goo. Each touch singed the warriors' armor. The bipods had a star-shaped body anatomy similar to humans—two legs, two arms, and a head. Thick webs spanned from their triceps to their backs. These faux wings abetted the creatures in gliding and attacking from the air. Some managed high jumps into the sky thanks to oversized quadriceps. They matched Pures in speed.

The creatures were feral, their wide jaws snapping. Their weapons were their large incisors lining the top and bottom rows of teeth. Oh, and long steel-like claws. Except for two nostril openings, their heads were black hairless eggs. I recalled this creature from my introductory studies at Invicta. This was *hamangi*, listed under common demons known to breach black lines regularly. I didn't recall them coming in a swarm of dozens, though. They were supposed to be small group dwellers of four or five.

The good guys were P6 warriors and a group of Seraphs. I couldn't tell whether Xavier was among them or anyone else I knew. The action blurred as drones moved to a safe distance for recording. The drones were not designed for combat. I didn't know whether Earthbounders had such technology at all.

The Exiousai, Seth, had a private office at the end of the command room. He'd come out of it on multiple occasions to assess the situation. He inclined his head to acknowledge me. Each time he addressed Rae and Elias, he asked questions and provided guidance. Then he'd disappear for a considerable stretch of time. I didn't understand it. They were his men, sort of. I understood P6 warriors were independent like assassins, yet this place was their hub. Shouldn't he lead them?

After hours of an ongoing battle, the Earthbounders surrounded the last of the enemy and dispatched them. Zaira's voice came in over the comms device on Rae's desk. She and a couple of others planned to stay behind and conduct an analysis of the rupture area.

"What's the team's injury profile like?" Rae asked with stoic calm as if this was a normal occurrence. I guessed it was.

"A few bumps and bruises, no open wounds. Vex will need a burn wound kit, though." My eyes shot to the screen with warriors' vitals. Vex's picture flashed red.

"What happened?" Urgency spiked Rae's inflection.

"He was being an idiot. He jumped in front of me, and I had these two stalkers all lined up for beheading. You've got to talk with your man, Rae. He's insane." Zaira's words turned into a disgruntled rumbling. She was annoyed with Vex, all right, but not just because he spoiled her plan. She was upset because he got hurt.

Rae snatched my hand, hauling me off the chair without warning. She held on until I could control my own feet and not fall flat on my face. I jogged behind her into the corridor, taking the second elevator. When the elevator doors slid closed, I expected it to lift us. I was hyper-propelled toward the door and stumbled to my knees. Not only was the lateral motion unexpected, but it also knotted my stomach in the worst ways possible. I grunted, hoisting myself up with the sidebar.

"How thoughtful," I grumbled. The car traveled at high speed. I clung to the side bar as if it were my personal "oh, shit" handle. Rae had not moved since we entered this tricky box of steel. She leaned against the opposite wall, facing the back of the elevator. Ha, there were sliding doors at that end, too. Rae was deep in thought. Worry radiated from her in waves. I chewed on my lip, not knowing what to say or do. Vex must have gotten gravely injured.

As the elevator slowed down, I dug my feet into the floor to avoid yet another embarrassing spill. The opposite door glided open, revealing a medical unit. Steel cabinets locked with a key and a thumbprint pad lined the reception area. Reclining chairs that resembled transfusion stations, tables with laboratory equipment, and several microscopes connected to laptops filled the space. The far wall held five doors leading to private rooms. One door label read *OR*. That's where Rae headed next.

I trailed after her. I wanted to help, but my medical knowledge stretched only as far as Band-Aids and makeshift bandage wraps. The operating room door popped open with the force of decompressed air. I stayed by the door, hesitant to enter.

Rae prepped the table, set up an operating kit on a silver tray and some IV fluids, and moved a large lamp over. I wanted to offer to help. Each time, my tongue would tie up. I bit the inside of my cheek, my eyes going out of focus. I worried for Vex. But he wasn't the only one occupying my mind. Piercing chocolate brown eyes kept flashing in and out. I hoped he didn't get hurt. Not badly, anyway.

"Arien!" Rae snapped. She stood by a large steel fridge door, motioning for me. I shook my head, clearing the fog. Rae pulled out the bottom drawer filled with dozens of ice packs.

"When they come in, distribute the ice packs." She pushed the freezer door shut and opened a cabinet, pointing to Band-Aids, gauze, scissors, and more first-aid supplies. I bobbed my head numbly each time she pointed at an item. I blanched when Rae opened a drawer containing vials and syringes. She noted my reaction and shut the drawer with a sigh.

"Don't worry about it. All warriors train in first aid. They'll manage." She turned toward a single wall in the room made out of metal. Her forehead puckered.

"They're here."

The wall grunted and began lifting. A thick steel platform descended to the floor level. The sounds of car doors opening and closing and chatter inundated the room. Kole and Talen carried in an unconscious Vex. Time slowed down as they passed me. Vex's face was lax and ashen. His arms dangled helplessly by his sides. This was wrong. Vex was full of life.

That couldn't be him. The demon cut his abdomen from the breastbone to the pelvis. Charred skin surrounded internal organs swimming in a pool of blood. I clasped a palm to my mouth to stifle a gasp. My other hand gripped the edge of a countertop behind me. The two warriors entered the operating room and the door closed behind them. I hung my head low.

"He'll be fine," I muttered.

Rubbing palms over my thighs, I studied the small crowd in the healing center. Four warriors rested on the infusion chairs. Others were slumped over benches. They suffered bruises, cuts, and some burns from the *hamangi*'s touch. I rushed to the freezer and grabbed several ice packs. Setting them on a tray, I rummaged through shelves and grabbed jars of salve for burns. I loaded up my tray and stopped at the closest warrior. He scratched his head, squinting at my tray. His lips widened into an inviting smile. He guided me through my hectic attempt at applying first aid and advised that the salve worked best when applied thick. When I finished, the warrior grinned. There was a hint of playfulness in how his lips curved at the corners, perplexing me. I left his station and went on to the next warrior. When I glanced over my shoulder, another warrior joined my first patient and clapped him on his back, lively discussing something. I frowned.

By the time I reached my fourth patient, I'd become efficient at the first aid routine. I made a full round, gaining more confidence. Minor burns and cuts were healed by now, leaving only faint scars. I imagined these would be gone before long, too. As Rae had predicted, warriors administered the infusions themselves. My worse-for-wear patient was helped by another warrior. He maneuvered a bag around a stand, his shirtless back facing me. Two nasty gashes of charred flesh crossed from one shoulder to the opposite hip bone. A pink line of flesh lay above as his body had already healed some of the damage. How had I missed this warrior? I grabbed two jars of salve and set them up on the side table.

"Stay still," I repeated the memorized line. I smeared the salve an inch thick across the wounds. I worked in a total trance, enjoying each stroke of my fingers across his flesh. My eyebrows drew together. That was an odd feeling to have. I forced my hand away and closed the jar extra tight. Concern struck me when the warrior didn't acknowledge me. His shoulders bunched and relaxed in ripples. I scanned the expanse of his muscular back, making sure I didn't miss any spots.

The warrior turned around, slowly. Or my mind played a trick, slowing down his movements. His thick dark hair registered for the first time, then his strong stubble-covered jaw, and those intense eyes. His deep gaze captivated me. Was he angry with me, tense from the pain, or perhaps even something else altogether? He was one big walking conundrum.

"Thank you." I read his lips before the velvety tone of his voice reached my ears. Warmth soaked my body, weakening my knees. My eyes morphed into saucers as fear surged up my spine. My reactions to Kole weren't natural. That fact alone scared me. I didn't know the Power except that he was pushy and sulky. Kole noted the change in me. Backing away, he seized his shirt and stalked toward the elevator. As the door slid shut behind him, I was finally able to breathe again. As if a line connecting us had loosened, letting more air into my lungs and reason to return. I kicked myself for overreacting around Kole yet again. I had to get over my debilitating tendencies. What warrior would I become if I couldn't shut out distractions and stay on target at all times? Vex paid a hefty price for deviating off the course. Thankfully, he'd heal within the next couple of days as if nothing ever happened. I didn't have that luxury.

Flustered, I rubbed my face. I walked over to the cooler,

and many eyes in the room followed me. *What?* I wanted to ask. Conflicting emotions ran rampant through me. I even blushed when I recalled Kole's exquisite eyes and the way they scrutinized me. What was I thinking treating his wound? Without even asking if I had his permission to. *Ugh.* The situation was eating me up, and I needed to stop obsessing.

Talen acknowledged me with a curt nod before pouring himself a cup of water. Dirt and sweat mixed together stained the sides of his face and neck. His forehead grooved in concentration.

"How is he?"

Talen stroked his chin, gazing at the floor. "He'll be all right," he rasped. He crumpled the paper cup in one hand and tossed it into a trash can. His actions and the tension in his body were at odds with his words.

"Talen, what's going on?"

A dry laugh escaped Talen's lips. "What's not going on? They're coming out of the woodwork lately, and we're struggling to keep up."

"Is this unusual?" Part of me knew the answer, but I hoped I was wrong.

"Something changed a few weeks back. Ley lines have gone haywire. Our servers are crashing under the volume of predictive possibilities." My palms clammed up again. Could this be related to Paulie's blunder?

"Today, for the first time in...as long as I can remember, I wasn't certain we'd come out victorious." Talen swept his hand in the air, pointing to the warriors.

"Look at us." He amplified his tone. I took a quick sweep of the infirmary. These warriors were running on their last fumes. Of course, with my limited exposure, I wouldn't have expected much better after hours of intense fighting. They had the stamina to last this long, that was for sure. No human could've faced those demons and survived. Warriors began clearing out of the clinic as most finished infusions.

"The infusion helps with the recovery?"

"The serum, yes. We may face the enemy as soon as tomorrow. We can't be unprepared, even though the serum supply is low."

My eyes wandered to the elevator door.

"Kole didn't take it," I said. Heck, he didn't even see to his wounds. But he assisted others.

Talen grunted. "That old bastard. It takes a lot to slow him down. He'll be like new in the morning." Still, seeing those wounds, I bet that hurt like hell. I took stock of Talen's body. He'd suffered similar injuries.

"You must be an old bastard too, then?"

"Old, yeah. Bastard? That depends on who you ask." He ran his fingers through his soot-covered hair. He veered his attention to the operating room window once again. Rae pushed the curtain open. We moved in unison closer to the glass. The surgery part was over. Vex lay still, hooked up to an IV drip. It worked miracles as color resurfaced on his face.

"I doubt any of these warriors would've taken the serum if Kole didn't order them to," Talen said. I tilted my head.

"He ordered it?"

His lips curved.

"No one defies Kole." His eyes skimmed over me. "Except maybe you." Talen peered inside the OR, his features morphing into contemplation. I risked a glimpse. Upon seeing lifeless Vex covered with a white sheet up to his neck, my heart wrenched from pain. What if *I* did that to him? I pivoted on my heels, turning away.

I made another round. Some stragglers lounged about striking up a conversation, and more than one made it clear they were interested in more than a working relationship. I deflected but used the opportunity to ask them about the fissure and commit to memory the unique details they supplied. The warriors were all too happy to recount how many kills they had or what techniques worked best. They began challenging each other's narratives and bantered. I rested my back against the wall and listened with a faint smile on my face.

Talen emerged from the OR and headed for the elevator. I peeled myself off the wall and followed him. I'd done all I could in here. The warrior held up the door. I threaded my arm over the side bar while Talen took on a wider stance in the center. We traveled in silence. Exhaustion set into my limbs, and sorrow ravished my soul.

THIRTY-TWO

S omeone once said that "knowledge is half the battle." After leaving the clinic, I planned to grab some food, shower—I hadn't done so since training with Vex—and lie down. My nerves were frayed, and my body craved rest. Instead, I ended up on the library floor with my legs crossed and surrounded by piles of books. Some stacks surpassed the top of my head. Among them were titles like *Demonology, Myths of the Dark, Earth's Grid, Stargates and Portals*, and *The Convoluted Universe* volumes.

Unfortunately, not a single book in the library was dedicated to Archons. I knew because I'd swept through the shelves one book at a time. *Demonology* had a chapter on the subject, but the information in it was generic. Young Earth-bounders read that stuff before breakfast. I hunted for particulars about Bezekah and the Great Archons.

"Ha," I whispered, intrigued by the map of Earth outlining energetic grid lines. Blue ink marked ley lines. The author used black ink to draw black lines. The note beneath the map said, "Depiction of Black Lines alignments in 1958." The next pages showed the same map in chronological order.

The lines shifted with time. I ran my thumb over the edge, locating the last map from the year 1984. Over the years, the black lines got closer to New Seattle's city limits. I frowned and laid the tome on my lap.

Through a crack between book towers, my eyes snagged on a jeans-clad pant leg. I sprang up, disturbing the stacks.

"Shit!" It fell out of my lips on impulse.

"I'm...sorry. I thought you heard me come in." Kole's eyes softened around the edges. He smelled wonderful, fresh and spicy all at once. Like sandalwood. His moussed hair was damp. I cleared my throat.

"I didn't." I lowered my gaze to the books strewn all around me. For some reason, I hated the idea of Kole thinking I wasn't warrior material. He'd never grace me with his deep chocolate eyes again if I was less than, weaker, or more mundane. I inhaled deeply, struggling with inner impulses—those desiring to be close to him and those wishing to flee in equal measure.

"Are you looking for something in particular?"

My chest seized. He was still here. Looking up, I nodded.

"Archons." One word. I couldn't form proper sentences around this warrior. Silence stretched between us. Honestly, I didn't understand why he lingered. Was this his favorite place to stand in the entire cabin? A snicker bubbled up. Covering my mouth, I dropped to my knees, busying myself with re-stacking books. I went for alphabetical order, which would take some time. Surely, Kole could take a hint.

A book hovered before me through a cascading curtain of my hair. I accepted it, donning a small smile. Part of me rebelled at his obvious and intentional ignorance. Maybe he was trying to prove a point. I just couldn't figure out what that was. The vibe he gave off was pleasant, and his presence mellowed my mood. We kept at it until all books were reshelved in order, except for a few I put aside for paging through later.

"Er...thanks for your help." Our gazes locked for a nanosecond. Kole tipped his head. His gaze never left my face as if he wanted to say something. Or, well, stare. I shuffled toward the door, forcing my sore legs to move. Why couldn't I heal faster? I should ask Rae for some salts I could soak in.

The hairs on my arms prickled. I didn't need to check behind me to know he had followed me to the door. I pushed it open and halted in my tracks at the picture before me. Half of P6 was in or around the kitchen. Boxes of pizza kept their attention away from me. The aroma of freshly baked dough, melted cheese, and various toppings hung in the air. Although my stomach growled in anticipation, I contemplated retreating to my room. Except this maneuver would require me to face a certain stubborn Power. Had Kole predicted my dilemma and barred my escape route? I hoped not, but I wouldn't have put it past him, either. I needed to socialize, but I preferred to do things on my terms.

The sound of creaking leather drew my focus to a recliner nearest the fireplace. I blinked rapidly.

"Vex?" What on Earth was this warrior doing up here, kicking back and grinning from ear to ear? My feet carried me to him. Warmth reached me from the crackling fire, melting some worries along the way. I longed to hug him but restrained myself. I collapsed onto an ottoman by his side and fidgeted with the hem of my shirt. Moisture pulled into my eyes. I sniffed, wiping at a stray tear with a sleeve.

"Hey there. I'm not dead yet. I have a rule—you can only cry at my funeral." He winked.

"Not...crying." I looked away. Guilt gnawed at me. If Paulie was correct, I was putting these warriors in danger by being here. I startled when a beep sounded behind me. A medical device with an IV drip stood in the corner. Rae rushed over to replace an empty bag with a new one. Vex grimaced.

"Never in my entire existence have I needed this stuff. Isn't one enough?"

"You need it." Kole's voice was void of any emotion, no inflection signaling his concern. I studied his features as he sat down on the sofa, placing two pizza boxes in front of him. From the time I'd spent with Seraphs, I learned Pures weren't accustomed to displays of emotions, and some didn't possess them to begin with. Kole was as difficult to read as Xavier, but there was no denying he took care of this group.

"Eat." He extended a paper plate my way. The single-word command promptly notched my opinion of him down the scale. Emotions boiled up in me, with confusion overshadowing the others. I hesitated, my hand in midair. I willed myself to push through the uncertainty and grab the freaking plate. That's all it was, a plate. He wasn't passing over sharp knives or battle axes.

I jolted when the pads of my fingers touched Kole's longer digits underneath the plate. My gaze snapped to his face. His fingers shouldn't have been there. I grabbed as little of the surface as was necessary. Kole opened the box and turned it around, encouraging me to take the first slice. When our eyes met, there was no surprise reflected in his hypnotic irises. He lifted an eyebrow.

"So, what's the diagnosis? Will you be up and about, putting me through more torture tomorrow?" I grabbed two slices. Vex snickered.

"Not tomorrow."

"It's a girls' day tomorrow." Rae plopped next to Kole.

"Eww. I hope you're not counting on me, sister." Zaira's face screwed into horror. "I don't do...girly things."

Rae hid a snarky grin behind a slice of pizza.

"What will we be doing?" I pinned her with a questioning

stare. Although I hadn't had a chance to do many "girly" things growing up, I had an inkling of what to expect. In the human world, that was. In the Earthbounder world, "girly" activities could mean anything from training to more training to polishing weapons. Another question that begged to be asked was whether Rae meant tomorrow as in later today or the next day. By my estimation, it was the middle of the night. Rae lifted a shoulder.

"I say we plan the day as we go," she said.

I had to admit I liked that. I scooted off the ottoman and rested on the carpet, cross-legged. Flames bathed logs in delicious heat, then snapped them in half. As with people, some things drew you in with their marvelous promises of comfort, only to scorch you from the inside out. What remained was a hollow and brittle form. I shivered. Voices carried on, discussing events from today and making predictions for the upcoming days. I half-tuned into them. I stole glances at Vex, who had snoozed off. His complexion lacked that radiance he possessed, but he'd recover. If he had died, I'd never have forgiven myself. I cast my eyes down. Winding a finger on a loose thread, I tugged until it broke off. Losing those I cared about had been my life's theme. I was foolish to think I could turn back time. I clenched my fist, sucking in a trembling breath.

"Arien, you okay?" Rae asked.

"I..." My gaze shifted to Kole. He glowered, perched at the edge of the couch. The air between us was electrified, rendering me speechless. "Excuse me," I said before I hightailed out of there because that's what cowards did.

THIRTY-THREE

I jogged down the steps, eager to see how Vex was doing today.

"Vex, stop that," Rae scolded. What was that about? I reached the point where I could peer into the living area and the kitchen farther out. About a dozen warriors milled around here this morning. Rae stood in the kitchen, hands on her hips. But where was Vex?

"Ahhh!" Vex jumped out from his hiding spot and scared the living shit out of me. I tripped up and slid the last few steps on my butt.

"Gotcha." He beamed from ear to ear. Catching my breath, I didn't react at first. The room imploded with laughter. I accepted Vex's proffered hand and let him pull me up. I socked him in his overgrown bicep. Not that it hurt him. I fought the urge to rub my sore bottom and flexed my fingers instead.

"I'll get you for that." I narrowed my eyes before abandoning his ass. Sure, I'd laugh about his antics later. Right now, my pride suffered. How was I ever going to earn a shred of respect among Earthbounders when sabotage hit me at every corner?

I joined the female warriors and others in the kitchen, aware of Kole's eyes following me. He and Talen occupied bar stools, forearms propped on the countertop. I picked out a chocolate chip muffin from an assortment laid out on a tray. Remembering the chocolate chip debate with Zaira, my eyes connected with Rae's, who smirked from behind her coffee cup. She grabbed another cup from the cabinet and filled it up for me.

"Thanks," I said. With a plate and cup in hand, I pivoted for the kitchen bar. I froze, blinking rapidly. Kole sported a fresh black eye, a cut on his lip, and bruised-up knuckles. And those were only the injuries I could see.

"Was there another attack?" I stepped toward him but restrained myself in time from invading his personal space.

"Your lover boy called on you," Vex said.

"Huh?" I grimaced. This wasn't a good time for one of his jokes. "Which one, Vex? Because there is a line, you know," I said in a strident tone.

Kole puffed out air.

"What happened?" I asked again, pressing Rae for an answer with a deep frown. Why had no one told me about this?

"Donovan," Talen said.

My jaw unhinged. That wasn't the answer I expected. "Oh, shit!"

"Exactly."

"He did this?" I swallowed. Kole's eyes turned stormy.

"He got off worse," he said. He sipped black coffee, his stare unwavering.

"Why was he here?"

"I told you—" I scowled at Vex. Recovering or not, he was getting on my last nerve today. And the day had barely begun.

"To retrieve you. He insisted we hand you over to him and insinuated his interest in you runs deeper than a mentor-protégé relationship," Talen said. "He brought four golden boys from Invicta with him. I guess he thought that would intimidate us." Talen crossed his arms over his chest and widened his stance. I doubted anything intimidated this warrior.

"How come Kole is the only one bruised?" I knew his beautiful face would soon heal, but I couldn't stand there and do nothing. I scoured the contents of the freezer and fished out a cold pack.

"The Exiousai advised we use diplomacy. Some of us lack the skill." Vex grinned, patting Kole on the shoulder. Kole shot daggers at the offensive hand, his lip curling. Vex removed it. I extended the cold pack over the counter. Kole raised an eyebrow.

"Just put it on your eye." I rattled frozen peas in the air in front of his face.

"Will it make you feel better if I do?"

"Yes!" Silence fell over us. I cleared my throat. "It will help with the swelling." Kole's lip quivered. He took the peas from my hand and pressed them to his cheekbone.

"Anyway, you should've been there and seen that. Before Donovan could finish a sentence, my man here shut him up with a classic fist-to-nose connection." Vex imitated the punch and Donovan's appalled face, and I couldn't resist but laugh. Talen smirked around his mug.

"Maybe I'm old school," Kole said.

"Nah, you're no school. It's the quality I adore most about you, my friend." Vex patted Kole twice more, which earned him a growl, and he scooted toward Rae, who pulled him the rest of the way.

"When are you gonna learn some boundaries?" Her voice was quiet, intended for Vex only. He dipped his head and whispered into her ear; Rae's face flushed. I averted my eyes from the two lovebirds. Heat crept up my neck. Vex and Rae's relationship awakened a want in me. Deep inside, I wanted that—to be loved and love in return. But I buried these desires long ago, and I didn't intend to resurrect them. Not now, not ever.

"Donovan thinks a lot about himself. He's one douchebag I don't mind never seeing again," I said. "Thank you for sticking up for me." Kole's contemplative eyes shone brighter. I broke the eye contact.

"Whether you like it or not, you're not going anywhere anytime soon," Zaira said. "You're one of us now, a P6-er." Her words warmed my heart.

"You're right. I don't like it. I like my independence. But, P6 may just grow on me." I winked at her.

"Aww. Our lost lamb is finally home." Vex engulfed me in a hug. Geez. He wasn't letting go either, waiting for me to embrace him back while Rae complained about respecting others' boundaries again. *Oh, what the heck.* I circled my arms around him and patted his back.

Rae parked the Jeep at the foothills of mountainous terrain. Stepping out, I stretched my arms. A small smile played on my lips. Any day Donovan got a whipping was a good day. I trudged to the back, joining Rae and Zaira in packing the rest of our hiking gear. Rae passed me a backpack and two trekking poles. I'd be the only one using poles. Neither of them needed aid while hiking.

We trekked at an incline with water pools and streams flowing in the valleys below. The crowns of the trees swayed in the winds high above, filtering out sun rays. Rae led the way, and Zaira held the tail.

"This place is breathtaking," I said.

"Wait until we get to my favorite spot," Rae said.

At the highest point, the trees thinned out, and rock plateaus jutted from the ground. I folded and stashed my poles in the backpack, needing to grip rough edges for balance. Sweat dripped down my nose. I hoisted myself up the last few stone platforms. The white noise that lingered in the background for some time now intensified.

"Please tell me we're there," I said, panting. I rested my hands on my knees and hung my head. I was right in suspecting "a girls' day out" among the Earthbounders meant working out or torture.

Zaira slapped me on the shoulder. "Look up."

I straightened. Rae stood a few feet away on the edge of a promontory overlooking a raging waterfall. Water traveled down at a high drop into the circular basin. From there, easy-flowing water trickled out from one side of the basin, forming a wide stream. I strode over, grinning. Rae closed her eyes, taking deep breaths. Zaira plopped down, dangling her legs over the edge. This place was magical.

"I didn't know there were waterfalls near New Seattle," I whispered.

"There is only one, and it's a secret P6 has been guarding for centuries," Rae said.

"Can we get to the fun stuff?" Zaira wrinkled her nose. Without opening her eyes, Rae lifted an index finger.

"Fine, one more minute." Zaira plonked on her back. "I'm counting. One, two, three..."

I spun in a half circle, admiring a panoramic view of the waterfall, mountains, and lush greenery. Zaira jumped to her feet, fishing a harness out of her bag. Sure enough, I found a harness in my backpack, too.

"You're sure about this?" I asked as we traversed the terrain around the cliff to where wide-trunked trees grew near the precipice. Rae helped me attach my harness to the rope tied around a trunk. Zaira swayed at a forty-five-degree angle from the cliff, connected to her rope.

"Remember, you control your speed. Pull down for the break and up when you want to release it," Rae said. With her hands on my shoulders, she guided me to the edge.

"Bu—"

Zaira leaped down, hollering from excitement. My pulse skyrocketed, and I grasped Rae's arm, my eyes wide.

"You can do this," Rae said. I closed my eyes and pushed off. I dropped fast, forgetting about the hand brake. Zaira's form came into focus, her grin fading away. Shit. I fumbled for the handle and yanked it down, stripping the rope and braking in time for my feet to touch the ground. Zaira applauded.

"You're a daredevil. I think you beat my record." She beamed.

I let out a long breath. Unhooking myself from the vile trap, I collapsed to the ground, giggling. I couldn't remember the last time I had done something so thrilling. Perhaps I had never truly lived? Rae slid down her rope with grace.

"You don't think that was it, do you?" Rae asked, the corner of her mouth lifting. I sobered up and stumbled to my feet. The adrenaline still coursed through my body.

"Whatever you have planned next, sign me up."

THIRTY-FOUR

"Wine?" I arched an eyebrow. Rae had stashed a picnic basket full of fruits, bread and cheese, and drinks between two boulders at the end of our water rafting route. After the daring jump off the cliff, we'd donned wet suits and relaxed in the magnificent blue pool the waterfall cascaded into. Rae retrieved self-inflatable tube floats we used to drift down the stream. That was the most relaxing thing I'd done in my life. I lay on my belly, watching multicolored fish and turtles swim in the limpid currents. The sound of the waterfall quieted and the sounds of birds calling and critters scurrying around filled the air. We floated like this for an hour or maybe even longer. At one turn, a small, pebbled beach greeted us, and Zaira gestured toward it. We maneuvered our floats out of the water and settled on a patch of grass, basking in the sun.

Rae uncorked the bottle and topped off two plastic cups.

"Uh…you know that stuff still affects me, right?" I asked.

"It's your day off." Rae waved off my concerns. "Besides, no one will judge you."

"We all wish we could get wasted." Zaira sighed. I tilted my head.

"I thought you could. I saw secondborns drink some sort of fizzing green liquid at—"

"That's illegal," Zaira said through gritted teeth. "Besides, that stuff will get you high. There is a difference between that and getting drunk." She tore a butter roll open with firm fingers and stuffed it with cheese. Her explanation made sense. That's why Paulyna and her crew kept to themselves. Did Donovan condone her proclivities? Did he know?

"What's it made of?" I asked.

"The key ingredient is the blood of brownies, small household faeries, although some live in nature. They are subjected to torture when their blood is collected. That's key to the drink's potency," Rae said.

I got sick to my stomach. What monster would do such a thing? Torture innocent faeries. I recalled them from my handbook. They were the size of a human child with large soulful eyes.

"Those secondborns are degenerates. Next time, point them out to me," Zaira said. "I hear the Council added more jail cells, and they need warm bodies to fill them with."

"That's good to know," I said, picking at my roll. I'd lost my appetite. Rae heaved a sigh.

"This was supposed to be a fun day. No more serious talk." She forced the cup into my hand and clinked hers with mine, making the sound with her mouth. I sipped the wine. It was fruity and sweet, just as I liked it. Zaira left soon for her shift in the command room. The P6 operated on a tight schedule that synced into everyone's devices. I did not have a P6-issued device or duties since I was still in training.

"I'm a transplant myself," Rae said.

"What do you mean?"

"I grew up away from all of this. My grandma raised me.

She had a cattle farm in the stinking middle of Kansas. I swear there were days I thought I was gonna spew my guts out from the awful odor wafting in from a nearby meat processing plant." Rae made a funny face.

"How did you end up here?"

"About two years ago, Vex showed up on my grandma's front porch, looking completely out of place. He was investigating recent cases of missing cattle—he introduced himself as an agricultural researcher—but he didn't know my grandma had a built-in bullshit detector. He looked and smelled wrong to her. She pulled out a shotgun she kept by the front door and bang." Rae imitated her grandma pulling a trigger. I held my breath. "I'll never forget his eyes. They turned into saucers. He peered down at his chest, then straight at me, and said..."

"What? What did he say?" I squeezed Rae's arm.

"He said..." Rae whispered, "'I didn't see that coming.'" She grinned, and I gave her a gentle shove. "I swear on the angels."

"Nooo... Your grandma wouldn't shoot an unarmed man."

"Ask him." Rae shrugged. "Grandma ran into the house to call the cops. I kneeled by his dead body when he jolted upright and freaked me out. My grandma didn't know what my parents did for a living. She wasn't *in the know*. I witnessed things as a child before my parents were murdered. Right then, I recognized what he was. I told him where to hide, and I lied to the cops that he ran away. Grandma's eyes narrowed to slits when she listened to my story. No one would've survived a shot to the chest from only feet away, but she couldn't deny the body was missing. I wasn't strong enough to have done anything with it. The rest is history. I moved here, blah blah blah..."

I washed down the last fruit with the wine. How horrible it must have been to lose both parents at a young age. Rae was an orphan like me, like Brie. She reminded me of Brie, too. Her liveliness, steady head, and selflessness. Brie always made it easy to forget the world's problems when we were together. And yet, she ended our friendship, which went against everything I'd known to be true about her.

"Why are you twisting your face like that?" Rae asked.

"My friend lost her parents in a car accident when she was only ten years old. I know how hard it was on her. How old were you?"

"Eight." She cast a forlorn gaze on the ground. "Where is your friend now?"

"She lives in the Fringe. She's engaged. And I, apparently, am not welcome there." I reclined on my elbows. "It's weird. We were the best of friends, always looking after each other, and then one day, she tells me she's moving in with her boyfriend, and that we can't see each other anymore." I picked up pebbles and threw them into the stream, one by one.

"Arien?" Rae scooted closer. "You are aware of the types of beings who live in the Fringe?"

My next pebble fell short. Speechless, I shook my head.

"We call the Fringe a shifter town."

I stared at her, mouth agape. This couldn't be.

"Bric isn't a shifter," I said with conviction. She couldn't have been. I'd go berserk if she hid this from me.

"Regular people reside in the Fringe as well, but they're bound to secrecy. It sounds like your friend got herself a shifter fiancé." Rae took another sip of her wine, sighing with delight. This was not news to her. But, to me, this information flipped my world upside down again. Somehow Brie had stumbled upon this supernatural world that she had kept secret from me. We used to never have secrets between us. But hadn't I withheld information when I tracked Brie down? I didn't tell her about the Earthbounders because I didn't want to put her in danger. She would've done the same. She did. I emptied my cup.

"I need a refill," I said, reaching for the bottle.

"I walk alone. I walk alone…" Rae and I bellowed Green Day lyrics in her Jeep. The sun was diving below the horizon. My head buzzed, and my spirits rode high. I broke out into hysterical laughter at something Rae said as she parked the car. She hauled me out of my seat, and we rounded the cabin. P6 warriors lounged around a roaring firepit, carrying lively conversations. Some wore their uniforms of black tactical shirts, pants, and utility boots. Others dressed casually. The divine aroma of barbecued chicken wafted over from an open grill. I skirted over to it, separating from Rae. I salivated at the chicken leg quarters perfectly basted in a gooey red sauce.

"Plate?" a male warrior asked.

I scrutinized his familiar-looking features and pointed at him.

"I know you from somewhere."

"We may have run into each other at an abandoned stone factory." He flashed a cocky grin.

"Oh, yeah," I said. I cringed internally, recalling the hellish kelpie.

"I arrived today. But what are you doing here? Weren't you stationed at Invicta?"

"They kicked me out." I rolled my eyes, piling one of the larger chicken legs on my plate. I couldn't wait any longer. The warrior guffawed.

"What did you do?" he asked. "I've never—"

"Emmett, I need to steal her for a sec." Rae's smile didn't reach her eyes. She slinked her arm around my shoulders and pulled me away. I wrinkled my nose at her.

"That was rude," I said.

"I'm helping you make smart decisions."

"I am smart. Most of the time." I grumbled the last part.

"You're drunk, and you're flirting without knowing it."

"What. Am not..." I glimpsed Emmett checking out my ass. Ew. "I was just being friendly," I whisper-shouted back at Rae.

"You can be friendly here." She pressed me down into an Adirondack between stoic Talen and scowling Kole. I shot her a reproachful look. She raised a single brow. I stuck out my tongue. Vex plopped in a chair by us and was scrutinizing our exchange with his shrewd eyes.

"I knew it." He pointed one long finger at Rae. "You drank the wine." He pushed off from his chair, gaining height over her.

"I don't know what you're talking about," Rae said, her nose twitching.

"Aha! You're lying." His finger came close to her face.

I hiccupped and slammed a hand over my mouth. Vex swiveled his accusatory finger my way. "Aha! She's drunk."

"Fine, Sherlock. We drank your wine. What are you going to do about it?"

Rae shrieked as Vex pinched her sides. She twisted out of his grasp and fled into the grass, Vex in pursuit. I burst into giggles, not able to help myself.

"Protect it with your life," I said, shoving the plate into Kole's lap. I sprinted on jelly-like legs across the patio and onto the grass. Vex had Rae in a tight vise, tickling her.

"Hold on, Rae. I'm coming!"

I dove onto Vex's back. Rae kicked his leg from underneath him, and he fell like the ogre he was. We bounced to our feet, laughing our asses off and high-fiving. Vex twined his fingers behind his head, smiling up at us. We did a weird, uncoordinated victory dance around him. I had to hold my side from laughing so hard.

"Now, help me up. I think I sprained something." Vex outstretched his arms and we both latched on, concerned about his recent injury. His eyes sparkled with mischief for a second before he tugged us down on either side of him. I had no balance and fell splat on my face.

"Ow." Before I could push myself off the ground, Vex rolled me over, brushing hair out of my face.

"Nothing's broken," he said. "Come on." He kicked up to stand and pulled me to my feet in no time. Rae wrapped my arm around her neck on my other side.

"Guys, I can walk." I strode forward, and my knees buckled. If it weren't for them supporting me, I'd have been down kissing the ground again. Was I that wasted, or had Vex served me with a concussion? I hobbled to an Adirondack.

"I'm an invalid," I mumbled, throwing my arms over my eyes.

"If your arms are working, you can at least be an invalid enjoying some barbecue chicken," Kole said. I peered at him from between my forearms. I'd forgotten he was here. He held the plate out to me. A single vein throbbed by his temple.

"I will, thanks."

THIRTY-FIVE

I awoke with a start. Schemes jostled around in my head while I slept, forming an action plan at the culminating point. And I needed to be fully awake and functional—cognitively and otherwise—to enact this plan. Pulling the curtain away, I glimpsed a hazy morning with low-lying mist stretching in all directions and plunging into the forest. That was my destination this morning.

Rae had stuck a note to my door instructing me to get breakfast and to join her in the command room. Glee knocked in my chest. This was perfect. I didn't want anyone coming with me this morning. This was a solo mission and a covert one. The house was quiet. Empty pizza boxes sat in the kitchen corner. Someone had wiped the counters clean. P6 warriors cleaned for themselves around here, which made sense with heightened security at this compound. I'd offer to help with cleaning next time I saw Rae.

A chill ran up and down my body as soon as I closed the patio door behind me. I traipsed across the courtyard. Even if no one noticed me through the windows, I suspected security cameras recorded the surroundings 24/7. If I acted natural, the warriors were less likely to stop me. I strolled to the edge of the forest. I chanced a glance towards the cabin. Spotting no one outside, I slid into the cover of needle-laden branches. I stopped after five minutes, deciding this place was as good as any to begin my experiment.

I picked the largest tree around me and placed both hands on the bark. I closed my eyes and concentrated on Paulie. In my mind's eye, I brought forward an image of him—the way he looked when we arrived at his makeshift house. And I waited.

"Paulie, Paulie, Paulie..." I began chanting. I cracked an eye open. Nothing was happening. None of those sensations from when Paulie appeared to me in the woods returned. It could have been that I was too far away for his powers to reach me. And it was possible that P6's magic barrier canceled out the druid's powers the same way Invicta's allura did. I tested a few other trees. I tried different contact positions, like hugging and touching my forehead to the tree trunk. Morning dew seeped through my clothes, but I pressed on. Racking my brain for more ideas, one popped up. If Paulie could communicate through the trees, perhaps he could also receive messages through animals. As far as I knew, wildlife could cross allura. If I could call on an animal, encode it with a message, and send it to Paulie... I doubled over with laughter. This plan could work if I had experience in these things or was a druid, a witch, or a gifted Earthbounder perhaps. I wiped the moisture from my cheeks and rolled my shoulders. *Let's try this*. I tapped my mouth, settling to call on a pigeon. No harm done if this didn't work.

After a minute of concentrating on nature and fidgeting, I abandoned the idea. Nothing had happened, and nothing was going to happen. I needed a new plan. I fell into a jog heading back to P6. Chirping sounded off in the distance. The wildlife thrived in the warmer climate of the alluras. "Kwin," a bird called out. Why did that sound familiar? I slowed down and listened to the sounds. They got louder with each second until a fuzzy chikaka jumped on my leg. I shook him off and stepped backward, scrutinizing nearby bushes for more extraterrestrial vermin. My eyes returned to the chikaka in front of me.

"Kwiiin," the creature drawled out. He dropped onto four paws and crept towards me.

"Stay where you are." My palms shot out. The chikaka froze. I drew my brows together. Hmm, that was... interesting.

"You understand me." The chikaka perched on his hunches and bobbed his head.

"Kwin, kwin, kwin," it cried out in a high-pitched whimper.

"Fine, fine. Me Kwin—although my name is Arien—and you are..." I said. I beckoned it for an answer with a wave. Its nose twitched.

"Do. You. Have. A. Name?" I tried a different approach. The chikaka whimpered, lowered to the ground, and skittered away, all the while wailing like a banshee. I gawked. My arms rose and dropped.

"What did I say?" I wondered out loud.

"It's not what you said. It is my presence." The authoritative, deep voice carried from behind me.

I pivoted and assumed a ready stance. I fought the urge to cover my eyes as the blinding light expanded and burst in front of me. A tall male silhouette came into focus. He resembled a warrior with sleek black armor embossed with golden markings. Power and magic oozed off of him in waves. I dared not to tweak a single muscle when faced with such a powerhouse.

Jet black hair framed his hawk-like face with penetrating saffron eyes. On his head, he wore a gold circlet with an antler design and a citrine-yellow gem centerpiece. His hair cascaded straight down his back, drawing my attention to his pointy ears. This being was not human—for one, he'd materialized in a flash of light!—but he didn't resemble any demonic beings from the books, either. He didn't appear to have a weapon, but I had no doubts he was dangerous. He craned his head sideways like a researcher studying an inferior life form. Hands clasped behind his back, he raised a quizzical eyebrow.

"You are the queen?" The *r* rolled on his tongue.

"Wha-what?" I risked a cursory peek behind me. Surely he wasn't referring to me?

"Are you deaf?"

"No." I pulled down the hem of my tactical shirt. "I think you have me confused with someone else."

"I, confused?" The man's jaw tightened as his eyelids slit closer together. "I don't have patience for games."

I shrugged. "I don't know what you're referring to. And I have no idea who you are."

The stranger's features morphed into puzzlement. "Many years must have passed since I last visited your realm. What year is this?"

"Two thousand twenty-three?" It came out as a question.

The stranger nodded to himself. "I will forgive your ignorance."

My eyes widened at a realization. I should've been offended, but I was in awe instead because the man—er, being—in front of me sounded ancient. I roamed my eyes over the space behind him, worried he wasn't alone.

"I am King Cygnus of the Andromeda Fae race." He connected his pointer and middle fingers and touched them to his heart. One of the golden markings there flared up to shimmery brilliance for the duration of contact. This was a formal salute of sorts. There were other markings on his attire as well. They resembled symbols but nothing I was familiar with.

"And you are..." The curtness in King Cygnus's tone was palpable.

I blinked. "I'm Arien...of the Earthbounder race. Second-born." I bit my tongue. I did not intend to divulge so much—it was none of the Fae's business—but my tongue got possessed and answered for me.

For the first time since he'd arrived, King Cygnus's lips upturned halfway.

"You're oblivious to the ways of the Fae," he mused.

"I guess." Why did I even answer that?

"Tell me why my"   he spoke a word in a language I didn't know—"call you their queen?"

"Who?"

"I believe you call them chikakas in this realm." His tone bordered on impatient again.

"Oh, them." Queen? Is that what they'd been saying? I thought they'd given me a nickname. I smacked my forehead before I remembered the impromptu audience with a Fae king.

"There's been a misunderstanding. I don't know why they call me what they call me. Well, I helped them this one time. But I am not their queen. I have no aspirations to be anyone's queen."

"Hmm." The king considered me. "To think I risked my presence be known for this..."

"Pardon?"

"I've come here to face my challenger to the throne."

I couldn't speak. What King Cygnus was insinuating was...insane. I placed a hand on my chest instead of a question. *Me?*

He affirmed with a stately nod. "You're not vying to rule the Andromeda Fae. Yet, my—*he spoke that language again*—are never mistaken." He lowered his voice as he spoke until his words became whispers and internal musings. The king's brows narrowed, and his eyes lost focus. The words "challenger" and "throne" played in my mind on repeat. My heart hammered, albeit with a steady rhythm, ready for what was to come. Reason told me I had to get away from the king. Otherwise, he'd have my head. I slowly shifted to the side. The king hadn't noticed. Something rather odd was happening to him. His body was fading, turning more transparent with every second.

I took that moment to flee. I didn't take two steps before I hit an invisible barrier and bounced off of it.

"I created a time bubble to delay my detection."

I spun around to find King Cygnus standing in the same spot, holding a gold-trimmed book.

"I wish you no harm, secondborn." He sifted through the pages. What if he planned to spell me?

"You said it yourself. The title made me your challenger to the throne, and chikakas make no mistakes." I doubted chikakas knew corn from potato, but if the king said so...

"I granted you clemency. Didn't I?"

He did.

"Arien of the Earthbounder Clan. Do you concede your claim to the Andromeda Fae throne?"

"Uh...yes?"

"Excellent. There is one last step to complete your concession." The king extended the book towards me. "Place your hand on top."

I squinted an eye.

"Why are we doing this?"

"To end your supposed challenge. According to the Fae law, when the challenger concedes, the winner will grant him one wish. What do you wish for, Arien? What's your deepest desire in this moment? I can make it come true for you." The king's words made little sense. The winner would grant a prize to the loser? His words replayed in my mind. They felt so...right. They carried a soothing melody. This was the right thing to do. I deserved a prize. Didn't I? The melodic chant removed the last fog of doubt. Yes. Now, what was my deepest desire? That wasn't hard at all.

I smiled at the king. My reflection stared back at me from the depths of his dark pupils.

"I have it."

"Excellent." His voice sent a reassuring vibration my way. I watched as my hand rose and floated toward the book. The motion didn't feel like my own, but I ignored the sensation. I was getting my wish, the one thing I wanted so badly right now. His hand dwarfed my own, resting gently on top. I shut my eyes and focused.

"It is done." The king's voice startled me, ripping the daydream sensation away and throwing reality into my face. I withdrew my hand, feeling puzzled. Maybe wronged? Definitely used.

"What did you...?"

"It is done." King Cygnus pinned me with a death stare. "Challenge me again, and your concession will be null and void. I will kill you to reclaim my legacy. This magic pact is now binding." With those words, the king vanished with an explosion of light. I braced myself against the tree trunk, squeezing my eyes shut. Still, tears pulled into my eyes from the intensity of the flash.

"Who the hell was that?" a voice boomed feet away. Kole's voice.

THIRTY-SIX

"Andromeda Fae vanished from Earth several thousand years ago. They claimed an island in the Atlantic as their home after they fled Andromeda. Their home planet was invaded. Earthbounders, as you can expect, did not approve of the Fae's presence on this planet. To ease tensions, King Cygnus vowed to monitor demonic activity on the island Fae selected as their new homage and around a family of islands surrounding it. He also gave his word to back up Earthbounders in times a calamity should strike." Seth shared an abbreviated version of Fae's history on Earth. He occupied a cushioned chair in the library positioned opposite the sofa I was dumped into—courtesy of Kole.

Kole's sudden appearance in the forest had spooked me. My vision was blurry—the waterworks wouldn't stop. I didn't trust my own ears. So, I'd swung at him when he approached. I missed, of course. He hoisted me up on his shoulder in a fireman carry and threatened not to let me out of his sight ever again. He said he'd lock me up in my room or put a tracker on me. Strangely enough, his rough voice lulled me into compliance and a sense of security. I ceased demanding that he let me go, and at one point, I rather liked the physical contact between us, which disturbed me.

"What happened to them?" I asked.

Seth gave a short-lived laugh, anticipating my question. "That's what they call a million-dollar question, I believe." He extended his arm and pulled out a book. "There are stories, legends of the Fae. No one can know for sure. Except now, perhaps." Flipping through the pages and stopping on one, Seth placed the book in my hands. A portrait of King Cygnus stared back at me. The artist used watercolor, which could be flimsy, but the being I encountered and the object of this painting were the same.

"That's him."

"Wait a minute," Vex called from a corner where he stood with his arms crossed, listening. "Fae have many talents, and they're crafty as hell. What if some other Fae simply used glamor?"

Seth rubbed his chin.

"To what end?" he asked.

Silence.

"What could motivate a common Fae to reveal the entire race's existence to us and risk their king's wrath?"

I knew the Fae I met was who he said he was, a king, but I questioned his motivation myself.

"Why would he feel threatened by me? Surely chikakas are not reliable informants."

"I've never heard of chikakas naming someone their queen. They are simple creatures to most, but they possess cognitive abilities that can be astounding. I don't know why they pronounced you their queen. However, I can see why this development would trigger the king's response the way it did."

My gaze dropped to my lap.

"Arien, is there something else?"

I winced. "I think I know why chikakas gave me the title." I swallowed, aware of all eyes on me. "During our team challenge, at Invicta, I kinda released the chikakas I caught." I shrugged a shoulder.

Vex guffawed with obnoxious snorts.

"The female was expecting!" I shot daggers his way. He put his hands up.

"No judgment here. We don't resort to barbaric training techniques at P6." A suppressed snicker escaped him.

Heat crept up my neck. "Her partner gave me the nickname when I freed them." I lifted my eyes to Seth's, and he nodded, scratching his chin. He didn't seem to care I had failed that challenge. I relaxed deeper into the couch, combing wisps of hair behind my ear with my fingers.

Seth withdrew a cell phone and speed-dialed someone. We—P6 members, except for Talen commanding a patrol and a few P6 warriors with him—waited in silence. A warm male voice picked up the line and after a curt greeting, Seth asked the man a series of questions about P6's allura.

"So, we never spelled the P6 allura against energetic signatures of the Fae?"

Some movement was audible from the other side. "I've searched all records on P6, and the Fae are not mentioned. The answer is no. Why are—"

"Thanks. I'll catch you up soon." Seth hung up the phone. "That answers that question." He looked worried.

"I will call local mages. Perhaps one of them can add anti-Fae protection to allura." Seth gave Rae an affirmative nod and she took off at a brisk pace down the stairway.

"Until we learn King Cygnus's intentions, he is not welcome here. If you'll excuse me,"—Seth rose—"I have a few phone calls to make."

"Will you alert Invicta?" This was the first and only question Kole asked so far. I found it unusual too. Even I under-stood Seth would alert the Magister. King Cygnus posed a threat to all Earthbounders. Why would a race of formidable warriors hide for thousands of years and suddenly reemerge? What if they were conspiring with Archons? Unless that wasn't what Kole was asking about. Seth's eyes fell on my face briefly.

"I will stall them from sending reinforcements in."

"Good."

I rubbed my forehead. Kole's speaking in code made me dizzy. Or maybe it was the Fae and his magic. After I conceded my claim to the Fae throne, there was a hole in my memories. I had this feeling there was more to what the king and I had discussed. A recollection of speaking to King Cygnus and him smiling upon me flashed in front of my eyes. I frowned.

"Everything okay?" Zaira handed me a bottle of water, and I pressed it to my forehead.

"Does it feel hot to you in here?" I tugged on the collar constricting my neck.

Zaira asked a question, but its substance escaped me. Something about a lavender bath. That sounded nice. I pushed up. The water bottle fell from my grasp. I watched it roll across the floor in slow motion. Each turn of the bottle wound up my stomach into a tighter knot, and when it hit the wall and settled with a counter-roll, my stomach did the opposite.

"Son of a bitch!" The cold pack slid down my face as I sprang up. The room was shrouded in darkness with streaks of moonlight breaking through the gossamer white curtains. After my sudden sick spill, Zaira had helped me into a shower and tucked me into bed. I was spent and needed the rest, although I hated checking out early and feeling so fragile. A constant reminder that I was mostly human.

I hadn't expected to sleep for the next twelve hours, either. I threw the heavy covers aside and fell back on the pillow. The chill in the air ran up my legs, inducing small shivers. I needed it. I didn't want to lay here any longer. I couldn't afford to. While I "rested," I uncovered missing memories from my encounter with King Cygnus. In my dream, I saw myself speaking with the king. The moment I conceded the Fae throne to the rightful king, an ungraspable force attempted to pull me away. The movie playing out in front of me fuzzed and paused. I applied all my dreamy might to push through the fog, and when I reached my dream self's side, it was as if someone pressed "play" again. King Cygnus tricked me into wanting the Fae to grant my one wish. And he blocked this memory from me for some reason.

I didn't have enough knowledge about the Fae to understand what having a wish granted meant for me. Did I now owe the king a favor he could cash in on at any time? I sure hoped not. I didn't consent—not freely, anyway. I splashed cold water over my face and stared at my reflection in the mirror.

I dressed in tactical gear and arranged my hair into a tight ponytail. I hoped I'd find Seth at the library. I did not know where Seth's suite was or whether he'd even be there at this time of day or, more accurately, night. I glanced at my nightstand clock, which pointed to a few minutes to midnight. Not too late to find somebody around here. The kitchen would be a good start, and it was on the way, anyway.

"Shit." My heart vaulted into my chest. Vex was leaning against the wall, right outside my door. He pocketed a yo-yo he'd retracted with a fluid upward motion. He had shadows under his eyes, and his irises lacked their usual luster. My anger dissipated into concern.

"How long have you been standing here?"

Vex wrinkled his nose. "How long have you been asleep?"

My jaw slackened. "Who... Never mind." I had a decent idea who had ordered Vex to guard me. "Come on, let's get you something to drink."

Vex followed me without a single word. That told me he was exhausted. He'd just recovered from a deadly injury—was it a day or two ago now? And Kole had stuck him as my security.

"Coffee?"

Vex bobbed his head, sliding onto a bar stool.

The P6 kitchen reflected the different culinary tastes of its occupants. A red single serve Keurig stood by an old-fashioned multi-cup coffee maker. On the shelf above sat a French coffee press and a menagerie of coffee beans in labeled containers. I took out a coffee grinder after grabbing a bag of whole-bean coffee. Before long, I had the coffee press spouting out brewed dark liquid, and on the next burner, milk was rising. I fished agave nectar out of the pantry and assembled a lip-smacking-good cappuccino complete with frothed milk.

Vex's eyes sparkled brighter as I carried one large cup his way. He sipped it and sighed.

"I took a rather long nap today, and I need some serious debriefing. What's been happening?" What I wanted to say was "Where is everyone, and why are you assigned to keep an eye on me?" The cabin was oddly quiet.

Vex raised an index finger while he chugged down the whole cup.

"We continue to monitor the site. A few of our warriors are there, but Invicta is now in charge. Rae is arranging for a mage to examine the magic of the P6 allura and conduct tests specific to ancient magic. We've communicated the Fae king's unexpected return to top Earthbounder intelligence, and our mage is currently in high demand. This is effectively pushing P6 to the bottom of the list..."

"But Rae found this guy." I shouldn't have been surprised at the goings on where Seraphs were concerned, knowing their attitude toward other Earthbounder groups and their societal standing above everyone, and yet I was appalled. The king had appeared at P6. Therefore this fortress had priority. He chose P6 because of me. The unease resurfaced again. My situation was complicated. I was lucky to have been at P6. If the king had visited me at Invicta, I'd be under lock and key right now. I chased away less savory thoughts of the Soaz getting involved. I grabbed Vex's forearm.

"Can you take me to the Exiousai?"

THIRTY-SEVEN

V ex punched in the fourth level on the elevator's panel. Of course, the levels here went underground instead of scaling upward. The fourth floor was two levels below the command center. What else lay within the cabin's inconspicuous front? The elevator door opened to a long corridor illuminated by strips of lighting running parallel on either side of the walkway and up pristine white walls. The metal security doors glided apart, revealing Seth on the other side.

"I will take it from here. You're relieved until further notice, warrior." Seth's words confirmed my suspicion. Vex was assigned to guard me. Vex gave a curt, jerky nod.

"Exiousai." Retreating, he backpedaled a couple of steps and winked my way before turning around. The heavy door closed the gap between Vex and me with a swoosh. I trailed Seth into a room to our right. Custom built-in wall bookcases and cabinets lined the farthest wall. A matching redwood executive desk and black leather office chair perched in the middle. The longest wall reflected the office to us like an oversized mirror.

"How are you feeling?" Seth motioned to a sofa.

"Fine. Thank you." I sank into deceptively firm cushions. I expected Seth to join me. He leaned into the desk, crossing his legs. A warm smile graced his lips. Not for the first time, I wondered how he did it. Seth asserted authority and inspired loyalty and respect. He did all that without threats or public displays of prowess.

"What's on your mind, child?"

"King Cygnus erased some of my memories from our encounter. They came back to me when I woke up." Seth's lips flattened. "He said because I ceded my claim to the Andromeda Fae throne, he'd grant me a wish." The statement sounded foul, nonsensical even. Why would a loser get a reward? This logic had escaped my discombobulated mind while in the presence of the Fae. I sighed.

"I'm sorry. I know this doesn't make any sense... That's what I recall. I don't think I was in full control of my mind when he offered to fulfill my wish."

"Did you make a wish?" Urgency underlined Seth's tone.

I straightened. "Yes. But I can't recall what I wished for."

"Trickery." Seth's eyes took on a withdrawn look before focusing again. "The Fae are masters at deception. He tricked you." But why would King Cygnus bother to bestow upon me a wish? Seth pressed a single option on his touchscreen office phone.

"Elias here," the voice from the speaker announced.

"Reach out to all our contacts and inquire about their predictions of unusual energetic alignments locally and on a global scale. I expect a report today." After a pause, Elias responded in the affirmative. I leaned forward, threading my fingers together and worrying my lower lip. I was missing chunks of a puzzle, and the realization didn't sit well with me.

"Let me explain. Fae possess gifts, and one of them is compulsion. Most Pures are immune to compulsion. Secondborns can learn to resist it. The skill is a difficult one, but it can be learned." Seth walked up to the bookshelf and pulled out a book. He handed it to me.

"King Cygnus wronged you in two ways. The first offense is infringing on your free will. The second is infinitely more offensive. Each time a Fae fulfills a wish, the Fae draws up some of the victim's life force in a way of remuneration. The substance of the wish is irrelevant. They can use this energy to create powerful magic, more powerful than what they can manifest themselves. Earthbounders' life force is precious and more potent than that of a human. By ingesting a portion of your life force, King Cygnus has now become a threat. Even more so than when he revealed himself after the thousand years following his presumed death."

Many questions begged to be asked at this moment. One jumped over the next to the top of the list.

"How would I know if King Cygnus granted my wish? I don't feel any different."

"It is true what they say—the Fae cannot lie. I don't doubt he followed through. The manifestation of a wish can be instantaneous, or it may require a longer period, days or even months sometimes. You will know it in time. The Earth realm is built upon different laws than the Andromeda stars. Time and space work differently here. This affects the timing and result of each wish manifesting. I once knew a man who asked for a thousand golden bricks; the bricks rained down from the sky and buried him alive."

The Fae couldn't lie. The Fae could charm and deceive. The Fae would use anyone they could to get what they wanted—lesson learned the hard way. And there was a chance my wish would kill me. My day had just gotten infinitely better.

"Can you try recalling your wish again?"

I concentrated. The scene unfolded in front of my eyes.

King Cygnus had me lay a hand on a gilded book. He asked what I wished for most in the world, at this time. I tuned in to listen to my answer, but only silence filled the space. I exhaled, disappointed.

"It's as if I'm blocked. And I can't think of anything I'd wish for."

Seth strode over to the mirrored panels on the wall. He tapped something with his finger and the reflective tint dissolved, transforming panels into fully transparent windows. The view revealed a cylindrical space about twenty feet in diameter with a round, chalky platform in its center. A thin filament barrier tinted in a burnt orange color stretched from the base to the high ceiling. There was something about this barrier that called to me. Humming inundated my ears, and soon, my entire body vibrated in waves. The dark orange hue floated around, painting a mosaic pattern. The sight mesmerized me. I allowed my feet to carry me closer and stepped to Seth's side.

"What is this?"

"Alluron. You've seen one before?"

I shook my head, my eyes were glued to the magi-tech barrier.

"I was...new." A euphemism for an orphan no one trusted. I knew Invicta's alluron was located underground, and only Pures had clearance at that level.

"You must see it up close." Seth's eyes sparkled. I followed him down a narrow corridor separating his office from a larger observation center and down a flight of stairs. The humming intensified. The hairs on my arms stood on end. I circled the structure, ogling it wide-eyed and leaving Seth behind.

On the ground level, clear two-foot tall quartz obelisks stood erected at regular intervals. Blue light connected the obelisks, anchoring P6's allura to the base. The alluron was created out of allura via specialized technology. Unlike its predecessor, Earthbounder scientists developed alluron in their laboratories. Its sole purpose was capture, transfer, and containment, also referred to as the CTC process. Any demonic being who breached allura landed within the walls of the alluron. All other life forms including people who crossed the barrier unaware were transported to the other side, maintaining the illusion of a continuous landscape. Most people didn't notice the transition; some may have experienced vertigo-like symptoms. That was what the handbook said, anyway.

"What do you think?"

Magical came to mind, but that sounded cliché.

"It's impressive."

A puff of dark orange dye billowed upwards, constrained within a thin, glass-like barrier.

"The handbook doesn't mention colors."

Or how they swirled as if someone had trapped paint within the alluron's thin wall.

"Do they change?" I asked.

"No two allurons are the same. The outbursts of color are its energetic signature. Our scientists don't yet understand how the hue manifests in allurons since alluras are semi-transparent. They suspect it's a result of unique frequencies pinned to their location. Ours is orange ochre—the color of ancient art." Seth extended his arm, letting it go up to the elbow through the alluron. Once half of his arm was inside the demon trap, he flexed his fingers and waved. My eyes rounded.

"We can penetrate alluron to quickly and effectively dispatch the enemy."

"Can I?"

Seth nodded.

As I drew my palm closer, questions whirled in my head.

How many demons had been captured this way? Would I ever see Invicta's alluron? Xavier's face flashed in my mind unexpectedly. In my last few days at Invicta, Xavier and I formed a sort of understanding. He stopped being my monster. Of course, his rushed, irrational claiming of me as his *Ashanti* had diminished the bit of hope I'd placed in him. Xavier had an agenda when it came to me.

I hit a wall. Literally. My palm, which I expected to pass through the alluron as Seth's did, was now stuck to the invisible hard surface. I yanked, but it wouldn't budge. The twirling hue glided my way. I dug my feet into the ground and jerked until my shoulder popped.

"Seth!"

The Exiousai jumped toward me but froze mid-step as if time suspended. My head swiveled back to my palm. The orange reached it, circling it. While it rotated around my hand, I glimpsed new imagery inside the circle—a forest. The circle exploded and sucked me in without warning.

THIRTY-EIGHT

The serene scenery rushed toward me. Or was I traveling in ways unknown to a human? I hovered in space, my arms flailing and desperately trying for purchase. On the last leg of my transport, I got an extra push, hurling me toward a mushy forest floor. My arms twisted beneath me, and my chin caught the brunt of the fall. *Shit. What was that?*

I jumped to my feet and whirled around. The tranquil sound of birds and the rustling of leaves greeted me. Large trees reminiscent of the types I'd come across at P6 surrounded me. Shivers ran down my body because wintry temperatures weren't counteracted here. The ground vegetation was dense, and I couldn't tell if I was close to anything or in the middle of a forest. One thing was for sure—I was outside P6. Why did the alluron dump me out here?

The gibbous moon gave off abundant light. Unfortunately, I was no expert on night navigation. Searching for the north star was useless since tall trees blocked off most of the sky. I tested a few trees for climbing potential. One tree's branches hung within my reach, the lowest branch hovering just a foot above my head. The wind picked up, and a flurry of leaves and sticks hit my back. I backtracked a few feet from the tree. Now or never. From a sprinter-ready position, I kicked off loose underbrush and threw myself forward. My hands circled the branch, and I interlaced my fingers to fortify my hold.

"Arien," a severe voice called out.

My eyes located the source of the voice before me, just a couple of feet below my line of vision. The tree bark became an animated version of Paulie's face. My eyes rounded, and I lost my grip. I plopped on my ass.

"Paulie?" Surprise, relief, and anger filled my voice.

"Before ye com' swingin', I've been tryin' to reach ya. This fuuckin' magic." Paulie's wooden face contorted in one of the ugliest grimaces I'd ever seen. I took a minute to compose myself. Putting aggravation aside, I replayed Paulie's words, or rather what he wasn't saying in his response. It wasn't like Paulie to show emotion, and he sounded troubled. I swallowed.

"What's wrong?"

"Fuuck... Soleil is gone. I lost it. I had a plan in plais, I had it all arranged for and then it disappear-red. It's o-ver, Ari-en. I only wanteed to make sure you're protecteed before I turneed myself in. Seth will be alert-ed once I do. And Kol. He'll protect ye. He's no choice. He'll protect ye with his own laif. I guess it waz meant to be. There are no koinsid-ences in life." Wait, what? Paulie's tirade gave me whiplash. Who was bound to protect me with his life? Seth or Kole, and why?

"Why are ye outside allur-on? Neve' mind thou, this will—"

"Paulie. Paulie!" The haze over my memories dissipated. I knew what happened to the soleil!

"Soleil was returned to the Emporium," I said on one exhale.

"Returned? How?"

I nodded my head with a smile painted on my face. I did it! I helped Paulie. Although I'd never forget King Cygnus's deception, which stained my opinion of him forever, he acted as a catalyst on this quest. I could see it now as if the Fae's magic block retracted. He asked what I wished for most, and I said, "to stop Bezekah from reuniting with his soleil."

"Explain, child." I bristled at Paulie's tone. The hardness in his voice was unmistakable. I recounted my encounter with the Fae and the conversation with Seth that ensued. Paulie listened, his wooden lips puckering.

"Paulie?" Did he freeze?

"Still here," was all I got. His tone was lackluster, deflating my spirit.

"Fae's magik of wish fulfilling is convoluted. The strangest kind kno'n to us. One nev'r kno'ns how it will manifest."

"But it worked. Soleil was returned. You said yourself, the Emporium is the only place Bezekah can't get to."

His carved lips carried a low whistle, which I presumed was a long exhale.

"While that solves one problem, the biggar problem remainz and now I have nothin' to allure Bezeka-ah into the trap I set ove' the past few days."

"But..."

"Bezeka-ah does not kno!"

Oh. I thought... What was I thinking? That one wish would solve all aspects of a complex situation. Well, it didn't.

"Shit."

"There were no witnessez. The traitor who disclozed my pozession of soleil to Bezeka-ah was dealt with. Besides, Bezeka-ah wouldn't believe the soleil waz returnd. It's impo-sible."

"He can't check with the white dragon?"

Paulie scoffed. It was a stupid question. Archons were blacklisted with archives, the Emporium, weaponry—in short, anything the other side of this ancient conflict possessed.

"The Fae used ye." Paulie paused. "Hmm, he's after somethin'."

Seth had said as much. A fleeting thought of the Fae and Bezekah working together slipped through my mind again. The Fae were too proud of a race to make deals with demons, though.

"What do we do now?"

"You do nothin', ab-solutely nothin'. Do ye hear me?"

Paulie's words hurt, but his accusatory undertone stung even more. I had wrecked his plan, so I couldn't blame him. My eyes fell to the ground, moisture gathering in the corners. Way to feel sorry for myself when Earthbounders and humanity were at stake. Because of me. I was the epitome of the worst secondborn ever.

"Now, child, it's not yer fault."

I sniffled. This was, to a great extent, my fault. If I'd studied as expected and learned countermeasures to Fae magic, I wouldn't have fallen for the king's trick. Why hadn't I wished for fortune, family, or independence in the Earth-bounder world? Those were all reasonable requests and plausible in my current situation. Well, maybe not the fortune thing. Money was nice, but I had yet to find that millionaire who lived in absolute bliss and happiness. Money equaled happiness—not.

I grabbed the hem of my shirt and wiped my wet face clean. As a chill ricocheted around my abdomen, I was reminded this was still winter season.

"There must be something we can do. That I can do?" My eyes lifted to the rough bark absent Paulie's engraved face.

"Paulie?"

I turned in circles, examining each tree around me. He'd disappeared.

THIRTY-NINE

I marched in the direction of... I couldn't tell. I spun in a circle, hoping to recognize something about this area. Paulie's revelations occupied my mind. I didn't notice a clearing ahead of me until I stepped into it. I froze. The air buzzed with supernatural presence and two winged figures stood at a distance. Their bodies were the size of my pinky, but I recognized Talen's profile. His natural blond curls were unmistakable, after all. One other P6 assassin was with him. Behind them, a lava-like substance shot out into the sky and fell across the surrounding perimeter. It sizzled and bubbled until the earth extinguished it.

I jogged toward the warriors. Talen spotted me and used his hyper-speed to meet me near the clearing's edge.

"What are you doing here?" he spoke in a monotone while scanning the area behind me.

"You have no idea how happy I am to see you."

Talen's shrewd eyes narrowed with skepticism and curiosity. Brief suspicion flashed across his face, replaced by concern, or more like worry that I'd turned into a nutcase. I wrinkled my nose. I was in no mood to explain. Honestly, I wouldn't even know where to begin.

"Look, call Se—" An uncomfortable ball of pressure settled around me as if an outcrop of cacti that prickled with the slightest movement surrounded me. The largest of the thorns swooped down from the sky. His large red wing swept my side roughly before retracting into Xavier's back.

"What is *she* doing here?"

My face twisted with displeasure. Invicta's Pures refused to acknowledge secondborns even when in their presence, inches away. We were below their level, but according to Xavier's flawed ideology, we were oh-so-happy to stay there. To serve.

Talen read my body cues. "Step away from her."

Xavier huffed. He pinned the P6 warrior with a daring stare. The hostile energy between them intensified. I stepped in sync with Talen, grabbing his arm.

"He's not worth it. Call Seth. *Please*."

Talen raised a quizzical eyebrow and cracked his knuckles for good measure.

"Pretty Invicta boy gets saved by a secondborn," the warrior quipped as he turned his back on us, a major dissing move. Xavier's jaw ticked. To his credit, he didn't bite. Maybe because he ended up getting what he wanted—my time—in a wacko-kind of way.

"You're staring." The corner of his mouth twitched as his eyes shifted to my face.

"Oh, now you're speaking to me," I said, hiking my eyebrows. Xavier's lips flattened. He squared his posture, towering over me. The air stiffened.

"Last I heard, you were being coddled at P6. I didn't expect to see you outside. Unprotected." Funny how his words sought to insult but landed on a serious note underlined with worry instead.

I chewed on my lip. Part of me wanted to tell him about the alluron accident. I trusted him, even though we failed to see eye to eye. The other part of me despised Xavier for his highhandedness and listen-to-me-because-I'm-a-Pure attitude. He was a seasoned warrior set in his ways.

"Arien?" Damn the man. The softness of his tone affected me.

"Fine. I'll tell you what you want to know. You will listen, and then you'll give me your honest, undiluted opinion."

"You have my word."

"Seth invited me to inspect the alluron. I'd never seen one before, you know." Xavier listened with intent. Occasionally, his gaze fell to my lips and remained there far longer than necessary. "I ended up in these woods, not far from here." I pointed in the direction I'd come from.

Xavier's throat bobbed. He looked at the woods, me, then behind me again. He said, "Hmm" and twisted his mouth to the side.

"Sooo...that happens, right?" I shrugged a shoulder.

"Never," both warriors said in unison. Talen had rejoined us partway through my storytelling.

"Exiousai corroborated her story," Talen answered Xavier's unspoken question. Wait a minute. *Did they doubt me?* I massaged a new aching spot near my temple.

"I was instructed to return you to P6."

Xavier widened his stance, his neck muscles swelling.

"Can I have a minute with Xavier?" I asked. Talen hesitated. "Please." He crossed his arms over his chest. "I need to ask our pretty boy from Invicta a few more questions. It won't be long." Talen's expression softened at the reference to his jab. He inclined his head and strode off.

"Why not go with him?" Xavier's rigid posture slackened, his eyes trailing the P6 warrior before settling on me again.

"Simple. We had a deal, and you haven't delivered on your end yet."

He raised an elegant brow.

"Why do you think the alluron transferred me here?"

"Careful what you wish for, little secondborn. You may not like the answer." Xavier ran the pad of his thumb over a raw spot on my chin.

"And you have the answer?" My voice lilted with hope. He proceeded to lift my chin up and I swatted his hand. I'd live, bruised or not.

"Answer—no, suspicion—yes." The wind blew my loose hair forward like a sheet in the breeze. I slicked it back and twisted it into a bun. Xavier wore a funny expression when I looked at him, a mixture of bewilderment and surprise. He sniffed the air around me, I placed a palm on his chest and nudged him out of my personal space.

"What?"

"The wind carried your scent to me. You reek of the sweet vanilla scent Pures have in the days preceding their transformation."

"My birthday was in April." I nosed my shoulder. "I don't smell vanilla, just detergent."

"My olfactory abilities are heightened." He studied me. I wasn't buying it. I told him there was nothing angelic about me during our first encounter and my stay at Invicta and P6 only proved my case.

"How does my scent connect to the alluron issue?"

"It doesn't. Take me to the spot—"

"That won't be necessary," boomed a familiar male voice. Kole's long, swift strides spoke of determination. His irises turned to coal and flashed with lightning. Thunder roared nearby. Storm clouds brewed on the verge of a moonlit sky. The storm was coming.

FORTY

Seeing Kole was equal parts frightening and thrilling. My pulse kicked up, and heat crept up my neck. I knew well that both warriors would notice the change in me. It was up to them to interpret it. I'd keep my secrets close to my heart.

"What are you doing here?" A tinge of breathlessness stained my tone. Darn it.

Some of the darkness left Kole's eyes. He blinked. "I was near."

I waited for Kole to extrapolate. No such luck. I glanced at Xavier, who was no help either. His unyielding glare was locked on the Power.

"Well, I was going to show Xavier—"

"You're not going anywhere with *him*."

My palms rolled into tight fists. Kole was insufferable and unbending. I cast a longing gaze toward my alluron dumping spot. I weighed my options.

"Xavier, thank you for your help." I pasted a genuine smile on my face, which I wiped away when I addressed Kole next. "Where's your car?"

As Kole pointed to an outcropping of vegetation, I took off in that direction. I expected Kole to follow fast on my heels, brooding all the way to P6. To my surprise, he stayed with Xavier. Maybe he was being congratulated on the way he willed me to obey. And possibly I was being sour and unreasonable. Kole and Xavier worked side by side on this energetic fissure and were probably discussing it. The real problem. One which, if not taken care of, could cost many innocent lives. I kicked myself mentally once more for forgetting the big picture. A bolt of lightning struck somewhere in the surrounding forest to drive the point home.

A path led to a grassy area used as a parking lot. Black SUVs with Invicta's emblem occupied half of the space. Kole had parked his dark green Jeep slanted, on the level above the designated parking area. The passenger side sat on moss-covered rocks. I sighed with disbelief and frustration as I scaled the slippery incline. Gaining purchase on the car's roof, I opened the passenger door and slipped inside.

The interior of Kole's car was cozy and warm. The scent of a brewing storm mixed with pine dominated the air. It soothed my frayed nerves. I relaxed into the cushioned leather seat. There was an array of buttons on the steering wheel, the console, and a large touchscreen. I was no expert on cars, but there appeared to be more buttons than necessary to drive. Hopefully, some of them activated weapons against demons, like the Batmobile. I imagined Kole used this vehicle often because the exterior of my door had deep welts on it, and the back door sported a few dents. The other side of his car must have suffered similar damage. I didn't dare leave the warm interior to satisfy my curiosity. I reclined my chair, rolled to the side, and tucked my legs in. Kole was nowhere to be seen, so I closed my eyes to enjoy a minute of blissful solitude.

Something brushed my arm, and I startled. I hit my head against a hard object. *What the hell?*

Someone grunted near my ear. My eyes flew open, meeting chocolate charcoals only a few inches above me. Kole stilled, his expression one of indecision. Something tumultuous pressed against my rib cage.

"What are you doing?" I asked.

"Your seatbelt." He stretched it in front of me.

"Oh, thanks," I mumbled. I grabbed the seatbelt, taking care not to touch him, and busied myself by punching it in.

Kole slid back into the driver's seat as if nothing bizarre happened between us.

"Welcome."

The Jeep rocked as Kole backed out, and the passenger side of the car leveled with its counterpart. I must have fallen asleep—in Kole's car. Playing with my hair for no reason, I stole a sideways glimpse of Kole in between my fingers. An inflamed pink circle covered his temple.

"Sorry for hitting your head," I said.

His eyes skimmed over my face. "It's already healed, but we should probably find some ice for your bump."

I touched the sore spot on my forehead. It was bulging out as if a unicorn horn was about to spring up.

"Fabulous," I murmured. "I don't think ice will help much at this point. We'd better head straight back to P6."

He nodded. We pulled out onto a dirt road, and the car quit jerking around.

"You're jumpy," Kole said, his words taking me by surprise. I didn't expect him to speak to me. He'd outdone himself by avoiding me while at P6, and when he was around, he glowered more often than not. It was mind-bending because I'd been feeling an invisible pull between us, and at times I had thought the feeling was mutual.

"Um… It's a survival instinct, I guess." I said, placing the ball back in his court. If he was opening up to me, befriending me, he'd carry on with this conversation. Folding my arms across my chest, I waited. With each passing—silent—minute, I berated myself for reading into something that was not. With a sigh, I turned to the passenger-side window. We entered the highway but soon exited south. I pulled up a mental map and dropped our location onto it. Living within the confines of highways which formed a square-like perimeter around New Seattle my whole life, I'd gained decent navigational skills in the city. I hoped by points of reference, I could learn the lay of the land outside New Seattle.

"Arien?" Kole's voice drew me out.

"Hmmm?" My hand tightened on the armrest.

"I'd like to…apologize." He raked a hand through his silky hair. "It's been pointed out to me that I may have stepped out of line at the junkyard. You had no reckoning as to the danger you were in. My harsh words and direct actions scared you. That was not my intention." He stared at the road as he spoke. Tiny crinkles etched in the corner of his eye.

"I thought you were going to kill me." I recalled Kole's murderous stare when I'd tipped the pile of metal scraps over the three warriors. At the time, he, Vex, and Talen were a bigger threat than the Archon with his snake pet put together. After all, they'd defeated the Archon and killed his nefora.

Kole's knuckles whitened, gripping the steering wheel tighter.

"Trust me, I'd be the last person to ever harm you," he gritted out. His words incited fuzzy feelings in my chest, and I scolded myself for feeling that way. The way he spoke wasn't romantic. I didn't know why Kole had appointed himself my protector. He studied my face, nodding once. That was... intense. When he turned back to the road, I released an overdue breath.

We drove in silence for the next several minutes.

"What are you thinking?" he asked.

"Xavier."

Kole scowled into the road.

"He suggested my transformation hasn't happened yet. He detected a pre-transformational scent on me." Kole's forehead furrowed.

"I am still confirming some information. We tracked down your original birth certificate written in French. Whoever filled it out used numerals. They did not spell the month. They wrote four-twelve-two thousand five."

"The twelfth of April."

Kole shook his head. "Most countries, including France, use a day-month-year date format."

"That's December fourth," I whispered. Only a few days from today. Was this possible? The idea that my date of birth was not my correct birthdate disturbed me on many levels. I never knew my parents or any family relation, and I wasn't allowed to know anything about my mother other than the day I was born was also her last day on Earth. Except for my mother's bracelet, my birthday was the only piece of my past I had. Now, even that was an unknown. I fell deep into my thoughts.

"Hey." Kole's mild voice brought me out of my inner shell. "We're here."

A massive gate emerged from the fog surrounding us. Kole pressed a garage opener attached to his visor, and the gate engaged. Was it that easy to get in and out of this place?

"The clip has a built-in fingerprint technology that requires clearance," Kole said.

It unnerved me he could read me that easily. I slumped in my seat. But a dangerous thought soon lightened my mood. I now had access to a back door leading out of P6, and it appeared the alluron worked only for me.

FORTY-ONE

The storm advanced. Frequent lightning outlined tall red cedars in the bright light. Each time it struck, our surroundings went from total darkness to a flash of hundreds of immovable sentries, long and wide in girth—dark monuments on a blinding white backdrop. A tenacious wind stirred, bringing with it strewn pine needles and broken-off branches. The sentries began swaying to the rhythm of wailing gusts.

One side of my head throbbed. Kole pulled into a cavern in the mountainside, cutting us off from raging nature. My eyes watered with each motion-activated LED light bursting to life as we traveled through the tunnel. The car lift's droning sound was amplified in my ears. When we descended to the infirmary level, I was fighting nausea. My legs numbed, and I tripped on our way to the elevator. Stupid legs.

Kole caught me before my mind even registered I was falling and carried me inside. His face distorted, and his chocolate eyes morphed into black cesspools. I blinked until Kole's dark orbs came into focus again. He set me on my feet in the corner of the elevator, caging me in with his warm and towering body.

"You're pale." His eyes roamed my face. Worry lines marred his forehead. His nearness had an effect on me. I blushed, beating myself mentally for feeling attracted to him under these circumstances. If it was possible, my face heated even more and I swallowed hard. If I ever wanted the ground to split and swallow me whole, this moment would have been it.

"It's just a migraine. I feel better already," I said to his Adam's apple, shifting from one foot to the other. I needed space. Kole's body vibrated, calling to me for unknown reasons. If he didn't relent, I was bound to do something stupid, like seeking his heat and embrace.

With enough force, Kole pinched my chin between his fingers and tilted it until our eyes met. I schooled my features as my stay at Invicta had taught me to. Kole's eyes narrowed.

Danger always lurked behind his dark foreboding stare. But I think this time there was something else there, and he wanted me to see it.

"Arien." The whisper fell from his lips.

The elevator ground to a halt.

"I'm sending Kole there right now." Seth's voice carried from the corridor beyond the elevator's now open door.

Kole's expression closed off, and he took a step back. He plucked a small brown leather book from his back pocket and extended it to me.

"I think this may be what you were looking for—at the library," he said, stoking my memories.

"Oh." I wrapped my fingers around the book, prolonging the moment.

"Come on now." Seth motioned for me to join him. I stepped out alone, hyper-aware of Kole's eyes on me. Part of me was disappointed our paths were splitting here and now.

Kole divided his attention between Seth and his smartwatch as he logged the details of his new assignment. Without a single glance my way, he jammed the button, triggering the elevator door. I bit my lip, kicking imaginary dirt like a pouty child. *Kole and I had a moment, didn't we?* I had a sinking feeling we might not get another one. My shoulders slumped. I was about to turn away when he unexpectedly locked his eyes with mine. A coy smile formed on his lips. He winked—at me. My eyes rounded. That was the weirdest, most unexpected behavior I had yet to encounter from Kole. It felt intimate, too. A sheepish grin slowly spread across my face. Too soon, the door cinched shut, snapping me back to reality. I tilted my head up and closed my eyes, savoring this fleeting moment.

I fell into a jog after Seth. The movement rattled my migraine-ish brain, but I had no choice if I wanted to catch up with him. Seth led in silence. We entered the command room, joining Rae and Vex at the holographic topography of the rapture terrain. I craned my neck to scrutinize the fissure. Its length was that of a football field, the width only about a few feet. The zigzag pattern deviated on one side, drawing an arch.

"Look at this." Rae skimmed her fingers over a holographic toolbar, activating unfamiliar settings. The fissure turned a vibrant red that stretched from the surface deep into the underground. The crimson matter pulsed and spewed high into the atmosphere.

"Last reports displayed a new trend. Our fissure ceased closing. Up to this point, the contraction was slow but steady. Seraphs evaluated the site for supernatural activity and detected none. They called in a disaster management crew to physically secure the area and prepare a statement for the media. But things weren't adding up with me." Rae drew in an overdue breath. "You see, it wasn't supposed to storm tonight."

"The weatherman promised an unobscured view of meteor showers," Vex interjected.

"The atmosphere was charged with negative ions out of nowhere. I scanned the site with modulators and I was able to capture a very low frequency. A signal of sorts."

"Let me guess. The frequency this operates on cannot be detected by Invicta's devices," Seth said, crossing one arm over and propping his jaw on the other. Shadows of gloom overcast his usually bright disposition.

"I've never seen anything like it," Rae said.

"Black linc implosion," Seth muttered.

"What does it mean?" I asked.

Seth's lips flattened. "It means the attack two days ago was only a preview spurred on by some unfortunate idiots. Something far more nefarious is about to encroach on our realm."

I sucked in a breath with a hiss.

"How much time do we have?" Seth asked.

"Five days, give or take. I'm running a modeling analysis to pinpoint a precise point of manifestation on our plane."

"Bezekah." As the word left my mouth, my feet left the ground. Seth held me up by my throat, single-handedly. On instinct, I kicked out and tugged on his sleeve.

"Stop," Seth boomed. The hard angles of his face jutted out, his brows grew fiercer, and the veins in the corners of his eyes turned blacker. I heeded his command. I stopped moving and instead struggled for each breath Seth allowed me to fight for. My eyes prickled from the exhausting effort.

"Exiousai, I'm sure there is an explanation. Allow her to speak." Rae crept up closer, never dropping her eyes from Seth.

She was there in an instant when Seth released me, catching me mid-fall and helping me to a chair.

"You fooled us all. Are you working with the demon realm?"

"No!" My eyes filled with unshed tears.

Seth weighed my words, his jaw grinding. A bout of coughing ripped out of my chest. Damn it, that hurt.

"Bezekah was banished from Earth centuries ago. He'd be a force to reckon with, even without his full strength. You must be aware that as part of his banishment, Bezekah was stripped of his greater power."

I nodded.

"Without his soleil, he's vulnerable. He can be killed now. If he's returning to Earth, there must be something worth risking his own existence for."

"The soleil was removed from the Emporium a couple weeks ago, but it has since been restored. Paulie thinks Bezekah is after his soleil. He wouldn't know it's been returned."

"Paulie?" Seth hedged.

I dug into my memories. What did Xavier call him?

"Kwan...Kwanezerus?"

"Your former protector?"

"My friend."

"When did he communicate with you?"

"One day after a field exercise last week. Paulie revealed himself to me through a tree. That's when he told me about Bezekah. Paulie claimed Bezekah was after him, and me, and he made me swear not to tell anyone about it."

"Is that all?"

"No. When the alluron dumped me outside P6, Paulie appeared to me again. He said Bezekah wouldn't believe the soleil was returned. We were too late," I said, massaging my throat. It felt like a firecracker had exploded in my neck—

shredded and singed. "That's all I know; I swear it on my life."

"Innocent denizens could've perished if we didn't mitigate the breach in time." Seth's eyes were cold, unforgiving.

"I didn't know." I shook my head, my voice cracking.

Seth's steel gaze trapped mine.

"Vex, track down Kwanezerus." The warrior engaged his comms device as he sprinted out of the room. Seth's eyes shifted to Rae.

"You know what to do."

FORTY-TWO

We walked in silence as I fought despair, shame, and rising anger. My heightened emotions propelled the pounding in my head. I didn't dare to glance at Rae. My eyes latched onto bare gray walls and stone floors. Rae kept silent. She'd turn around and back forward again. We both knew I was following her, so she wasn't checking on that.

Walls turned into glass, revealing cells beyond it—all empty and austere-looking. Rae unlocked a compartment with a glass front and dragged the door ajar. I didn't wait for an invitation or order. My shoulders slumped down lower as I hugged myself and shuffled inside. I faced the wall. Rae sighed and locked the door in place. I stole a glance at her retreating back. She paused two units down and leaned her shoulder into the glass barrier.

"I know this is a misunderstanding. The Exiousai will see it too. Just...don't give up on us." Rae's voice was loud and all around me. I scrutinized the walls inside my cell. There, beside the door, was a small white panel with one button.

"Rae..." My throat was on fire. What should or could I ask

her about? Did she think me a traitor too? I feared her answer would crush me. "Have you heard of the alluron transferring people, Earthbounders, before?"

Rae turned around. Her eyes were rimmed with red. Her features morphed into those of a scholar searching for answers in her internal catalog.

"All the knowledge we possess about the allura and alluron is their affinity toward demonic energy. To trap lower density energies, to be exact."

"Oh." My mind pointed me to one conclusion alone, and I refused to acknowledge it.

"No, Arien. We would've known if that was the case."

I bobbed my head against the glass. Its cool touch soothed my migraine. But I wasn't convinced either.

"Some Earthbounders have a unique gift—Kole's gift of persuasion, for example—but no one knows why or how this phenomenon occurs. I think you have a gift too, and your gift involves allura manipulation. You jumped in space this time, but with practice, you may be able to do even more."

Rae's eye shone with wonderment, which stunned me. I expected everyone to treat me like the freak I was. An Earthbounder freak. The information she shared about Kole surprised me, too. How had I not known this? It was inconsequential now. I doubted Kole would ever look at me the way he had gazed into my eyes in the elevator after these revelations.

"Thank you," I whispered into the box. I held her gaze, silently communicating all that I was thankful to her for—her unwavering friendship, her belief in me, and her relentless support. I had not known Rae long, but if I'd ever had a sister, I'd be honored to have her fill those shoes. She drew in her lower lip, considering. Sadness entered her eyes. She turned her back to me and marched down the hall.

I crossed over to the bare mat and collapsed. My eyes

burned, but not from unshed tears. Closing them was my only reprieve. I forced the lids open, though. I pulled out the book Kole had lent me earlier today. It contained information on Archons, and I was desperate to learn more about Bezekah—especially how to stop him. Maybe if I had set aside my trust issues and told Seth about Bezekah's plans earlier, Vex and the other warriors wouldn't have gotten hurt. And I wouldn't have lost the new friendships.

I began with the index. My finger ran over the Bs, and it bypassed Bezekah before my brain caught up with it. I retraced my finger. There it was, the name *Bezekah* and a few page numbers mentioning him in Kole's book. This almost seemed too easy... Page seventy-eight was the only page number in bold following Bezekah's name. I leafed through the pages until I got there. The author had dedicated several pages to Bezekah, which gave me hope. I read line by line and gasped at the sudden realization. I flipped to the front pages and blinked. The year of publication was 457 AD, which was before the press had been invented. How was this possible? I shook my head to clear the white noise erupting from my inner ears.

Choosing to ignore this disturbing fact, I thumbed back to the Bezekah section, which was written soon after Bezekah's banishment. The author of this book thought Bezekah was annihilated by someone he called a *Traveler*. I grunted. The author was mistaken. Bezekah was alive and well. He didn't possess his usual might, but he was not dead. I wanted to scream. Information in this book was questionable.

I took a deep breath and returned to scouring pages for something of value. My eyelids grated against my eyeballs, and it was only a matter of time before my brain exploded from the constant pounding. Never a quitter, this book was all I had right now. I couldn't rely on anyone but myself. According to the author, Bezekah had been the most powerful Archon to invade Earth. He'd come to our planet through the Ninth Stargate in a galaxy I couldn't pronounce and had never heard of. History wasn't of interest to me, so I skipped along to paragraphs describing Bezekah's powers and limitations. I grew hotter with every power discussed. *Damn it, give me something here—one weakness I could explore.* I soon ran out of pages.

"That's it!" I threw the book down and folded my arms over my head. Damn it! Dam... I jolted upward with a gasp. Dragging myself on all fours, I picked up Kole's book and paged through to the one line which could be our salvation. I ran a finger across it. *Ability to read Earthbounders' minds upon physical contact.* If this was true—and I had my doubts about the author's credibility at this point—but if this was true, I had my chance.

I lay down on the mat, desperation twisting my guts. As long as I remained in this cell, I wasn't able to do anything. I needed Paulie to come through for me. Once he did, I'd be leaving P6. Absent magical protective borders, Bezekah would locate me. The Seeker had marked me on that faithful night at the junkyard, but Paulie failed to mask my marker when Xavier barged into his house. The rest I'd have to figure out as I went. Asking P6-ers for help at this point was out of the question. Perhaps the relationship could be mended in the future, but right now, all felt lost.

My entire body weighed me down. I touched my head to the cool stone floor. Ahh...that felt sublime. My eyes leveled with the book. Faint blue highlights bled to the edge of a page. Was this something Kole was looking at? A struggle between my innate curiosity and respect for Kole's privacy ensued. He'd lent the book to me and didn't say not to read parts of it. Running my fingers over the floor, I poked my index finger at the marked page and nudged the book open. I was close. A couple more pages over and the blue highlight appeared over a paragraph. Letters blended, and I blinked in rapid succession to clear my vision.

Ashanti Rosa.

The One True Love.

Rare.

Twin Flame.

Connection.

Unavoidable...

I racked my brain. Something about this sounded familiar. Something Nelia had said... Ah, what was his name? Oh, my head was splintering. The drumming intensified into a high-pitched note. My lips moved, but I heard nothing. Something popped, rendering my arms useless. The sensation of a thousand ants spreading all over my body dominated all else. And even though I couldn't hear it, I screamed louder than I ever thought possible.

FORTY-THREE

Sky Ice. Sky Ice. Sky Ice. Who said that? I whirled around, blocking the blinding light with my arms. The hair whipped around me as I rose into the air. My eyes flew open and locked on a mesmerizing male face. His beauty was surreal. The silver undertones of his golden hair shimmered in the light like strands of satin. As I was being lifted away, his eyes shone with determination.

"I will find you again," he said.

I closed my eyes, drunk on a beautiful feeling.

A breeze picked up my hair again and tossed it around. I cracked one eye open. A green valley spread before me. I stood on a stone balcony etched into a mountainside, overseeing the land. I caught movement to my right. The long pale gold and silver hair of a woman danced in the wind. Her white gossamer dress billowed around her. She faced away from me, standing perfectly still.

"Hello?" I dared a few steps in the stranger's direction.

Silence.

I inched closer.

When I was within reach, I raised my arm. The woman's head snapped to the side, and I yelped. She opened her mouth, and the sound *she let out echoed through the valley and boomeranged into my ears, amplified tenfold.*

"*WAKE UUUP!*"

An outcry of heart-wrenching agony startled me out of sleep. The clinic's curtain flew open and concerned faces hovered above. Zed was among a trio of secondborns surrounding me, all scanning my body with expert precision. One technician advanced towards the small machine by my bedside and began touching the screen. I struggled to breathe, taking in shallow gasps.

"What's going on?" The last thing I remembered was being sick, fainting... And there was something important happening in a few days... I scoured my mind for more information, but couldn't quite get there. A sense of desperation rooted itself deep inside me. I raked my hair, pulling at the ends.

"How are you feeling?" Zed's gaze remained fixed on my neck, where his fingers peeled off two circular nodes. They fed data to the device by my bed.

"Fine," I lied. I felt like a stampede of demons had run me over—sore and deflated. A pretty female I'd seen around the infirmary before removed a drip from my arm. I frowned. I'd never needed an IV infusion because of fainting. Zed browsed through his tablet. My mind was a web and I concentrated to see through the nebulous threads. What was I forgetting?

"Are you ready to remove the catheter?" the female asked. I inclined my head and lay down. Zed and the other medic stepped outside the privacy curtain. A slight pinch-and-burn sensation followed the procedure that seemed to awaken my senses by a margin. A fog of sorts lifted.

"I'm finished here," the medic chirped. "I'm so glad you're recovering. Everyone's been worried sick about you. May I say you have quite a fan club." She tossed the catheter and other medical implements into a wastebasket. I reexamined my circumstances—IV infusion, catheter, Zed's avoidance... I bolted upright.

"Who was here?" I asked. It came out demanding.

The girl blinked.

"Oh, well, the P6 unit to begin with. They looked amazing in their fighting gear, so awe-striking..." No! The black line implosion! I forgot about the black line implosion.

"Zed!"

The secondborn stepped into my treating area, his eyes betraying him.

"You weren't going to tell me, were you?" I swallowed down the emotions. Of guilt, of anger, of worry...

"Arien," he pleaded "I have strict orders to keep you here until—"

"From who?" I cut him off.

He pursed his lips. He didn't think it was a good idea to reveal my jailers. I waited, though.

"Damn it all to hell. The orders came from Xavier, the council, Exiousai Seth, Kole, and..."—he hesitated—"the Soaz." My stomach rolled when I heard the name of my least favorite Earthbounder of all time. What did he want with me now? I pushed the question to the back of my mind. There were more pressing matters at hand.

"How long have I been unconscious?"

"Five days."

I did the quick math in my head. My eyeballs bulged with a startling realization.

"It's today? Is it over? What happened?" I needed to know the Earthbounder warriors prevented what could've been an infestation of demons and demonic energy on a scale never seen before. I had to make sure my friends were safe.

"Zed?" I prompted him when he did not reply.

"Arien." Once more, the pleading manner in which he

spoke sent shivers down my spine. "I don't know the status of the P6 units. Invicta's finest are scheduled to leave in the next hour to brief with local Watchers."

There was time. I threw off my covers and swung my feet over the bed's edge.

"What do you think you're doing?"

"I have to...see someone," I lied, for the second time in a span of a few minutes. I was setting personal records today. "Where are my clothes?" The black hospital-like gown wouldn't do in the outdoor weather. Zed folded his arms over his chest, his stance widening.

"There is no way in hell I'm letting you leave." His voice rose a notch.

"You don't have to yell," I said, wrinkling my nose.

Zed sighed with exasperation. He rolled his eyes to his right. I glanced past his shoulder to the computer station. Other medics congregated there, many shooting us curious glances. Oh. Playing my part, I hung my head low.

"I will arrange for apparel for you."

The curtain rippled as it separated me from the rest of the infirmary again. Biting my lip, I flexed and pointed my toes, then rolled my shoulders. Five days of lying around would never be my hobby.

I stood by the bed, introducing more movement to my body when Nelia's face peeked in. She was upon me in a tight embrace before I could react.

"Hello to you, too," I whispered.

She pulled away, a large grin digging into her cheeks. Her eyes shone in the dim light.

"Don't do this again," she hiccupped.

I nodded, a crease forming between my eyebrows. I couldn't promise her that. Until I knew what "this" was, my life and my future rested on fate alone. She dropped a backpack on top of the bed and fished out jeans, a long-sleeve thermal shirt, and fur-lined boots.

"The Magister demands an audience with you. I'll wait outside."

My face had shock written all over. What would Hafthor want with me? The beautiful warrior raised both eyebrows in a "you buying this BS?" gesture and tapped her ear before hiding behind the divider. I sagged against the bed, massaging my chest. I guessed a certain level of deception was in tall order. Did Nelia know about my imprisonment at P6? Seth must have notified the Magister. Shame and hurt resurfaced as I recalled Seth's reaction. He thought I'd betrayed P6—that I was a plant.

Beads of sweat gathered above my upper lip. I pulled up the sheet and wiped my lip dry. Tremors ran up and down my body, and I wondered if I was ready to do this. I tossed the sheet down. It wasn't as if I had a choice. I inspected the small medical case left on the nightstand and pocketed some items.

As we were leaving, questioning glances trailed us. Nelia tightened her hold on my arm. We turned corners and took several staircases. The crowd began thinning out. Hallways became grander. A door cracked open, revealing a couple. A half-dressed Seraph whispered into a female's ear on her way out. Her cheeks flushed red.

"Don't stare." Nelia tugged harder on my arm. There'd be a bruise there once she let go, but I couldn't bring myself to care. If my plan panned out, my chances of seeing tomorrow were pretty thin. Non-existent even.

The next turn brought us to a dead end with one door. Nelia used a key to get us in. Shelves of sheets, towels, and cleaning products lined the walls and ran parallel in the center. Fingers snapped in front of my eyes.

"Concentrate." Nelia unhanded me and began pacing back

and forth, mumbling under her breath. Something about "them" having all her addresses and not being able to hide me.

"I don't want to hide. I need to get to the fissure in Sector B. Can you help me?"

Nelia's eyes widened. "No. That's not safe." She shook her head.

I snorted. "Nowhere is safe for me. But I think I can stop Bezekah. At least I have to try."

Now it was Nelia's turn to snort her way into a chuckle. It was short-lived.

"We have legions of Seraphs observing the situation over there. If they can't stop the evil bastard..." Her somber eyes finished the sentence for her.

"I don't intend to fight him. Just get close enough so he can read my thoughts. The soleil he's after was returned to the Emporium. Once he finds this out, he won't be sticking around. He's exposed without his power."

"Even if you could get near him, that's a suicide mission." She threw her hands up. She wasn't having it.

I straightened. "You said it yourself, I don't have a future here. Maybe in the dungeons or at the mercy of the Soaz." Nelia winced. "And whatever this sickness is, it's not letting up. I know you felt how many times I relied on your strength to keep me walking. So, I'm going to the battlefield. I only ask that you get me out of Invicta. Can you do that? Please."

My speech did something to the warrior. Her features hardened as she tapped on her wristwatch displaying a holographic map of the building.

FORTY-FOUR

I slid down a laundry receptacle to the underground washroom, where an older grayish man waited for me with a secondborn laundry master suit. He smiled as I donned it and pushed a cart my way. He ambled away without a word.

I'd memorized the layout of this floor, and within minutes, I was pushing open the door leading to the underground dock. Headlights flashed at me. I abandoned the cart on the side and strolled toward them. Nelia sat behind the wheel, waving me in. I jumped into the back seat and rolled into a ball on the SUV's floor.

"Are you sure they won't inspect the back?" I asked for the hundredth time.

"I have special clearance; they won't even peek. Stay there until I say it's safe."

I pillowed my head on one arm and closed my eyes. Each time Nelia stopped or slowed down, I fought to keep my breathing and heart rate steady. At the gate, a guard warned Nelia to keep away from the fissure before Invicta's gate opened. I welcomed the laborious grunts and shrills of the gate rolling out. Several minutes passed before Nelia announced we were in the clear. She adjusted her rearview mirror once again.

"Thank you," I said, guiding the seatbelt across my chest.

Nelia's brows pinched together. "For what?"

"For helping me. For believing me. For believing in me."

Nelia's throat bobbed. I rested my forehead against the passenger window. In an hour, we'd be arriving at the fissure site and saying goodbye. Maybe forever. I'd listened to Brie's advice and cracked my shell open a smidge, allowing people into my life. But I wasn't going to get the happy ending Brie had envisioned for me.

The highway was busy. Unsuspecting humans traveled to their destinations. Many looked like they'd just left their offices for the day, loosening their ties and folding up expensive shirt sleeves. The ramp off the highway took us through the industrial district into farm fields. The red-ochre sun dipped towards the horizon.

"How did I get to Invicta?" I asked.

"Rae brought you in. Your sickness put you in a coma and her attempts at waking you failed. We have more medical resources at Invicta, but we couldn't even tell when you'd recover. Any idea what made you sick?"

"I—I don't know. I fell sick before,"—like when the Soaz assaulted me and following King Cygnus's visit—"but I don't know if any of it is connected."

Nelia nodded.

I chewed on the inside of my cheek. "When P6 came to Invicta, was Kole among them?"

A corner of Nelia's mouth hiked up. "He arrived later that day and beat up a few guards at the south gate."

"What... Why?" Nelia had my full attention.

"Kole's been blacklisted by my brother." Nelia's eyes

flicked to meet mine. She sighed. "It's a long story. Anyway, Kole wasn't happy about it."

"What happened?"

"Rae went out to the gate and talked to him. That seemed to calm him, and he left. One guard suffered a broken arm."

"Oh." I recalled Seth's harsh words, which triggered a strange ache in my chest again. Was Kole motivated by our friendship or revenge? A few days ago, I cared less what he thought of me. I'd despised him and he'd returned the sentiment. Funny how our relationship had flipped. And now it flopped, leaving only a thin layer of maybes.

Vegetation obscured the sunset. Forests surrounded the one-lane road Nelia had picked. My body hummed with anticipation, recognizing we were close now. I tuned into my body, testing tiny movements and fighting the growing despair within. What if I didn't make it on time?

Nelia pulled over and cut the engine off. Reaching into a concealed storage compartment, she retrieved two devices and armed herself.

My despair funneled into anger. "What are you doing?"

"I'm coming with you," she said, her tone terse. Her eyebrows drew low over her large doll eyes.

Sighing, I acquiesced, but panic gripped me on the inside. She was as stubborn as her unbearable half-brother. I watched Nelia round the hood toward my door. I dipped my head low and faked tumbling down as I stepped out. As I predicted, Nelia caught me in her arms.

"Are you all right?" Worry underlined her voice.

Bent over, I uncapped the syringe I'd grabbed earlier from the infirmary. I squeezed Nelia's shoulder for purchase and jammed the syringe into her arm.

"I'm sorry," I whispered. Shock registered on Nelia's face as she swung at me, but she failed to connect. I grasped her limp body and lowered it gently to the car floor.

"Why?" Nelia croaked, her throat refusing to obey her.

"Shh, it's a sleeping agent. You'll be fine," I promised as stupid tears leaked out.

"Why?" she repeated.

"I won't let you die because of me."

She fell silent as the sleeping agent stripped her consciousness away. My eyes landed on her wrist, and with an already guilty gut, I removed her smartwatch and strapped it to my own hand. After a few tries, I pulled up the map of the terrain. The map revealed my destination was to the left, across the road, and opposite where Nelia said we'd be heading. She'd lied to me. One sly warrior friend she was. A smile tugged at my lips, but the moment flitted away as I stared at Nelia's motionless body. She breathed softer than an angel's whisper. There was a teeny tiny chance this beautiful warrior wouldn't hate me forever for this deceit. I expelled air on a shaky breath and closed the door.

I jogged until my recovering body couldn't carry me any longer. I sagged against a giant spruce, defying the throbbing in my legs. Shit, maybe I should've paced myself. A wry snicker escaped my lips. I was going into a battlefield. How in the hell was I supposed to pace myself? A flock of birds flew over the forest, squawking and wailing, heading away from where the fissure hissed into the air. My pulse quickened. I pored over the map again. I was right on target. The small blinking dot depicting my position showed an open field where the fissure was a couple of hundred feet away. The closer I got, the more my muscles tensed and coiled.

A large black bird landed at my feet. The beveled-out saffron orbs ogled me with hidden intelligence. I backpedaled. The bird cawed and in a flash of blinding light, morphed into a man. I gaped. King Cygnus stood in person mere feet away. With my eyes trained on the Fae king, I widened my stance. I wouldn't go down without a fight.

The king raised one thick black eyebrow and leaned against a trunk. He tossed a red ball of something into the air and snatched it in midair. An apple. His foreboding eyes studied me as he sank his teeth into it.

"May I ask why you are heading into the battle?" he asked around the mouthfuls of apple pieces. "It's a lost cause if you ask me."

"It's good I didn't." Irritation got the better of me.

The king spat bits of apple onto the ground. He threw the core across the bushes as his orange-hued eyes turned dark and stormy.

"Look, I never challenged you for your throne, and trust me, I don't intend to. I'm only trying to get to the battle before it's too late."

King Cygnus narrowed his eyes. "You'll get slaughtered as soon as you step onto that field."

I threw my hands in the air.

"Why do you care?"

"I don't. I find myself—" He paused, eying me. "—*curious*. You're a puzzle, and I bore easily. But now, I guess, the only thing you're going to be is dead."

I winced. The truth stung.

"You're powerful, right?" I asked.

King Cygnus's chest puffed up as he pushed away from the tree. "I am."

"Then why don't you help the Earthbounders destroy Bezekah?" I had a strong suspicion King Cygnus could do a lot of damage with merely his pinky.

He tsked. "You've got much to learn. You never interfere when your enemy is on the path to self-destruction."

With those words, the king levitated, collapsing into a bulbous dark matter with black wings. The matter condensed into a very real bird that soared into the sky. Soon his silhouette faded away. His words stumped me.

Who was his enemy—the Archon, the Earthbounders, or both?

FORTY-FIVE

I staggered into the clearing and sank to my knees. The view in front of me was that of an absolute melee. In the center, the mother of all black worm creatures reared and thrashed, fighting off attackers. In its corporeal form, the nefora was half a football field long and at least twelve feet in diameter. More than one weapon bounced off of its slick and tough exterior. Individual segments rotated in different directions, making scaling the creature impossible. Its only weapon—sharp rows of black teeth where the head ended in a ring-like orifice—snapped at approaching warriors. One by one, varied weapons and tactics failed to slow it down. The warriors surrounded the worm and began lassoing with a black rope. I shook my head. Was rope the best they could do? Where were the onyx blades?

The fissure erupted at the far end of the clearing with black goo oozing out. Blobs of goo transformed into scores of demonic beings. Each one was uglier and more terrifying than its predecessor. Above the expanse, high in the air, Bezekah levitated. His face was a dark, smoky hole. The Archon was

motionless as if in a trance. Battle cries drew my attention
back to the surface. Dozens of demonic figures formed from
the goo, clashing with the first line of Earthbounder warriors.
Several warriors sliced through the creatures. Others used
zappers, frequency jammers, and weapon launchers to disable
the enemy before dispatching them. The Archon did not let
up in his attempts, however.

With time, more and more demons emerged out of the
goo and at a faster rate. Warriors switched to disks, zappers,
oscillators, and any other means they possessed to conserve
their energy and dispatch scores of demons at once. Despite
that, warriors were getting hurt. The razor-sharp claws
slashed their armor, drawing blood. The slithering goo
trapped many of them. The scene played out so fast no one
could reach the warriors in time. The black pitch enveloped
them and collapsed to the ground in a dizzying drop as if
nothing had ever been inside it to begin with. The scene paralyzed me, rooting me in place.

Over the past few weeks, I'd trained to become a warrior,
but I wasn't ready for this. I'd never be ready for this. It didn't
matter anymore, anyway. Regardless of the personal cost, I
was here to fix this because I didn't want my friends to get
hurt. However, I had serious doubts my presence would
change the outcome of this battle. Not if I failed to garner
the Archon's attention or was killed before I reached him.

My eyes scoured the battle landscape, resting on Xavier
cutting through demons in a blur of nonstop motion. He
partnered with a secondborn who dispatched zappers ahead
of them, allowing Xavier to weave through the throng. The
secondborn, who I recognized thanks to his signature blue
hair, tossed batons toward the closest demons and ducked
low while Xavier cut through hordes of assailants within a
matter of seconds. He headed for the fissure. Without a

doubt, he'd formed a plan. He yelled out, and many Seraphs adopted the same strategy. I sighed in relief at the sight of Seraphs getting the upper hand on the demonic enemy.

"No!" a breathless voice said to my right.

I spun around to face Paulie's appalled reflection carved into a tree trunk.

"I sensed a potent blast of energy invading this forest,"— Paulie's voice carried this time—"and I set out to inspect it, but then I felt your signature. I couldn't believe it, but here we are."

Here we were. Paulie must have sensed King Cygnus. What else was Paulie capable of?

"Why are you here?" I asked.

Paulie harrumphed. "I told you I've been working on a plan to stop Bezekah." I nodded. "Those plans have altered since I no longer possess the soleil. I'm here with a group of my closest allies to give Bezekah a taste of unadulterated druid power and seal him away from this world forever." Paulie's rigid face stilled. "It's time. I must go."

"Oh..." I didn't know what to say. Was *good luck* appropriate?

"Arien, go back to where you came from." An impatient note of warning stained his tone.

I straightened my spine. "I can't do that."

"Bezekah is my responsibility!"

"And now he's mine as well. I can help."

Paulie's rigid eyes hardened with a deadly stare. "Very well. Forgive me."

A vibrant purple current flowed from Paulie's tree to the adjacent gnarly monstrosity.

"Rise!"

"What—"

Paulie's visage disappeared from the surface of the tree

with a plume of green smoke. My gaze shifted to the tree
Paulie had juiced with something. I regarded it with unease.

Popping and crackling filled the air before my brain registered a large branch swinging at me. I crouched in the nick of
time. Tiny branches and leaves scraped across my scalp and
yanked hairs out in their wake. When the branch swung back
with momentum, I flattened myself to the ground. This thing
aimed to knock me out cold. The earth at the base of the
trunk stirred, and roots dug their way up. *Oh no, Paulie zombified a tree!* I ran deeper into the forest, hoping abundant vegetation would slow the tree in its tracks. But I was drained,
and the underbrush and the above-ground roots tripped me
at every turn. I chanced a glance over my shoulder and
shrieked when my foot hit a slant, sending me on a descent. I
rolled down through ferns and splashed into a shallow creek.
I groaned, lifting onto my elbows. My eyes widened as I
looked up. The tree emerged from the forest wall and
stepped forward onto the decline. My heart fought to leap
out of my chest as the tree leaned toward the creek and froze.
Its roots burrowed into the soil to stave off a fall. Before I
could celebrate, the roots snapped in sequence, and the
crown plummeted down—where I lay. I scrambled over slick
rocks in the creek's bed and threw myself out of the way. The
tree fell with a wet thud.

I heaved myself up against a rock and wheezed. My lungs
burned as did most of my body. Yet, I couldn't deny myself
feeling a smidge of smugness when the Frankenstein tree
remained still. I'd defeated it. I could do this. I straightened,
doing my best to ignore a throbbing in my side and a sprained
ankle. I was going to have words with Paulie if we survived
tonight. I followed the creek to the battlefield.

A shadow of a winged man was cast onto the battleground, and my eyes darted towards napalm-colored skies.
My heart stuttered. The grace and precision with which he

glided distinguished him from the others. Choking worry constricted me. Kole was on a head-to-head trajectory with the Archon. He was a torpedo about to collide with this powerful ancient mage, and there was no telling the outcome. A sonic echo erupted about six feet away from the Archon, where Kole collided with an invisible barrier. The energy sphere surrounding the mage cracked on the side of the impact and sizzled with electricity. And Kole plummeted...

"No!" I shouted. Legs carried me forward before I realized what I was doing. Kole's lifeless body disappeared among the throngs of warriors. He didn't fall anywhere near the fissure or the demons. But that wouldn't make much difference if he was already dead. I lost sight of him. I pressed forward, but I was too far away. The clearing was larger than I thought. My legs protested. I faltered when a sticky black substance began bubbling near my feet. I jumped over it and spun in a circle. There was a discernible pattern of goo permeating from the ground up, forming a line across the surface, opposite the raging battle. I panted from physical exertion and panic. Surely, the Earthbounders patrolled the terrain for any fresh developments. But to my horror, no one raised an alarm. I backed away from the oozing goo. It crawled and stretched slowly but with surprising ease. At one point, it jerked in my direction, climbing to a foot above the ground as if some intelligence was lurking inside it. I hurried toward the closest group of warriors. They had to be warned. Kole weighed heavily on my mind, but I suppressed the urge to go to him. If these demons surrounded us unbeknown to the warriors, it would be the end of us all.

"Over here!" I flapped my arms above me as I slogged along at an excruciatingly slow pace. A contingent of Earthbounders squaring off against the nefora fixed all their attention on the task. I trudged closer.

"Here!" *Come on! Look this way. Please!* I waved until one of them noticed me and sprinted over the remaining hundred yards separating us. I doubled over, clutching my side. The warrior was upon me before long.

"You must evacuate." He turned me around and shoved me away. I wasn't sure he knew who I was, but I was certain I'd seen this warrior before at Invicta. He was a Seraph—and a Pure—which upped my chances of being ignored.

"Black goo is leaking out over there." I pointed a finger the way I'd come. "He's surrounding you." The warrior hesitated. He glanced past me and back at the roaring nefora, weighing his options. At last, he nodded.

"Wait here," he ordered before sprinting towards the tree line. I let out a sigh of relief. Now that he knew about the goo, they'd contain it. I surveyed the battlefield for the best path to Kole. I hobbled to the left, skirting around the threat in the center. The warriors entangled the giant nefora in glowing snarls. They circled the creature, immobilizing it, and waited. The coils sank into the worm's tissue and snapped with an audible popping that ricocheted across the opening. The nefora stiffened, its mouth gaping wide. It toppled onto the ground in a pile of severed sections like a tower of blocks, its mouth wide open but immovable. The warrior lines at the back of the battle took notice and roared in camaraderie.

I squinted into the sky. Would Bezekah retreat after this loss? His hooded face swiveled. My breathing seized. He was staring right at me. I shuffled backward. Thudding rocked the ground beneath my feet. I peered behind me. The tree Paulie had revived limped on its shorn, stumpy roots. I stalled. A zombified tree pursued me from one side while a Great Archon hung above me, ready to strike. Talk about being stuck between a rock and a hard place.

I tried to avert my gaze from the Archon, but I couldn't. I attempted to move, but I crumpled to my knees instead. A thousand tons of pressure crashed down on the crown of my head, causing hot tears to well up in my eyes. I cried out in pain. Someone yelled my name.

Bezekah's outline became clearer. His figure grew bigger and taller. Within mere seconds, he drifted closer with only a few feet separating us now. The electrical shield that protected him earlier no longer encapsulated him. The Archon materialized a blue sphere onto a smoky form where his palm should have been. Within it, blue slime swirled, erupting outward into a thin bubble gum layer that enclosed us. The darker blues swirled within the sphere, obscuring the view. Shadowy silhouettes approached from the outside. The battle was at a standstill.

I gasped when the incapacitating force let up, falling to all fours. I wiped the tears away and pierced the Archon with the sternest expression I possessed. He wore a coat over black, smoky hollowness. He lacked a face. And yet I felt him scrutinizing me.

"The soleil was returned." I outstretched my trembling hand, offering it so he could see into my mind and see for himself. He didn't take it.

"What are you waiting for?" My weak voice shook. It was too late for me. But I'd do anything to save the others who were collateral damage. He was here for the soleil, which he could no longer have. Black smoke poured from where his head should have been. It hovered in front of my face. My eyes rolled backward. I willed them open again. Particles of light lifted off of the surface of my skin and fed the black cloud. That was it. I allowed my body to surrender, eyes rolling backward again. Out of all the ways to die, this wasn't the worst way to go.

Shouts from outside the sphere intensified. More than once, a ripple of vibrations initiated by the warriors attacking the barrier skimmed over my skin. Would this evil leave once it sucked in my life essence, or would it attack the Earthbounders with renewed force? I thought of Paulie, Brie, Nelia, Rae, Kole, and the others. All of whom I'd disappointed and who deserved to live out their lives. A tear rolled down my cheek. I wouldn't go out this way. For them, I'd fight. My eyelids flew open. Gritting my teeth, I forced my legs beneath me and rose.

FORTY-SIX

I concentrated on the flow of energy between us. The Archon faltered. Whispers reached my ears. A strange language I didn't recognize played on a loop. It began as a murmur but soon grew in crescendo. Several voices chanted in my head or all around us. I couldn't tell. My enemy did not acknowledge any of it. My vision tunneled to a flicker of blue light flashing between me and the Archon. The light crackled as it expanded, forming a ball. Within it was a powder-blue stone. *Sky Ice*. I extended my arm.

When I made contact, all at once, a gust of air and visuals assaulted me. On instinct, I ducked when 3D objects were hurled my way. I felt nothing as they collided with me. They passed right through me. Multifarious geometric shapes in a selection of vibrant colors zoomed by me and through me. Drawings like symbols careened above my head. Another sensation—one of buzzing and lightness—penetrated my defenses when ghostly-looking feminine arms appeared by my sides, overlapping with my own. They lifted and began sorting the symbols right in front of me. I gasped, my eyes growing to saucers. I wanted to get away, but the apparition rooted me in place. Hyperventilating, I inspected my body. My arms hung loosely by my sides. Whoever the female specter was, I wasn't her or in control of her. When I looked askance, I caught sight of long pale golden hair flowing in the air. On closer inspection, I spotted silver tones within the gold. The specter was a woman, her semi-transparent silhouette an overlay of my body. I strained against the force holding me hostage, which turned futile.

The woman outstretched her arms, her delicate hands gliding through the space as if she conducted a symphony. She matched different symbols and constructed something out of them. I focused on the visuals. It was a chain of sorts. A sequence. Whatever did not match, the being tossed back into the electrified stream of air. She'd catch another. At times, her actions blurred. When she completed her work, the gusts subsided, and the flying symbols dissipated into nothingness. I stared at the string of symbols she'd put together. They bent and stretched, blinking through a kaleidoscope of colors. The sequence flared up with fire and collapsed on itself into a bright ball of light. The transformation was so abrupt I cried out from the blinding light.

"Shhh…" A loving voice said, "Watch." My eyes snapped open. The light no longer blinded me. Something akin to invisible polarized lenses protected my eyes.

Calmness came over me. As if my newfound clarity had given her permission, the woman raised her right arm, palm up, facing her masterpiece. The sphere of light spun faster and faster until it hurled itself at the Archon. The impact generated a lightning strike. The Archon was there one minute, then the light flashed and everything disappeared—the Archon, the specter, and the sphere bubble.

The connection between me and the apparition weakened. Before it was severed completely, the woman whispered to me, "Remember how to shine."

I gasped for breath, clutching my chest. Warriors surrounded me. Their faces were blemished with a blend of astonishment and rage.

"Arien!" Kole wrapped me in his arms. I yelped on contact.

"Sorry." He loosened his embrace and created space between us. I blinked hard. Kole's actions and words caught up with me. My eyes snapped to his to find sorrow reflected in the charcoal-warped depths.

"That's not..." I shook my head, lips unwilling to move. *That's not it,* I meant to say. I shrugged instead. His eyes cleared with understanding.

"Let's get you—" he began.

"What the fuck, Arien." Xavier's menacing voice zinged me back to reality.

What did he mean, *what the fuck?* My eyes refocused on his cerulean orbs shining with potent emotions. I flattened my lips and gawked. What did he expect me to say? What just happened was inexplainable. However I or *she* did it; it appeared to me like we'd saved everyone's asses. Couldn't I get at least a minuscule break from the scrutiny of Earth-bounder overlords for that? Xavier's jaw ticked. I used to associate that with his pissy mood, but the angle of his brows revealed a twinge of worry.

"You will return to the infirmary with Mezzo. I have to deal with the aftermath here." His eyes bore into mine. "Then you'll tell me what happened inside that pulsar." His words brooked no argument. Why didn't that surprise me?

"I'm coming with her." Kole stressed his point with raised eyebrows. Kole was making a statement—for me. He dared Xavier to refuse him. The palm of his hand found its way to my lower back, warming my shaking body. I trembled, but not from the cold. Waves of tremors weltered up and down my body. My teeth chattered. I clamped both hands over my mouth. Next thing I knew, someone had turned off a switch, and I was out of it. I opened my eyes to Kole propping my weightless body with his right arm and tapping on my cheeks.

"There you are." Concerned eyes scanned my face. "Better?" he asked.

I closed my eyes, sensing my body. The feeling returned to my legs, and I put some weight on them.

"Yeah, sorry." I exhaled. Xavier and a small group surrounding him lingered. He addressed Kole—something about a briefing. I lost focus.

Something brushed against the rib bones on my back and my breath caught. The sensations intensified and my back heated. I tried to grab Kole's arm as I fell to my knees and hands. Loud ringing in my ears canceled out their voices. Hot tears dripped down my chin. Liquid fire entered my veins. Why wasn't anyone doing anything? I breathed out hot air, burning my throat and nostrils. *Where was I?* I lost the sense of time and space. Shrouded in darkness, the excruciating pain became my only companion. My blood boiled; my bones melted away. Hot pokers nudged the skin in between my shoulder blades and the spine. *Ahh!* What did they want from me? I was already tearing up all inside. Stop! *Leave me alone!* Screams echoed. I crawled. Where? I didn't know, but I had to escape.

My head was in shambles. The poking resumed. *Stop!* But they were incessant. My skin flaked off where the poker pressed. It was going to cut through to my internal organs. I couldn't allow it. I thrashed and collapsed. They succeeded. A fissure opened, and heat sizzled out from the left side of my rib cage. *Mmm...* That was...nice? A small reprieve amid hell. The ringing abated, and a pinch of lucidity returned to me. The invisible enemy I fought was contained within me, and it needed to be let out. I willed it all out when the next wave of unbearable heat erupted.

This time, I heard my high-pitched cry. Accumulated heat burst out of my back. Tearing and popping noises accompanied it. Hot liquid spilled out from where my skin tore open. The outdoor air cooled it before it could burn my skin. My vision came into focus with an image of a patch of grass. My forehead rested on the ground, and my knees were tucked under. I sobbed in relief.

"Arien?" Kole's soothing voice reached me, but I didn't trust myself to respond yet. Out of the corner of my eye, I spotted Kole's knees on the ground next to me.

"What's happening to me?" I rasped out in a small voice.

"It's done."

I twisted my neck to see his face. I faced his abdomen instead, as he pulled the combat shirt over his head. Weird time to be undressing, but maybe he was as hot as I had been not so long ago. Holding the fabric in his hands, he surveyed my face and body, pausing on my back. Yeah, there was something not right over there. As always, Kole betrayed nothing.

"Can you sit up?"

"I would, except something heavy seems to be weighing me down. Can you move it?" I swallowed. My throat still burned.

An amused smirk won over Kole's stoic expression. That was so out of character. I considered the chances that this was a dream, a parallel universe, or something. But the painful twinge between my shoulder blades proved this was my new reality. Kole assisted me up, covering my chest with his shirt. *Oh, wait.* I grabbed the shirt and pressed it closer to my chest. I was naked above the waist! My cheeks reddened. My clothes lay in pieces, splattered with blood. Dark red fluid stained the grass. I questioned Kole with wide eyes—What had just happened?

He sat on his haunches, his biceps bulging out and distracting. He leaned forward and plucked something from my hair. I fixated on his face as he studied the item with awe. He twirled it in his fingers before lowering it to the space between us.

"It appears you grew a pair of wings."

No, no, no. This can't be happening!

The feather in Kole's hand was a silvery-white beauty with gold streaks.

FORTY-SEVEN

Why today? Of all times and places, the enigmatic wings emerged today—on the battleground. This meant I was a pure-blooded Earth-bounder. This meant I belonged to some order with the silver wings gene. This meant...I was screwed. My life choices had just been drastically curtailed. I sank into the back seat of Kole's SUV. Rae had tied Kole's torn shirt for me in the back. She monitored the frequency activity at the fissure site from a nearby stationed van. She assured me no P6-ers suffered any major injuries. Nothing that was beyond their healing powers anyway.

I replayed the events of the last couple of hours in my mind. I couldn't explain what happened out there—what happened to me. The symbols, which were so clear at that moment when Bezekah froze and the apparition sorted them out, were now a blur of color and faint shapes. None of it made any sense. The only detail I could grasp was the woman's hair. The pale blond coloring with silver undertones. There was only one other time and one other being I met with this same hair, and I had dreamed of her. Unless all of it was real—the woman, Sylvan, and the crystal? Blood drained out of my face. I was losing it.

Rae placed a reassuring hand on top of mine and braced me with a sympathizing smile. I couldn't return her kindness. An emotional void rooted itself in my heart. She'd tried to teach me for the past twenty minutes to fold my wings back inside. I couldn't get them to twitch. They hung as numbly as I felt inside. At least they were short, the tips brushing against my waistline, so we didn't have to make any special accommodations for the travel. Their coloring didn't resemble any warrior wings I'd seen before, except those of Sylvan's—if he existed.

"Does it hurt still?"

"No. I know they're there... I can feel them, but the pain is gone." I chewed on my lip. *Was that a good sign or a bad one?* What if they were broken or something? Rae said I should be able to fold them. It was instantaneous for everyone else. They grew them out, flapped them, and folded them when-ever they wished. The flying part took a little longer—a few weeks, tops.

"What a way to spend your birthday, huh?"

My birthday? I turned eighteen today, and not a few months ago, as I'd believed.

"Don't worry." Rae squeezed my hand. I released a long breath.

"Fine, Rae." I composed myself. "What happens now?"

"Oh." Rae dropped my hand, wincing.

Yeah, Oh.

"Well...I suppose..." The car swerved off the road and stopped, the force flinging Rae across her seat. As usual, Rae had forgone a seatbelt. She ended up on the console between the front seats.

"Kole!" Rae yelled.

He was already outside the vehicle, ripping my door open. My heart pounded as I scanned the area for the threat.

"Shit." Kole cradled my face. "It's fine, Arien. Everything is fine, I *promise*." The intensity of his words carried conviction. Rae leaned against the hood with her back toward us, hands in her pockets. Convinced no Archons or their hellish pets were in the vicinity, I propped a shoulder against the back seat, feeling exhausted from this stunt alone. Kole's hands fell back to his sides.

"What are you doing?" I asked, perplexed.

Kole shifted his stance, his gaze traveling to the ground, then heavenward before settling on my face. A storm of emotions brewed in his eyes. He was considering something, and I feared whatever it was, it bore serious consequences. He expelled hot air on a long exhale. It tickled my cheek. I soaked in the sensation and studied his proportionate face, thick and defined brows, long eyelashes, and firm lips unabashed... I suspected I wouldn't be seeing this infuriating warrior for a while. Rae's non-answer revealed as much.

"Screw it." He ducked his head inside the vehicle, caging me in with his arms on either side of me. "I cannot let them take you to Invicta." His eyes bore into mine, imploring me to understand.

"Kole, we both know I have to go with Xavier. As much as I hate the idea of being a Pure, I can't change who I am." My voice was calm which surprised me. When had I resigned myself to this fate? The Magister had called an urgent meeting as soon as the word got out about Bezekah's annihilation. He expected me. Xavier had conceded to Kole's request to drive me there, even though he was hellbent on interrogating me on the field. The Magister wouldn't tolerate any such leniency.

"I'd never ask you to change." A declaration. "This..." Kole ran the back of his fingers down the outline of my silvery wing with reverence and delight that sent chills down my spine. He shook his head and withdrew from the touch. "Changes nothing." His head dipped lower, and I waited.

"Kole." His name escaped my lips. I'd never known a whisper could carry a mixture of a plea and anticipation.

"Am I interrupting?" Condescension saturated the air. *Xavier.* My head snapped in his direction as if on marching orders. He stopped mere feet behind Kole, a black SUV pulled to the side of the road behind him. A slight stiffness in Kole's shoulders was the only sign that Xavier's appearance affected him. Kole pushed away and within seconds faced the Seraph.

"Xavier. We're checking on Arien. We're ready to get back on the road." Rae climbed into the back seat beside me. Xavier's shrewd eyes studied me. A hostile sound came from Kole. My shoulders bunched in anticipation. This subtle warning meant something. My intuition knew what it stood for, but my logical mind rejected it. Xavier had a different reaction to Kole's threat. His stance relaxed, and he cocked a brow.

"Now you tell me?"

Kole strode up to Xavier. Both warriors' chests puffed up and palpable tension charged the air.

"You will stay away from her."

Xavier's eyes narrowed. "I don't think so."

Another growl. The sound of it was doing something to me. Drawing me to Kole, awakening a desire I'd tried to stash away. This wasn't me. This was the bond acting up. A hot flash spilled from my core outward, triggering my wings. They bristled with agitation and I cried out. Warm liquid dripped down my back. Rae dabbed at the blood with fabric. Hiding my face in my hands, I peeked through parted fingers. Both Xavier and Kole ended the standoff, their eyes intent on me.

"No more stops." Xavier's eyes fell away from my face as he stalked off.

A dark blue Humvee squealed to a stop. Donovan emerged from behind the driver's wheel, rounding the hood. His scowl deepened when his eyes landed on Kole. His tactical gear suffered tears as if claws had ripped his pant leg open. Rivulets of dried-up blood clung to the exposed knee and calf. His displeasure morphed into an enraged sneer when Xavier blocked his path. Donovan looked past Xavier's shoulder at me. On cue, Kole stepped into my line of vision. If Donovan wanted to reach me, he had two powerhouses standing in his way. Xavier ordered Donovan to leave. I didn't hear his reply. A car door slammed, and the Humvee sped away.

When we reentered the road, we'd become part of a convoy with Xavier's vehicle behind Kole's.

"Kole, what's the plan?" Rae asked. I whirled at her.

"Oh no, no. There's no plan other than me returning to Invicta, and you two...well...doing whatever it is you do."

"You are one of us. And we don't leave P6-ers behind." Annoyance flashed in her eyes.

"Rae, I didn't mean to... I don't question your integrity or friendship. But what you're suggesting is suicide. Kole?" I wouldn't risk their lives to make my own easier. It was about time I took the reins of my existence. Rae grimaced into the rearview mirror, her eyes boring a hole in Kole's head. He glared back, pressing his lips into a firm line. Was I missing something?

"What was that?"

Rae dared to turn away from me. She conveniently found the passing trees quite captivating at the moment.

"Please." I scooted over to the middle seat, gaining a view of Kole's profile. He ground his jaw.

"Rae learned something interesting while she stayed at Invicta."

I bit my lower lip. This must have happened while I was in a coma. Rae jumped into an abbreviated story about how she'd sleuthed her way around Invicta's research laboratory. She knew Invicta had sent my blood and DNA samples for analysis. Standard practice when the family line couldn't be established. During her stay at Invicta, Rae discovered the initial results returned. And they were inconclusive.

"Inconclusive?" I popped my knuckles, trying to stave off the wave of worry crushing me. "There is more to this finding?" I hoped I was wrong.

Rae nodded. "The DNA sequence contained unknown polymerase links. Something we don't see in humans or the Earthbounders. They seemed to hide in what we call junk DNA. The clinical analysis showed the lead examiner suspected these links caused your illness. However, now we know your transformation induced the condition." Rae paused.

"Go on." I inclined my head.

"The lead also noted certain properties of these links resembled...foreign DNA." Goosebumps erupted on my arms. Rae never stumbled when in her scientist mode.

"How foreign?" Wariness punctuated each word.

"Before I answer your question, I need you to know this means and changes nothing." Her brows drew upward. I stilled, readying myself for the blow.

"His notes mention demonic attributes." I sucked in a breath and held it. *Holy shit*. My fingers dug into the leather cushion.

"They rarely examine the junk DNA, but the Soaz put a special order in." My heart leaped to my throat at the mention of his name and title—a lethal combination. The important question of why the Soaz requested additional tests begged to be asked, but it would have to wait. As bad as this news was, there was more at stake here. Still.

"Rae got her hands on the access code to one of Invicta's systems," Kole said, "and Talen reviewed the access logs. Someone from the Soaz's office has viewed your test results. It's not a far stretch to think that *he* knows." Electric chocolate eyes veered to mine through the rearview mirror's reflection. "Talen also learned that the Soaz has been communicating with Invicta, demanding further interrogation." My mouth opened and shut. This was too much. I felt like someone had ripped the ground from underneath me—spiraling toward a black hole. How could I not have seen this coming?

"Xavier has kept the Soaz away." Kole answered one of my unuttered questions.

"But you don't think he will stop the Soaz now. Not with the new information about my lineage..."

"*Unconfirmed* lineage," Rae corrected. Unfortunately, I didn't think that mattered much in Earthbounder politics. I rubbed my face.

"What's your plan?"

FORTY-EIGHT

No amount of persuasion would dissuade Kole and Rae from their fallible plan. No amount of reason, either. Kole planned to fake my abduction through the allura, relying heavily on my ability to transport two people besides myself to P6. A task I'd never attempted before. Rae insisted she and Vex spent hours studying the magnetic field configuration after my infamous first encounter with the alluron and concluded other warriors could enter and ride the frequency I *supposedly* initiated on contact with the magic barrier. She explained I carried the key and coordinates, and through physical touch, they could tag along.

"So, it's like hitching a ride?" I struggled to wrap my mind around it. Was this what quantum physics was all about?

"Exactly." Rae beamed with excitement. If anyone could find a silver lining in this dire situation, it'd be the optimistic Rae.

"What about the coordinates? How do I direct where we travel to?"

Rae shifted, and my stomach squeezed.

"Your gift is rare, but we located two other records of Earthbounders who possessed your gift in the history books. They used two methods: blinded coordinates or sensory recall. We're going to rely on the latter."

I dipped my chin. It made sense—in theory!

"There's a caveat." *Oh goodie.* "The endpoint must have matching frequencies. For example, you can't use allura to hop on a bus going to who-knows-where." Her eyes focused on my face. "It must be a portal in itself. This means you can jump us to P6's alluron." She winked.

I sucked in my bottom lip. The longer I contemplated the idea, something just didn't sit right with me.

"Let's assume I can do this for a second—for the record, we all know that theory doesn't always translate into practice —Xavier will figure out where we've gone the instant we disappear. You're putting P6 in danger. The Exiousai wouldn't want that."

"I will bear sole responsibility for *my* actions." Kole cut off my argument. He held my gaze in the rearview mirror. I knew well enough that any further conversation was pointless. He, once again, took it upon himself to protect me, regardless of my wishes. It hurt to be overlooked. Although I believed his heart was in the right place, my heart begged to be sought after as an equal.

"We have to do this, Arien. We're out of options." Rae squeezed my hand.

I smiled at her, knowing well the smile didn't reach my eyes. I slumped in the seat. Wings flattened along my back as if they commiserated with me. I flinched when an object scraped my waist. Stretching a hand to adjust the feathers around me, I came across a sharp tip sticking out of my jeans' back pocket. I pulled it out slowly and ran my fingers over its expanse. This feather wasn't one of my small and soft new additions.

I peeked sideways at it to confirm my suspicion. I'd totally forgotten about Mezzo's gift. It wasn't in the suitcase Nelia had packed for me. I thought I'd lost it. I had read about it in the handbook since. The text said the feather would follow the owner in mystical and unexplainable ways. It would always present itself as an option when needed. This phenomenon presented me with choices I didn't have only minutes ago.

We remained silent. Kole and Rae exchanged inconspicuous glances I saw by chance. I had a sinking feeling they were hiding something from me, still. We approached the gates of Invicta with the allura veiling the building ahead. The car caravan stopped. I hoped Mezzo was near, but I restrained myself from checking. The action could alert Kole that something was amiss. I silently crushed the feather in my palm. I scooted over to the door when it was flung open. A large hand reached in and pulled me out. In one fluid motion, Mezzo shut my door, exposing an infuriated Kole.

"Kolerean,"—Mezzo inclined his head—"your services are no longer required." The broken feather fell out of my opened palm and spiraled to the ground. Kole's accusatory eyes bore into me. I didn't flinch. With time, he'd understand why I had to stop him.

"Don't do this." The low octave of Kole's voice set off alarms in my head. In my hypothetical scenario, Kole heeded Mezzo's orders and returned to P6. That was the first and critical part of my plan. Yet again, I miscalculated Kole's reaction. His neck muscles swelled, shoulders rounded and engaged.

"Kole, don't..." I wasn't sure where I was going with this. My brain bucked at possibilities thrown at it, without a single desirable outcome.

"Stand down, warrior. Arien is under Invicta's protection now." Mezzo wrapped steel fingers around my bicep... My eyes widened as Kole zeroed in on Mezzo's hand. A fist shot out, connecting with Mezzo's stomach. *Oomph*. Mezzo folded in half, the force of the impact sending him several feet backward.

"No!"

Mezzo released his hold on me, but not soon enough. I went down, ramming my elbow into the car door. In a flash, he collided with Kole. Panting, I pushed myself off the ground. *No, no, no*. Couldn't I do anything right? Kole's SUV grunted and bounced as a body was slammed on the top of the hood. A head of strawberry blond hair—Rae—fussed over the pair. I froze in place.

"You know..." Xavier's smooth voice startled me. He was standing by my side—who knows for how long. "I've often wondered what it would take to chip Kole's calcified exterior. And here you come along..." I sensed rather than saw Xavier inspecting my profile. I breathed hard, my body shaking. Would Kole get hurt? Would Mezzo?

"You've all but destroyed him." Xavier's voice rumbled with pleasure. A deep, prolonged shudder stripped my emotions bare. He was right. I'd only ever caused pain to those I loved. Love... I mulled it over. Was it possible? No. I wasn't capable of love. Ever since I could remember, I was called a "worthless rat," "unlovable," and "a plague on society." Over the years, I'd only proved it to be true.

The struggle ceased. My legs carried me around the car. Kole's prone body lay on the ground, his head resting in Rae's lap. I sank to my knees. Except for a purplish bruise on his beautiful cheekbone, I didn't spot any other injuries. I ran the tips of my fingers over his unruly hair.

"What happened?" My voice sounded broken.

"He's fine." Rae stared down at the fallen warrior. I didn't blame her for not wanting to look at me.

"I had to subdue him. He wouldn't listen to your friend

here." Mezzo placed a reassuring hand on my shoulder. "Let me help lay him in the car."

I pushed to my feet. Mezzo and Rae hefted Kole's long body. As I watched them walk away from me, tears threatened to spill from my aching eyes. I turned around, hiding from scrutiny. *They* didn't tolerate displays of weakness. I meandered toward Invicta's border, aimlessly at first. I wiped my cheeks, gaining clarity and confidence with each step.

Someone called my name.

I broke into a jog.

Calls turned into shouts.

I jump-sprinted forward.

"Ariieeen!" One angry voice distinguished itself from the others. It carried closer with each syllable. Xavier chased after me. I pumped my legs, kicking up loose dirt. My useless wings contracted in place, reducing the drag. Thank heavens for that. The last thing I needed was to go airborne. Booming snarls were closing in.

I didn't dare glance back.

Almost there.

Nothing and no one would stop me.

I crossed my hands in front of my face as I took a long leap forward and crashed into the liquid plasticity of the allura.

DEAR READER

I hope you've enjoyed Arien's story! She's back in GLASS WATER, book II of The Earthbounders series, get it here: https://amzn.to/4bdFV2i

And enjoy this short story OF SERAPH'S SONG which takes place between books I and II and is written from Xavier's POV for **FREE** here: https://dl.bookfunnel.com/qzvi3kru5l

May you soar high always!

www.egsparks.com

ABOUT THE AUTHOR

E. G. Sparks is an award-winning dark fantasy romance author. Her debut novel, "Sky Ice," won the Silver/2nd Place award in the 2024 Feathered Quill Book Awards for the Fantasy category and was a Finalist in the 2024 Wishing Shelf Book Awards.

She delights in sharing fantasy worlds and making her heroines' lives difficult. When not in her writing cave, E. G. can be found hanging out with family and friends, traveling, gardening, doing yoga, and (you guessed it!) reading.

E. G. resides in sunny Florida with her husband, three beautiful daughters, two dogs, and a cat.

She invites readers to get first looks, bonuses, and more by subscribing to her newsletter at: www.egsparks.com

Made in the USA
Columbia, SC
18 March 2025

55321481R00205